The Solitary
Slocum

Robert Blondin

Adapted and translated
by Hedley King

NIMBUS
PUBLISHING

Nimbus Publishing Limited
P.O. Box 9301, Station A
Halifax, N.S.
B3K 5N5

Cover design: Arthur Carter, Halifax
Photo: Public Archives of Nova Scotia
Printed and bound in Canada by Best Gagné
Book Manufacturers Inc.

Canadian Cataloguing in Publication Data

Blondin, Robert

[7° de solitude ouest. English]

The solitary Slocum

Translation of: 7° de solitude ouest.
Includes bibliographical references.
ISBN 1-55109-002-3 Hardcover
ISBN 1-55109-026-0 Softcover

1. Slocum, Joshua, 1844-1909—Fiction.   I. Title.
II. Title: 7° de solitude ouest. English

PS8553.L66S4613 1992   C843'.54   C92-098510-6
PQ3919.2.B56S4613 1992

Contents

An Apocryphal "Autobiography"

Reconstructed from
pieces of a puzzle found in the attic
of our hero's legend.

CHAPTER ONE

My Childhood

What I know of the years before 1844 all comes from others, those who had fought the fight of life before me. Just as Faust was being rejuvenated by Schumann's inspired music, I began the process of growing old, tenaciously biting into my own desire for life and sharing from the table of others on the same path.

But before I cut my teeth by gnawing on raw potatoes, I had to start by sucking, like everyone else. For me that started at the end of February, 1844.

My beginning was buried in the cold, cunning mists which shroud the Bay of Fundy on Nova Scotia's southwest at that time of year. The fog climbs inland as if the Atlantic herself was trying to reach into the hearts of those ashore and blight their lives.

In those days a sea captain's certificate was a passport to success, especially if its holder hailed from Nova Scotia. They called us "blue noses" (blue with cold some say, others blame it on the Caribbean rum we traded for our potatoes). So my place of birth made a form of distinction available to me. It is a fine thing indeed to be born in a port opening onto such a prospect. But I did not wait on destiny to provide me with everything; that is an attitude as fatal to man as salt is to sails. I made my own choices and took initiatives when fate alone failed me. The distinctive seal of man is that he can shape his own future. It may not always be attractive to be stamped in this way, but it is the sign of authenticity.

Having to accept events passively makes me feel suffocatingly swaddled, as if I were a helpless baby again, back in the arms of my begetter in Wilmot Township.

I was my mother's fifth child, and again the delivery proved difficult. Old Edith Landry ruled the household throughout the vigil with all the authority of an adept in the mysteries of midwifery. Her time-honored skills were fully extended in damming a heavy hemorrhage. In the gravity of this exclusively female drama, my father

1

was relegated to a supporting role. I had been quickly bundled and delivered into his care.

It was an uneasy provider who cradled me.

Mankind becomes more refined. Men used to be able to repay a woman's sexual favors by bringing her food. Then he was found guilty of causing the labors of pregnancy and charged with the responsibility of supporting the product of his pleasures. Looking down on the bundle of swaddled cries with which he had been charged, my father wiped the tears of oppression from his eyes. Our ancestors had been Quakers. A guilty conscience had long ago been developed to take away simple enjoyment in the satisfaction of a desire. Culpability was a burden he had to carry until the Final Reckoning, and I was the straw too much. He felt incapable of carrying his cargo of responsibilities any further. Unlike the pelican, my father was unwilling to serve up his own entrails to his insensible progeny.

But it is impossible to stop the progress of mankind. The epoch when maternity was knowledge and paternity only belief was over. Socially enforced fidelity ensured that the father could not escape or deny his offspring. Man's recourse is to sweeten the bitter pill of responsibility with a coating of authority. The more bitter he finds the pill, the more sugar he adds. Like so many others, my father became dependent on his drug. He took it to be an inalienable right, a fundamental aspect of masculinity.

The only guidelines for his exercise of authority came from the barracks and monasteries. His overloaded imagination confounded rights and duties. The duties of responsibility were autocratic rights, unfortunately for us. Unfortunately for him, his lifelong rights became a painful duty; he was being asked to do a job he had not been equipped to perform. He had been appointed general without any training. He knew how to domineer, but not how to influence.

So I became the symbol of his sad dilemma. The bitterness of impotency was hidden behind a mask of authority. My arrival in the world was already having an effect over which I had no control. I did not live the rest of my life like that though. Time is inclined to slip silently by, but I did not simply wait for chance to bring me what I wanted. This fatalistic attitude of most sailors has often annoyed me. I tried to take the offensive, relying on willpower and action; to be a pilot rather than a passenger on the ship of life.

I proudly plead guilty to what I have accomplished in my life. Its events may interest you, but they were not undertaken for you. My life belongs to me.

I attempted to pass my childhood unseen, hiding behind others to escape my father's eye.

That night, when my mother fell asleep finally out of danger, father gladly returned his burden to the midwife's arms. He had no heart to look at the journal of the Rochdale Society of Equitable Pioneers he had been sent, with its dull news of sales of wood to the pulp industry. They had almost convinced him to join with their arguments about the social and economic advantages of the new co-operatives movement, but my arrival finally convinced him that an increase in numbers was not the answer to his particular problems.

New ideas were not something he put his trust in. A ship has to be run by an individual, not a committee; a hierarchy is essential.

In February 1844 the valley of Annapolis still had no thought of awakening from the stubborn Canadian winter. Being frozen by the winter cold for half its life made progress dishearteningly slow. The polka may have made its triumphant arrival in England from Bohemia, but it was still far from Wilmot Township. Deep-frozen Methodists like my father take a long time to thaw.

Two springs later, father was still forcing himself to weary labor in orchard and potato field. Mother was close to giving birth to a sixth child, having missed the intervening year with a miscarriage.

Holidays the Annapolis valley dressed seductively in rolling hills and meandering streams. Workdays revealed the capricious fertility of her stony red soil. Father had to devote all of his energy to her, only being spared rare moments for nostalgic recollection of his seafaring past. Now he slaved with mattock and spade to remove the roots of the great spruces with which she had been clothed. Their timber had made a fine reputation for our shipyards, building ships of supple strength to travel the world over. In its wild freedom that land had been able to produce proudly perpendicular mast timber. Now a man had to break his back to wring a meagre crop of potatoes out of its grudging ground. After so many centuries of freedom it did not tame easily.

It could be forced to yield sufficient for survival though. At least we had a harvest—a privilege at a time when famine was the order of the day in Europe. Dutch, Belgians and many Irish, forced to emigrate by imminent starvation, overflowed Halifax, right into our valley. I can still remember how their sad faces lost all trace of dignity when they were offered a "poutine rapée." That was the national dish of the Acadians who were now returning to Nova Scotia from their forcible deportations to the Caribbean, Louisiana, and elsewhere back in the eighteenth century. As they crept back, these Frenchmen kept to themselves, fearful of a repetition if the Anglos found them out. The only thing we shared with them was animosity. We could be intolerant because we were in the majority. Any pretext served as a basis for mockery and sarcastic abuse. The braver lads who dared to court the Acadian girls returned from their incursions with mixed sentiments. The girls were certainly beautiful and their folk music full of feeling, but eating their food more than paid for any pleasure.

"Poutine rapée" was always served. Potatoes are first grated, then left to soak in water before hours of boiling. The resulting glutinous, blue mess is formed into small homemade cannon balls. By working a finger into the heart of this ball, a hole is made to receive a good-sized lump of fat. After making good the wound, boil again. Serve with a sprinkling of brown sugar. And that was one of their delicacies! Even the impoverished Irish found it a cruel way to treat a potato. The unfortunate Acadians had forgotten that their ancestors had taken the recipe from Germans living in Lunenburg, on the other side of Nova Scotia. They were regrouping themselves around a borrowed cuisine.

If they avoided Acadian cooking, the immigrants still tasted misery, from the first sip of their morning cup of chicory to the bottom of their evening bottle of moonshine. But they worked tenaciously, in shipyard, workshop and field, as if by work they could forget their troubles. From them I learned the profound happiness work can bring, when work is freely chosen with a goal in sight. Work undertaken unwillingly is no better than slavery.

It was easier to find traces of slavery in Wilmot Township then to see signs of the liberating ideas sweeping the big cities of North America. Many freed Negroes were to be found in the region, but they were even more ostracized than the Acadians or immigrants. They had not yet learned that freedom cannot be given but has to be seized with one's own two hands. Following your own path with all your mind, body and heart is the prerequisite of fulfilment. Build your own boat and sail her yourself until you and her become one. But I am getting too far ahead; I must return to the farm.

In that latitude the season is short, seeming to pass as fast as the phases of the moon. Apart from the very youngest, the whole household was forced to work. Ten-year-old Elizabeth was placed in charge of us nippers. She made a deep impression on my all too solitary childhood. It was only with her that I lost my fear and was able to release myself to pleasure. I remember slipping some fresh manure into her apron pocket and then hiding in the folds of her skirt from her laughing slaps when she discovered my trick.

She had seen off-duty seamen on the beach playing the new game called baseball. A homey version was concocted to entertain us. Lobster pot markers made bases, a stick for a bat and old potatoes for balls. The life of the "ball" was short if the batsmen were any good.

When Elizabeth turned her attention away from me to chase one of the others, I chewed out my jealous annoyance on raw potatoes. I gradually developed my biting technique into a new art of oral sculpting, forming little white boats from the tubers. An earthy reality was transformed into a briny dream. With Elizabeth's complicity I stealthily buried them in the rows, primarily to avoid a beating from father for waste, but secretly in the hope of collecting a full fleet at the fall harvest.

Throughout the winter I would watch carefully whenever Mama or Elizabeth were cleaning potatoes. But there was only codfish on my plate to remind me of the sea. My dreams remained buried.

I did not appreciate it at the time, but that unvarying plate was a symbol of my two aspects: the meeting of sea and shore. At once nomadic and sedentary, I would always be stopping and starting, uneasy either settled or travelling. Leaving to return better, returning to prepare for a better departure, my anchor would be forever aweigh. When it had too good a hold on the bottom, I would raise it before it could get fouled and stuck permanently. When it lay dry on the foredeck, I would look for a chance to send it down again. I was always itching to let go, forever in a state of nostalgia, at sea for the land and ashore for the sea. I fear both society and solitude. So I have tried to assimilate the two, incorporate them in myself, digest them like that plate of codfish with potatoes.

Now that I understand this of myself, I can comprehend the apprehension that kept me distanced from my father. I sympathize with him for the sterility of the situation into which he was forced.

The sadness in his eyes came from his own pendulum being shackled. He had lost the courage or felt he had no right to put the clock back in motion. But that shackled pendulum stuck in his craw. He should have been allowed to oscillate between land and sea but his time had come to an end.

Experiences at sea had brought my father the best years of his life. His father had been a captain like my great-great-grandfather, who had carried full cargoes of Loyalists from Boston to Quebec. These faithful people had clung to the English Crown as if it were their only identity, like born vassals who could only exist under royal command. As a result, my great-grandfather had received a grant from the King in Nova Scotia. Five hundred acres of Canada for maritime services rendered. But father's good years had long been over.

One summer did bring my father a temporary reprieve. Uncle George's ship put into Yarmouth to discharge one of those new milling machines which was to bring confusion and eventual despair to fat Mr. McTavish the miller. Father was not interested in the machine but took advantage of the novelty to have a look around the old spruce-built ships in the bay. Uncle George was short-handed, and a relation in trouble gave father an ideal excuse to sign on for a round trip to Quebec City. Somehow I was invited too!

Father's silent paternal gravity enwrapped me as I watched the stupidly indifferent longshoremen on the quayside. Did they not realize how incredibly adventurous was our daring departure? The poverty of my practical geography showed itself in my thought that we might well find gold, Quebec being so close to California.

I held father and he held the wheel. I was to learn later that taking the wheel is normally an inherited privilege, like any mastery. On the farm I dared not approach him. At sea he spoke almost gently to me and showed no impatience at my arm permanently holding to his leg. Being my support made him feel more solid.

For several days fog weighed down our sails. Then a wind dispersed the vapors, sending all idle chatter with them. We advanced into the Gulf of St. Lawrence in a silence enforced by delicate navigation and a cacophony of water music played with whistling strings, creaking woods and the bass groans of the old hull.

Like the explorer Jacques Cartier three centuries before, we furled our sails in Gaspé Bay, a majestic funnel which gives access to lands so rich in game, timber and fish that the British Crown maintained several colonial trading stations there. Under Imperial protection the company of Robins, Jones and Whitman exchanged the natural riches of the land against imported merchandise, profits ensured by their monopoly. Going down towards the quay from one of their houses, we passed alongside the Catholic church. Several young French–Canadian boys, scarcely older than myself, jostled to sell us model boats they had made during the winter. I made my sudden over-whelming desire to have one abundantly clear to father, with no result. My tears of disappointment were at first muffled sobs but increased in volume in proportion to our distance from their cause. All I received was a slap behind the ear and the benefit of some prejudiced advice.

"These papists don't even have enough common sense to speak English like everyone else. Look how scruffy they are. And God knows what plots they cook up against us in their churches.

"You can't trust people who don't have the sense to accept defeat. When you've been conquered, you have to obey your new masters. These peasoupers would rather save their crazy religion than make money. And they only keep that obsolete language to annoy us."

"I gave up buying models from them years ago," added Uncle George, "when they started rebelling and carrying guns. Fortu-nately those so-called patriots have been crushed now. They deserv-ed worse."

"Come on Joshua, Papa will make you a better one with real sails. That's a promise."

While I was being treated to this lecture, the sails were being set. Fluvial breezes were to dry the tears on my cheeks. At the mouth of the Saguenay some days later, my mourning for the model boats was ended by the sight of belugas swimming alongside the ship. With friendly eyes, the white monsters gently rubbed against our hull in complete trust.

Now we had to work the tides past silent or noisy islands, often sending up flocks of soaring white geese or clouds of gulls. Quebec City greeted us with her magnificent waterfalls. The torrents of water created a misty veil to hide her legendary secrets. The seamen whispered with knowing looks, stirring my curiosity.

"Look. She hides her face like a bride."

I was afraid because something was being kept from me.

The order was passed for all hands on deck to beat through the hundreds of ships cluttering the roads. These naval dockyards were amongst the most important in the whole of the Americas and huge volumes of commercial cargo transited through the port. Gigs came skimming over the water, coxswains steering with effortless dexterity. It was a race to deliver the first pilot aboard and offer the facilities of a particular private wharf. They scrambled aboard while we were still under way. Once a deal had been struck with Uncle George, the whole gig's crew came on board to help us in to their patron's quay.

As soon as the hold was cleared and cleaned, gangs of stevedores set to stowing the ship with tons of cordage for Halifax. Levi's quay had a warehouse belonging to the Consumer's Cordage Company of Montreal. The superior quality of their Manila ropes made them easily saleable anywhere in America.

I remember there was a festival going on in honor of one of their saints, but I was not allowed ashore to see any of it. The appearance of a "blue nose" might well have turned rejoicing into less friendly activity. I amused myself watching the trapped seamen occupying their enforced idleness with handicrafts: elaborate ship models, frigates in bottles, paintings of sea scenes on canvas offcuts or ditty bags. One thickset Newfoundlander chewed sadly on his quid as he engraved a whale's tooth with a sail needle. I still remember the tobacco pouch lying beside him, fashioned with the finest of workmanship from the webbed foot of a Cape Horn albatross.

Looking through a newspaper Uncle George brought aboard, I was shocked by a drawing of six men hanging from gibbets. The caption read, "A Reminder of the Hanging of Patriots at the Pied du Courant, Montreal." Further on was another illustration, this time showing several men garlanded with flowers. They were "the great patriots who had brought independence to Hawaii."

Uncle George managed to further confuse my ideas of what patriotism was when he spoke about the attempts to have amnesty granted for those Quebec patriots held in prison rather than execution or exile.

"Those guys have rebelled against their conquerors. They've already lost once. Now they want to be conquered again. They've got no excuse. Even their goddam papist preachers have got the message now. They're cunning enough to speak English for business though. As this Adam Thom says in the *Herald*, they're English now, so they might as well act like it."

"But what about the Hawaiians?"

"They won."

So I came to understand which side to be on in a fight.

With a fresh northwesterly we dropped down river towards the Gulf, my father frequently turning his gaze from the maritime horizon to the rich crops and rural animation produced by this corridor of fertile land. At sea his thoughts turned to farming.

Later I came to appreciate those peasoupers with their love of laughter, song and dancing, but then it seemed that the Anglos would stifle French Canada. The "Canayan" trappers who had first tamed the land with audacious energy were already sprouting the old French warts. After a courageous start, they had settled into domesticity and timid xenophobia. Wandering wings were gradually being gnawed away by the predatory teeth of a sedentary religion.

I was to receive more political instruction on this early voyage. Because of more thick fog ahead, we put in to the Magdalens, several small islands set peacefully in the centre of the great Gulf where rain and snow never fall. The clouds, like everything else, just pass around them. Insulated isolation has made the people stubbornly autonomous. By consensus they live close to anarchy. Being mainly fishermen and seal hunters, they had come to put more faith in their own knowledge of the sea and its ice floes than grand political speeches for their survival. Personal freedom was their passion.

Independence was Uncle George's *idée fixe*. Encouraged by the free-flowing potato beer, he launched into a speech praising our hosts and their rejection of outside control.

"One of the finest consequences of the absence of government, for those rare people able to do without it, is the development of each individual's strength. Each man has to learn to think and act for himself, like at sea. No external power could ever look after all our needs anyway, so it's no good expecting it to. Look after yourself, then you can be proud and will be respected by others. That is America's lesson to us all, my friends."

Satisfied with his effect, he swept up the bowl of clotted cream I had been spooning into the crashing waves and demonstrated his point by helping himself to it with great relish.

Retreating to where the other children were sitting on barrels of smoked herrings, I listened to the fishermen telling their tales. Tonight the subject turned to "ponchons," the small tubs they sent messages in, using their knowledge of the currents to direct them to the right destination. But many a mishap occurred when a miscalculation sent a love letter to the wrong place. A fisherman might be welcomed home by an unexpected alliance or a very angry wife.

Around me the older boys were treating the girls with a familiarity I had never witnessed in Nova Scotia. To help the seduction along, the boys boasted of arcane knowledge hinted at with typically masculine condescension. So the girls learned that a ship's compass turns towards red but away from married women, especially if pregnant, garlic eaters, and perjurers; that the moon must always be saluted when coming on watch; that the word "rabbits" must never be used on board; that one must never sail on a Friday or at midday; and that to appease Neptune a young maid should be thrown into the sea before sailing. When the boys took advantage of the girl's excitement to become more intimate, the hubbub had to be suppressed by the men, who could no longer talk above the squeals.

If I was not needed on the farm, the weather was good enough, Miss Landry was not busy at a sickbed, the call of the sea was not too strong and Elizabeth was not available, I went to school. But I went without enthusiasm because, although I wanted to learn, I did not have much interest in good manners or the Holy Scriptures. The only things of interest to me in my school satchel were the barley biscuits and buckwheat rolls my beloved Elizabeth loaded it with. Burying my nose in that satchel, I felt myself safe in the protective folds of her skirt again. There I could forget my mother's eternal weariness.

How often I had labored to help my mother by cutting firewood or cleaning out the stable. By the time I was seven she was into her eighth confinement. There were six of us children still alive. I loved her, but she never had time or energy to spend on me. I was ready to do anything. In spite of being the oldest living son, I even committed the treachery of helping with female tasks, seeking to win her attention by being close to her. This made father furious with shame.

"There are enough girls in this house, young man, for you to be able to hold to your masculine rights. If anyone should see you peeling potatoes or scrubbing the floor like you have been doing, they would think I had a degenerate for a son, and I can't afford to rear a degenerate."

He could not understand that I was just a child and still wanted to be held in her arms. That desire stayed in me like a festering boil, never treated and never cured. Always something came between us: household chores, another baby, illness, or my father's anger. I had to resort to tricks to get anywhere near her, playing a baby or playing a man. She had brought me into this world but would not come into it herself.

Slowly I came to accept the shell she lived in. There was only the shell. The illusion of sound coming from inside was produced by an empty life turning in an endless spiral.

I came to believe later that the "maternal instinct" is not an instinct at all but a learned social role. Women make children, and since there are children, women have to become mothers. The function is not the individual. Necessity is the inventor of mothers.

Happiness needs to be encouraged like any other feeling. Smiles beget smiles. "Melancholy is not good for your health," Miss Landry warned me. Elizabeth was generous with her welcoming smiles. When mother did notice me, she just stared like a daguerreotype fixing on the plate. So, naturally I turned my attention to Elizabeth.

The procession of pregnancies and hardships inured mother to emotion. She seemed barely to notice when another matrimonial submission threw out another child from time to time like an inhuman centripetal force. Another child was just another cause for sadness. I did not live with my mother, I merely ate in her house. I could never bring that photograph to life.

Fortunately, I sniffed the barley biscuits often enough to learn to read. Once Elizabeth had read the weekly *Scotian* to father, I devoured it without leaving so much as a crumb of a comma. One of father's cousins was a crewman on board the *America* so news of its famous races became a topic of conversation. Father could not understand anyone building a boat just for the pleasure of going faster than someone else. Sailing without a mercantile purpose scandalized him.

"Don't go to sea without a good reason. It's ready to swallow you forever if you don't treat it with respect. Never play with the sea. But have you looked at her lines! What a boat! Just think how quickly you could get to Australia in a boat like that."

He was obsessed by the reports of a gold strike at Summer Hill Creek. As his own position grew more wretched, so his interest in the possibility of sudden riches increased.

With the acquisition of a new rotary press, the *Scotian* brought out

11

two issues per week that year. To help fill the new space, they serialized Melville's *Moby Dick*. When the newspaper was finished with, I cut out the story and carried each section to the shed. There I sat in our ancient decaying dory to read and reread each chapter. That Captain's inexorable need to meet and master his whale fascinated me. He was ready to sacrifice his reputation and life to satisfy his craving for a final encounter. His mania took him out of reach of death, his excesses made him immortal. Though he turned his back on civilization, he could never be forgotten. His pagan stamp had been printed on the world.

The new milling machine proved more profitable to the smith than the miller. Forever taken aback by its own mechanical complexity, it produced more laughter than flour. New respect grew for the old water mill, still slowly turning while its replacement rusted in silence. Never try to steal the scene from an old pro. Bready McTavish poured out his woe to his clients.

"All of last year's profits are being eaten up by the payments on this goddam machine. And that goddam smith is devouring this year's."

"Goddam progress, it sticks in my throat. I'll never go to an agricultural fair again. Their newfangled machines are one almighty swindle."

He raised enough steam to drive a paddle boat.

The Annapolis valley spreads out flat at the foot of a spine of hills thickly wooded with thorns parted here and there by patches of bald rock. From those hills tumble the streams that irrigate her flower-filled meadows. It is their water that pumps up the apples until the skin is ready to split under the pressure of sweet juices. McTavish's millpond was fed by one of those tributaries of the Annapolis River. And that pond was my first ocean.

I was just a nipper then. A five acre pool offers plenty of challenges and dangers for an eight-year-old-lad. It had the added attraction of being strictly out of bounds. Too wide to swim across, too deep to wade, its water mysteriously black under the shade of the overhanging trees, banks cut away and crumbling, current running irresistibly into the maw of the great wheel—how could I keep away?

At first it was enough just to sneak close and look, but I soon grew bolder after that went unpunished. I would pry a rotten upright from the surrounding picket fence and throw it into the current. Running to the mill, I watched it being sucked in by the wheel to be pulverized by the pounding paddles. Filling my picket-boats with imaginary passengers, I was either the world hero saving shipwrecked waifs or the evil despot destroying hundreds of human lives, depending on how I felt that day. Omnipotence was mine.

The individual is so tyrannized by society that we all try to reverse the process, whether in our play, dreams, or struggles for power. Power carries the right to assert oneself. Though still only a novice, I liked the feeling. With power one can be bold.

First you dominate your own fears and turn them into a source of courage. Then you can dominate others by manipulating their fears. I watch with interest as one gull falls from the sky to the masthead to dislodge another, which then frightens another from the shrouds, which in turn attacks another sitting on the water. I wanted to increase the number of my subjects, measuring my domain by the count of those dominated.

So that my boats could carry more people, I ripped out ever larger chunks of wood. Thousands were sent to their deaths each day. My best was a whole fence post, which made such a hollow anarchic clatter as it passed through the wheel of destiny that I recovered it from the bank below for further trips to purgatory.

Uncle George had a saying: "If you poke one finger into the forbidden fruit, you'll end up loosing an arm."

I was lucky enough to escape intact. One day when the household was preoccupied with the latest baby, Alice, I made my preparations and slipped off. A print of *The Wreck of the Medusa* had been my inspiration. Imagination had done all it could with throwing in sticks: the game had grown stale. Familiarity had removed all sense of danger, and danger was the thrill I was seeking.

Collecting together a dozen good sized dead branches, I lashed them together with rusty fencing wire. It took all my strength to get it into the pond without it all falling to pieces, but once in I found that it would bear my weight so long as I did not move much. I was not launching myself into the wheel, of course; I knew the currents well enough by now to avoid that fate. Brave but not reckless, my goal was the opposite bank. As the mist revealed that far shore, I stepped onto the new land with all the wondrous pride John Cabot must have felt so long before when he first reached North America.

It was probably my sister's green wool overblanket I used as a sail that gave me away. The great explorer was greeted at home with a good thrashing and an endless list of ignoble punishments. I felt this martyrdom expiated all the murders in the mill wheel. My final heroic act deserved a better reward, but I was in no position to argue. Father was six feet tall and weighed two hundred pounds.

I had to sew my sail back into a blanket. Elizabeth was given my coverlet, and from then until I left home I slept every night with the rancid smell of that green wool. That smell and the sight of that shade of green still remind me of how I was punished for being daring, found guilty for stepping out of line. To me they are the smell and color of affliction.

The next summer my mother grew even weaker, my father became even more discouraged, and I had a great time. Mama confined herself to bed. Father dashed around like a demented windmill as successive clouds of beetles ate their way through the potato field. Heavy rains rotted the fodder before it could dry and washed away his last remaining interest in agriculture.

Sitting hunched over the Canso stove, he fed it from a meagre supply of apple tree prunings. The feeble fire barely managed to budge the thermometer on the oven door. Buckwheat biscuits inside dried rather than baked; there had been no molasses for those biscuits since the beginning of June. A large pot simmered on the griddle, but it held only a few old potatoes and two yellowing onions. On the right, over the water tank, the teapot tried to draw a last drop of flavor from recycled leaves. The Canso's chrome was tarnished. Father would not have wanted to see the despair in his face reflected back to him anyway, an unmanned vessel seemingly trying to crush the fender with his boot, scraping off the sterile red mud. With the poker he opened and closed the airvent in a forlorn effort to coax some life from the fire.

Elizabeth signalled me to follow her to the stable where the cow waited to be milked. There I knew I could get some real heat from my budding sensual imaginings. At that young age they come to the boil very easily.

The pattering of rain on the roof made a wall of sound to cut us off from the world. All we could hear was our own panting and the cow's slow, heavy breaths. Gaps in the old clapboarding lent an air of conspiracy. We could see out, but nobody could see in.

My russet-haired, fifteen year old sister had acquired the air of mystery surrounding young women. Her child's shape was already changing to more mature lines. I sipped fresh warm milk from a tin mug, watching as she squeezed the cow's well-washed teats. It is impossible for a woman to milk a cow modestly. As I leaned over her to dip my mug into the pail, I felt my eyes draw me to the edge of the abyss. I could only stay there a few seconds or I would have fallen.

In my dreams I did indeed leap into that fertile valley. These reveries were so vivid I was sure she must have been aware of the part she played in them. Her smiles encouraged me in that belief.

"Joshua, come and help me move the cow. I need to talk to you."

It was my last treat. Elizabeth sobbed as she told me of the plans which had been made for me. An aunt in Hall's Harbor had heard of the family's desperate plight and offered to take one child for the rest of the summer. I was to be removed one hundred and fifty miles from the only person I loved.

The wrench was as difficult as weaning. I have never touched a drop of milk since.

The Bay of Fundy is a funnel with two throats. The highest tides in the world run down that funnel twice every day. When they are compressed into the throats of the Chignecto and Cobequid bays, they reach nearly fifteen feet on a spring. A tidal bore is forced up the Petitcodiac River all the way to Moncton, thirty miles inland. Hall's Harbor is on the channel to the Minas Basin, where the tide enjoys its fullest range.

My cousins had always haunted the quays and soon taught an enthusiastic pupil all about the boats and their owners: the local guys who regularly crossed the sixty miles to Saint John, New Brunswick, through treacherous currents and dangerously short seas; the Acadian fishermen from St. Mary's Bay who rarely mixed with Anglophones; and sad Portuguese in from the Grand Banks.

A skipper could occasionally be persuaded to take a couple of us out fishing on his boat. Generally around forty feet long, their bows reached high towards the sky while the stern spread out low and flat over the water. The only accommodation was a small wheelhouse with a coal cookstove. An unlucky spell could force a fisherman to work in the mines at Sydney to pay off his debts, and the coal scuttle was a silent reminder of that possibility. These broken-toothed, bearded fishermen who smiled enigmatically from under their salt-encrusted toques brought me to understand that the quest for fish is more than an economic activity. I experienced the triumphant satisfaction of returning with a full catch of mackerel or lobster, the individual independence and the collective rivalry.

On board those big boats I enjoyed eating for the first time. At home or in my aunt's kitchen, the portions were measured out frugally to ensure enough for the days ahead. At sea it was as if there were no tomorrow. A black iron cauldron was boiled up on the stove with one-third salt water, two-thirds sweet. Into this went small lobsters, mackerel fillets, scrubbed potatoes, and onions to make ample stew for everyone. Returning to the house, I gained great merit from my aunt for the modesty of my appetite. I maintained a humble silence as she held me up as an example to the others. Since then I have always been suspicious of humility, wondering what it is covering up.

At Hall's Harbor, salt water got into my veins, port odors infused my flesh, and thoughts of the open sea began to fill my mind. The oceans presented me with lessons enough for my whole life: the calm after a storm, each successive wave obliterating the last, ripples rolling untiringly onto the beach, the ship moving on and taking apparently impossible waves one at a time, lying quietly ahull while the worst of a gale passes, the rocks eternally battered by crashing swells, yet never moving.

However, these are reflections belonging to chairbound old age. In the hungry world of reality, seamen do not dine on words, for words are not meat enough to face a struggle where lives hang in the balance. When there is work to do, an oar is an oar, a mast is a mast, a wave is a wave. Only the idle make them symbols of something else.

My aunt's attitude to her husband was changeable in a way I did not then understand. She was more loving towards him just before he set off on a trip than when he returned home. I broke the enigma later by living through it myself. Departures are pregnant with possibilities, whereas returns are more trivial. Leaving is always more dignified than coming back. I did not understand this then, but I was frightened of becoming like one of those broken-backed gadgies on the dock unable to pull sail or shift anchor, their horizons limited to the torn nets passing through their twisted hands. A shorebound sailor has not a future, only a past.

The final departure should be the most glorious: it could be one's trip to immortality.

When I returned to the farm in the fall, I felt like a stranger. Mother was permanently ill and father had sunk into depression. The farm was no longer viable, so we had to move. I thought this was entirely father's fault, not realizing how important a role the wife plays on a smallholding.

There was fever in the air, but was the illness caused by fear of the new or regret for the old? The bitter taste was certainly failure, and failure gives no one confidence for the future. But I fought against the prevailing feeling of resignation. I tried to give myself the advantage of thinking of it as a decision with dignity. Resignation, accepting change imposed from outside, can only lead to alienation. You are only true to yourself when you exert your own will. There is nearly always something that can be done. If you cannot alter your ship's course, there are the sails to trim to control her speed.

Personally, I was happy to be leaving because our destination was Westport, on Brier Island. My mother had family there and would be able to surround herself with their attention. It might not cure her, but it would ease her decline. Her mother was dead, but her father held the noble office of lighthouse keeper. Father had bought out a struggling boot business. Elizabeth would not look up from the trunk she was packing.

I only suffered one moment of sadness on that fateful day. All around me rose cries, sighs, oaths, alarms, childish tears, groans and protests, all the rumbling apprehension of fearful stomachs faced with the unknown. But I was returning to the sea; the road of change lead straight to where I wanted to be. Nevertheless, when I was sent to the stable to see if any tools had been overlooked there, I stumbled.

When I saw the empty desolation of that familiar place, tears broke from my eyes, provoked by the sudden awareness that my years there had not left a trace. Everything I had lived here was evaporating; my life had disappeared. Was my past so volatile that I could not take it with me? Was there to be no witness of my passing?

There were still a few things left with which I could make my mark. A full five-gallon bucket of lard would make a good preservative. Improvizing a ritual of consecration, I collected my testimonials: the best of my lobster claw hoard, the jute sack I sat on watching Elizabeth, my old rusty knife, a brand new penny given to me by my Hall's Harbor aunt, a pot of mulberry jelly stolen from the store last winter and hidden for a secret feast, the seat of the milking stool, and my tin mug. Everything was crammed into the bucket and well covered in lard. Sealing the lid on my life in Wilmot Township, I scratched the top with: Here lies the Ghost of Joshua S.

My treasure was stowed under the false floor of the potato store. It was easy to get to because the potato store was as empty as usual. I had often hidden there to daydream, and pretend I lived in a happy family with a loving mother and a laughing father.

It is strange that I felt I had to do this secretly, but I was sure that if father found out he would never let me leave my mark. Anyway, it drove off my momentary sadness by overcoming its cause. I was leaving but also staying. Nothing was to be forgotten.

Walking back to the house, I kicked my feet through the brilliant autumn leaves lying thick on the ground. Soon they would be gone, buried and rotting. Fate was not going to play that game with me. Not if I could do anything about it.

Proud and lonely Brier Island; an outpost of Nova Scotia, but ready to cut its moorings one fine day and sail off on its own. Meanwhile it lay anchored fast to the ocean bottom riding out the tireless Atlantic rollers that tried to drive it onto the lee-shore of the American mainland.

Westport stands at the threshold of the island. The lighthouse was on the other end, a sentry under grandfather's command. Anchored to its granite rock, in a perpetual salt sweat, my craggy grandfather stood guard against the waves. With its light sweeping through the mist, the lighthouse drove off the giants, only allowing the meekest ripples past the gate to St. Mary's Bay, like a sturdy lion tamer lashing the ocean's wildest instincts into submission. At its feet the sea boiled in frustrated anger.

What frightened me most about my mother's illness was that I could not understand it. There was nothing tangible enough for a child to grasp. Nobody would tell me she has this or she has that wrong with her. But the whole household was organized around this mystery.

The house itself might have been designed by a geometry teacher. Exactly rectangular in plan and elevation, its rigorously regular roof sloped up to a ridge, plumb on the centreline. Since it had been built, the chimney had introduced its own anarchic ideas and the pine shingles had grown grey in the salt spray. Deeply conventional, it preferred the security of village life to any isolated adventures.

As I see it now, mother was simply suffering the chronic symptoms of creeping maternaphobia. Unable or unwilling to perform as society expected, she took refuge in illness. Not prepared to perform the only role offered to her, she created her own character as an invalid. The new persona needed careful cultivation, for if she lost it she would have had no identify left at all.

Physiologically she had all the necessary organs to be a mother. But the social function of a mother goes much further than bearing a child. Having a womb and breasts does not ensure that a woman will enjoy rearing children, and my father certainly did not see it as his job. Sexual desire, pregnancy, childbearing, motherhood, fatherhood, love, affection, dedication, friendship, tenderness—these are all separate things not to be confused or expected to follow one from another.

How could she escape from the guilt of not being what she was told she ought to be? All the other women seemed to be able to cope. She ran before the storm, straight into the safe harbor of incapacity. Hidden in her illness, nobody could make any demands on her. Sickness spread her welcoming arms to a woman who had no other way to escape from a gale that had already damaged her beyond repair.

Mother consulted the sadness within her, and together they called in the midwife to confirm the diagnosis and, above all, the treatment. The patient must have total rest and constant company. In default of love, she needed frequent doses of sympathy diluted in a syrup of kindness. When the midwife proposed a last-ditch treatment delivered with a novel instrument of torture, a syringe that pumped the remedy directly into the blood through a hollow needle, mother measured its efficacy by the suffering she would have to endure. Who would suffer that dreadful torture unless they were genuinely ill? Twice each week we had the privilege of listening to her resigned complaints.

"Don't go too far away this morning, I am growing so weak."

Then later, "The mere thought of that needle brings me out in a cold sweat. I can see it. Joshua, stay close to Mama."

In the afternoon, after martyrdom had been administered, came the dose of self-commiseration.

"I'm completely finished now, but perhaps it will help me to improve. You do want Mama to be better, Joshua?"

I was not convinced that I would ever get a real mother, not if it was just to be a repeat of what I had known before. My attitude towards her may have been hard, but a child is very selfish in his needs and I needed love.

"You see what a mother has to endure for her sons!"

I was more aware of the children's point of view, including that of the girls. These scenes left me with a healthy fear of needles. Nurses with giant syringes often pursued me in my nightmares.

But another event gave me stuff for sweeter dreams. A frigate made a short stopover at the Westport government quay. We were fascinated by a fisherman's dory, so you can imagine the excitement an elegant frigate caused. The whole male population gathered on the dock to discuss the merits and demerits of the ship and her rig. The women kept respectfully out of sight, under the shadow of the sheds, punctuating their giggles with arpeggio screams of delight. The ship's crew studiously ignored all the brouhaha, but their presence entitled us to share a little in their prestige.

As the ship lay port side to, it's two passengers, Mr. Heinrich Steinway and Mr. Samuel Colt, propped themselves against the starboard bulwarks, backs to the plebes. Mr. Colt was demonstrating to Mr. Steinway a new weapon he held easily in one hand. Shot followed shot without any sign of reloading. How was it done? Even the gulls that served as targets were taken by surprise.

Suddenly a miraculous bouquet of multicolored sound burst out from the ship's open hatchways. Music slipped and coiled into the ears, soothing any pain. Here was a true remedy, the medicine of music. The frigate carried several prototypes of Mr. Steinway's pianoforte. Mr. Colt's gun suddenly lost all appeal for me, for I was being baptized into a new faith. It was not until five years later that I found out what the music was. Hearing Mr. Liszt's "Faust" for what I thought would be the first time, I recognized instantly what I had heard as a child. Then the title had been unimportant. I had just let the strains flow into my blood.

The sound of hundreds of notes joining into an harmonious whole took me into myself again. The music dissolved everyone else, rather than making me one with them. I took it inside myself and then there was just me and the music; escape.

How could people discipline hands to produce those wonderful sounds? This talent I still admire without envy: my only regret is that

I do not have it myself. And how can a simple mortal weave all those patterns of notes together on paper, knowing exactly how they will join to entangle and catch another's emotion? The music made me forget the crowd and became my only companion. I could let myself go and know that it would guide me. All was banality compared to the ability of a musician to play upon my emotions, equipped only with sounds and silences.

The air of tragedy in the house surrounding mother was so awful, you could smell it from outside. From the increased activity, I guessed she had fallen again. For some reason the adults tried to keep the secret from us children. We were ushered out of sight when they held their whispered assemblies. But on one occasion I was overlooked, hidden in the linen closet, probably waiting to ambush a tribe of marauding Indians or surprise a passing warship. I was not there with the intent to overhear, but who can resist listening to a "private" conversation? What I heard pass between my mother and the midwife was not elevating.

"In the circumstances, Mrs. Slocombe, I think it would be best to stop the injections during your pregnancy."

"Are you sure? Without their help—the pain is so strong—without it I will never get through."

"Please understand, my dear, pregnancy is not a contraindication for this medicine, but it's not for me to take risks with new techniques. I have a family to consider."

"You can't do this to me."

"Try to be reasonable, Mrs. Slocombe, I can probably arrange a queen's delivery for you."

"It is really painless? Really?"

"If it's good enough for Queen Victoria."

"They say she slept right through Prince Leopold's birth, so she felt nothing."

"It is more like a swoon, brought on by chloroform. I have John Snow's book at home. He's the one who performed the delivery."

I thought to myself that, as much as wanting to escape the pain, she wanted to sleep through the birth so she could pretend it was all just a dream. Then the child would never have to enter her reality. I quickly dropped a line of reasoning which could only hurt me.
"If I don't have the anaesthetic I will never survive."

Mother was good at mothering herself. Perhaps she had never

known a real mother but had learned to look out for herself early in life. I do not know.

"Count on me, Mrs. Slocombe. You can sleep without fear."

So the family was going to grow painlessly. But a queen's delivery does not ensure an equally painless life for the offspring. Why did she keep having more children? Nobody even thought to ask the question in those days. When I returned to Westport many years later, (by then I had changed my name to Slocum), I was told that my elder brother, John Ingraham, who died just after I was born, had succumbed to anaclitic depression. Rejection was too much for him to cope with.

That night it was my turn to be mother's sleeping companion. She insisted on never being left alone for a moment. As I lay stretched out on the bed beside her, she turned over in her sleep and her nightdress fell open. My first sight of a full female breast shattered all my imaginings. A limp lump of vein-streaked flesh wrinkling up to a great brown wart was not what I had envisioned. But I was frozen to the spot: I could not drag my eyes away from it. Were all breasts like that? What I had glimpsed of Elizabeth's led me to believe not. How could I be sure? She turned back, leaving her breast imprinted upon my memory.

When I was relieved of my watch, I ran off to hide my guilty knowledge in the drying yards. The cod dries were sheltered behind a windbreak of pines at the end of a cul-de-sac which started at the salting sheds. The path ran across shore rocks. It was a good secluded spot to calm an agitated mind.

When I returned home there was not a glimmer of light in the house. I was sure father would be waiting up to pass judgment on me. Everybody would know what I had seen, how I had stared, what I had thought. Of course nobody knew, but I went in fear for days.

I never particularly liked school, but I did miss it when I was taken out at the age of ten. Probably it was getting away from home into the company of other children my own age that I missed more than anything else. At ten I started work in father's bootmaking shop, a patched up old shed appropriately sited next to the canning factory's rubbish dump. There father further jeopardized a business that was already running comfortably downhill on its own. I do not know if the business made father depressed or if his depression sent the business into decline. My own aversion to the work made little difference.

Father's own skin had soaked in the acrid smell of tanin so deeply that he carried it with him everywhere. A bundle of hides reminds me of him and the workshop. It brings back that nausea I suffered every day.

In those days a master exercised as much authority over his apprentice as any Southern slave owner over his slaves. He had more power than a petty god, and acted like one too. Setbacks were worked off in a grand bout of despotism. I was never free. Anxiety turned him into a tyrant. Trapped between the rocks of a father's fears and a master's will I was crushed each time they rolled to the waves of misfortune. Before my bones were properly formed they were bent under the weight of working from dawn to nightfall. Days are long in the northern summer.

All day I was bowed over before stinking fishing boots, abject servant at the feet of tyrant after tyrant. In father's rare absences I would hike myself to my feet and peer out at the sailors fleetly entering or leaving the harbor on the swift tides. From here they looked like courageous heroes incapable of any petty thought. When I turned my nose back to the repair of the boots those same sailors wore I breathed the rancid odor of decaying life. Making boots from cow hides; stretching dead skin into shape to encase stinking unwashed feet. Every day I was sick. My stomach retched, vomited up, rejected it all. That smell formed the walls of my prison.

As our supplies of hides arrived by schooner, prolonged gales would sometimes see us completely out of materials. A seaman never hopes for bad weather. I prayed for it in those days. Then I took refuge in grandfather's lighthouse until a break brought the arrival of the next cargo of emetics.

Grandfather's character was in keeping with his appearance: short and squat, on legs bowed with arthritis.

"The price you have to pay for living with this fog, my son."

With him it was nothing for nothing. Anything you did not deserve you had to pay for or be punished for. If you had not earned it, it was theft. He was puritan but just, straightforward, and fair. He had my total admiration. I attached myself to him with all the love I could not give to my parents, because he gave me love in return.

Together we scoured Westport's small dockyard. He taught me all about a boat's skeleton and ribs, how to tell its condition by ear. Tapping on old and new frames with a maple axe handle, he showed me how to separate the weak from the strong. Each note had its meaning. Did it ring flat, or clear as a bell? A boat was a musical instrument to this man who had long dreamed of becoming a renowned violinist himself.

"My son, if that great inventor Wagner could hear me, down in his corner of Germany, he would put me in an orchestra with a full set of hulls and rigging just as sure as that lighthouse is taller than me. Just imagine it."

The isolation of Brier Island and the creeping paralysis of arthritis had only allowed him to develop his playing to a modest extent. The local popularity of the gaunt Cajun Zacharie Leblanc pushed him ever further into obscurity in his lighthouse.

"That Cajun is always fiddling at his reels and quadrilles. They are so busy with their high-stepping chasing after women that nobody has time to listen to melodies. There is no music any more. Just wild, top-speed stomping. The pleasure of music is for the ears, not the feet."

Grandfather's own light had not been dimmed by time. He spoke of old age as if it were a disguise. Looking down from the dominating height of his light, he could despise anyone who had no respect for age. The swaggering pretences of youth he abhorred.

"You see, my son, the peace of wisdom comes with age. Grow old quickly while you are still young enough. Then you can enjoy it longer. Just arrange to stop before you reach senility. I'll let you into a secret: the old age the slowest."

I could not understand.

"It's not that complicated. The young pity the old, they think they have some advantage over us. But I am old myself and it's the young I pity. Youth is nothing to be proud of, my son."

I did have one reason to want to be older: so I could escape that infernal workshop.

"You're right there. That workshop won't last half as long as the boots you make in it. You'll have to start thinking about yourself, my son. You can only last if you accomplish something. Don't waste your time messing about with kids' things."

I told him I would like to be like him and own a lighthouse one day.

"I don't own this lighthouse, my son. It's a bloody sight too important for that. And my job's a bloody sight more important than just owning it. I am responsible for it."

Suddenly, Grandfather Southern wrinkled up his brow in an effort to see more clearly.

"Get the telescope and take a look out there, to the southwest."

The very first Cunard steamer was heading back towards Europe, after its record-breaking crossing to America in nine and a half days. The great steel hull smashed its way past. It needed to pay no homage to our Nova Scotian pines.

I was full of enthusiasm, but my cries of excitement stuck in my throat when I saw the look of sadness which came over grandfather's face. He took me by the arm and gently led me away. Then I began to wonder just what I was so enthusiastic about. I learned from him to question "progress."

"Leave the telescope alone. You'll have to get used to seeing for yourself, my son. It's the only way you'll get your freedom. Think about that tomorrow while you're cutting hides. It might help you."

Leaving the lighthouse road, I cut through the woods towards the cod dries. I was headed back to captivity, so why not take the longest route? Like a returning slave I walked slowly with bowed head. A sound must have made me look up and see the seaman just before I came into the clearing. He was weaving through the racks but keeping an eye in the direction of the cannery. From the way he clung to the racks I presumed he must be drunk. I froze, afraid of his reaction if I should surprise him. Then he turned and I could see the crooked grin on his face as he relieved himself all over the cod as they lay with bowels exposed to the sun. With a sigh he stowed his tackle, spat a parting farewell on another cod, and trod heavily back towards the quay.

I had to give him time to clear the road so he would not suspect I had seen him at his work. I stood and looked at the defiled fish in uncomprehending amazement. The man was quite unknown to me, but I felt sure that if we ever came face to face, the monster would be able to tell I had witnessed his crime and would eliminate me. I fled for home.

A battle between conscience and fear was raging inside me by the time I reached the house. If I told what I had seen, the monster would seek his revenge; if I did not, I would be an accomplice. Fear won. To avoid suspicion, I did not make straight for my room. I had to pretend I had nothing to conceal. Squatting at the top of the stairs seemed a good compromise; I was not hiding, but I was alone. Thus I came to hear another conversation between mother and the midwife.

Their talk covered the eternally topical subject of illness. Sicknesses, preferably grave, were the only events capable of raising an emotion in mother's heart. The midwife brought new delicacies of information for mother to receive with cries of alarm. Discussing other people's maladies was the only way she could overcome and temporarily forget her own. By becoming an expert in disease, a professional hypochondriac, she could open up a whole range of possible new futures for herself.

Today Portuguese sailors were going to infect us all with cholera. There were thousands of victims in their native land, eight thousand dead in Lisbon alone. We must avoid them like the plague.

The strange woman who was battling to save the lives of wounded soldiers in the Crimea, a Miss Nightingale, was received with distaste. Washing messy wounds was not treating proper illnesses. Finally I had had enough of this and crept off to bed. A young woman came to my dreams to wipe the sweat gently from my excited body. After that night she often brought me her cures.

The grave, austere atmosphere of home ensured that my conscience made me feel guilty if I was ever idle there. Any pleasure had to be obtained outside, in secret, and out on the waters of the bay if possible. My maritime audacity dragged a band of scruffy accomplices in its wake. Our crazy craving to be afloat sometimes made us take careless risks. Of course, none of us could swim; no seaman feels the need to learn. We expect to be on top of it, not in it. Besides, it held no fear for us. Respect, yes, you can respect something you intend to master, but if you fear it you will fail. Death lurks close behind fear, ready to unravel the mystic ties bonding a sailor to the sea.

Cobbled up rafts were the best thing we had until we found the wreck of a ship's longboat lost in a small rocky cove. We worked on it for weeks, patching holes with whatever we could find. The looms of two broken oars were lashed together for a mast, but it took hours to sew together enough rags to make what we called a sail. For us that sorry heap of jetsam was as good as the brigs that traded with the West Indies. What marvellous business we would do. A full cargo of fish could easily be caught to barter for slaves in Africa, sell them in the West Indies and fill up with rum, then back home to a hero's welcome and endless riches. We would even keep a few slaves for the menial jobs, like making boots. So we would sit in our boat on the beach and outdo each other in bold adventures. I capped them all when I suggested a voyage around the world.

Meanwhile the boat stayed on the beach. It would be seven miles of sailing to round Brier Island.

Tears of frustration trickled down my cheeks and dripped onto the leather uppers of stinking boots. Surely this could not be my destiny. They left me with an aversion to feet, even pretty ones. I only had to see feet and it brought back that bitter smell. I had to get out of that dank workshop and away from boots at any price. Smelly, thick-soled boots reaching up to the knee, boots that were proof against snow, mud, and sea water. I ought to be wearing these boots, not sitting here sewing them.

Although the old dory had been repaired to our satisfaction—that is, all the obvious holes had something nailed over them—the day for our exploit never seemed to arrive. When we did find a time to suit everybody, the tide or the weather would be against us. Those tides are dangerous and have to be taken at just the right time. A light boat like ours would be swept away. The range is so great that the flood starts before the ebb has finished. The incoming current passes under the outgoing stream, breaking up to the surface with a roar like thunder. At low water, shining ochre mud flats stretch as far as the eye can see, slimy rocks poking their heads out here and there. Peace reigns while the sea gathers itself for the next onslaught.

We had no need for tide tables, we could tell when to prepare a boat "by pig." At low water the village's pigs ventured far out on the mud in search of clams. When they saw the rising tide, they made for shore, squealing fit to burst. Two hours after this warning was the ideal time to weigh anchor. So long as the wind was right, that is, because if it was wind against tide the chop kicked up was too much for an open boat. Father knew all the tricks of tide and current around Brier Island from his own sailing days, but the knowledge had to be teased out of him during the rare moments when he allowed himself to think back to those happy times. Words came out uneasily, squeezed between long silences. Memories of better days made the present even harder to bear. I stored away every drop I could get.

As the village was mainly Quaker, there was no tavern. Men gathered in the post office to gossip, which was good for me because I could slip in and listen. News of Mr. Livingstone's exploits was discussed for hours. The discovery of the giant waterfalls in the middle of Africa which he named for Queen Victoria would suffice for his name to be recorded in history. When a Westport fisherman was lost at sea, he was soon forgotten outside his own family. This Livingstone was still alive but assured of a place in prosperity. I had to start doing something outstanding soon or I would disappear too.

An outbreak of vermin in the workshop, probably attracted by offcuts of leather from the rubbish dump next to us, meant the workshop had to be treated with quick lime and sealed up for two whole, marvellous days. Wonderful rats.

At six in the morning I woke to the sound of running pigs and made straight for the dory hidden in its cove. The rest of the gang would be in class when the school bell rang at eight, but there was no school for me. It was the first time I had been glad of working in that awful shop. True, it did give me an edge over the other lads; they still had their heads buried in books while I was part of the adult world. I used my difference, my solitude, to command respect from them. It had to have some advantage. I exploited my own misfortune by emphasizing that difference. Now I had a chance to stand out again, to claim what was planned as a communal glory for myself, undiluted. I had no scruples about my friends. Why should I pretend now that I had? I am a seaman, not a saint: I follow a deeper calling.

The dory was right at the water's edge, but it was still a struggle for me to launch it alone. I urged myself on, shouting encouragements to myself in that wayward pubescent voice that tries to be gruff and then suddenly turns into a squeak. I pretended I was my grandfather, the old seadog John Southern, who had heard the thunder of Nelson's cannon and served on the *Bellerophon* when she transported Napoleon into exile on St. Helena.

Sitting back, with the sail pulling us along, I was totally confident of my success. When this voyage became known, I would be rushed to the Paris International Exposition to be feted by the multitudes. Was I more intoxicated by the adventure itself or by the fame it would bring me?

After the lighthouse point, the true nature of our boatbuilding ability began to show itself. A puff of wind had the sail back in rags. In tears, I started rowing back to the cove. Tears of frustration at first, then tears of exhaustion as my twelve-year-old muscles began to weaken, and then tears of fear as the water slowly crept above my ankles. I felt so alone. Would I ever step on dry land again? Was I to die like this, unseen and unsung? That damned Livingstone had all the luck.

Nearer the cove, columns of spray shot up as waves bounced off the rocks. I had to row looking over my shoulder, fighting to keep clear of the patches of foam that seemed to draw the boat in with a fatal attraction. Never was a sinner more repentant. They say that mountaineers sometimes throw themselves into the void as the only way to free themselves from the fear of falling. Do they simply take the initiative before they are overcome or do they answer the siren call of death? But I was too young to die yet, to die in the shame of failure.

I spread my clothes to dry on the sand while I bailed the dory. There was nothing to be done about the sail but remove the remaining tatters and plead ignorance. There must be no suspicion of what had passed. If nobody knew what had happened, then there would be no failure. Defeat without witnesses is like success without recognition; nothing at all. My fear of death was transformed into a fear of being found out. By the time I walked back into Westport, I was still shaking. It was not yet midday and nobody had even noticed my absence. I had got away with it.

Nothing gained then, but nothing lost, and I had come face to face with fear. It had lost its mystery.

I made for the lighthouse. There I could revive my spirits talking about Mr. Livingstone's adventures again. Grandfather patiently let me chatter on, but there was a look of gentle reproach in his eye. He walked me to the end of the point, the head of the headland.

"Listen to me carefully. Do you know why heroes and adventurers go out looking for something to achieve? It is because they don't understand the difference between strength and violence. Strength is like this." He used a stick to roll a boulder over onto its side. "You see? Concentrated energy with a solid base. Violence wastes its energy on the wind." Now he beat the bounder wildly with the stick but, of course, it did not budge. "Effort wasted and I'm worn out. The great exploits you're so full of are just like that. They achieve nothing. Like this lighthouse you think is so important, they are only signs, nothing unless other people know how to use them."

I fell asleep there on the rocks, wrecked.

Even though my sister Elizabeth was six years older than I was, our feet were identical, short and wide like seamen's forearms. We used to lie on our backs, legs raised and feet together, continually amazed by their complete coincidence.

Playing that game just after our brother Ingram Bill's birth, I suffered a terrible shock. I had seen blood stained cloths being carried from mother's room that day, so I knew that women bleed when they give birth. As we lay giggling, I could not resist the opportunity to let my eyes run up Elizabeth's legs. I knew there was some kind of secret hidden up there. Then suddenly I glimpsed a patch of red on her knickers. My laughter froze in the chill that came over me. If she was bleeding, then she was going to have a baby too, a baby that would take my place and leave me in the cold.

My legs collapsed. I could not stand, so sat hunched up on the floor. Elizabeth knew me so well she guessed exactly what had happened. She came over and sat with her back to mine—our backs fitted too—and started to give me a gift of words in proof of the bond between us. She whispered to me all the great secrets of womanhood; she told me how women follow a special calendar whose high priestess is the moon, unlike men, who only know the seasons of the sun. She spoke of the original female sin which had to be expiated with blood every month, how marriage would lead to the stopping of this flow for nine months, followed by the torture of childbirth. I knew enough about what came after that. So I became an initiate and never again had to climb that wall of secrecy separating men and women.

In 1856 the first refrigerated ship had carried a cargo of fresh meat from Argentina to Europe. I had cut out its picture from the *Scotian*. When I stacked firewood in the cellar, I formed a secret hiding place I could slip into by removing a few logs. In this pirate's cave I dedicated all my free time to making a detailed model of that ship. All of my twelfth winter, when I was not working, that was where I went.

The hull I rebuilt three times. The two sides never seemed to quite match, so there was a list when I tried the flotation test. Finally I had to settle with ballasting her with two pennies I had saved, carefully concealing the subterfuge so I could forget it myself. Before fixing down the deck with tiny treenails cut from Eddy matches, I stowed the carefully folded illustration in the hold. I studied that illustration so often, I think I could reproduce it now. I even remember what was on the back, the end of an article on the abolition of privateering and a headline announcing the mysterious suicide of a composer, Mr. Schumann. Interminable sanding with a piece of dried shark skin removed every last knife mark. I rubbed it till it was as smooth as ivory.

The secrecy was as important as the model. Here was something known only to me, a concealed weapon I could draw on if anyone threatened my self-esteem. In its varnished glory, it needed a suitable setting. Mounting it on a cedar shingle, I shaped a sea from offcuts of leather, meticulously forming and glueing each individual wave. My ship ploughed majestically through the swells.

One Sunday morning I was left alone on watch by mother's bedside while the rest of the family attended church. My father had become as committed to the Methodist Church as I was to my little model. A brand-new deaconship increased his authority and straightened his back so he now stood his full six feet again. Sunday morning was his moment of glory, when he took his proper position in the Methodist model of eternal happiness.

When mother fell asleep, I took advantage of the rarity of an empty house to fetch my model from my secret cellar room; I needed to see how it looked in the full light of day. Lost in admiration, I forgot time until I heard voices below. All I could do was try to hide it under my bed.

Father found it somehow. Religion had made him eager to hunt out sins. Then I had my vision of the Methodist model of hell.

Why?

Because I had stolen the leather, the glue, the shingle, the wood, and the varnish; because the model represented a novelty; because I had missed the morning's display of religious righteousness; because he resented me for having a dream of my own; because he had not ordained the work; because I had hopes from life when he liked to preach death; because enforced celibacy was filling him with frustration? I do not know. All I remember are his great hands beating at me, and the maledictions he screamed at the demons he had to beat out of my body. I accepted it. It was the price I had to pay for having a dream. Hours of work had gone into creating it and now it was being baptized.

Resentment came only when the punishment turned to injustice. Magnified to a giant by my lens of tears, the deacon turned into a monster. Fixing me with enraged eyes, he took my model and crushed it in his hands, tore it piece from piece. In a final fit, he threw it to the floor and stomped it with his feet in the grotesque jig of a man possessed.

When he stormed out, he left me without a father. My tears had stopped before the door slammed. I could only laugh at his performance. He had made himself ridiculous, a fat prancing puppet with his slave's religion that only preached suffering. And if I did not suffer, it would not be through any lack of effort on his part.

Fortunately for me, I still had a grandfather at the lighthouse.

"Joshua, the young wolf has to turn on the old wolf one day. When the old wolf fights the young, it's because he knows that day is near."

Chronic nausea and dysentery from the workshop tortured my stomach. Years of undernourishment ensured I would never reach my genitor's size. But aping only makes apes. Indigestion and cramps plagued me for the rest of my life, always returning in times of stress.

The primary result of my various forms of isolation was an early termination of social education. Values can only be transmitted through ties of respect, through attraction, through daily familiarity. I had no model from which to copy myself. That need to be needed, to be liked and approved of by everyone I met, grew to the proportions of a vice. When I could find some continuity, I clung to it, trying to create an identity for myself.

It makes for a strong man; strong but brittle.

We controlled Westport quay. Well, the south side of the quay anyway. That is, we controlled the other lads who came there, so long as there were not too many of them.

But I was uncontested leader of the gang. I had established my position by owning a new knife and being able to throw it more effectively than anybody else could their's. I soon learned to handle the gang with the same dexterity as we huddled together amongst the piles of broken fish crates at the end of the jetty. Once I had them caught, I enslaved them with superior knowledge until they believed every word I said.

How did I come to have this superior knowledge? It was simple. Grandfather was the only person in the whole area to take the Halifax newspaper and I delivered it to him each week. I read the most interesting articles as I walked up to the lighthouse. Like that Sunday morning in 1858 when I let them know that the explorer Speke would soon be back from Africa, news that he had discovered a huge lake at the source of the Nile and named it Lake Victoria. I told the tale of his exploits as if I had been there with him. Sure enough, a few days later, they found out it was all true. In the same way, I let them know about the British researcher who was claiming that men were really apes and how the tightrope walker Charles Blondin had crossed Niagara Falls on a wire. I even suggested I would give them a demonstration of his technique between two warehouses on the dock, but fortunately nobody could lay their hands on a rope long enough.

When they wanted more details, I could always supply them from my abundant imagination. That source normally proved just as reliable as the newspaper. With these amazing powers of premonition, it was easy for me to maintain my position as head of the gang. Reality seemed to have to conform to my words. When I invented details, I knew I was taking a risk, but normally time proved my intuitions to be inspired. Nature differentiates between the liar and the visionary, the Indian and the chief.

I never allowed myself to be disabled by lack of information. Whichever is more interesting is always more readily accepted. I understood things immediately and took decisions in a flash.

We always talked in the same boastful way to assure ourselves as much as everybody else that we were strong and powerful. Anyone our age who came into our territory without showing proper respect could not be tolerated, unless they were too numerous, in which case we would try to get them separately later.

One day the gang on the north side of the quay, mainly Acadians, began scoffing at the choice of the old Bytown as a new capital for a united Upper and Lower Canada. So we were forced into becoming fierce partisans of the nascent glory of Ottawa, even though most of us had never heard of it. All retired to the drying racks for a confrontation, the weapons to be dried cod. After a while I realized how hard it was to get a real advantage over an opponent by beating him with a flabby fillet. Bare fists had a much more rewarding effect. The rest of the gang soon followed my example and we gained the advantage with our sudden change of tactics which gave us superior firepower. It was like muskets against the bow and arrow. The Acadians accused me of cheating, but I became even more of a hero in my own camp. I had tried something new and been successful. Nothing brilliant, but a leader has to deliver victories and needs luck on his side.

I called a celebratory meeting at the lighthouse headland. Walking along, boosted by my triumph, I kept up the excitement by telling how I would be off soon for Lake Victoria, Africa, the whole world. How could a person like me stay in Westport? I needed liberty. They should break free from their parents and follow my lead. I did not know enough then to realize that just moving does not bring liberty. There is liberty of limb and liberty of heart. The liberty I wanted would only come with independence.

Arriving at the headland, I was forced to dampen the fire of my eloquence for the very parents I had spoken of were gathered there to watch the passage of the biggest ship in the world, the S.S. *Great Eastern*, with its unique combination of screws and paddle wheels.

We kept together under the lighthouse and I continued to talk about leaving, out of earshot of the crowd. I encouraged them to be bold too, but left myself a path of retreat by never being too specific about my plans. I could always claim they had misunderstood me.

As the S.S. *Great Eastern* dropped below the horizon, the parents started moving back towards Westport, calling their children to follow. All my accomplices submitted to the word of authority, leaving me alone. Turning after them, I glanced up at the lighthouse, only to see grandfather's enigmatic face looking down at me from a window. Had he heard everything? I ran.

If only the gang had not given in to their parents so easily. "Do this, don't do that," was becoming burdensome to me, so why was it not the same for them? They would not be able to put off manhood forever and remain children fed, protected, guided, watched, and controlled by others. Or would they? It was probably as much that I dared not face grandfather's eyes again as to get free of father's tyranny, but I realized I was committed now.

The brigantine *Sophia* had been alongside, provisioning in Westport for several days now. None of her crew were local, so everybody felt free to spread the wildest rumors about her mission. The story of surveying to lay a cable under the sea from America to Europe was too incredible to be believed. All the speculation about what she was really up to did not interest me. For me she was just the shortest route between my father and liberty.

Before the sun had put in its appearance, I slipped under the tarpaulins covering the banks of extra gear lashed down all over her deck. I knew she was leaving that morning, and I was going to leave with her.

When she let go around midday, my stomach was making as much noise as the crowd on the quay. I was so tense; sick. Was it the fear I would be discovered before she was well out at sea? Was it regret at leaving everything I knew? Was I sick from knowing my friends could not see how brave I was, being a hero, and nobody to witness it? Whatever it was, I was sick. I kept my attention away from my stomach and my remorse by imagining the gang's reactions when they found out how courageous I had been. I saw their faces struck with wonder at my audacity, putting superlatives of admiration on their lips. I went through it again and again until my dream lulled me to sleep.

The sound of anchor chain running out of the hawsepipe woke me. We should not be anchoring, we were meant to be deep-sea. What was happening? The mate must have been standing close by, because he caught me as soon as I poked my head out from under the tarpaulin. I had thought I had already bought my liberty. However, not only was the officer's grip crushing my arm, but the open sea was even further away than when we had left Westport! The *Sophia* had crept right into the mouth of St. Mary's Bay. Her captain's itinerary had not led to freedom but to another port to collect two engineers and a new type of echo sounder. We were tied alongside the fishing schooner, *Effie M. Morrissey*.

The officer eased his grip a little after he had dragged me over to talk with a sailor scrubbing the fishing boat's dodgers. It was hard to pretend I was a hero now. My balloon had been pricked and I was sinking into ignominy fast. I could not recognize Alex Lundgren through the tears of my shame, but he knew me well. He was a regular customer at father's workshop. Here I was in the depth of despair and they were chatting and laughing over their catch. I was handed over to the *Morrissey* like an unwanted cod.

Alex Lundgren stood bare-chested, a white body with a ruddy head driven into the top, forehead and chin still pushed out from the blow which had planted it there. He might have been blond once, but now his lye-washed hair had taken the hazy color of harbor mists. He just leant over, took me under the arms, and lifted me clean across both taffrails. Holding his shoulders, I took measure of the route I would have to travel before becoming a real man. His arms made mine look like matchsticks. Mine had more bone than muscle. It is true Alex Lundgren had a reputation for strength even amongst seamen, who tend to come tough. His short, bowed legs were naturally adapted to moving about on a storm-tossed deck. I never found out if his nickname, "Leg of Mutton," came from his bulging, sweat salted arms or the fact that he worked in the galley. But in spite of his appearance, he became an angel to me when he said he would get word to my father as to my whereabouts and ask the captain if he could keep me as galley boy.

Captain Kerouac was completely unknown to me. That is, I had heard the most sublime and sordid rumors about him for so long that he had become more of a mystery than a man. He never commented, contenting himself with a muttered, "Never mind." You were left to make what you could of that. And it never seemed to be directed to you but rather to be part of a conversation he was having with himself, or his rum bottle.

Just as effectively as Mr. Lundgren's arms, Captain Kerouac's inaccessibility kept others at a distance. He laughed and became angry, but not when other people would. You were either attracted or repelled by his thorough alienness, or both at the same time. He even looked different, tall and thin, silently ungraspable. This mystery man had broken many hearts.

Once he arrived on board, Mr. Lundgren did not have time to make a proper plea on my behalf. He decided a "Never mind" could be taken as an affirmative and I was now one of the crew. Mr. Lundgren became my tutor and I followed his every instruction. He found a hammock for me and showed me how to rig it inside the galley door. Now I had a home that felt more like a home than the house in Westport. I had a place like the others. Soon I would be able to say "we" and be one of the crew. If only the old gang in Westport could see me lying in my hammock, stuffed with bread and herrings, opening and clenching my fists to build up those forearm muscles.

When the anchor came up the next morning, I started my life all over again, as I would have to do many times.

By noon we were passing Brier Island, with Westport just a blur in the mist. There must have been a mist because it was hazy in my eyes. I could not see my future clearly either, but I was doing something about my present. My arms felt stronger already. I was somebody; I was a cook. Standing in the galley, I tried to follow individual waves. As they came in from port it was easy, but how could I be sure it was the same one as they moved away to starboard? One big breaker would stand out from the rest.

The boastful ways I had adopted in Westport would stay with me for a long time. I thought then that humility could only diminish one, arrogance was nearer the truth and modesty would only attenuate it. Over-ambition taught me that modesty is not starvation, it is just saving yourself from gluttony, in the way that having to swear an affidavit checks exaggeration.

Fishing on the schooners was done by line. Everybody fished. I also had to keep up the fire for hot drinks, always in demand. The peggy is at the beck and call of the whole crew, so I was constantly having to tie off my line and run to the galley for a mug of tea. By tradition the captain inhabits the poop. As we were too small a ship to carry a steward, I had to run aft and serve him too. I hoped to follow tradition myself: peggy, deck hand, then able bodied seaman. After that it would be goodbye to fishing and look for a ship going deep-sea.

For now though I was as green as a cabbage, a mere sprout with small leaves. I had to take in, learn all I could, nourish myself. Each day when I served him his evening meal, Captain Kerouac would have me stay with him on the poop deck, singing to himself in a French different than that used by the Acadians:

"*Un petit mousse un soir chantait.*"

A mouthful of rum.

"Ah, who could give me back my mother's smile?"

He passed me the empty glass.

"Never mind."

That grave voice carried straight to me. I could hear him clearly even from the bowsprit end. In my hammock I could hear him singing softly. He reached me even in my dreams. One evening he did not sing. He gave me the beans left on his plate to eat. Normally he would glare at me and throw them over the wall. He did not like beans. Those looks of his frightened me more than a blow or kick from one of the forecastle hands. Later he walked into the galley were I lay in my hammock, staring at me with fire in his eyes. I wilted in the heat. Taking a small book from his pocket, he pushed it into my hand and turned to go back, muttering, "Never mind."

It was a book of seamanship I read as my Bible:

Why do they stay, with miserable wages soon wasted in port on ale-houses and brothels? Because a seaman's job is his only home and he returns to the warm camaraderie of the crew knowing nothing better. They come to love the sea and the feeling of freedom she always brings, even to the most deprived. ... Captains hunt for the best seamen. An A.B. is strong, healthy, obedient, knowledgeable in nautical lore. He neither smokes nor drinks on board, does not have strong sentimental attachments ashore and is never sad. The virtues required in a seaman are to be hard working; faithful; never quarrelsome; attentive to himself and his work; and quiet. He never forgets to give his best hand to the ship and keep the other for himself.

Here was my father in black and white. He always prided himself on turning sharply and with a will. I remember him saying: "A good seaman, Josh, is a shoemaker, helmsman, caulker, topman, carpenter, sail trimmer. He knows that he has to submit, make himself liked, not feared."

For now I was just a drudge, a peggy at the service of the crew's only apparent pleasure: eating.

Alex Lundgren noticed the captain wanted to encourage me, so he made me responsible for the whole meal. Fear and pride boiled up inside me like beans in lard. In my excitement I forgot to desalt the cod, rather a large oversight. The crewmen beat me as if I were a slave. They bruised my new muscles and then took away my new pride by demanding whether I would eat the food myself or run to the protection of that peasouper I was so fond of.

I had seen myself becoming a real seaman, but instead I was reduced to a poor aching knot. That night I dreamed that Dame Celeste came to save me and take me away, like she did in Captain Kerouac's song, and that the nurse from the Crimea soothed my wounds. I thought so highly of myself that I blamed myself entirely, for I could not accept that I too could make mistakes like other people. The captain appeared in the galley, holding out a bottle of rum towards me, but he could not bring himself to part with it. He just gave me his all-purpose comment.

"Never mind."

I listened to his footsteps returning to the poop. The *Morrissey* seemed to be endless; he was going an infinite distance from me and

I would never be able to reach him again.

So I stuck to Mr. Lundgren and the galley. He gave me the secrets of his special recipe for cod with onions and potatoes; similar to my aunt's stew but far better. Whenever I felt in need of relieving my isolation or remembering my youth, I made a plateful and thought of the friendship Alex Lundgren had extended to me.

By the morning a full gale had blown up. Still weak from the beating, I could barely keep my feet, so Mr. Lundgren sent me back to my hammock out of the way. A wave broke open the galley door and swept in, taking pots and pans before it, until it reached the stove and burst into clouds of steam. Mr. Lundgren was everywhere, looking to the boiling water on the stove and saving the fresh water butt from upending. While I lay in the hammock immobilized by fear, he responded to the chaos with perfect calm.

In my early years at sea I learned many things, but the chief lesson of all was how to get on with the job and not let fear overwhelm me. A seaman gets frightened like anyone else, but he soon learns that he cannot escape by running.

The great day came when I was replaced as peggy and promoted to deck hand. I had earned a new berth in the forepeak. I was no longer Captain Kerouac's servant but a crewman on the *Effie M. Morrissey*. I could be sarcastic about the cooking. I was cocksure and full of myself, certain I was better than the rest of the crew. "Leg of Mutton" soon disowned me. Even my captain seemed to turn away from me. I am not sure of that though, he was so hard to fathom. The general atmosphere was such that I decided I had best leave before I was invited to. I had had enough of the smell of fish anyway. I wanted freer air to breath. I could handle sails with the rest now and move around the rigging as nimbly as an older hand. I dreamed of a berth on a big three-master heading out of this foggy corner of the world.

It was just before my sixteenth birthday and winter still held Westport in a tight grip. I walked up the quay, kit-bag on my shoulder and seaman's boots on my feet. Two of the old gang were sitting on the piled fish-boxes. They rushed up to me shouting their welcome and pouring out their questions. "How was it?" "Have you had many gales?" "The work, I bet it's hard, hey?" But I was not thinking about the sea. My mind was back in Wilmot Township.

How does a house know that someone is dead? All the family were there but inside it felt empty and cold. Elizabeth greeted me with her tears but Father's eyes were dry; dried by the fire of his religion. And to me, now a seaman, used to living with seamen, his stature had shrunken. I saw for the first time how working over a bench had bent his back. It was not the type of work which makes a man hard and proud like a seaman's work does. When I was a child he had beaten me with his belt but he would never be able to do that again.

"My son, your mother is now free of the trials of this world. She has gone on to a better place where she can devote herself to praising the Lord. It is a terrible loss for us but in heaven she will be happy and receive the reward for a good and humble life."

For me she was just dead. Now I would never be able to win her love. I had returned a man, thinking she might admire, but she had denied me even that. And Father? I had broken out of the trap in which he was caught, but he could not admit that so how could he admire me. There was nothing for me here. My mother had gone ahead of me and I had left my friends and family behind. But as this world closed up another one was already opening. I had started to explore it and knew I would make my new home there...on the sea.

I followed Elizabeth in the procession.

She wore mother's greatcoat, the same rust-brown color as the soil in grandfather's garden. Grandfather's rheumatism prevented him from walking in snow, so he could not come. The hood on the coat bristled with soft down, just like Elizabeth's arms.

When the procession stopped, I clung tightly to Elizabeth's arm, my cheek against the fur around her hood. I did not look to see what we were waiting for. Scraps from the morning's paper were chasing through my mind, making me dizzy: Livingstone's expeditions in Africa; a criticism of Thoreau's *Life in the Woods*; the papists reaffirming Mary's virginity; Shuman's suicide explained by madness; *in memory of Sarah Jane, wife of John Slocombe of Westport, who died in her forty-sixth year, after giving birth to her eleventh child, leaving her husband and nine surviving children in mourning*; Livingstone in Africa, Thoreau in the woods, Schumann gone mad, *Sara Jane Slocombe dead...leaving her children in mourning...in mourning. ...*

CHAPTER TWO

Apprenticeship

I considered myself a special person. I had not finished testing the boundaries of my capacities but had learned the necessity of making choices, of being responsible for my own life. Life would no longer lead me by the hand, not if I went to it and took it in my arms. As a child I had thought I was the centre of the world. Now I could move around in the world and look at the possibilities. My fears were there still, but they were no longer phobias. Like the gulls, I could pick around the quays or fly off over the sea to find my nourishment.

As September began to turn the trees red, I shipped out on the *Marco Polo*, a lumber-carrying vessel shipping out of Saint John for Dublin. The hull was slimmed down to increase speed at the sacrifice of a small amount of capacity. I managed to lose myself in the intricacies of her three decks as I searched for the crew's quarters.

Her captain was Nicol "Bully" Forbes, who enjoyed acclaim for his legendary acrobatic ability as topman, navigational prowess, and outstanding courage. For reasons he never discussed, Captain Forbes kept company only with ecclesiastics when in port. This religious bent made our departure from Saint John somewhat unusual. Instead of the normal vulgar cries of whores and longshoremen, we had the prayers and hymns of a congregation of pious well-wishers. This solemnity seemed more appropriate for a shipwreck. Any doubts amongst us new crewmen were soon dissipated. As she was towed down the fairway, we were assembled for a short speech.

"Religion is indispensable. Its truths were revealed to us ashore nearly two thousand years ago, and ashore is where it belongs. At sea you can only depend on your own courage. Standby to set sail. Dublin awaits us."

Climbing to the yards with the topmen, I had the feeling I was mounting towards heaven, consecrating myself to the mast. A smack from another seaman to clear me off the ratlines soon brought me back to reality. They already knew I had no right to be up there with them, the elite, from the way I moved. I would receive more than one punch before being fully ordained into this privileged group who considered themselves the only true seamen on board. I had a taste of how that status was earned a few days later.

Bully Forbes was forcing the pace in a gale, all sail set and pulling strong, when a topsail ripped clean through. It had to be cleared away immediately before it could do too much damage in its wild flogging. Our watch was off on a hundred-foot climb before the order was finished, dodging flying ropes that threatened to send us back to deck or sea, depending on the roll. Spars, sail, sheets, and guys were hopelessly entangled.

"Use your knives and cut it all away," came from the deck.

Slipping on the ratlines, I was caught and pulled back by someone I did not even have time to thank as he rushed on up. Reaching the main-top, I was sent out on the main yard foot ropes to work from there. Torn sheets cracked like whips, one blow enough to turn a man into a memory. As everyone around me worked frantically with knife and axe, I was paralyzed. I could do nothing but cling on for dear life. My neighbor saw my condition and quickly passed me an end of rope to tie myself on with. I watched with awe as they confidently went about their task; chaos was being tamed. Bundles of sail and fragments of spar were lowered to the deck.

"Heads up below there."

Our ship had come through with only minor damage.

"Up helm," from Captain Forbes, and we were off again.

It was several anguished days before I accepted that nobody was going to comment on my freezing up on the yard. They had all known fear themselves and knew how it could penetrate the best trained defences to strike at the soul and bring down a veil of darkness. It would probably shoot its cunning arrow at them again one day.

From then on, I was less proud and worked at any task with extra zeal. Like all the other unspecialized seamen in the watch, I had little free time, unlike the true topmen, who lounged in the well chatting idly while keeping a sharp ear for a call from the bosun's whistle.

When not hauling sheets or winching halyards with the capstan, we were scrubbing decks, painting bulwarks and coamings, cleaning the exposed hull to keep her moving at top speed, daubing rigging, or transporting water, coal, and wood. We played caulker, smith, and carpenter.

My time was strictly controlled every day by the list of captain's orders fixed to the forecastle door. My humor depended on the tasks listed by my name. Those orders were unquestionable, and they had to be to maintain peace aboard. One never asked why, but my name was "Helmsman" even though we had no assigned helmsmen and every seaman stood his trick at the wheel. Neither icy water down the neck, salt-crusted eyelids, nor the threatening rumble of a wave coming up from astern could detract from the feeling of power each spell at the wheel gave me. The concentration necessary to hold a straight course is such that no extraneous thoughts are possible. At first you just work to bring the ship back on course after she has gone off, then you learn to anticipate the effect of each wave and meet it before she has time to go off. A moment's lapse can lead to five minutes of struggle to quiet her down again.

At the beginning I had more time at the helm, until all the seamen had sobered up enough to be trusted with the job. I have always detested drunks. I remember them being trundled up to the *Marco Polo* on the agent's cart after he had been sent to round them up, sprawled on top of each other and stinking of alcohol and tobacco. The crimps carried them to the forecastle, assuring the mate they were all worth their price. By the end of the first day at sea, the officer's rope's end had put a different sort of spirit into them. It was an effective method, unless used too liberally on the wrong man. Many an officer has lost his life to a knife from a seaman who felt unfairly punished.

Conversation forward generally centred on food, gossip and whores. I tried to read. Unlike most of the crew, I did not intend to spend the rest of my life before the mast. But I was young and green, so it was hard to ignore exciting tales of exotic places and immerse myself in my Norie's or Thomson's or just Waldo Emerson (his father's story was interesting: marooned on a desert island, equipped only with a pocket knife, he managed to build himself a raft and escape).

The prices and quality of whores always sparked long debates. So I learned that in Boston one could be had for twenty five cents "all night." Someone reminisced about his favorite, a fat Neapolitan who let him have it on credit. She used to serve him a secret aphrodisiac called tarantula juice.

"And how the old bag used to rig herself. Oiled cloth jacket, oiled wool stockings, and the speciality, red draws."

What he and the others never mentioned was that the "trollop" they laughed at had all their money now. I preferred to save on money and remorse. The only pussy I came near was the ship's cat, as soft with me as she was sanguinary with rats. When the crew caught a shark, a pastime which was supposed to bring good luck to the ship, I was detailed to keep her away from it. This new food might have spoiled her taste. I did not want my taste spoilt either.

I spent hours stroking that cat while I read my books. I must have come near to wearing out her coat. She never liked to be outside and ran to the warmth of my lap as soon as her hunger was satisfied. For my part, I had companions, a trade, a ship, and plans. Above all was the hope it would continue that way.

We reached Dublin in record time but found the city full of misery. My thoughts were fully occupied with my final destination, London, the capital of the Empire. I had heard tales of the temple of civilization at home, and the reports of its attractions from my fellow seamen only increased my excited anticipation.

I rented a room in one of London's most famous pubs around West India docks, the Railway Tavern. The landlord, Charlie Brown, had his praises sung all around the world by every seaman who had visited London. At Charlie Brown's you could drink (I stuck to ginger beer) and dance without fear of the dangers frequently met with in other establishments. Charlie Brown was a remarkable man, giving freely of his money for good causes and of his judicious advice to his younger customers.

He noticed how timid I was but never remarked on it to my face. Instead he introduced me to people I would not approach myself. One was a dancing partner, a slender mulatto with velvet smooth, milk chocolate skin who made a living for herself, her mother, and her sister by taking the floor with lonely seamen in the Railway Tavern's dancing room. With her I learned why everybody was crazy about the polka. The desire to please her inspired me with a rhythmic talent I had never known before. Jamie and the polka taught me how to feel the music with my whole body. Spinning around the floor with her became my sole interest in life. She seemed to prefer me as a partner too. Perhaps it was because I stayed sober and was too prudish to make the lewd comments she was used to from seamen. When she told me she performed occasionally as an extra at the Royal Academy of Music, I invited myself to see her perform.

Leaving Jamie at the stage door, I went to buy my ticket at the box office. Queuing in the foyer, I overheard the gossip: a scandal about Wagner in Paris, and the new trend for soloists to play without music—that sounded as impossible as navigating without compass or chart.

My programme told me the strange story of Faust's rejuvenation but did nothing to prepare me for the intense feeling raised in me by the impossible complexity of sounds, as the conductor's baton directed divine voices to every corner of the auditorium. I was so involved that I completely forgot to look for Jamie on stage, where illuminated miracles were transporting the audience from one scene to another as if by magic. And that old man becoming young again—I would have given anything to be initiated into the mysteries of music and theatre.

As soon as Jamie appeared at the stage door, I grabbed her in my arms, babbling like a baby. I had no words to tell her what I felt. She spoke to calm me down, but it was Elizabeth's voice I heard. The stink of Well Street did not reach my nose, instead I smelled warm milk and the stable. Jamie had to lead me by the hand around the stacks of bales unloaded from West India docks. I could not see for tears.

All of my emotion transferred itself to her. I took her in my arms and kissed her, and unbelievably she did not resist. My hands moved excitedly over her body, exploring curves I had only dared look at before. Her sobs suddenly brought me back to my senses and made me realize that it was her, Jamie, I was doing this to. I excused myself and reassured her, walked her home, apologized, said goodnight, and returned to my room. I lay awake all night, yawed between shame and desire.

The next day she was not at the Railway Tavern, nor the day after. Then the tavern was almost empty. Everyone had gone to see the

Prince Consort Albert's funeral procession. I wandered into the White Swan alone; alone, but with my body shouting instructions in my ear. A redhead came up to me, made my body an offer, my body accepted. I was not even consulted, my body had taken control.

And what did I feel afterward? I felt empty and alone, more that I had lost something than gained. Jamie could have filled that emptiness, but though I searched for her and waited near her house, I never saw her again. Soon my money was gone. I had seen the sordid and the sublime, so what was I to do now? Like any seaman, I went to the "pool" and asked for a berth. I ran from all this confusion to a certainty I knew.

The *Tanjore* was bound for China under British flag and very much under the command of a nasal-voiced despot called Captain Martin. Rank was the only thing of importance to him: I chanced to see him faced with a lord, whereon he was all courtesy. All I had was my A.B. certificate. That seemed a noble title to me, but to Captain Martin I was just another member of the rabble he had to put up with as crew.

When I presented my papers to sign on, the officers learned I was merely a colonial from Nova Scotia. They did not even want to handle my papers but passed them with their fingertips over to the bosun with the instructions, "Return these to Slocum." Captain Martin gave me a look of disgust: fancy allowing foreigners on his ship. I refused to react. Let them take my dignity for submission if they would. I had time enough ahead to show them who was superior to whom.

Hiding behind my bunk curtain, I read the letter I had received from Elizabeth.

Dear Josh,

We were all very worried about you, especially me, but your letter has delivered us from our anxiety. I am busy looking after the family and that takes all my time as you can well imagine. Papa is very pleased with me. He says he would be in a bad way without me. And it is true. He has not mentioned the money you sent, but that is his affair. Above all keep writing to me. The widower, Mr. MacGregor, spoke to father about me, but nothing has happened. I am glad because he does not interest me. Papa still needs me anyway. I have to tell you, Josh, not to dirty yourself with the filthy women in the ports. God gave man his passions to make families with or maintain the ones they have, like I do. I think about you a lot and am enclosing a piece of cloth from the new dress I have made myself as a keepsake. Please do not forget me. You promised to tell me all about your life at sea. Tell me all, I will not tell anybody else.

As always,
Your sister forever,
Elizabeth

Had she guessed what I had done in London? I was overcome with remorse about the redhead and Jamie when I feared Elizabeth might know. At night the three of them were confused in my lewd dreams. I was confused about friendship, complicity, and desire, so I confused their recipients, desiring where friendship was appropriate. Even when mature I had problems with this: my background and personality made me unwilling to examine my own emotions.

So I left for the Cape of Good Hope and China, torn between imaginations of debauchery and tenderness. I would have to sort it all out later, but for now I would bury the problem under a mountain of work. If you are too tired to think, then you think no troubling thoughts.

The officers were in great excitement about the use of a new innovation: weather reports. These I have never been happy about because they try to turn an art into a science. Certainly, one wants to know as much as possible about the weather, but I feel that can best be done by studying the sky, the clouds, and the barometer, rather than by looking at a piece of paper. The apparent accuracy of what is written on paper gives the impression that weather is controlled by those who write it, but Nature does not reward such impudence.

My first steps towards China were made tramping in circles around the capstan, leaning all my weight on a bar, hauling the *Tanjore* away from her Londonian connections.

It was rumored that the mate had far more experience than Captain Martin but that posed no problem for the latter, for his arrogance left no doubt in his mind that he was superior. I already knew from experience that the sea takes little account of age, only the essence of a man is recognized: his ability to sail and command. Young or old, friend or foe, the master always rises to the top. When things go well, he is the one who takes the credit; when things go badly it is the mate who does the bailing.

We were bending our backs to maintenance before she was clear of the London River. Every trace of the city's grime had to be scrubbed from her decks. The cunning ones made a dive for the long-handled "bears" so their behinds would not be presented for an encouraging kick from the mate.

Once the northeast trades winds had run out, there were long days of drifting through the doldrums before the South Atlantic's steady winds sent us on our way again. Not all were idle days, for every breath of wind, every squall, had to be taken advantage of to clear this dead area. The crew fished for shark by towing great iron hooks baited with a good-sized chunk of salt pork. I never involved myself in this sport, but I happened to be the only one watching over the rail when a great white decided to clamp its iron jaws onto the bait. I had contributed nothing to the catch, but the mere fact of being there at the important moment meant I received all the congratulations as the beast was hauled on board. Nobody can become a hero unless they put themselves in the front line.

Hung over the deck, the shark suffered his punishment. After the execution, his stomach was cut open to verify his guilt: had he eaten a seaman recently? That is the crime all sharks are accused of. Every shark I have seen thus condemned has proven his innocence, but it has cost him his life to do so.

The judicial error caused no regrets, thanks to the superstition that this type of witch hunt would be rewarded by a fair wind. The ritual continued: it had to be completed to achieve the full effect. The jaw was cut away as a votive offering, the backbone removed for fashioning a walking stick, while the tail hung from the bowsprit end as an amulet against foul weather. I declined the offer to take a leading role in the ceremonies. The officer's derisive looks confirmed to me that credulity and power do not walk together.

Quietly I went below to my bunk, preferring not to let the rest of the crew see my disgust. While they were all busy on deck, I took advantage of this unusual moment of privacy to write to Elizabeth. Each line attaching me to her pulled me out of the mob; she became present to me and drove away troubling memories of the redhead at the White Swan.

1861, off Africa

To my sister Elizabeth,

Here, for you my dear sister, my secrets for you to share as you asked, hoping they will bring us closer. Be discreet with my revelations, I am not a captain yet so I should not be bringing a woman aboard. I could not bring you anyway as you are my sister and I could not protect you as I could a wife. Remember the perfume of a secret fades with each nose sniffing it. Be equally assured I will not stop until I have told all. I live under the foredeck of this ship, a clipper running the tea route. My bed is always being tossed by the waves, when there are any that is. At the moment there have been none for a good week. But we are slowly nearing the Cape of Good Hope and it will not be long before our courage is tested.

There are no ports to light our quarters, just two smoky lamps swinging as we roll and accentuating the apparent motion by flinging shadows around the cabin. The only natural light comes through the hatch, and the same for ventilation. That is always insufficient or excessive. If it is closed we cannot breathe, if it is left open we are periodically soaked with spray or worse. Sea water is also liberally sprinkled on our bunks from open seams in the deck.

My neighbor, I can tell when he is there by the smell, says it is greed for profit which restricts our space. The owners want as much room as possible for cargo.

Obnoxious odors from some deliquescent cargo filter through the supposedly watertight bulkhead separating our quarters from the forward hold. It is presently packed with salt cod and green hides and the combined stench makes me vomit just like in father's workshop. At least it stops me getting fat. The same neighbor tells me he has sailed with guano, ground nuts and nitrates and they are even worse. I should also mention that the stink of tobacco juice is everywhere and the smell of stagnant bilge water, dead rats and tared rope wafts up from the lower peak below us.

You want me to tell you everything but never repeat to anyone what I am about to say. You are the only woman I would tell this to. To satisfy calls of nature we have to go right forward on deck and climb out on a grated platform suspended above the sea between the heads. When the sea is rough it is a very uncomfortable place to be exposing oneself, especially if the bow digs in to a wave. Do you remember that time I caught you doing it in the stable? I hope you are not mad at me for that any more.

It is said they might change the rule prohibiting us from wearing beards or moustaches, although it is true they are not very neat when streaked with tobacco juice. Do not worry, I do not chew a quid. Tobacco does nothing for me. I think I would rather chew a clove of garlic.

I know you like me to keep clean but you should see how we bathe on the ship. Well actually you will never see it because the whole crew are on deck naked, jumping up and down on our dirty clothes. We stack our clothes on deck starting with the trousers then the jacket, shirt, neckerchief and finally our underclothes. We wash standing on top of them then scrub them in the soapy water that has run off of us. Back on top of them again, a bucket of fresh water suffices to rinse both our bodies and our clothes.

I have crossed the line for the first time! We were given double rations but the captain would not submit to the custom of disguised seamen giving him orders. The rituals were much worse for the tyros than for me. I just had a cut-off oilskin leg pulled over my head, tied around my neck then filled with seawater. I swallowed quite a lot before they let me go. Then I had to respond to a litany of insane questions I cannot repeat to you. Honest women should not even know what they were about.

The peggy is hated because he is a nephew of the captain so they took the chance to make him suffer. They stripped him then painted him with a repulsive mixture of soot and rancid oil, left him to dry in the sun, then plunged him head first in a barrel of seawater. Being the captain's favorite cost him dear.

Your able seaman brother
Josh
To be continued.

I suspended my writing there hoping to be able to complete the letter with a description of the famous Cape, but we rounded well offshore and never sighted it. The rest of the trip blurred in the routines, which is the reality of most time spent at sea: a routine which eats up the days, leaving little trace.

Memories of my adventures in the capital of the West made me curious about the lascivious possibilities of the East. Then I would feel guilty and become excessively puritan for a while, moods changing with every roll of the ship.

Hong Kong harbor swarmed with junks and sampans. I could not believe the washlines of fish and squid would ever dry in the humidity of those dogdays. A multitude of kneeling workers waved their punkahs over the floating confusion in an effort to stir the air a bit. In its shallow basin, the town receives a lava flow of air from the surrounding hills, heats it further and adds its own spices, before sending it out to hang sweet and smoky over the port's limpid water. The East stood open before me, and I was curled up with a fresh attack of dysentery.

Anchored out in the bay lay a horror in black, waiting to strike terror in any honest seaman's heart: an armor-plated warship said to be invulnerable to any weapon. Sinister sounds rose from its bowels to complete the feeling of death lying in wait. The Prussian navy had sent it to encourage the completion of a commercial treaty with China.

We waited out in the bay until the next day, while the mate cleared our cargo with customs and all the crew's papers with police and immigration. We did not have the advantage of the Americans who had all their stamps and visas collected together in a small "passport." Captain Martin talked with some Chinese merchants on the poop in his muttering, nasal way. The conclusion was passed down to the crew by the mate. A large quantity of ice was to be loaded and we were to do it, saving the price of hiring labor from ashore. We ran from steaming heat to icy cold, pouring with sweat despite the blocks of ice that froze our shoulders. Captain Martin watched with the satisfied smile of a man turning a profit, while the officers laughed at our protests. The merchants shuffled off, leaving behind one to keep the tally.

I was already like a dishmop, shrunken and weakened by dysentery. Menacing fingers with long dirty nails riffled through my insides, searching for the worms eating at my guts, consuming me before I was even ripe. My legs collapsed and the block of ice flew skidding across the deck.

Later, the bosun had me transferred to a Dutch ship whose captain was famous for his medical skills. Captain Airy of the *Soushay* had spent years in Batavia in the pestilential Dutch East Indies, where he had become familiar with tropical fevers. Several days passed before I reemerged from a nightmare in which death walked by my side. I was exhausted, my bones aching as though I had been stretched on the rack. Fortunately, Captain Airy and the Chinese nurse he had appointed to me knew their job well. Hou Ying stayed with me constantly, bullying or cajoling me to take the noodles and apple juice that were waiting for me every time I opened my eyes. I abandoned myself to his care.

The fever left me with even more determination to make something of my life. I had nearly disappeared without accomplishing anything: now I would have to drive forward even harder. Hou Ying taught me how to channel the energy I drew from this new awareness. He oriented my oscillations between feebleness and excitement to produce efficient development. He guided me along the path I had to follow to bring body and mind together.

Going through the facts in my head, I decided that I could make a case against Captain Martin for neglect of human life. Members of the crew who had found different ships agreed to bear witness for me at a tribunal. A writ was issued, forcing the *Tajore* to stay in harbor until my case was heard. When the judge found in my favor, I received three months wages in damages but, more importantly, the satisfaction of having stood up for myself. Hou Ying guided me again in this matter, showing me how to obtain justice through the law and making me reflect on the idea of justice in itself. Learning the law under his tutorship, I gained the confidence which comes from having knowledge others do not possess. People began to treat me with respectful admiration. I cultivated the air of mystery which surrounds one who is initiated. My Chinese nurse helped me to understand it all.

One evening Hou Ying took me out on a small sampan propelled silently through the crowded junks by a taciturn old man. I had no idea where we were headed. Hou Ying spoke as we glided along.

"Do you remember in your fever you were an apple being eaten?"

Lanterns on a junk lit several cormorants tied by one of their feet to a fragile bamboo raft. They fished for their owner, prevented from swallowing their catch by a tight collar.

"The apple is the universal sign of wisdom. In every race's orchard the apple is the fruit of wisdom and desire. A key to immortality, it is eloquent, seductive, sharp tasting."

We passed floating families, their boats weighted down to the brink of disaster by accumulated goods and persons.

"It smells both sweet and sour because it is neither one nor the other. It changes with the apple as it changes from green to red. The seeds it keeps in its heart contain the whole of the heavens and an infinity of possibility."

In the labyrinth of waterways, the air was thick with the odor of roast meat and opium.

"The apple is flesh and spirit. She protects the knowledge of her flesh with a robe of beauty and dignity."

We nearly hit a withered old wreck of a man hanging out over the side of a junk.

"The apple does not hold on, she falls. So our sages say whosoever eats of her no longer feels hunger or thirst, sadness or illness."

Our old oarsman clucked to himself as we saw a row of identical sampans and smelled the perfume of women dressed up like actresses.

"She is round like the earth and reflects the world's desires. She is virginity and sensuality. The apple, young man, represents the inescapable necessity of making choices. If you hesitate too much in choosing, you lose the right to enter the orchard of the dignified great. Then you are left with the pitiful illusions of the masses."

We disembarked at the end of Woonoon quay amongst the salt soup and sweet grill stands and Hou Ying stopped in front of a small booth. Pushing me in with a hand on each shoulder he solemnly declared:

"You have tasted of desire and knowledge. Now you must carry her mark on your flesh so as never to forget."

The ritual marking on my behind took a month to heal fully. A representation of an apple, bitten into once. I have seen seamen being tattooed in idle hours in the forecastle but never was it done with such ceremony. Branded like this, I could not set aside the duties of knowledge and excellence. I had chosen to live them and reject the banalities of everyday life.

My first encounter with justice had shown me the most flagrant example of injustice, the inequality of people's abilities. Now I was tattooed with the sign of a marginal.

Eighteen years old, I was soon leaving on another trip, out of Liverpool for the East Indies. My application to the study of seamanship had effected my removal from the forecastle to the after end of the ship for the first time. I had always worked to be popular with everybody on deck, so the jibes and taunts I received as I packed my gear caused me some discomfort. But I was glad enough to be moving out of that smelly, crowded hole, so I was not distressed.

On the quarterdeck I had to bury my pride. I was the new boy, the most junior mate, and the officers did not hesitate to remind me of that fact. I protected myself with voluntary isolation from both officers and crew. I do not know which was the stronger, my pride at having excelled as a seaman or the shame at being the least amongst the officers. My competence at following orders had been proven, now I had to show if I had another ability, the strength of will to command.

To command effectively one needs the men's respect, and one needs sometimes to lead by example. That is how I got a scar over my left eyebrow. On a gusty day in the mid-Atlantic, I went out on the upper topsail yard to give a hand tying in a reef. With both hands full of flapping sail, I was unable to stop a sudden lurch, cracking my head on the mainyard. Thus an officer earns his stripes.

CHAPTER THREE

An American in Command

I touched my first U.S. dollar bill in the port of San Francisco, discharging English coal and loading American grain. The financing of the Civil War that was to spill men's blood on the soil of Antietam and Gettysburg had forced President Lincoln to issue the Union's first paper money, "greenbacks." Our mate from Boston felt called to lend his hand to the cause of freeing slaves and keeping his country united. His patriotic spirit earned me promotion to the rank of first mate and even more isolation. I did not suffer from that isolation though; I profited from it by retiring to my cabin to study navigation further. Johann von Lamont on the workings of the ocean's great currents was absorbing me at the time. All of the useful knowledge I have was acquired in this way: practice and private study of the best books I could find. Later, when I became captain myself, I always preferred to employ autodidacts, considering that the effort they had made to search out knowledge themselves rather than be handed it at a school meant they must have had more energy and self-confidence.

As first mate I had more time for study when at sea, this ship carrying a sailing master who relieved the mate of many of the duties he would normally have to perform when not on watch. Maintenance of rigging and sails was in his hands, as was the building of new sails to the designs made by Captain Hayet on the backs of old charts.

My cabin was confined, with barely room for a chair: damp and fetid with the smell of mouldy glue, thanks to my predecessor's bright idea of carpeting it. But in spite of the constant humidity, the impossibility of opening the single port when at sea, and the cockroaches, I could not but enjoy my privacy. It was the first time I had known it, and I resolved to do everything possible to maintain this privilege for the rest of my life. Privacy and isolation had other benefits too. As another one of the crowd, I only knew the ships I was on in part. Gaining the right of access to the whole ship whenever I pleased made me feel more complete. I no longer just worked on a ship, I was second in command: a high priest.

Captain Hayet often compared the life of deep-sea sailors to that of monks. Draped in his greatcoat, he resembled a vicar who had exchanged his cross for a pipe.

"We are just like monks, gentlemen. Monks and nothing else. With the difference that we are useful. Ships are our churches. Like monks, gentlemen, like monks. Look here: isolated from the world, under a rigid regime day and night, up in the middle of the night at our work. Monks, gentlemen, monks. No women; that's abstinence isn't it? Monks. Loving in poverty; that's religious isn't it? Gentlemen, our life is controlled by the clock like them. Rising early, working, simple meals, sleep. The compass light is our sanctuary lamp, gentlemen."

The captain let himself be carried away by his favorite metaphor, his voice rising as he developed his sermon.

"The anchor, the mast, and yards, they're all so many crosses; the filled sails are the vaults of our cathedral. The mighty rumbling in the rigging is the organ leading our prayers. Gentlemen, like monks we live mortified by privations. Hmm, pass me a light, gentlemen, my pipe seems to be out."

I took to command as willingly as I had taken to obeying orders. They say no man can give orders unless he has learned how to take them. The green, young peggy had taken little more than four years to become a mate, and that was through the discipline of willingly accepting orders. And now that I was giving orders, I expected them to be obeyed.

There were few mysteries left to me concerning the intricacies of the rigging, the handling of the sails, or the caprices of the winds. I had devoted myself to the study of them all, trying to understand where others just accepted. Now I was learning how to control men too: which to trust with what job, who should be sent up to the topgallants when a squall called for them to be furled quickly. I learned what sail the ship could safely carry as the wind increased to a gale and how to keep her driving and under control until the last possible moment. Once she is under bare poles, there is nothing to do but make all secure and wait.

When I carried my kit-bag ashore at San Francisco in 1866, I left seamen behind me and withdrew to soak up the beauty of the bay alone. Memories of my Nova Scotia childhood brought tears to my eyes. I wanted to put that bitter past behind me too, to be reborn in this city and forget it all.

"Do you know Slocum? Slocum from San Francisco."

Perhaps I could do it.

The bay held some of the most famous sailing ships in the world. After surviving trying months at sea, the terrors of Cape Horn, and the pox of Valparaiso, they disgorged materials to feed Frisco's voracious appetite: cement, iron, rats, bricks, machines, coal, men, everything. Gold fever was in the land, devouring all.

One had to be particularly cautious to do business in San Francisco. Seamen were lured by the attractions of Kearney Street, where anything could be had for a price. Captains and officers patrolled the streets and bars in an attempt to curb the activities of the shanghai boys, the kings of the area, like Shanghai Brown, Calico Bill, and Honest Arnold, whose trade was the abduction of seamen to sell to ships short of crew because their seamen had also been abducted. The whores would offer a bed and free sex, receiving their payment from the merchant when he collected his recumbent goods. Calico Jim, for instance, worked through the "Lion's Cage," which carried a staff of more than two hundred whores of every race, color, and speciality.

Many seamen woke from a drunken haze to find themselves back at sea after only one night in town. It all depended on whether they had been unlucky in their choice from the three thousand bars, one for every one hundred inhabitants of the city. A thousand men jumped ship each year, attracted by the city or the gold fields, only to be shanghaied onto another ship.

The city boiled with controversy, with most discussions leading to scuffles. The Congress had just abolished slavery, but that did not mean civil rights for Negroes was accepted on the streets. The first Finian uprisings were taking place in Ireland, and San Francisco was packed with expatriate Irish staging miniature re-enactments of the troubles in their native land. These confrontations had been kept on the boil ever since the S.S. *Great Britain* had laid the telegraph cable from Europe to Newfoundland, bringing a constant flow of fresh news. Adding oil to the fire were arguments about the rules the

Marquis of Queensbury had codified to lessen the brutality of boxing in England.

Moving in the direction of California Street, I was still considering the possibility of making San Francisco my new home. Climbing a steep hill, I had to wait behind a team of oxen slowly pulling a cart and closely controlled by Chinese drivers. It was loaded high with the first consignment of nitroglycerine to arrive safely, destined to ease the tasks of railroad construction and mine digging. The crowd ahead parted apprehensively, so I followed in the clear path of its wake.

I was attracted by a Eurasian fortuneteller's booth. My own future was very much on my mind at the moment. After she silently scrutinized my face, she took my hand:

"Music, you must have music, but you only know how to listen. You want to shine, but take care not to dazzle. I see affluence, luxury, beauty. Why do you want to shine so much? Look out, big boy! There will be bad times, very bad, obstacles, trials, which you do not want to undertake. But you will force yourself because you want to shine so much. What pride. Look at me. That's it. I see women in your blue eyes, but as you blink so they will pass. I don't know if your eyes are trying to follow them or avoid them, beautiful American. That's all, twenty cents please."

She had taken me for an American. So, I was not alone in seeing myself so. That was enough for me: I decided to get naturalized. Disavowing Canada would be a rejection of my father and family, but I could not be faithful to both my origins and myself, and I could not reject myself.

My new American papers would be my passport to adult life.

It would take several weeks ashore before I would be issued my new papers, so I needed to find a temporary job to keep me in funds. Work on a ship would have been easy to find, but I needed something ashore. Finally an acquaintance came up with an opening which seemed to be suitable, as bodyguard to a young lady and her child. Their house was up at the top of the hill overlooking the Barbary Coast district where a nucleus of important Italian immigrants sheltered their families from the vice and violence below, while the money they earned to protect their families came from that very vice and violence. When I reached the Heights, my view encompassed the whole bay, right across to the small fishing village of Sausalito.

My prospective boss's bushy beard topped a tough, domineering body. I was told he had earned his money from mining. George Hearst certainly talked like a miner round his quid of tobacco, and his rough manners and flashy dress spoke of newfound wealth. His four passions were power, poker, bourbon, and his young wife Phoebe. He spat; the full protection of his wife and two year old son William Randolph must occupy all my energy. He spat; and any undue attentions to his wife would lead to my immediate castration. Did I understand? Right; start tomorrow. He spat again as I walked out, perhaps as a reminder.

Phoebe was a languid, musky Southern Belle of just twenty. Spending so much time with her, especially after years with no other company than seamen, was too much for me. I could see only too well why Mr. Hearst had felt his final comment to be necessary. I had to find an outlet before I made a stupid mistake.

With the help of a clarinetist from the Golden Note called Eleanor, I was able to maintain a respectful attitude. Phoebe praised me to her husband for my discretion and complete incorruptibility, reminding me of my aunt's praise for my modest appetite. When my naturalization papers arrived, Mr. Hearst showed his satisfaction and confidence in me by offering me the post of manager at one of his mines. I refused his offer but was encouraged by it to ask him to join me in establishing a shipyard up north where good pine was abundant. Phoebe sat by with little William, smiling at me. That smile encouraged me to ask, and it may have encouraged him to accept, a proposition that would remove me from San Francisco. Soon I was partner in a company with five hundred dollars capital in its account. The clarinet called me to a celebration.

Before departing to the land of the Douglas fir, I spent some time around San Francisco yard, collecting together all the equipment I would need. That was how I met Mr. Griffin, a builder of small boats for the Columbia River fishery called gillnetters after the special nets they employed. They seemed the ideal size considering the investment I could make, but I would have to attempt some improvements if I wanted to break into the market. Working on a set of plans, I decided I could increase the sail area to raise the speed and fit fairly shallow ribs to the bottom, reducing leeway without deepening the draught, which was limited by the river work. Armed with my new drawings and full of confidence, I managed to persuade the owner of a canning factory in Astoria to place an order for seven.

He was not mistaken: my gillnetters proved more efficient than the traditional model.

This immediate success confirmed my decision to break with my predecessors and become an American. Nobody was going to crush my talent any more.

Against my wishes, the seventh gillnetter was to be painted green. As I laid on the paint, its fresh gloss reflected my image back to me, an image which reminded me of my father. I slapped on more paint in an effort to obliterate the face staring out at me from that unlucky green paint. Never has a hull been so well protected.

The good Mr. Hearst was very happy to pocket an unexpectedly good profit. Phoebe and little William Randolph were not in the house to bring me luck this time though. He tried to convince me I could earn good money with him as the distributor of a new contrivance, a box with a motor attached which somehow stayed cold inside. I told him I had complete confidence in the efficacy of ice and declined the offer. I had my own plans to buy back one of my own gillnetters and try Columbia River fishing for myself. He almost swallowed his quid when he heard this.

"Buy! Buy! You have to sell, not buy. I'm rich because I sell gold, not because I buy it, goddamit. Stupid crazy buying. Unless it's an investment. See this picture here? Have you ever seen such a blurred bridge? All distorted and warped. They claim it's closer to reality—a funny impression of reality. But this painter, some Frenchie called Carot, his work'll be worth a fortune soon. You wait and see. So I haven't bought it, it's just there to make me money. Can't stand it meself."

My eyes wondered over the painting, trying to pick out details, but they eluded me. It was more like music than a picture.

"It's people like you, hot-heads like you who're ruining the Union. Have you heard their latest trick? Buy a whole Alaska full of snow and mujiks who can't even feed themselves. Have you ever heard of anyone finding gold in the snow? And just when we don't need it any more, thanks to this new ice chest. Now I'll give you one more chance to be sensible."

He was still spluttering into his beard as I turned the corner and headed for California Street. At Astoria Post Office my sister Elizabeth was waiting for me in an envelope:

Westport, Nova Scotia
Canada
22nd. May 1868

My Precious far away Joshua,

I always feel as if I am shouting against the wind when I write to you. Please let me know as soon as you receive this letter. Very bad news; grandfather was found dead at the foot of his lighthouse. Nobody knows how he could have come to fall. There are rumors going round but you must not believe them, Joshua. There are so many evil gossips saying he did it deliberately that I still cry every night. What do you think? Papa made the funeral speech and everyone was very impressed. Some people ask after you from time to time but I never know what to answer, your letters are so rare. I have followed your good advice and now confide in a diary too. It does me good. Sometimes I imagine you reading it which makes me feel very strange. You know that our Province is now part of the new Canadian Confederation? Everybody has been talking about it for ages. They say Nova Scotia even sent some advocates to London to try to stop it. I do not understand these political things though. The Acadians have kept quiet, not like those papists in Lower Canada who are supposed to be recruiting in Italy. I hope you will never become involved in that sort of stupid thing. Anyway, everybody says Lord Durham is right and they will have to speak English like everyone else and forget that old religion of theirs. Are you not frightened on the West Coast with all those Chinese and Japanese? I think you are very brave, and Papa does too. He also says he is pleased with the new law to prevent men working with women on the plantations. He has been preaching and praying for it. They say all sorts of alarming things about the West Coast. I hope you are maintaining the dignity of the family name. Write to me soon in this new Canada which seems so complicated to me after what we had before. Your sister who thinks of you more than you realize,
        Elizabeth

I had abandoned ship just in time, just before the old one sank. And I needed to be mature now, as I had lost my grandfather, my substitute father.

I decided that with my new gillnetter I would excel at salmon fishing so as to prove its worth. It became a tripartite adventure, the boat, my Indian friend Joseph, and me. It was more than an identity of interest or a complementary relationship, but rather a complete coincidence of purpose which directed our eyes and the boat's prow straight on to the salmon.

These boats are only about twenty feet long, double-ended with a spritsail set on a single mast well forward, like a catboat. On longer fishing trips the sail was draped over the sprit at night to convert the boat into a tent. Our success brought us to people's attention early in the season: famous, if only on the Columbia River.

At night Joseph had yarned about the sea otter hunting around Port Gray so enthusiastically that at the end of the salmon season we decided to give it a go. The hunt was mainly in the hands of Indian riflemen who take the otters in the shoals. Great stealth had to be employed, as the otters had become very leery, smelling the scent of humans several tides after they had passed on the beach, and staying well clear once they had. We were as successful at this as with the salmon and made more money, skins selling for anything from fifty to three hundred and fifty dollars. Joseph was soon ready to rejoin his tribe on the Prince Rupert reserve for the winter. Each autumn he returned to his family, and each thaw he set off on his travels again, following the seasons like the son of Nature he was. Like Nature, his life was made up of a series of separate parcels of time, a continuity of discontinuous moments. He could thus avoid the monotony of daily repetition by living in a longer time cycle.

I took a tack across to Vancouver out of interest, where a chat with a local newspaperman in a Chinese restaurant led to my first attempt at writing. He thought an article on sea otter hunting would interest his readers. I spent days working at it and in the end produced something I was quite proud of. When it was printed, I rushed off a copy to my sister, strongly urging her to pass it on to my father. The article started with the newspaper's own eulogy of the author's prowess at salmon fishing, otter hunting, and boatbuilding, which is what I really wanted him to see rather than my own modest presentation of the facts. I recalled the time when the sea otter was to be found from Kamchatka right down to the south of New California and alluded to the Russian colony in Alaska and the first development of the North West coast. I learned from the Chinese how the main market for the furs was in China, so I told of fortunes made by New York and New England traders who rounded the Horn, loaded furs in Oregon, Vancouver, and the Charlotte Islands, and then crossed to Canton to barter for tea and silks. In this very trade, Captain Gray in the *Columbia* out of Boston discovered the great port site and important river which carry his and his ship's names respectively. He finished that voyage back in Boston in 1790, becoming the first captain to make a circumnavigation under the American flag. His trip made a profit for the backers of more than seven hundred percent. I admired both the exploit and the profit.

Of course, my first written work ended up as wrapping for Chinese cabbage and chips, but I knew there would be one copy yellowing amongst Elizabeth's treasures.

Joseph had expressed the wish to see me again before I left the area, so I took this as an invitation to visit him on the reserve up in the north of British Columbia. I was pleased to see him again but must admit to being shocked by the conditions I encountered: colonialism gone rotten. The officials, colonists, Métis, and Indians spent every mosquito-infested day cultivating individual and collective hostilities. The Indians bit the Métis, who stung the colonists, who tormented the officials. Even the ancient pines wilted in the atmosphere of mordant hatred.

I was impressed by the ability of the native fishermen and their seaworthy pirogues. The quality of their lives and their lives themselves depended on those pirogues, so they spent time on them. They were better than those of the settlers, even though the natives had only the most primitive tools to fashion them with. They made up for lack of tools with a plentiful supply of time, their one luxury: time to wait for a tree to become ready, time to season it fully and to carve it into the exact shape to suit their water, time to talk to it and listen for its reply.

My roots felt in need of a little salt water after all this time, so I headed back down to San Francisco to find a ship. I would try for a command of my own this time. The first thing to come my way was a coastal schooner carrying grain to Seattle and returning with coal. The owners wanted to know if I was experienced in the transport of grain. As my own conviction is that competence is mainly a matter of intelligence, I declared myself fully competent and the command was mine.

For two years I worked in this coastal trade, justifying my master's stripes. It was demanding work, since grain was carried on deck and great care was needed to prevent it from becoming damaged by a stray wave. The ship had to be worked like a dancer, swaying clear of the grasping hands of each passing wave. Confidence grew until I was happy and content to be controlling the mechanism of control over others: a twenty-five-year-old chief ruling my own small tribe, submission a thing of the past.

The only news from Canada which interested me concerned the Métis rebellion and that was only because a likeness of their leader, one Riel, reminded me of my father. I was more inspired by pictures of a new clipper just launched in England, the *Cutty Sark*. What lines! She would certainly earn her owners a fortune on the tea route. Great things were happening elsewhere in the world too, as I read in *Whitaker's Almanac:* in South Africa a huge diamond had been found, called the "Star of South Africa"; in Australia more gold strikes. Here on the West Coast the situation was deteriorating, with gold becoming harder to find and bizarre social developments, like in Wyoming where they were talking about giving women votes! Fortunately, maritime tradition kept them off ships. All this made me think of going deep-sea again.

The relentless competition of the times made no allowance for the youth of a master: he was still the "old man." A seasoned temperament was needed if one was to stand the trials of the trade. On all the great trade routes of tea, coffee, spice, and grain, time was important in achieving the best prices, and now there were not only other sailing ships to beat but steamships too. The rivalry was merciless. A master was always having to choose between safety and speed, with speed normally winning, because failure meant demotion to cement, guano, or coal.

A young officer had to be especially gifted to rise from the ranks and become an "old man" responsible for everything on the ship, even in port: navigation, recruiting and training crew, passengers, cargo, repairs and maintenance, discipline, sails, administration, and even politics. The sea itself was often the least of his worries when compared to the knavery of agents, the paperwork for endless officials, power-crazed customs officers, and the greedy machinations of the shipowners, without taking into account the wiles of local chiefs, contrabanders, shanghaiers, and pirates.

Shipowners were always looking out to make a fast profit, so gold fever in California and Australia affected them as much as the hoards of immigrant prospectors they crammed onto their ships. I remember a typical description of conditions on such a ship: "I followed the mate down the ladder to the first tween deck. It was terrible. The stench nearly laid me out and everyone groaning. The light of our storm lantern showed a swarming mass of creatures, racked with seasickness, on filthy, split palliasses covering the whole deck, so they could not move without stepping on someone."

For the unscrupulous shipowners, immigrants were an ideal cargo. In those conditions they did not need much food: they could not keep it down, so why waste the money? If they died it was no problem because they had paid in advance.

So many crews jumped ship in San Francisco and made for the gold fields that the shanghaiers often failed to make up the numbers, even for top prices. By 1869 there were more than one hundred ships abandoned in the bay for want of men to sail them, run aground, or converted to hostels. Even so, the owners could turn a profit in one trip, so they just bought a new ship on the East Coast.

Many years later I discovered a clipping from the *National* amongst Elizabeth's belongings concerning conditions around Australia. The article was written by a French prospector, R.F. Anthier, who turned to ink when gold failed him:

The *Begum Jeanne,* a three master built for the opium trade, loaded some serious trouble in Macao. Four hundred and fifty coolies were crowded into her nauseous tween decks with little more space than black slaves. The owner/captain, M. Butafuego, kept them locked in, only allowing ten on deck at a time to cook for the others. The hatchway was re-enforced with a heavy metal grill and constantly guarded by armed marines. Retrenched aft, the officers and crew slept with weapons in their hands and when on deck carried two loaded pistols and a long kris. In Macao, ten pirates managed to infiltrate themselves amongst the coolies. Ten days in the tween docks sufficed for them to foment a revolt, convincing the coolies of the wealth to be gained by seizing the ship. The cargo of tea, silks and porcelain in the holds was worth its weight in gold.

The attack was launched in full daylight without success. Six of the pirates took refuge in the rigging. Knowing they would be condemned to death anyway, they started cutting sheets and guys. Then, leaping from mast to mast, they hacked through jib and forestaysail halyards. The yards swung free, damaging the rigging with every roll, striking against the masts with blows like cannon shot. As the crew fought to deal with this revolt in the rigging, a rumble came up from the hold. The four hundred and fifty coolies, terrified by the masses of water coming down the hatch, thought the ship was foundering. Their frantic struggles were working the grill free from the hatch despite the bosun's systematic hacking off of their hands with an axe. The captain blew off two emerging heads with his pistols, then, maddened with rage, set fire to the tween decks. The terrible Butafuego, torch in hand, was insensible to their cries. The crew launched the longboats, as the *Begum Jeanne* sank crackling into the sea, and made for Singapore. An enquiry was opened, but the authorities are expected to cover up the scandal.

A few hundred yellow monkeys more or less did not interest the Europeans and the mandarins made a good profit from the trade in coolies and so did not insist. But six months after the drama, Captain Butafuego died of food poisoning: his cook was Chinese.

The appalling conditions I witnessed in San Francisco made me resolve never to become involved with human cargoes, even if they did show a good profit. The temptation has sometimes been very strong, but thankfully I have not succumbed.

After so many years on the coast, I felt ready to go deep-sea again. Confidence in my authority showed in a new elegance of dress and manners. Even the shipowners started to be polite to me. So I applied and was appointed to the command of the three-masted barque *Washington* sailing for the Pacific Islands and Australia. Being towed out of San Francisco Bay early in 1870, I was as proud of myself as of my ship. If only grandfather could see me.

Crossing the Pacific consists of days of abstract points on charts suddenly broken into by the appearance of an island ahead. As the island drops away astern, it becomes just as abstract as the points on the chart.

Slightly unsure of myself, I stuck rigidly to my new status to combat the insidious slackness of island life. Only with the assurance of experience would I be able to relax enough to enjoy and accept their ways. This passage, self-denial was the order of the day. Memories of life in port when I was on deck were locked away behind my captain's buttons. The only flesh I came close to was the sweating bodies of stevedores, and my conversations were mainly with annoying officials.

From my high position of isolation, I watched a melange of multicolored parakeets, turquoise lagoons bordered by pressing seas of white foam, louis d'or, silver ecus, laughter, smiles, white-brown-black-copper skin tattooed and velvet smooth, mother of pearl, shell necklaces, fish and birds rivalling each other for brilliance, girls under palm trees, girls dressed only in pareos, shining black hair brushing naked breasts. My head condemned the inevitable desire stirring in my stomach. I was frozen in this tropic of frustration.

My crew felt none of my inhibitions: they had no dignified status to uphold. They would return aboard laughing, pockets stuffed with momentos of the previous night: scraps of pareo or strings of flowers. They displayed their trophies like medals won in the glorious war of love. I envied them, even as I reprimanded them in the name of the good society to which I aspired. I wished I too could strip my smart new uniform and sacrifice myself to a dusky heathen goddess, forgetting my education, my prejudices, my anxieties, my seriousness. But the thought of baring body and soul was humiliating to me: I must have been suspect of what might be revealed.

Conflict between body and mind congealed in the return of my chronic stomach cramps. I had laid aside my seaman's clothes, but my captain's uniform I could not undo: it held me like a straight jacket, preventing me from going where desire called. My seamen only listened to their desires: I only to my mind. Neither of us were complete men.

Under the control of this social restraint, I starved my body and nourished racial, colonial, and religious prejudices instead. I limited myself to the company of administrators and missionaries. Finally I was somebody, but only amongst a group who deluded themselves with illusory superiority whilst fearing the Third Republic or the artistic audacity of painters like Pissarro. I had made the desperate mistake of leaving one crowd only to become lost in another. In that society, which covered its corruption in immaculate clothes, they had a comfortable habit of judging without attempting to understand and of relegating desire to the level of an unmentionable bodily function.

I blamed my internal dissensions on the monotony of an insular life and carried my cramps from island to island, so blinded by my blinkers that I could not see I was in paradise.

With all sails set and sensuality well battened down, I turned the bow of the *Washington* towards Australia. My head was held high, but my body was struggling for breath.

CHAPTER FOUR

Love

We sailed into Sydney Harbor with my pride unabated. My navigation had brought the *Washington* to the harbor entrance without any last-minute changes of course. That is how one has to approach Australia: boldly. My voice rang with assurance as I called out the orders which brought us up amongst the hundreds of ship anchored at the de-ratting station. They were being cleaned of the sweat of immigrants before that smell was replaced by the rancid odor of baled wool. All of the captains would have preferred something heavier than wool to ballast their ships for the coming battle with the Tasman Sea. Unfortunately for them, sheep reproduce faster than nuggets of gold.

After lying at anchor for de-ratting and customs inspection, and then the medical examinations at Cockatoo Island, we were allowed to move alongside at Circular Quay, close to the ferry berths. They served all the beaches in the bay where the Australians like to parade their loves or bury their problems in the hot sand. It was on one such ferry, running to Manly Beach, thick with white sunshades and embroidered parasols, that I fell in with Lionel Sutherland. Our only introduction was a common interest in observing the female passengers.

We spent the afternoon continuing our inspection on the beach, our conversation wandering aimlessly as our minds were concentrated on the view. I envied all those men who could lie contented alongside a conquered companion, with no desire to look around them.

On the return trip, backs propped against the ferry's saloon bar, I felt sufficiently surfeited with bronzed flesh to engage my mind with what he was saying. As he warmed to the subject of his singing career, his rich voice enveloped me in cotton-wool clouds quite invisible to the other passengers in the orange glow of the setting sun. As I showed an interest in music, he invited me to accompany him to work. Thus I attended my first opera.

First we had to stop off at the lounge of Muir's Hotel at the bottom of George Street to meet with his fiancée, Miss Walker. Each night at this time, when the sun sunk below Milson's Point, the animation in the bars increased. One could feel the tension between English and American colonials, in spite of the treaty just made to regulate the litigation between scions of those two lands. As usual, I kept out of any debate that looked as though it might become heated, but I liked this lounge for the view it gave me of the docks and the *Washington*'s rigging, which occasionally emerged from out of the forest of masts.

Miss Walker arrived and we were introduced by Mr. Sutherland, after which he spoke little to me, his attention being completely monopolized by her. The fact that the simple presence of a loved one could so rapidly caulk all interior seams opened up the cracks of my own solitude. My happiness was capsized. I attempted to make conversation, pretending to have an interest in Rockefeller's recent petroleum discoveries and repeating some of what I had read of Ed Whymper's conquest of Mount Cervin, but my heart was not in it. I foundered and then sank into silence. Other people had come here to Australia and found fortunes; perhaps I could find love. It felt far more important to me than money at the moment. I had no idea of how to conduct the search, no more than I have now, but subsequent events indicate that this time it was a premonition rather than a decision.

Miss Walker—who was also a singer—Lionel, and I walked to the opera, where I was told that Miss Walker's sister would meet us at the entrance, under the sign advertising Smetana's "The Bartered Bride." She had already arranged to attend this performance and would help me at the box office if there was a problem with tickets. She was there waiting, and we were introduced.

"Miss Virginia Walker, Captain Slocum. Captain Slocum, Miss Virginia Walker."

I vaguely remember Lionel and Miss Walker rushing off towards the stage door. I surprised myself by being able to emulate Mr. Stanley when he discovered Dr. Livingstone at Ujiji and hid my emotion behind polite conversation. Her presence brought home to me how little I knew of how to behave at an opera, causing me some embarrassment, but she took my arm and guided me through the formalities to our seats. I turned my head towards hers and found her eyes waiting to meet mine.

Throughout the evening, we turned to look at each other in this way, our eyes calmly speaking complete understanding as we interrogated each other's souls. I did not make out a word of what was being sung but found that, while words speak to the mind, the feeling in a voice goes straight to the heart with no need of interpretation. A night of heavy seas for a heart, to be assailed through the ears by music and through the eyes by a beautiful face.

I felt sure that the audience's final applause was for me, for having waited patiently through twenty-six years of preparation for this moment. Now everything would start, here in Sydney in the embrace of Virginia's eyes, an ex-American and a new American. They were applauding me for having found her: I was handsome and important because she was beautiful and important to me.

I had always distrusted women before, thinking them unfaithful, disloyal, traitorous creatures even at their most desirable, but Virginia I was sure was different. She was not just a woman, she was going to be mine. By simply looking at me, this firm-handed companion with tresses encircling her face like the tropics, making it the world to me, had suddenly changed all my expectations.

Mr. Walker had emigrated to America from Scotland and married Mrs. Walker in New York, where they became influential members of society. Gold took them to California, then the lure of Ballant and Sovereign Hill drew them to this new land of Australia. The metal did not work for them in Australia, but they did well from kangaroo hunting, selling the salted meat to ships for provisions. Virginia had been born to them on Staten Island, New York and was as proud of the Leni-Lenape Indian blood she had inherited from her mother as her father was of his Scottish origins. She loved outdoor life, starting with long horseback expeditions in the Blue Ridge Mountains of her American youth, free from the comforts of civilized life. In Australia she had continued in the same way, even becoming initiated into a matriarchal Aborigine tribe whose women shared the remaining men when their lovers left on long hunting trips.

The sun-bleached Australians seemed to have picked up this wanderlust from the natives. They did not need to travel over the immense Australian territories, but it had become a national pastime which everyone took for granted. Since the western part of the continent had obtained it own government, Cobb & Co. were making a fortune with their monopoly of public transport between the west and New South Wales, Victoria, and Queensland. A new submarine cable made communication with England simple, but at home they preferred to travel endless miles in person. Cobb & Co. used six thousand horses to pull their diligences over eighty thousand miles every week.

But this cloud of dust was being raised far from the isolated beach which refreshed our passion with its gentle surf. The rocks and sand of that beach were the only witnesses of our first kiss. Not a stolen kiss, but one we had both prepared well for and entered it as though it was our first home and shelter in which we would be safe. Pressing together as if striving to become one, that kiss bound us and welded our bodies into a single unit. Tears of joy did nothing to cool the heat of that kiss, a moment of magic in which our whole future became present to us with the promise of happiness.

That same day she told me she would not enter the water as she usually did because of a certain periodic inconvenience which troubles all women. Her frankness on the subject tied us even closer, just as it had done with Elizabeth and myself. Did I see something of Elizabeth in her? There were to be no secrets between us to obstruct the clear horizon of loving confidence. The fears of my Quaker antecedents and the taboos of her Victorian society were banished: we would choose our own way.

Mr. Walker cultivated the good taste proper to a resident of Double Bay. He was happy to give his daughter in marriage to a captain, but only in an official church ceremony. We felt our felicity needed no ornamentation, so the simplest of services would suffice, having our own ideas on how the rope of marriage should be roved to run most freely. There was some discussion on the subject, but in the end we had the highest trump card: Virginia was no longer a minor and she was in love. I made the arrangements at the presbytery of Christ Church and the guest list was short. The wedding itself was of no great importance to us: we had already been united on the beach with rocks for witnesses, our joy officiating.

In my life I have seen many married couples who do not share the house they live in despite appearances. The wife settles in, in a sedentary fashion, only leaving when necessary and soon hurrying back. For the husband, it is only a base from which to go out. Virginia and I were going to shelter our love under the sea's starry canopy, our home travelling with us. Our life would be at once stationary and mobile: unmoving love on an endless voyage, our only comfort each other's arms. Previously I had held to the traditional attitude towards women on ships but, as I say, previously I had always distrusted women. Virginia's arrival on board broke tradition, but I wanted sailing and her, and she had the strength of character to deal with a novel situation.

She installed herself in a tiny cabin already filled by desk, barometer, chronometers, and books; nothing in common with the staterooms she had seen on the White Star packet ships like the *S.S. Oceanic*. This cabin was lit only by a skylight above, giving a view of the helmsman's boots and a patch of sky showing between masts and yards. She was prepared to do it because a life without total sharing would have been an empty sort of existence for us. We were intoxicated with each other to the point of addiction, so we could not bear to be apart. We were not going anywhere without each other, but we definitely were going. Our love flowed in an endless steam of words, the fugitive syllables constantly renewed.

During the wedding ceremony the officiant had rambled off on a peregrination concerning the importance of remembering the good times when passion had abated in later years. We chose to profit from the richness of our pleasures by remembering them now, talking of them endlessly so as to fix them in our minds by reliving them in words. We drowned ourselves in love.

"Gentlemen, here is my mate: Mrs. Captain Slocum. Any comments? Any objections? If so, please take them ashore and stay there with them. Thank you, gentlemen. Single up, fore and aft."

Like so many other couples, in private we were almost childish with each other. Virginia became my "Ginny" and Captain Slocum rediscovered the "Josh" of his youth.

Although nobody had objected when I made my little speech before leaving, many of the men carried the old superstitions concerning women aboard. Amongst themselves they referred to "the mainmast's women" and "the Devil's ballast." When one man on a ship has a woman and none of the rest do, there is sure to be jealousy, but the happiness enveloping us like warm mist was not for sharing.

Ginny insisted on learning all about navigation and sailing. We only left the compass and charts to return to the refinement of more intimate skills, learning how to navigate and handle our own bodies, trying out many different approaches to the same safe harbor, discussing the advantages of varied routes as we relaxed once the sails were properly furled.

When our bodies were becalmed, Ginny worked at everything to be done on a ship: how to strop, rig, bend sails to a yard, take in a reef, steer, plot a position, take soundings, repair sails, splice an eye, handle a gun, tar. I had to portion her apprenticeship with regard to the tolerance of her female presence by the crew. A woman herself has never really endangered seamen, but they tend to be crude creatures and the routine of a ship can be boring. Their habits are deeply ingrained, for tradition is essential on ships: the men on the next watch have to know exactly where to find each sheet and how it has been belayed, even in the dark, otherwise an emergency can easily turn into a disaster.

But why should they be reminded of their isolation on board by the constant presence of an amorous couple? I understood that: I had been on deck too, but we found it impossible to hide our love. My linen-clad seamen disapproved, but underneath their linen they understood and envied me. It is good to be in a position to be envied. With the eyes of these witnesses upon us, our love intensified. Their jealousy fed our libido. I think we may have taken a vicious pleasure in reminding them of what we had, revelling in the exclusivity of our relationship.

Ginny had quickly consented to the presence of my own body enwrapping hers, responding to my caresses when she discovered the pleasure they could bring her. It was some time before she consented to my exploration of her body with my eyes, and she was right in that. To allow oneself to be looked at is the ultimate in submission and only with my eyes did I fully possess her. Throughout our marriage, that was the way I reassured myself of her love and I could feel the thrill go through her body as though my eyes had penetrated her.

During this first trip, everything around us was filled with under-tones of carnal pleasure: the obligatory discretion in front of the crew, flattering moonlight playing on her stern as she leant looking over the taffrail, the soft wind fluttering an open shirt, the swell moving to its own rhythm, the sound of a licking wave. Even our first row was over sex, with Ginny ending by establishing that in the intimate matters of matrimony we were to be equal partners.

"Josh, I have let you do anything you like to me and I regret nothing. But you must learn that each person's appetite is their own. Just because I have shared a meal with you it does not mean I cannot still be hungry. If you leave the table satisfied, then I can still help myself to more. I live on the ship you command, but you do not command the body I live in. Do you understand? I am warning you, I did not marry you to change you or to be changed myself. If you want to have all of me, you must not try to take anything away from me."

The situation had made me angry: I felt it was a rejection or an affront but I learned otherwise. Even solitary pleasures can be shared. Our respective desires were allowing themselves the freedom to accede to passion, a passion in which we would not lose ourselves but find each other.

In the Pacific there are no easy landfalls. The only pacific thing about the ocean is the immense distance that can separate one from the problems of the world. Navigation is never peaceful in coral reefs and tropical storms: it gave Ginny an arduous apprenticeship of the best sort. Taking account of winds and currents, a sailing ship has to travel about seven thousand miles from San Francisco to Sydney, and practically the same from Sydney to the River Kasilof at Cook Inlet, Alaska, our ultimate destination. A long way around just to get cold again.

I did not follow the normal route with the *Washington* but headed straight north from one end of the Pacific to the other: first through the treacherous reefs of the Coral Sea, then doubling Bauro Island in the Solomons, past Nauru towards Joliut atoll in the Marshalls. Under the equator the Pacific is pocked with coral atolls jealously sheltering their turquoise waters like a reservoir of royal jelly. Ginny sulked angrily each time I rebutted her attempts to persuade me to alter course and anchor awhile in a lagoon. It was hard to convince her we had to flee north and quit the area before the hurricane season: the owner's date for our arrival in Alaska was drawing nigh. When she finally came to appreciate the imperatives of navigation, she understood that a master does not have a free hand. She came to think and act like me, and I loved her more for it.

In the North Pacific, above the fortieth parallel, the colors become less pleasing to the eye, the pallet looses its pastels and half tones, keeping only brilliant colors or washing everything out in a terrible, concealing fog. The situation is similar to that on the Newfoundland Banks, with cold winds from the Bering Strait blowing over the warm waters of the Kuro Shio, or a warm breeze from the south meeting the cold waters of the Oyo Shio. Ginny was fascinated by the species of birds she had never seen before and raved over the sea otters, calling them "dormice." We came across thousands of them peacefully asleep on their backs, forelegs folded over their faces to keep the water from splashing their nostrils. They made perfect victims for the cook. At first she thought it cruel to kill them, but when she tasted the sweet fresh meat after twenty-four days of salted pork, she took the gun herself, keeping the cook busy with the gaff. Otter meat is ideal for fighting the bitter cold winds. The crew congratulated her on her marksmanship and thanked her for the fresh meat. From then on the "the Devil's ballast" was accepted as Mrs. Captain Slocum.

The *Washington* returned to her birthplace in Puget Sound, for me one of the most beautiful areas of the world. Here Nature provides for all man's needs and aspirations. The shipbuilder in me was attracted by the ranks of forest pines marching right down to the water's edge. Sawmills were built alongside the shipbuilder's ways so the handling could be reduced to a minimum. This was essential when planks of sixty meters were being turned out, long enough to make a whole strake in one piece.

We were there to refit and equip for a salmon fishing expedition in Alaska which I had persuaded the owners I could lead successfully. Ginny heard from me so many tales of my prowess as a gillnetter builder and salmon fisherman that she had to counter me with stories of her own equestrian adventures in the unmapped mountains. It took some time to load the hold with provisions and materials for building a base camp and prepare the deck for a cargo of gillnetters which we were to build ourselves on the way north—to my improved design, of course.

Sailing north, Alaska soon infiltrated our oilskins, trickling down our necks and creeping slowly on until it finally settled at the bottom of our boots. The crew worked on the preparations for our campaign. Anyone who could handle an adze or a saw was detailed to building the gillnetters, making them to a size to fit the space available on deck. Ginny became expert at the precise positioning of brass fittings and the laying on of varnish, though she found the smell of turpentine nauseating.

When I piloted the ship down the Shelikof Channel, Ginny took the helm. I gave her the names of distant Aleutian volcano peaks off to port and she responded by telling me that the cape to starboard was called Karluk. After forty-nine days at sea she could read a chart perfectly well for herself. She was becoming a lady captain, my Lady Captain Slocum, whilst still remaining my Ginny too. Life lay open before us, like the River Kasilof opening up ahead.

At that time the two-hundred-mile glacial fjord which constitutes Cook Inlet had the stern beauty of a scantily charted gulley which could be penetrated only with extreme caution. The sole bits of information available came from the summary reports of Russian sailors. Ginny made sure the lookouts kept a sharp watch, shocking them out of any inattentiveness with phrases which had no place in such a pretty mouth. I was proud to walk arm in arm with such an exceptional woman who knew her will and imposed it firmly. When we sent a boat ahead to sound for shoals, she went in it herself to ensure the job was done properly. Few depths appeared on the chart I had, so a falling tide could soon have us aground. The tides here reminded me of those of my youth in the Bay of Fundy, swirling in and out in unforeseeable currents and eddies. At springs we measured a range of some six fathoms, and I estimated the tide of icy water to run at five or six knots, full of small bergs, tree trunks, and glacial debris. In the narrows, deafeningly violent overfalls forced us to wait for slack water to pass.

Captain Vancouver had good reason to recall the inlet in his memoirs: "Being anchored on the left of the entrance to the inlet with the *Discovery*, the ice carried by the current broke my anchor cable and caused my ship to drift out to sea."

Although the Russians had come here in numbers to fish for royal salmon, I could find no sure anchorage. And there was no one to ask, because few American ships had used it since Alaska had been bought by the United States. To ensure a safe cushion of water under our hull, I had to anchor almost two miles off shore on a bank filling the bay beyond Cape Kasilof, off the mouth of the river I had selected for our base. Murmurs of discontent at our instruction came up through the water from the enormous glacial boulders covering the shallows. The ship was as well protected as possible with the Karluk reef offshore of us, but the fierce current tugged hard at our cable. I had her topmasts lowered to reduce windage, because squalls blow violently in these narrow inlets and the sudden strain as a ship pulls on her anchor when hit by a squall can soon break its hold on the bottom. The northwest winds are the most frequent in the spring and send down the most vicious squalls.

All the gillnetters were launched and put into service ferrying our provisions and equipment ashore. Kenia Indians who had watched our arrival came up to offer their assistance. Their legendary seamanship and familiarity with small boats made them perfect crew. Their energy matched their acrobatic abilities in running the shuttle from ship to shore, freeing my men to unload and transport ashore. With smiles which would be the envy of any Don Juan, their lithe copper bodies danced about the overloaded gillnetters, making landing and launching through the surf look like a simple, everyday activity. A soaking just made them roar with laughter, and Ginny joined in their merriment. Whenever I looked, she was there with one or another of them, laughing together. As soon as possible I sent the pack of them away, promising to come to them if I needed any help later. Ginny shot me a look and disappeared, not to be found for several hours, when I discovered her bad-temperedly sewing an oilskin.

Once we had completed our installations and started fishing in earnest, we met with such success that I found myself short of labor and so was forced to apply to the Indians for assistance once more. The ones I picked were mainly half-breed descendants of passing Russian fishermen. They worked well at first, but in spite of all I could do to prevent it, they soon sank into alcoholic depravity. Then Ginny became the object of their unequivocal attentions. She never responded to their advances, but I was surprised she did not make use of her new-found authority to repulse them. She gave the impression of drifting rudderless, vulnerable to a shipwrecker or pirate. One in particular looked very much like such a pirate to me.

I dismissed them all again and personally escorted them back to their village. Thinking I would be away all night, I made some recommendations to Ginny which were received in cold silence. The trip went faster than I expected, so I decided to return the same night, arriving in the early hours of the morning. Sounds of movement inside the tent aroused fresh suspicions in my jealous mind, sounds as fearful as the trickle of water in a ship. Barely breathing, I unlaced the tent door. The click of a rifle being cocked stopped me cold.

"Who's there? Answer quick or I'll fire."

She spoke calmly, her voice deeper than usual.

"Don't shoot Ginny. It's me, Josh. Are you alone?"

"Yes. And I'm going to stay alone for the rest of the night. Get out. You can come back tomorrow as arranged."

"But, Ginny."

"Virginia. Virginia tells you she is not spending the night with you and your jealousy. If you want to sleep with her again, you'll have to get rid of it."

"But..."

"Go and drown it in the sea. If you're alone tomorrow, I might forget it. I wear a wedding ring, Joshua, not chains. Remember that."

The wound to my self-esteem was more painful than the pistol shot which would have put a permanent end to my jealousy. I spent the night under an upturned boat, on the pebbles.

In the morning, cold and tired after a sleepless night, I went to the tent to discover Virginia had gone. Remorse aged me by ten years, remorse for being jealous. For two days we searched the whole area without success. At the end of the third day, a canoe turned the end of Cape Karluk and headed straight for our camp. In front of the crowd gathered to help the canoe ashore, Ginny slowly stood up and stretched, as if waking from a refreshing sleep. Calmly she stepped out and walked towards me, stopping to wave her thanks to the big half-breed paddler. He responded with a smile as broad as the bay. Still smiling, she turned back to me.

"Josh, we ought to explore this place together. How are you?"

The rush of happiness at finding her alive drove out all other thoughts. I decided I would have to live each moment with her as though there was a canoe waiting round a corner to take her away from my jealousy. I never questioned her about what had happened: perhaps I was afraid she might tell me the truth.

Fishing and life were generous to us. Ginny was more loving than ever and I was grateful for each day we had together. I felt that now she had chosen me, preferred me, was mine quite freely. Our ardor acquired new strength from that magic land. Alaska showed us many wonders.

"Josh, my love, look at the chain of the Aleutians over there. Those two high peaks, those are our twin monuments. The one behind,

Mount Iliana, that's me behind you, Mount Redout."

She stood behind me, clinging to my back like the baby koalas we had seen at the Sydney zoo.

"From out at sea Mount Redout is behind Iliana."

She laughed, holding me tighter.

"Do you see, my beautiful captain, how the glaciers have sculptured our two volcanoes? Fire and ice sculpture each other, but remain fire and ice."

Who says Eden was in the tropics?

Ginny and I rediscovered the happiness of our former innocence. We were enraptured by the joy of life, every living creature being family to us: the geese, the gulls, the half-breeds and Aleutians in their otter skins, the friendly belugas. We explored the River Kasilof to its source at a frozen lake deep in the heart of bear and wolf country. The course of the river could be seen for miles ahead, revealed by hundreds of eagles in search of salmon. Ginny always carried a Henry rifle and rarely missed her mark.

The bears also normally lived on salmon, but the smell of food sometimes attracted them to our camp. One day a kodiak approached us directly, without any sign he would keep a respectful distance. I had been clawed once before in British Columbia, so knew these powerful beasts will occasionally attack. I made to take the gun from Ginny, but she clung to it, giving me a look of reproach. Not until I removed my hand from the gun did she turn from me to the bear, which was less than a hundred feet away and still coming. She placed herself between me and the bear and calmly brought the rifle to her shoulder. As he reared for the final charge she fired and he sank gently to the ground without a sound. What had been a redoubtable beast had been turned into an immense fur coat covering a mountain of red meat. As I skinned him, Ginny sat stroking his heavy head, the rifle still smoking in her hand.

Increasingly frequent gales kept everyone in the camp, apart from a skeleton crew left aboard the Wa*shington*. Then a particularly strong blow from the southwest backed up by the force of a rising tide caused the ship to drag. The crew did all they could but being light, she was soon driven high up on the beach. As the gale blew on, day after day, masses of sand piled up on the beach, creating whole dunes between her and the water. By the time it blew itself out, she looked as though she had never been afloat. We shored her up tight and removed everything salvageable to improve the camp, spars and sails giving us extra tents. We no longer had a ship, but morale remained high.

We had reason to stay in good spirits: the fishing campaign was so successful that there would be a good profit even with the loss of the ship. As Ginny regularly assured me, I could still hold my head high. Nevertheless, the stranding left me with the serious problem of how to realize the profit. We had to transport the fish south to where the markets were. The nearest port, Kodiak, was more than two hundred miles away. In those waters, two hundred miles is a long way in a small boat, but we had no other alternative than to make the journey. The two largest gillnetters were prepared for the trip, and then we built a twenty-one-foot whaler, more suitable for open water than the smaller gillnetters. I enjoyed building that boat, mainly because it gave me another opportunity to display my skills to Ginny.

When the time came to strike camp, a customs cutter arrived and offered us assistance. For myself and the crew I refused, wanting to keep our independence and not look as though we had had to be rescued, but Ginny was suffering from giddy spells, so I allowed her to travel in the cutter. One seaman, Thompson, nicknamed the "Rocky Mountain Hunter," stayed behind to guard our carefully stored catch from raids by bears or natives. With his hunting ability, he would have no problem keeping himself supplied with fresh food.

With such small boats we had to wait for favorable weather, and the first part of the journey went well, an ebb tide and north breeze taking us the fifty miles to Kachemak Bay in six hours. From there to Cape Elizabeth was open seas, and so our supply of ship's biscuits and dried salmon stayed almost untouched during the couple of days it took us, the gillnetters not being designed to work through large waves. We were all very glad to step ashore in Kodiak and be free of the violent motion of the small boats.

Kodiak was buzzing with talk about an arctic whaling fleet that had been taken by surprise by early ice: twenty-nine ships lost, with a cargo of oil valued at half a million dollars. The crew members who had survived the escape across the pack ice had harrowing stories to tell.

That ice was fortunate for us. Ginny had found two ships set up for seal hunting that were sitting in harbor with empty holds because of the early winter. I immediately chartered them to recover our salmon stock from Kasilof and carry it to San Francisco. With that taken care

81

of, we boarded the Russian whaler *Czarevitch* in Kodiak; she was loading ice and bound for California. En route we witnessed the harpooning of a humpback whale, which excited Ginny's hunting instincts. I answered her endless questions to the best of my ability, but the crew could not help me out as not one of them spoke English. In the effort to unify the disparate cultures of the Empire, it was forbidden at that time to teach any living language but Russian anywhere in the tsardom.

When the whale was cut up, an almost completely formed whelp was found inside. Ginny was overcome with nausea and refused to join us at the captain's table to sample that particularly tender delicacy.

Back in San Francisco, the shipowners did not hold the loss of the *Washington* against me. In fact, they were so satisfied with the results of the expedition that they gave me a new command. Captain and Mrs. Slocum took charge of the barkentine *Constitution,* running the San Francisco–Honolulu line.

CHAPTER FIVE

Complicity

Our son Victor was born to us on board the *Constitution* in the port of San Francisco in 1872.

During the preceding weeks, Ginny had turned in on herself, putting a wall between us. She took everything I said lightly, and laughed at me when I tried to be serious, seeming to take pleasure in thwarting me. Her almost sadistic humor and loss of interest in sex diminished my joy at becoming a father. I gave my wife all the attention due to one in her state, but she still took the opportunity of my absence from the ship on a visit to the owners to be delivered of the boy. The child was asleep, already washed and fed, when I first saw him. I had expected to be overcome by pleasurable feelings at this moment, but instead I felt like an intruder coming between the two of them. I was told to keep quiet, not to touch. She announced her choice of name without any suggestion that I should be consulted.

But motherhood brought us back together, as if she now had room for me again. I recognized my Alaskan Ginny. She allowed me to gently massage her stomach, and I had to restrain the desire to embrace her and take possession of her body again. As I kissed her, she slowly turned her head, turning mine with it as if our faces were geared together, to look at the sleeping bundle.

"Look, Josh. Our child looks like you."

"You look pale. Have you eaten?"

"Do you know if he is perfectly alright? Are there any problems?"

"I've spoken with the shipowners. We have to be ready to leave with our passengers next Wednesday. They've bought us one of Lord Kelvin's new sounding machines. Do you think you'll be ready?"

"Pass me some cotton wool. I'm leaking and he's not ready for a feed."

"I wonder what it tastes like."

"Josh!"

"Just a little taste."

"You ought to be ashamed of yourself. Here, lick my finger, its covered with it."

I would have preferred to take it directly like my son but had to be content with sucking her finger, nursing my impalpable paternity on her manifest maternity. The effect this had on me became so obvious she had to send me away, falling into a contented sleep. I would have to contain myself now that she had become a mother to this child to whom she was already so attached. My thoughts on how to live with this baby had been hypothetical, whereas for her he had already been alive for months. I could not interpose myself between two people who knew each other so well. I walked out my parental solitude on the quays and down back streets. Perhaps I was listening for the sound of a clarinet.

I made no attempt to come between Ginny and Victor, and fortunately he did not come between us. Ginny and I, settled back into the plural "we," became indivisible once more. She took pleasure in sharing all my tasks around the ship, whilst I took my turn in caring for the baby. In port, while I was busy with cargo and passengers, Ginny organized the intense social life we had developed at the two ends of our regular journeys. The Hawaiian archipelago was then a rendezvous for all ships crossing the Pacific, a thriving provisioning centre and postal interchange, a crossroad for secret passions. And where passion roams, competition lies in wait, or is it the other way around? I kept Ginny on my arm and tried to mix only with other couples.

Our solitude melted in that intoxicating social omnipresence. The flow of our happiness put others in the shade, our obvious sensuality disturbing many for whom the social and legal obligations of marriage had become more like shackles and chains. We had only a silken cord woven of complicity and mutual admiration.

The *Constitution* lay at anchor, and we were moored to each other on the terrace of the Waikiki Hotel watching the locals prolonging their childhood by riding the waves on planks of wood, slowly sipping our tea and exchanging winks over the rims of our cups.

I was quite happy to talk about chiffons and crinolines, and Ginny could take part in discussions on navigation or economics. At that time we were partisans of the communal economics of the fashionable New Zealand cattle-breeding author presented in the novel *Erewhon*, although I think it was more to shock the conservative majority than from any deep conviction. However, we were vigorous opponents of the far fetched prophecies of that Frenchman Verne, who pretended his hero could circumnavigate the globe in only eighty days. To read him, one would think that sail was a thing of the past.

The modernists maintained that steam was here to stay, that progress could not be stopped, and that soon all the risks of sailing would be removed by the huge iron steamships already being built in Britain. Ginny and I could not believe the fifteen years I had dedicated to sail would leave me only with an obsolete skill. Our beings were so incorporated that any success or failure was never individual; on the contrary, our shared worldly progress cemented us in a dual unity which distinguished us from other couples. Always polite, we never restrained ourselves from expressing an opinion which might shock, pleased in fact to keep society at a distance from our happiness. We took enjoyment from being in the minority, not wanting to be infected by the bitterness of the majority.

Ginny was different from the other wives in many ways. She never carried a parasol and her tanned, mixed-blood skin went against the current criteria of beauty: rice flour being commonly used to cover any local deviation from a uniform white. Ladies giggled behind their fans at Ginny's "peasant" coloring but their husbands were obviously attracted by it. After a few trips, sunshades became less com- mon. A secret trade began in a mysterious balsam based on copra oil that could be used to darken paper-white skins. A tan brought the ladies closer to the appearance of the native Hawaiians their husbands had difficulty resisting too. Trips of locally printed cloth began to replace lace for sashes and scarves, soon becoming valued items of a woman's wardrobe. As soon as word spread of a fresh arrival of Marquesian pareos at the market, our friends would gather, finding it hard to maintain their manners in the bidding for the best pieces. Each cloth was marked with the artist's distinctive sign. I remember Ginny saying she had been surprised to see a Western name on one pareo showing the head and upper body of a native girl looking out from amongst flowers and leaves: "Paul G.," she said.

Ginny caused another scandal which must still be reverberating around the volcanoes: becoming bored with tea and fruit juice, she decided to enliven the latter with rum. Even the husbands were shocked by that.

At twenty-nine, I took command of a new ship, the *B. Aymar*, a three masted topsail schooner working the Orient routes. A second son was baptized on her, and our daughter Jessie took her first steps on her deck, Ginny and I holding her hands. All three children liked to walk holding hands between us, feeling the love flow from Ginny to me and back, going through their bodies on the way.

The sea is ever the same and ever different. Wherever one travels, it remains the same sea, but every watch the combination of wind and water produces something new. One's position is only of navigational interest, because one is always in the same place: at sea.

We wanted to hide ourselves away like lovers but with the responsibilities of parents, we rarely managed to be alone. Ginny became a prey I stalked to flush out from the covey of navigating the ship, infant illnesses, paperwork, reading to the children, sail changes, conflicts between crew, playing with the children, looking after the cargo, squabbles between the children, study, feeding the children, sleeping, our fears, our hopes, our illnesses, our pride, and our weaknesses. Fortunately our courses sometimes crossed, to give some sense to the long periods when they ran in parallel. Then we found ourselves alone, a quartering breeze blowing into the cabin off a calm sea.

Although we enjoyed the roles we played, we needed to apply the brakes when could not act out our parts. We were parents on stage, but lovers in the wings all against the backdrop of the China Sea.

Deep sea had been far safer than those coasts where, in addition to the chance of a typhoon, Chinese and Malay pirates lurked, ready to attack and pillage any ship that ran afoul of the many sandbanks and reefs. The Australian and Annamite waters were also frequented by black ebony merchants. In 1875 they still worked the New Hebrides and the Loyalty Islands, selling their prey in Brisbane to understaffed planters. It was in the context of pirates and slave traders that I made the acquaintance of a man I came to admire so much that I tried to emulate him before my children. Bully Hayes combined strength and determination, courage and panache, ambivalence and mystery. No matter what enterprise he involved himself in, he did it better than anyone else. His trade was piracy.

Bully kept his secrets well hidden, but his most precious treasure was not to be found locked in any coffer: he never feared change. He even went out of his way to encourage change if he thought it would be to his advantage.

The most lucrative years for his trade, when cutthroats of the sea could earn noble titles by taking a gold-laden galleon, where long past. When they were forced to descend from the heights of bullion and church treasure to the commonplace of money and merchandise, the nobility of the sword was finished. Privateer heroes became pirate criminals. No more titles, their only public recognition came when they had the opportunity to perform a quick dance at Tyburn Dock. When the *B. Aymar* sailed, there were only local juniors in the profession, apart from Bully Hayes, that is.

When I first met him, he was passing himself off as a missionary in order to avoid the death to which he had been condemned so many times. Early one morning we hove-to off Oulau Island, hoping to bargain for fresh supplies of coconuts, bananas, pineapples, yams, chickens, and perhaps a pig. In reply to my signals, a six-oared boat pulled out from the shelter of a cove and headed for us. Surprised not to see the normal canoes, Ginny watched them tensely, then went below.

As the boat came alongside, a heavily built man with impressively broad shoulders carried with easy authority stood out from the cutlass-girdled crew of tattooed beach pirates. That first meeting with the most famous brigand in the islands filled me with admiration. I saluted him with the respect due his extraordinary disguise. Then we settled to the matter of trading for our provisions. How much did he want?

"A Bible, by God. I've all but worn out these old Sacred Scriptures of mine on them damn heathens. My indigenous children wait in darkness for want of the Divine Word."

His crew, motivated by less pious dispositions no doubt, were already engaged in mutually profitable commerce with my cook, exchanging fruits and vegetables for tobacco and pipes. The old buccaneer became more pragmatic and added some less spiritual goods to his list.

Missionary publications had brought about this miraculous conversion in Hayes. When he bestowed a blessing upon my voyage, who would have doubted his sincerity? Leaving the ship he bowed low, sweeping the deck with his hat.

"May the good Lord always go with you."

"Hands to the topsail braces," I ordered. The yards turned and we headed offshore again, bound for Shanghai.

That evening I could not resist telling Ginny and the children some of the stories I had heard about Bully Hayes. The children soon fell asleep, but Ginny listened on, appalled that I would talk of such a man with admiration. It must be said that the blessed infidel had a list of exploits as long as any arm he had cut off.

He had shown benevolence to some of the local people in the past, but woe betide any white man who stood in his way. One day the methods of a German commercial organization raised his ire. He opened hostilities by turning the German consulate upside down, running through the building, axe in hand, destroying all the furniture. Outside he took the axe to the flagstaff, bringing the Imperial eagles tumbling from their flight. This audacious blow earned him the respect of the natives, who felt he had defeated the Emperor.

News of his prowess rebounded around the islands, making each successive victory easier. His trade increased with his renown, until he reached the point where his schooner could no longer hold all his booty.

"Josh, I don't like the way you look when you talk about that man."

"Listen to some more. You noticed the boat he was in today? It belonged to the stranded missionary ship *John William II*, which Bully Hayes repaired, refloated, and rebaptized the *Leonora*. One day when the *Leonora* lay becalmed, Bully grew tired of whistling for a wind and started foraging through old trunks in the hold. He found an old house flag, the standard of the London Missionary Society, ornamented with a palm fond, the symbol of peace and goodwill. This gave him a new idea. Listen, Ginny, listen. He hoisted the pious emblem up the mast and took the first wind towards the most promising island for a cargo of black ebony. The isolated people knew the old ship and the flag under which they used to gather to give praise to God but knew nothing of her stranding and new ownership. They trooped aboard and were invited to a prayer meeting in the hold. As a benediction, Bully Hayes closed the hatches over their heads. He sold the whole congregation to a sugar plantation. Pretty exceptional man, eh?"

"But Josh, what are you saying?"

"Forget the cruelty. It's the audacity of the idea that's interesting."

"But, you know…"

"If it pleases you to know, he was hunted everywhere. The Royal Navy was on his heels but could never catch him. You see, in spite of his cruelty, they feared and loved him for being on their side in times of misfortune. Do you understand? He is held in such respect, it is almost a cult."

"Josh, you should be ashamed. You've never seen the pitiful states of those slaves like I have. It's appalling. Especially the Chinese."

"But Bully Hayes was involved in that too. Don't you remember? Surely you remember that ship that was sinking in Sydney Straits that suddenly disappeared."

"No."

"When Admiral Bruce was running his campaign against the slave traders a few years ago. You remember."

"Yes, I remember there was something my father told me."

"That was Bully Hayes. He had undertaken to transport some Chinese from Hong Kong to Sydney but dared not enter Sydney Harbor because he knew Admiral Bruce was there waiting to hang him from a yardarm. So what did he do? He collected from each of the Chinese the money they would have to pay the Australian government as their immigration bond. You know the bond I mean, we collect it too, because the master of the ship is responsible for it. Well, off the lighthouse marking the entrance to Sydney Roads at Ocean Beach, Bully Hayes hoisted distress signals: "Ship Sinking," "Mutiny on Board," and "Immediate Assistance Required." Rescue ships and tugs gathered around the ship and Hayes called to them, "Take my passengers: the imbeciles have revolted, they're scared because we're taking on water. With them making all this trouble we can't save the ship. Put them ashore for me, then come back for the ship. They're so frightened that they'll kill all of us otherwise. With them gone we can keep afloat until you return." There really was water entering the hold and the Chinese were terrified. They clambered onto the tugs in complete disorder. When the tugs arrived at Circular Quay, the immigration officers demanded bond money and the tug skippers had to pay! I don't need to tell you Bully Hayes was already heading for the open sea, having closed the seacocks. The crew had to pump for hours to clear her of water, but they had a good bonus from the tax money Hayes had collected."

"Josh, that's enough."

"Anyway, after several other adventures, Bully Hayes was stranded on Oulau."

I thought about Bully Hayes on and off over the years, then one day in Manila I received a note from the United States Consulate telling me one of my compatriots, a certain Captain Hayes, had been arrested in Guam. He was accused by the Spanish authorities of attempting to liberate several political prisoners. Hayes insisted I was a friend of his and could speak for his good character. I told the Consul only what I knew from first hand: that Hayes was a God-fearing man working to save the natives of Oulau. I reasoned to myself that all the rest was only hearsay, so I should not repeat it. The Consul gave me the broad outline of what Bully Hayes was charged with.

In Oulau he had fitted sails to a large canoe belonging to the chief. He set out in this for Ponape with two of his own crew from the *Leonora*. There he took fresh provisions and sailed on for Guam. According to his version, he knew there were Spanish prisoners on Guam but presumed they would be well guarded and not be a danger to his boat. He claimed that he anchored under the lee of the island and went ashore just for a freshwater bath. As he landed, a dozen convicts piled into his boat with the obvious intention of stealing it, and he was powerless to stop them.

According to the authorities, Hayes had taken one party of prisoners aboard and was ashore looking for more when he fell into their ambush and was arrested.

When I went to pay a visit to Bully Hayes in gaol in Manila, I found him on the veranda of the Governor's house, surrounded by the Governor's family, discussing on the nature of the Trinity. I could not avoid admiring this man, leafing through the Bible I had sold him in Oulau searching for some obscure reference. In Manila he had rapidly adapted his view to the Catholic faith and been baptized in the Church of Rome. Once converted to the "true" religion, Hayes found a powerful friend in the Bishop of Manila who wanted to parade this "holy man" at every church festival.

The cruel and rapacious buccaneer turned penitent made a moving figure. Bent with age, drawn thin and ascetic-looking by the ravages of tropical fever, he was impressive in any procession. As if his superior height were not enough to satisfy his desire for notice, he always carried the tallest candle, holding it like a standard. I was ready to rally

90

to that flag, to wave my own flag over the heads of the crowd. Secretly, I was reassured by the fact that an uncompleted achievement can assure a place in history too. People are attracted by mystery.

In Manila the *B. Aymer* was sold. The family no longer had a ship for its home, so we lived in a hotel. A tropical downpour had soaked the island and I was distracting the children, and myself, from worrying about Ginny's prolonged absence by organizing races with paper boats in the rain-swollen ditches. Ginny finally arrived carrying three of our boats she had found stranded downstream and presented one to each of the children, adding, "Yours is waiting for you at Mr. Edward Jackson's house, Josh. You can collect it first thing tomorrow morning."

I knew from past experience that it would not do to ask too many questions of this extraordinarily mysterious wife. I knew Mr. Jackson was a medal-winning naval architect at the London Industrial Exposition, an important man in England and an even more important man in Manila, having become a leading merchant there. But how and why had Ginny made this appointment with him? I was at once happy and unhappy: that is to say, in love.

I met with Mr. Jackson in the morning, as arranged, to learn he had designed a one-hundred-and-fifty-ton steamship to trade in the islands under his own flag. I do not know what Ginny had told him, but he wanted me to take control of building this ship. In return, he offered me my own sailing ship, modest enough but capable of taking my family and a cargo to sea. Here was the big break, the chance to become a captain/owner. I could make my talents bear fruit for the benefit of the family. I accepted then and there.

The yard was in the depths of Subig Bay, seventy miles from Manila, at a place called Olongapo. Long ago, Chinese labor had built galleons for the Spanish here for the trade between Manila and Acapulco. Olongapo lended itself naturally to shipbuilding: the surrounding hills were well wooded and the foreshore ideal for launching.

I permitted no wandering in that treacherous vegetal ocean of tropical jungle. All the family was commanded to stay close to father, even Ginny. Our survival depended on the family raft. On the footpaths one needed to keep a weather eye open for boas amongst the branches. On the ground these immense, silent forces of death remained humbly inoffensive, but in the trees they were ready to seek their revenge for being denied feet. Even natives familiar with the dangers sometimes disappeared. The simple village sat timidly between ocean and forest, equally fearful of both.

We all worked together to build our own "nipas" house, a bamboo framework covered with interwoven palm leaves, raised clear of the ground by legs. The natives would lend a hand and give advice so long as there was no cockfight to draw them away. I showed them how the foundation could be made more firm if the ground was consolidated by pounding, which impressed them, but not so much as to make them copy my example. Perhaps if I had a way of improving fighting cocks they would have shown more enthusiasm. One day when I was busy on the house and Jessie was laid up with a fever, I found that Ginny had gone off with a group of native women and left her alone. I was about to remonstrate with her about her neglect when she placed my hand on Jessie's brow. The fever had gone. Ginny practised her Mona Lisa impersonation and I knew not to ask.

Ginny made herself completely at home in our well-ventilated house. Who else could have stayed smiling in that jungle where the flora was as poisonous as the slithering fauna tangled in the path's turnings or coiling up the steps of our stilted house? Centipedes and scorpions climbed the bamboo and lurked in the palms. Constant vigilance and calm control were needed to keep these beasties away from the children. Soon after our arrival, we made the unpleasant discovery that they liked to sleep in our clothes and shoes after we had removed them to bed ourselves down. Every morning Ginny searched and shook our apparel thoroughly before allowing the children to dress.

Ginny's calm voice was needed to reassure the children, who had only known the rumble of waves and the squeal of puppies before. They were often terrified. Olongapo nights were filled with the cries of crocodiles in the neighboring marshes, the chirruping of giant crickets, and other sounds of unknown provenance. The nocturnal uproar of the Philippine jungle insinuates itself into the native's primitive imagination, turning their dreams into fearful nightmares. For them the crocodile's cry comes from the Devil, calling your soul to him. Lying sleepless and listening to that at night sometimes drives the Tagals into an hysteria by which they are drawn to the forest to reply. At night their superstitions are proven right, for he who approaches the forest then is certain to lose his soul.

The crocodiles were as much a danger as the boas in the trees, so I led the family down to the edge of the swamp to show them the submerged saurians, nothing visible but the twin craters of their nostrils skimming the surface, giving little indication of the volcano lying below. With Ginny's rifle covering us against the possibility of a lightning strike of open jaws, I took Victor close enough to hear the whistle of their breath. Ginny described the beautiful coloring and texture of their skin: such a hypocritical covering for an evil heart.

After a while we even became used to the incredible commotion caused when a snake found its way in to the hen coup.

I took a great pleasure in the shipbuilding, which, combined with the prospect of becoming an owner, made it relatively easy for me to cope with the heat and mosquitoes. Twice before I had put aside travelling, to work at building the means of transportation, so the time at Olongapo was not a break with my past but a continuation. I guarded against thoughts that it might be a regression by spending hours with Ginny discussing our future.

Work on the ship had to be accommodated to the primitive means available. Noah must have used the same sort of tools we had. When the woodcutter's slow axe-strokes finally felled a tree, the monkeys flew crying from its branches, and the natives replied even more stridently. The fellers roughly cleaned up the trunk where it fell and shaped one end into a turned-up nose with a hole through the tip. The turn-up helped it to skid over the ground more easily and the hole took the cable from the team of water buffalo that dragged it to the saw yard.

In the saw yard, seasoned baulks are converted into planks by hand. A mechanical saw would have saved much time, but in the East all the manpower available is employed before anything else is considered. The baulk has to be raised to a level so the two-man saws can work, one man below and the other on top. The same pairs always work together, the boss on top and his assistant below, controlling the down-strike. The assistant's work of pulling downwards is much lighter, but the boss takes the top to avoid the falling sawdust and contact with the damp soil and its warming insects. He might even get a cooling breeze if the wind is right. Following the custom, we paid for the sawing by the yard.

Excellent Chinese shipwrights had been recruited in Manila. The Tagals have never liked Chinese and showed it quite openly, but I chose Chinese because I had worked with them before in Hong Kong and knew they worked well under white control there, turning out fine, clinkerbuilt, copper-sheathed boats. The Chinese foreman provided me with problems though, because he felt he was competent enough to run the yard himself and was jealous of me for having been appointed over him. There were not only snakes prowling the night: discontent and treachery hung in the heavy air. Ever devious, they waited for one of my regular trips to Manila to strike.

Virginia was alerted by the Tagals. The glow of their torches allowed her to see they had armed themselves with axes and staves. She divided them into small groups posted so as to encircle the house, each gathered around a watch fire. Thus they stood guard all night. The faithful Tagals had discovered a Chinese plot to assassinate the whole family. With their warning, Ginny had been able to take the initiative and establish sound defences.

We kept ourselves armed and guarded from then on, but I suspected they would make another attempt, with the ship as their target this time. I checked her over repeatedly and tried to spy on them to discover exactly what they were about, but without success.

The final preparations for the launching completed, we knocked away the chocks. She slid several yards towards the water and then stopped for no apparent reason. A close examination of the ways revealed that the rails had been deliberately bent. With the full weight of the ship now over the bent section, only hydraulic jacks could straighten them again, and the nearest hydraulic jacks were in Hong Kong. Looking at the sabotaged ship, my mind went back to my father destroying my ship model as a punishment for presumptuousness. Had I hoped for too much?

Our Tagal friends were exemplary, rallying round with the generous energy of Nova Scotians at a stranding. Running heavy Manila ropes from the catheads down the length of the way, they attached every water buffalo in the village. In tumult, the drivers mounted their beasts and prepared them to make their greatest effort. Every Tagal was called out to put a hand to the ropes. A low, rumbling chant began as men dug in their heels and buffalo sank their hooves into the ground. As the rhythm of the chant mounted to a crescendo, the whole assembly of men, buffalo, and ship, united by the warps, inched

94

triumphantly forward till the bent section was cleared and all rushed together into the sea. The watching Chinese faces lost their smiles and slunk furtively away. I was revenged for my broken model: I was deserving, not presumptuous.

The whole family had shared toil and fear for a year in the monastic isolation of Olongapo, so it was with great relief that we loaded our baggage aboard the new ship for the passage to Manila. A tug towed her there and I would be finished. I would have nothing to do with the fitting of her boilers and engine: only wood and sail for me.

Mr. Jackson pronounced himself more than satisfied with the ship, clapping me on the back like a proud father. We must go up to his villa for drinks and a meal and he would tell us all what had been happening in the outside world. The whole evening was spent in trying to impress us with "modernization," the progress of the white man's world: a ship which could travel under water but not sink, new remedies for consumption and sugar diabetes, a project to build a tunnel under the English Channel, someone swimming across the same, the marvels of the Universal Exposition at Philadelphia, Kelvin's new gyroscopic compass, an apparatus for talking over long distances. He even claimed the London School of Medicine was taking women students—all the ragbag of oddities reported in the newspapers we had not seen.

Giddy with sherry and feeling unsteady with all this modernity, we politely begged leave of the man and his miracles. We wanted to escape the glare of the new, the iridescence of the unknown, the brashness of novelty.

My ownership of the *Pato*, the ninety-ton schooner that was our reward for a year's work, was officially registered. The following evening's sunset found us at the mouth of the Pasig, the children asleep in their freshly painted cabin and Ginny and me waiting to welcome the moon rising to light our Oriental happiness. Our success in meeting the challenge of the last year had brought us even closer together.

The *Pato* was similar in design to the America's Cup-winning schooner yacht *Sappho*, so she promised to sail well. Our first contract with her was from an insurance company retrieving cargo from a ship stranded on North Danger Reef, some four hundred miles from Manila in the China Sea. The cargo was a valuable one from the China–England trade—tea, silks, and camphor mainly—so a salvage operation was well worthwhile. We found her caught precariously on the edge of the reef and managed to relieve her of three full loads before bad weather pushed her clear of the coral and she sank in deep water. From that propitious and profitable start, various cargoes kept us busy around the islands until an accidental occurrence in Hong Kong made us change our plans.

It was only a little thing; Ginny found a set of fish knives in a curio shop marked "Souvenir of Cook Inlet." This lead us to many nostalgic rememberings which did not sit well with the heat and smell of the harbor. When an acquaintance, Captain Eben Pierce of New Bedford, started talking about the fishing in the Okhotsk Sea, we decided we had been too long in the tropics and to try our hands at fishing again.

The Okhotsk Sea is in the lee of the Kamchatka peninsula, a country rich in timber, furs, and salmon-filled rivers. Off its coast the cod banks stretch almost two thousand miles between Cape Lopatka to the mouth of the Amur in the Gulf of Tartary. In 1877 it was the prime fishing ground for the American Pacific fleet, mining the water like a gold field.

We were fortunate enough to find everything we needed in Hong Kong. The Chinese even made dories similar to those used at Cape Ann. Merchants sold us the fishing tackle at good prices, and a crew willing to sail for a share of the profits was soon recruited from experienced men amongst the flotsam of the North Pacific who tended to get thrown by the sea onto the quays at Hong Kong.

Ginny and Victor steered as we left the mysteries and the smells of Hong Kong behind us and headed for Petropavlovsk, a Russian port near the south end of Kamchatka by the inshore route, through the Formosa Strait, and between the Japanese islands and the mainland. The Formosa Strait was always made hazardous by the huge fleets of fishing junks and heavy commercial junk traffic.

Victor started his own diary on this trip:

Papa tells me this northeast wind blows steady through the Formosa straits so we have to beat. We are on the starboard tack, so have right of way, but junks cross our bow with the wind free, never altering course for us like Papa says they should. He says the rules of the sea and the priority of the starboard tack mean nothing to the Chinese. Perhaps they have some other laws of their own. We are often forced to luff up to avoid a collision, twice when mother was steering. Papa says I have a very special mother... We left Tsu Shima to port in the channel in between Japan and Korea at about seven o'clock this morning... I have just seen the Oki Islands. Some fishermen in big sampans came up and threw us some fish. I think they are very polite. Papa says it is a good omen and Mama agrees... We moored today in Wakanai, near La Perouse strait, to take on water and fresh stores. This is the very north of Japan. I had to taste some of their raw fish they eat here. I think it is horrible and so does Papa, but Mama says she liked it... Two thousand miles from Hong Kong. Near Cape Soya, in a place called Shama, the men went ashore and found a little portable Buddhist temple. Papa says all religions are silly and it is better to get guidance from charts and pilots' books. Mama is not very happy about him saying that... We have cleared Amphitrite strait. The wind is freezing and the fog makes me think about the little temple.

I had some strong exchanges with Victor over his diary. It was encouraging to write everything which happened to us, but I also wanted him to reveal his feelings too. He was stubborn about that, and we argued until one day he and his mother challenged me to do the same. I took his point and we reconciled on deck before the grandiose summit of Mt. Villuchinski, its peak lit by the rising sun like a great lighthouse above the clouds.

As we carefully approached the coast, the sun burnt away the morning mists, revealing a shoreline of towering cliffs. Myriad gulls swopped down to the sea from their nests in the crags. On the narrow beach at the foot of the cliffs were troupes of sea lions, the adults still asleep while their young frolicked on the water's edge.

Sheltered behind a spit of protecting sand, the port of Petropavlovsk needs concede nothing to Rio, Halifax, or Sydney. We paid our respects to the friendly functionaries of this far-flung outpost of the Tsar's domain. The family was given the freedom of the village's scattered houses. Wandering around the village I had to shout above the noise of the wind to explain to Victor how the log houses with their pleasing red rooves were constructed. Around the village, all was lush green, the depth of color becoming attenuated in the distance until it faded imperceptibly into the everlasting white of the mountain snows.

Petropavlovsk housed three hundred souls, twenty horses, and forty cows. Apart from some subsistence farming, its economy was based on salmon and furs, and even the cattle and horses were fed on dried fish when the short summer's forage was buried by snow again. The rivers were so full of salmon that the bears came to take on a fishy taste themselves. Separately, the tastes of bear and salmon are delicious, but the combination turned our stomachs, even when served at the head officer's table.

Our host was delicate enough to notice our difficulties and did not press us with the dish, possibly having had the same experience himself when he was first posted here. He was giving Victor his own version of the history of this remote corner of the world in a voice which rolled the r's like thunder rolling around the mountains. Our company gave him a rare opportunity to practise his English.

"It is frrrom this verrry herrre place, Petrrropavlovsk, that left the expedition for explorrring Alaska which Peterrr the Grrreat personal orrrderrr them to do. It is 1740, young sirrr. They still think Alaska an island. Mr. Berrring, he discoverrr Alaska stuck to Amerrrica."

"Was he Rrrusian, sorry, Russian like you?"

"No, young sirrr, no. It is Denmarrrk come frrrom Mr. Berrring. But it is Mrrr. Tsarrr pay him. He have to carrry all this things forrr the ships in one carrravan. You knowing Rrrussia one verrry big countrrry, young sirrr. He taking too long. He arrriving herrre Kamchatka and so! Petrrropavlovsk beginning."

Fortunately, Victor was used to this type of English. Later our host took us to visit the colony's ancient defensive batteries on the birch-covered heights. Ginny pleaded a headache and returned to the ship while the children and I completed the tour. This head official showed Victor how to make a whistle from a young birch shoot, while I showed Jessie how she could draw on the inside of the birchbark with a pointed stick.

Back on board we found Ginny asleep on deck, sheltered from the wind by dories. I woke her gently when supper was ready. Once the children were in bed, we returned on deck to enjoy the quiet peace of the night. Alone at last, we made love there on the deck, hidden from prying eyes under an upturned dory like furtive teeners, like escaped prisoners. Thus we stayed young and free.

When I mentioned the next day that we should carry a guide, Ginny surprised me by saying she knew of somebody suitable and would ask him if he would accompany us. She disappeared into the village for about an hour, returning with an old native she introduced as a sea-otter hunter. The old man looked like an otter himself, with his hirsute face harrowed by intemperance. How she had met him I had no idea.

We followed the contours of the coast, looking for the banks where good shoals congregate. Once the bottom had been found with the lead, it was a matter of sounding the water with a hook to locate the fish. I sent a line down at regular intervals, with Victor watching the process closely, too closely I felt. I hauled in again and warned him: "Don't touch that."

As soon as I had walked away, he seized the line and sent bait and hook overboard. I had to chide him for his disobedience but was secretly proud of the way he had learned by watching me and the courage he had shown in defying his father and captain.

"I told you not to touch that. You are too young. Haul it back aboard right now."

His little muscles stood out on his arms as he hauled away at the line. The effort was obviously growing too much for him, so I put a hand to the line to help, taking good care to curse him appropriately. As I took the weight, I realized there really was good reason for his puffing and blowing.

"If you've caught a fish you're pardoned. If not..."

There were two fish in fact. The larger was the biggest cod we took on the whole trip. I rewarded him with promotion to the rank of honorary mate before the assembled crew. He was feted with cake and lemonade, and Ginny sewed two stripes on the arms of his oilskins. He strutted around like a genuine rear-admiral. Ginny whispered to me that Jessie was sulking at Victor having all the attention, so I organized a triumph for her too. During our trip to Alaska, Ginny had been given some fossil fish by the Indians and we had carried them with us ever since. Once the crew were busy working the shoal, I circumspectly slipped one onto a hook and lowered it over the side, then taking another line myself, I called Jessie to haul it in. When she landed the fossil on deck the whole crew gathered around her beaming face.

"Look what Jessie caught. Look, Papa. Look what Jessie's caught. Victor, come and see what Jessie's caught."

The seamen applauded. Victor turned away disgusted. I swung her up into my arms.

"Bravo. Bravo, Jessie. You are the youngest one fishing and you've caught the oldest fish. That cod must be a million years old."

"Much older than Victor's, eh Papa?"

She ran to show her prize catch to her mother, who gave me her most loving smile as she cuddled Jessie in her arms. Benjamin was quite indifferent to the whole contest, quite content to tally the fish others were catching.

I was made profoundly happy by being in a position to give the family these experiences. The children were saturated with new knowledge. That the success was feigned in Jessie's case made no difference, they both had known success. It gave them assurance, always more useful than reassurance. They could measure themselves against reality and find how to overcome its obstacles. I never asked them to be like me but tailored their challenges to their own abilities. We explained why something should be done, suggested how, and applauded each success. When they met with difficulties, I explained to them that if a ship is caught off a lee shore it might be difficult to work her clear, it might be arduous and even dangerous, but a way has to be found to do it.

Ginny and I saw the family as being like a lifeboat in which there was a place for everyone if they needed it, but only to be resorted to when their own means of transport had failed.

It took us only two weeks to fill the schooner's hold, each crewman keeping a tally of his own catch against the day when the profit would be shared out. Now we must sail back to America and realize that profit. During the first 2,900-mile leg to Victoria, British Columbia, we called at the Aleutian Islands to shoot geese for a change of diet. Ginny spent her free time playing on the old piano bolted to the deck in the saloon or teaching Victor how to handle a rifle shooting sharks. He enjoyed the sport, but Jessie rushed to my arms for comfort as she mourned the unnecessary deaths; Benjamin kept the score. Ginny would not change her ways just because Jessie, or anybody else, objected.

The stop at Victoria was a brief one, only made to re-register the *Pato* for commercial reasons. When the words "Victoria B.C." were painted on her transom and the Canadian Union Jack hoisted, I felt I was betraying my new country, returning to Oregon with a foreign flag. How they talked about us on the quay:

"Any idea what B.C. stands for?"

"Before Christ, as far as I know. Then, she's flying a Canadian flag."

"Must've been held up with another docker's strike."

I had a nightmare in which the U.S. army invaded Canada through Nova Scotia, ransacked Westport, and tortured Elizabeth into revealing the hiding place of my secret treasure under the potato store floor.

A paddle-wheel steamer towed us up the Columbia River to Portland. It was necessary to take the tow, but I was as ashamed of that noisy, stinking steamer on the bow as of the Canadian flag on the stern. I had hoped I had put the restraints of Canada behind me, but having that infernal American machine ahead did not make me feel any better.

We were the first ship into Portland with salt cod and I learned that no others were expected for some time, so I could expect the best prices and ensure a goodly profit for myself and the crew. I was proud of the profits we were making, in spite of Ginny's reminding me I used to say one should keep above the common run of humanity by avoiding grubby accounting. I was ready to swallow those words. To maximize profits, I decided to sell directly, so I berthed the *Pato* in Portland East alongside the new fish-packing factory, had the cod preserved in tin boxes under my own name, and became a travelling salesman. Victor accompanied me whenever he could so he could see as much as possible of the noxious, horseless carriages that were making the roads dangerous. For some unaccountable reason he was fascinated by them. I only hoped America would quickly follow England's example and pass a law requiring every such carriage to be preceded by a man with a red flag. It is the only way to make them safe, but it does nothing for the noise and smell.

Walking from store to store with a good Petropavlovsk cod in my hand, I soon found there was a resistance to my produce. It naturally had a brownish tint to the flesh, and they preferred the "fresh" look of cod which had been bleached white with lime. I could not bleach my fish, so I had to find a way to overcome the resistance. I decided to promote brown fish as "natural" and therefore "healthy." To give myself a slight advantage, I took two samples of fish with me on my rounds; the bleached one I left outside overnight and generally took no care of it so it soon did start to look "unhealthy"; mine I washed regularly to keep its rich shining "freshness." My stock was soon sold.

When the time came to share out the takings, the rest of the family had a part too. Victor stored away his three dollars, Jessie bought herself a doll that became her constant companion, and Benjamin laid in a stock of paper and pencils. None of them seemed to take after their parents. Ginny invested her sixty dollars in a Singer sewing machine which saved her hours of handwork.

Several weeks later in the Hawaii Islands, I had further proof that the real, or apparently real, quality of one's merchandise sells it better than any salesman's patter. I had the schooner up for sale. The famous packet schooner *Hilo* had left the quay and already cleared the pass through the reef which encloses Honolulu's lagoon when an agitated official arrived with a bag of urgent mail. Knowing the nature of the winds at Pearl Harbor well, I glanced at the clouds and then shouted all hands on deck to cast off.

"Pass the bag aboard. We'll catch her."

He handed the bag across with a shake of his head. Nobody could catch the *Hilo*, but at least he could report he had tried. Sails filled and we pulled clear, to the applause of the idlers on the dock. The wind here falls down from the mountains in squalls with only light breezes in between. I had seen the signs of the next squall and the *Pato* flew before it. If I could hold it for long enough, get close enough to the *Hilo* before it reached her, I would be home and dry. I manoeuvred the *Pato* into a position to take the *Hilo*'s wind and the mail bag was heaved across to her as we drew alongside.

The story of how the *Pato* had overhauled the *Hilo* spread fast, but not the details of how it was done. Offers came in and I sold her for a better price than I had originally been asking.

I had been tempted to go to the Universal Exposition, but instead we sailed on a German ship bound for San Francisco. Ginny was sprawled on a wide cane chair on deck when I placed a sack of gold in her lap.

"That Ginny, is our next ship."

CHAPTER SIX

The Blow

*I*n San Francisco we soon found a ship suitable for conversion to the trade we had in mind, running timber from the Philippines to China: the *Amethyst*, built at the famous Thatcher Magoun yard in Massachusetts. The scantlings of her American oak frames were generous and her copper fastened planking ran true the whole one hundred feet of her length. Some alterations had to be made to her for her new cargo: a new deck was added and a loading bay opened in the bow, her copper sheathing needed renewing, and a new suit of sails was added to her wardrobe—but all that was reflected in the low price I paid.

In spite of the weakness Ginny had suffered since the birth of our last child, she undertook the job of supervising the refurnishing of our family quarters in the passenger cabins in elegant mahogany and horsehair. While this work was being carried out, we moved to the Clipper Hotel, far from the downtown bustle. I did not feel at ease being in the center of town with Ginny, fearing to run into a pretty ghost from my past at any moment. As the work would take nearly two months to complete, I felt the risk was too great, so proposed we cross the continent on the new Santa Fe railroad and visit Brier Island. She declined, saying the journey would be too tiring, but now the trip attracted me for its own sake, so I decided to go alone.

The prospect filled me with nostalgia for my old country and the maritime frolics of my childhood. I felt my heart grow heavy in my breast, making it hard to breathe. Family obligations were invoked to excuse my hurried departure for the other side of America and Elizabeth. Used to crossing oceans, I was now to cross a continent. The relationship between Ginny and myself had grown a little stale from overfamiliarity, so a short separation would do us good and allow us to rediscover each other and reawaken our earlier ardor.

Leaving and staying are not contradictory, but are the two essential elements of a man, like doubt and certainty in a woman.

Voyages at sea had always forced me to explore my internal resources. On land I again opened myself up to receive the outside and tried to see everything, hear everything, understand everything, and profit by it. On land I could take advantage of the aura of mystery surrounding a sea captain. The advantages started right from the beginning when a San Francisco newspaper asked me to give them an account of the journey from a seafarer's point of view. It enhanced the trip for me, because I had to see and hear all I could for my articles. With my press card, I was no ordinary passenger but someone of importance. I even met President Hayes. Considering his position analogous to that of a captain at the helm of the ship of state, I asked him how she handled.

"She sails close to the wind," he replied.

Each mile the train took me away from Ginny brought her closer to me in my mind; the hot air blowing through the carriage windows drew new flames from the fire of my love. In Chicago, New York, Washington, and Boston I saw many beautiful women, but their eyes were not Ginny's and their voices did not say what her voice said to me. In San Francisco I had looked forward to being alone, but now I was just lonely.

The steam ferry approached Brier Island.

My thirty-five years, my status as captain, my authority as head of a family, my favorable pecuniary position, my journalistic writings, my meeting with the President—they all were baggage I was proud to carry. Also in my bag was a model of the *Amethyst* for my father. He would have every reason to be proud of me at last. I had been admired by others, but that bears no comparison to one's own father's approval.

Brier Island had scarcely changed, always a surprise when you have changed so much yourself. Nobody seemed to even recognize me and there was certainly no great welcome. Elizabeth greeted me with tears. Between bouts of coughing she told me of our father's remarriage to a linen dealer in Lunenburg, leaving her to fend for herself.

"Josh, oh Josh. If only you knew the life he led me."

She clung to my arm, digging in her fingers as if she hoped they would take root there and draw strength from me to help fight her consumption.

I stayed with her all the time, apart from occasional walks to the other coast: to the lighthouse where my grandfather had quit the struggle too soon to see what I had become. During one of Elizabeth's better periods, when she could almost sleep soundly, I took my model of the *Amethyst* on one of these pilgrimages. From the rocks I threw it clear of the waves, to be carried off by a current to join him. Tortured by my sister's failing health, my father's inexcusable desertion, and my grandfather's unexplained death, I broke down in tears, sitting on the rocks and looking out at the emptiness of the sea. So, this was what it was like to return home triumphant. What was my success worth now? The tears relieved my tension and it was with a lighter tread that I returned to the house, even telling myself that Elizabeth might recover. There was a letter awaiting me from Ginny:

Dear Husband,

Excuse me for writing such a short letter. I was very ill after your departure. As you well know, I miss you terribly. It is a strange illness which I do not understand.

I am beginning to be able to eat a little again now but my hands tremble so much I can hardly write.

Josh, be brave. Our daughter died the day before yesterday. I think it was partly to do with her teeth. She often cried all night when they were coming through and the gums had to be cut to let them out. The night she died she had convulsions. I gave her a hot bath and some medicament and felt easy, thinking she was better. Then she gave a gentle sigh and was dead.

I wish you had been with me Josh.

Our Elizabeth awaits us in the beyond.

My greetings to your family.

Virginia

We had named the little one for my sister. I looked now at that sister who had to chase after every breath like she was running on the scent of life, but I saw she was now the quarry and the horsemen were close behind. Was there to be no end to this misery? Fresh tears came running down my face, but this time they were not tears of self-pity.

Elizabeth coughed weakly and I went to her. With a great effort she reached up to take my face in her parchment-dry hands, moistening them with my tears. As I looked down at her, her eyes became hazy, then clouded to the color of the warm milk we had shared so long ago. At the corner of her mouth the saliva bubbled. She had never once spoken of death, though she must have known it was coming. Was she glad it had finally arrived? Perhaps it would treat her better than life had.

I made all the necessary arrangements for her internment. I needed to get back to San Francisco as soon as possible. I felt surrounded by death, mocking immodest death who would not dress herself properly but was indecently attired in a stained handkerchief and a baby's swaddling clothes. Something seemed intent on taking all my people from me. With my perfect, virginal sister Elizabeth, I buried all that was left of my innocence, parental respect and illusions, leaving me no past.

Coming down into the village from the cemetery, I saw some boys playing with the battered remains of a model ship. They found it wrecked on the beach. Death all around was forcing me to face the fact that I too would die. I ran from that fact, back to the West Coast, back to Ginny, back to life. On the railroad journey west, I scarcely noticed the country parading past the carriage windows. Like a captain returning to his cabin after facing a storm, I was weary at heart. Slumped in my seat, I raged against time, angered because I could not harness it like I could the wind. My destiny was at sea; ashore was only bad luck.

Fortune showed cruel irony by sending the *Amethyst* a cargo of railroad rails for Honolulu. Designed for a career carrying timber, she was weighed down with iron for her first trip under my command. The whole crossing was plagued by constant heavy rolling, so bad it made us fear the cargo might break loose. Instead of rocking my disquiet to sleep, the Pacific was making sure it remained awake. I needed Ginny's soothing hand, but she was still weak and had to conserve her returning strength for maternal duties. My solitude was being isolated in a shell which the family tree seemed ready to let fall. I was glad to discharge that iron and the immigrant planter passengers in Pearl Harbor.

Cleaning out the holds, a kit-bag was found stashed away in a corner. In it were some old oilskins, a couple of empty rum bottles, and a letter addressed to a certain Angelina Desmarais, Chanal-du-Moine, Canada:

Greetings my Raven,

Do you vibrate as much as your harmonium? I was very pleased to receive your letter exploring the subject of solitude, but what are you complaining about? God damn it! Look at all those nobodies who rot away surrounded by other nobodies they have married or had as children. They have no solitude left to buy their liberty with. Reproaching others for having liberty is like envying the rich while hating the power of money. Amass solitude like gold, my beautiful raven. Then one day you might be able to buy yourself a liberty like mine—like mine but not mine. I have learned at last to cleave the wind by joining my rummy breath with it. I have become the wind. Never mind other people's solitude. I do not mind yours, my raven. If your calm and my storm meet one day in the sea of love we will make a tornado—and then blow back to our own hemispheres.

In all freedom,
Venant

I read and re-read that letter, stupefied. It was like receiving a message from the beyond, a cry from the past resonating in my present. Captain Venant Kerouac had been my first master on board the *Morrissey* more than twenty years ago. Before that he had been mate on this very ship. His words seemed to have caught me out like an errant schoolboy. He had taught me much then and now he was continuing his lessons across time, space, and our different solitudes. Now I understood the necessity of those buoys seen only by the heart, indispensable for navigating one's solitude to a safe port. Such buoys and markers do not need to be followed exactly, but they have to be recognized so one knows what they mark.

Ginny might be a light buoy for me, but you cannot moor to light buoys. Sometimes I felt like dropping my anchor and chaining up to her, but that would be like a little boy trying to hide under his mother's skirt. Surrounded by my wife and children, I sometimes felt as alone as an unanswered question. That solitude cannot be escaped, it has to be navigated courageously. The "Neighbor" of the Gospels is not someone one knows: if he lives in one's house, how can he live next door? Henceforward I would try to invest in my solitude, like a life insurance policy for liberty, in case of future need, in case of peril.

The next day I posted that old letter, hoping the addressee still lived up there in the cold of the northeast. One never knows. In a time when frozen sheep were being carried all the way to England from Australia, a loving French–Canadian might have conserved her passion on the ice of Chanal-du-Moine.

I headed for Manila, promising Ginny a stop in Guam on the way. The Spanish romanticism that still lingered on Guam from the days of the great galleons might revive the emotional excitement which was fading with time. I hoped for an opportunity to share our solitudes alone there, but one of the children became ill and Ginny had to stay aboard with him while I walked the streets trying to ignore the local ebony-haired attractions.

My mother had preferred her illness to me, and now my wife seemed to prefer her children. Does one have to be ill or a child to win a woman's attention? Women are more than nurses and mothers, surely.

All I got in Guam were supplies of fresh fruit, so we doubled to the north of Luzon and gained Manila with a fair wind. There Ginny was impressed by my many highly placed friends and my knowledgeable way of dealing with business matters. Her approbation gave me an assurance that multiplied my talents. At the end of my negotiations I was able to report to her that I had obtained a loan at a very good rate of interest from the Peele, Hubble and Co. banking house for the purchase of a cargo of timber from the merchant Henry Brown of Lagumanoc in Tayabas Province.

Lagumanoc is on the north bank of Tayabas Bay, where a lofty volcanic chain bears a forest of excellent hardwoods, undoubtedly amongst the best in the world. Almost all of the Eastern tropical species can be found there: ebony, camagon, narra, and tindalo for fine furniture, and at least fifty shipbuilding timbers. I knew some of those species would bring me a fat profit when sold to distant shipyards. For instance, molave is as good as American oak but has the advantage of being resistant to worms. I had that prepared in twenty-two-foot lengths with a diameter of at least five feet. Curved pieces I took, too: always in demand for cutting knees and other sharp curves. Betis, another worm-resistant wood, was used for keels. The cargo was completed with antipolo, completely inedible for teredo, so perfect for underwater planking.

Just touching and smelling the treasures piled in Mr. Brown's yard brought me sensuous pleasure: dugan, an ironwood as heavy as a rock and used for keelsons; batitinan, with its sweet smell, good for planking; the diabolically grained luan which the Spanish used in their Olongapo galleons when they discovered cannon balls would not splinter it; the springy and velvety textured mangachapuy, which makes good masts and deck planking; and the sawdust from the ipil, bansalangue, and banaba, giving off their perfume. I spent long hours with Ginny describing the qualities of these marvels we were loading, lauding the nobility of such a cargo, and reflecting on the profits we would make. She showed a great interest, questioning me until she knew as much as I did.

When I was completely drained of information, I proposed a family picnic. It seemed appropriate to mark this coincidence of pleasure and profit with a celebration. A native boat hired for the day and piled with Sunday treats took us upstream as far as a clearing made at a good spot for careening. We played together, me a wild beast on the attack, with mother and children beating me off. I wished that simulacrum of combat could be followed by a long, slow disarmament, but I knew that sailing and parental duties inevitably lead to tired silences of fatigue. I knew the sun would always shine in my sextant mirror once the clouds had cleared, but sometimes I doubted that Ginny's eyes would ever twinkle at me again: they were so full of cumulus.

While we were there, I showed them the route the timber followed on its way down to the yard. Walking the warm brown humus of the river bank, we had to keep a weather eye out for scorpions while I described how the Filipinos work.

"See, Ginny. They use the same axes as at Olongapo. Do you remember? Look down there, children. See how they square up the trunks."

"Papa, Papa."

"Victor, stay close to Mama now. The water buffalo are coming."

"You see, Victor, they pull the baulks all the way down the stream from the mountains to the river. Hold on to me and we'll take a closer look. Are you coming, Ginny?"

"Don't worry, Josh. I'm coming."

"What a beautiful beach. Come and sit on this tree trunk with us, Ginny. Come close. Come closer."

I explained how the trunks had to be supported on rafts of woven bamboo to be floated down the river. Ironwood trunks were lashed between dugout canoes. A whole week's work could be lost if the lashings failed and the trunk sank. I belabored my point about the importance of solid ties. Ginny smiled at me and then turned to watch a bird. Her spirit sat up with that bird on its branch while I talked to the children about trunks.

The loading progressed well, facilitated by my alterations. A sudden brouhaha brought everybody out on deck to see what was happening. The hatch gang had found an immense boa coiled around a rosewood trunk and, by the time we arrived, had managed to trap it by holding down its head with a forked stick. Ginny asked me to watch the children and then calmly approached the snake to stroke its satin skin. The Filipinos could not believe her temerity. The action filled me with desire for her, but I was called away to check some problem over stowage details. She had not looked at me, just at that trapped wild creature: it was only a small incident but it stays in my memory.

Along the coast of Bantigui we took advantage of a very light wind to anchor in the emerald waters of a sheltered bay. Ginny choose to stay aboard and fish with the children rather than accompany me ashore. Just inland we found a giant rosewood tree. I decided to offer it to Ginny, like a huge bunch of flowers, and set to with an axe without even stopping to remove my jacket. The crew joined in, ready to seize this prize, and it came down with a crash. Unfortunately, try as we might, we could not transport it those few yards to the water. Instead of bearing a gift, I returned aboard with a bitter feeling of defeat. Somehow I blamed Ginny for my failure, for not inspiring me enough to find a way over the difficulties.

On my thirty-sixth birthday, two years later, Ginny coiled herself in my arms with the old fervor. We were in Antimonan, on the opposite side of the isthmus where the clock tower marks the entrance. A fine Sunday morning had brought out the whole population for Mass. The first thing we noticed was a grumbling noise coming from the anchor chains, amplified as they passed through the hawsepipes. As Ginny came to me to ask what it was, the whole ship began to vibrate. Shaking with fear herself, she threw herself into my arms, burying her head in my shoulder. With the water in the bay boiling, she shouted in my ear how she loved me—without mentioning the children at all. She did not even notice the clamor of the faithful as they tumbled out of the church in panic, she just clung to me and repeated the old words. The bells rang out with the swaying of the clock tower.

Some minutes later the trembling ceased, leaving the clock tower leaning and Ginny with a definite list in my direction.

The market for shipbuilding timber began to decline as the Chinese took to metallic construction. This treasonable desertion of the most noble of materials went under the name of progress. Abandoning the traditional junk was the first death knell of their civilization. We were forced to vary our cargoes, becoming unwilling accomplices of the metal monsters ourselves by carrying coal from Nagasaki to Shanghai and Vladivostok.

I became fond of the Japanese of Nagasaki because, even though they soiled their hands with the present, their hearts stayed with their traditions. When we entered there our children were always excited by the smell of beefsteaks and onions coming from the pilot's sampan galley as he came out to meet us offshore and guide us in. I always took a pilot there, as the entrance is particularly dangerous: to starboard steep cliffs, their slopes covered in dwarf pine clinging to the rocks like the roots of tradition; to port a reef, just awash at low water.

Going against the current, I did my utmost to promote wood and sail in every port we entered. In Chinese and Japanese ports, the *Amethyst* was always having joinery work done both above and below decks. The native craftsmen excelled in decorating the fine woods with which we glorified her. The value of the ship was increased and she became a floating advertisement for the precious wood I carried from the Philippines whenever I could make up a cargo.

I kept the *Amethyst* one more year, enough time to discharge a cargo of coal into the bunkers of a Russian warship in Vladivostok. The poor prisoners impressed into carrying the coal on their backs were driven like animals. And time enough to go north to Hakodate and fill with natural ice for Hong Kong: struggling against an icy gale in the Tsugaru Channel, the *Amethyst* became a polar phantom. The whole crew, including the family, had to work to keep the rigging free of ice. The children slid around the deck like penguins and sucked the hanging icicles.

From Hong Kong, the *Amethyst* sailed east for Singapore. Against Ginny's wishes, I had agreed to carry a lucrative cargo of gunpowder to Shanghai, destined to help drive the Cantonese rebels from Formosa. Off the mouth of the Yangtze, we were boarded by a pilot, needed to guide us through the sand banks. Virginia pointed out a well armed junk lying off to windward which made both of us suspicious of the so-called pilot's intentions. Ginny sent the children below and returned to my side. At that time, all junks were armed to protect themselves from pirates, so we could not be sure. Thinking there were shallows to leeward, I demanded of the pilot, who was working the leadline himself, if there was enough water.

"Plenty water, honorable Captain, plenty water. Very much water here."

"Here then..."

I seized the line from his hand and quickly ascertained that the depth was very little more than our draught. I shouted to Ginny to put down the helm, and we tacked just in time to avoid running aground. The pirates here are unwilling to attack a ship under sail, and so the junk bore away to stay clear of us. We did not wait to see if the pilot managed the swim back to his sampan.

We were happy to be rid of that cargo and sailed immediately to Hong Kong, where the *Amethyst* was sold.

Virginia took the opportunity to mix with the ladies of Hong Kong and to reprovision the family with clothes, books—and another child! We named him Garfield, for the American President, even though the man was not popular in Hong Kong for effectively banning Chinese immigration for ten years.

I kept myself busy looking for another ship while Ginny dosed herself with ample measures of gossip, rumor, and the occasional real news, all of which she retold to me in the evenings before I fell asleep. The biggest news was of the Boer revolt in South Africa and the British M.P. who was not allowed to take his seat and was even imprisoned because he was an atheist.

Hidden in the docks behind an enormous tanker, the first, I believe, designed to carry petrol in bulk, I discovered a big square-rigged ship which I knew had once been the pride of the American fleet, the *Northern Light*. I had enough capital to buy the majority of her shares, even if I could not have her outright.

I could not resist writing to my father to tell him about my new command before we left Manila for our next cargo. The *Northern*

Light was five times the size of the *Amethyst* and my pride had grown in proportion. Coming on forty, I did not want to repeat the disappointment I had had with my grandfather. My father would know how successful I was. I made clear to him that my financial success and status placed me amongst the foremost captains of the American merchant marine. His admiration would be the greatest reward of all, in spite of the reasons I had to resent him. I noticed what the children did to keep Virginia's love, affirming her motherhood. The relationship with a father is more complicated, needing to be based on mutual admiration: we are never weaned from that. The link with the mother is through the heart, but with the father, through the mind.

From Manila, we sailed for Liverpool by the Cape of Good Hope, laden with the biggest cargo of sugar and hemp ever brought to England. The ship behaved as though she was proud to be under my command, which fed my pride in her. And I found my Ginny again. Strangely enough the presence of a fourth child gave us more time alone together because she had to organize her increased brood like a small army. She gave the children all the care and attention they needed but planned her time more systematically. In the ocean's gales we created our own calm; during its calms, gusts of amorous folly swept us along in our own storms. At ease and happy no matter what the wind, we embarrassed Banka Strait on the coast of Sumatra before penetrating the Straits of Sunda. The Indian Ocean would abuse us all the way to the Cape, and the approach to St. Helena in the South Atlantic was often dangerous, so not wanting to go off course we provisioned for the whole trip at Anjer on Java.

Ginny was so energetic about the stores that the officers were left with little to do: my beautiful Ginny. The anchor had not touched bottom before an armada of bumboats arrived filled with merchandise. We took provisions of monkey and musk deer, and Ginny insisted on buying some civet cats which proved to be the terror of the ship's rats. Yams, sweet potatoes, panniers of eggs, and cages of fowl were all piled on deck. The poultry were installed in a large coup build on the main hatchcover under Ginny's supervision. A boy had to be posted to guard them until the civets were taught the difference between hens and rats.

Even before we arrived at the Cape, the crew were protesting they were saturated with poultry and demanding "good old salt dog." Salt beef lies heavier on the stomach and keeps it quiet during the long night watches. The English sailors were already making up songs on the subject but I forbade them to sing them, thinking it out of keeping with the respect that should be shown for the flower of the American fleet. I even broke a seaman's guitar. When I found Victor making a model boat from the pieces, I ordered him to take it apart and return them to the seaman. Later I heard him sobbing in his cabin and I realized what my pride had led me to do: to repeat what my own father had done to me. I wanted to turn the clock back, to put the model back together, to give the seaman a new guitar, to join in the songs. How could I be so stupid as to break ties of admiration in this way? What price my success if it should lead my eldest son to hate me. I put my sextant to my eye to hide my tears. It took a long time to shoot that sight. Finding our position had become child's play to me, but I did not seem to be able to find the route that leads from a father to his son.

In Liverpool I let the seamen go off to their beer and whores while I applied myself zealously to my captain's duties. I engaged a team of Indians from the Langdon Graving Docks to clean the copper sheathing of the prodigious growth of barnacles which had attached themselves to the bottom in the hothouse of the tropics. Even in a seaport as busy as Liverpool this marine fauna attracts a crowd of curious onlookers. I encouraged Victor to try selling the most impressive of this *Lepas anatifera* under his mother's surveillance, thinking he could learn something of keeping accounts and the art of bargaining if I let him retain a portion of the profits. He did his best but was sadly lacking in self-confidence, always referring to his mother. I had to hide my disappointment.

After the sixty days of fighting the sea from Hong Kong, we had an easy trade wind passage ahead of us. Time to get the *Northern Light* shipshape for return to her home port. New York would be proud of her, and her captain. To the accomplishments of skilled navigation I could add the nobility of traditional sail. I would never change my sun-bleached, salt-stained ideas for the dirty face of a steamship sailor on their filthy vessels where they tried to replace knowledge and experience with the blind power of coal.

The arrival in New York in the spring of 1882 was a personal triumph for me. I shouted orders and uttered threats to "command-

114

ers" of dark steel ships who seemed totally ignorant of the bold manoeuvres we had to make, compared to their dead telegraphs transmitting their hesitations to dirty boilers.

The foresails slid down their stays. Then the courses and mizzen were brailed. One by one, skysails, royals, topgallants, and finally the huge topsails were taken in. The whole crew shared in the glory of the occasion. Slowly the sails were furled, leaving the heaviest to be handled by the longshoremen. The excitement of the *Northern Light*'s return would reflect well on me. The whole crew performed as a perfect team, forgetting the differences and dangers of the crossing. I even thought I saw a hint of admiration in Victor's eye as he stood beside me, holding the megaphone. The arrival of a steamer cannot produce this feeling of exhilaration.

Northern Light was towed to Pier 17 on the East River, just above the nearly complete Brooklyn Bridge. Her masts were so high that one of the painters working on the bosun's chairs slung under the deck of the bridge put a lick of paint on the main truck.

We would have to accustom ourselves to the incessant siren blasts of the small ferries running between Brooklyn and New York.

Virginia had bought us a smart, leather-bound scrapbook in which we kept all sorts of souvenirs. This cutting from the *Tribune* went into it:

At Pier 17 on the East River is berthed a typically American ship, commanded by a typically American seaman, whose typically American wife accompanies him on his long voyages, making their accommodation into a home as agreeable as any to be found ashore. Looking at the gracious lines of this vessel, her Yankee rig, her proud bow and nobel stern, nobody could take her for anything other than an American ship.

This is the clipper " *Northern Light*," property of Benner, Pinckney and Slocum of New York. A visit aboard this ship brings two thoughts to mind, equally sad as they are striking: the first is how few American sailing ships there are left, the second how few American sailors there are left. This ship is commanded by Captain Joshua Slocum, one of the most popular masters in the port for both his professional ability and for his benevolence towards his crew. One rarely sees such good maintenance aboard a merchant ship nor such neatness, from truck to keel and from bow to stern, she is as shiny as a new penny. The cover over the wheel was hand embroidered by the Captain's wife with the vessel's name and port of registry in silk lettering. On descending into the main cabin, one asks oneself if one is not entering a comfortable New York apartment.

When our reporter arrived on board, Mrs. Slocum was sitting busily occupied at needlework with her little daughter, her infant son lay sleeping peacefully in a Chinese cradle, one of her older sons was tidying his cabin while yet another was drawing at a table. The Captain's own spacious cabin is furnished with a double bunk in walnut which could be taken for a bed, bookcases, chairs, rugs, wardrobe and chronometer. This cabin is situated astern of the main cabin, which itself is furnished like a fashionable salon with piano, a central table, sofa, armchairs and straightback chairs. The walls are decorated with oil paintings.

Forward of the main cabin is a dining room which shines with the care that only a woman's hand can produce.

The Captain proudly showed our reporter the arrangements on deck, which include a steam engine located at the extreme aft end of the forecastle. This is used to drive a bilge pump, fresh water pump, fire pump, cargo winch or even to aid in handling the sails, although the Captain made it clear that this latter is only in case of an emergency. Our reporter was then shown the carpenter's shop, equipped with lathe, saws and all the tools necessary to repair the old or construct the new. We also visited the rope store, the sailmaker's shop and the smith.

The Captain's youngest son entered this world in Hong Kong aboard the *Amethyst*, the oldest American ship now working. He was baptized and registered before the United States consul under the highly respected name of James Garfield Slocum. General Garfield thanked the Captain for his homage in a letter addressed to the child. The *Amethyst*, which Captain Slocum commanded, is better known in Chinese waters as the "Old American Walnut" or the "Old 1822," the year of her construction. Her name did not figure on her colors but only the year of her launching in Roman numerals, "MDCCCXXII." These colors were made by Mrs. Slocum along with an ensign ornamented with stars in a circle. Captain Slocum thought he was going to end his sea-faring career on this ship when she was caught in a typhoon in the China Sea, only eighty miles east of Grand Loochoo. The *Amethyst* had a good turn of speed; the Captain says only the *Alaska* and a few modern steamers could catch her.

Returning below deck, our reporter was again reminded of a modern apartment when he discovered a Filipino butler. The butler has even been seen eating in a Fulton Street restaurant, which shows the affluence of this American sailing family. Mrs. Slocum often frequents the galleries and spoke with enthusiasm of her visit to Coney Island where she goes to hear the king of the military march, Philip Souza, and his orchestra.

It is clear to our reporter that Captain and Mrs. Slocum live a very happy life.

This article not only boosted my professional standing but also acted as a passport to New York high society.

It is true we were happy and proud of the life we were living. I had an incomparable wife who, in addition to her maritime courage, mastered many social arts, playing the piano, harp, and guitar and singing jolly songs. Social occasions also allowed her to display her talent for dancing. Ginny fed her many abilities, her love for me, and her devotion to the children from a vital inner reserve far beyond anything commonly met with. Even when her health failed her, she would draw on that reserve to calm her suffering and provide extraordinary power.

Dressed in our number ones, we visited the great world of New York. We were even invited to the American premiere of Tchaikovsky's "1812 Overture." I wished I had been rich enough to pay the orchestra to play it all over again.

We always put the children to bed ourselves before an outing. Each evening they waited impatiently for another episode of Stevenson's *Treasure Island*. I was always the first to read, or at least leaf through, any new addition to our considerable library. After that, the rest of the family were free to read it if they wished. I am not sure Virginia always obeyed that rule. Discipline is necessary in a family, especially aboard ship. Virginia was in total agreement with me on that and maintained a strict order in the children's activities. Except in bad weather, she gave them lessons every day, each according to their own abilities. Any transgressor fetched the cane themselves from its place in our cabin.

Two weeks after the publication of the *Tribune* article, I was putting some order in the library, which recent additions had swollen to more than five hundred volumes. Essays and history books went on the higher shelves, leaving the novels more accessible to the children on the lower levels. I had a deep veneration for essayists such as Lamb, Addison, and Irving and for historians like Gibbon, Hume, Bancroft, and Prescott. I also had some poetry, Tennyson and Coleridge, but my favorite book had always been Cervantes' *Don Quixote*. What nobody knew, not even Ginny, was that more and more I dreamed of finding my own name on the spine of a book, there on a shelf with the other great authors: Addison, Bancroft, Cervantes, Darwin, Gibbon, Hume, Huxley, Irving, Prescott, Slocum, Thoreau. And so nobody would think my name was in there by accident, I improved on the list, to read: Addison, Bancroft, Cervantes, Darwin, Gibbon, Hume, Huxley, Irving, Prescott, Slocum, Slocum, Slocum, Thoreau.

Lost in my dream, I did not immediately hear the seaman calling to me: "A Mr. Slocum requests permission to come aboard, sir."

I followed the seaman up the curved companionway and saw an old man leaning on the bottom of the gangway. For some reason I spent some time reprimanding the seaman for leaving him standing on the quay before I actually invited him aboard myself. I sent the seaman to summon the family and whistled "all hands on deck." Buttoning my uniform, I walked down to greet him, my feelings fluctuating wildly between the proud captain, the angry youth, and the frightened child. I took his bag and he leant on my arm to climb the gangway without a word passing between us. He did not look at me nor I at him. We both looked at the *Northern Light*.

"It's a good ship."

For the first time in my life I had impressed by father.

"My wife Virginia."

"Hum."

"My children, Victor, Benjamin, Garfield, and Jessie."

"Ah."

"You had a good trip?"

"Tiring."

"I would not have recognized you."

"She's a beautiful ship."

We installed him the mate's cabin and showed him every possible respect. Ginny was very attentive to him and I discovered he could respond with a gallantry I had never seen him display before. A quarter of a century of silence had passed since my departure from the family home and the boot shop.

He spent the greater part of his time aboard with the children, making them toys out of leather offcuts from the cobbler's store. The children thrived on his attention, and their laughing chatter continued even through meals, contrary to the rule I normally imposed at table. I found myself fighting Virginia and the children for his time so I could show him all I had done aboard the ship. He always managed to find some fault with my improvements, some minor criticism to be made. He could still overpower me; I wanted him to learn all the exploits of my career from my own mouth, but he would cut me down before I could finish:

"There's nothing special in that. You only did what had to be done."

The only subject he would discuss freely with me was my plans for the future. His complete absence from my past made him inferior in that area, but when it came to the future he could re-establish his authority over me. Before the unknown we were almost equal, except for the famous paternal experience, an advantage he used with delight. Apropos of that, I have noticed that I often end up talking about future projects with men and about the past with women.

One night, after he had helped me put the children to bed, I took him for a cup of tea at a restaurant near Wall Street. The subject of the construction of the new Eddystone Lighthouse came up and I took advantage of this to mention my maternal grandfather. He found several faults with him. I tried to talk about my mother but he claimed indigestion and we returned to the ship, limiting the conversation to his health, which he said was failing.

The next day Virginia and the children went to Coney Island for a picnic. In the evening my father and I were alone at the table; Virginia had sent a note saying she and the children had met some relations and were staying with them for a few days. I was delighted for them, especially as I would be away for two days myself to negotiate for some new sails at a lift in Rhode Island.

On my return, Virginia told me he had left, but there was a note for me:

Dear Captain son,
I must leave, important matters await me elsewhere.
I have repaired both your pairs of boots.
You should be well heeled for some time.
Your Father

I never saw him again. Several years later I learned of his death with little regret. There was still too much bitterness to mourn him. During his whole visit he had never once taken me by the hand; I do not think he ever had.

I kept my back firmly turned on steam. A ship's power should come from the sea's winds, from outside her, not from some sweaty, pressurized tin can inside her. How can you win the sea's favor if you do not work with her but try to fight her with your own power, the power of the land? A motor car with an internal combustion engine is not as bad, for it takes its power from the earth over which it runs. Happily, under the Brooklyn Bridge in 1882, the East River was still decorated with a forest of masts carrying cargoes from every sea in the world. Moored at the quays, bowsprits crossed South Street to almost touch the upper floors of the houses on the opposite side. Walking down the road, you had to keep an eye out for seamen perched high above, tarring the rigging; they tended to pay more attention to looking out for pretty girls than to the work at hand.

We reloaded the *Northern Light*'s holds with wooden cases, each containing two twenty-litre tins of refined petrol for Yokohama, Japan. I did not mind carrying the fuel so long as I did not have to use it. The crew sent aboard had been distilling their own dignity with large quantities of alcohol they would have to boil off as we worked the ship out to sea. Seamen had once courageously served the cause of civilization and commerce, but now they only served their own degraded appetites. Anyone who has sailed as much as I have in the company of these slaves of drunken bestiality cannot swallow talk of human equality. The people who preach that everyone should be treated on a strictly equal footing have certainly assured themselves of a large congregation, but I suggest that these great talkers should try taking a few trips at sea. If destiny had created us all equal then those drunks would be captains too.

120

Damage to the steering forced us to put in at Connecticut. It would be unthinkable to continue such a long voyage with a jury-rigged repair. Some of the do-gooder's egalitarian ideas had filtered their way to the rabble I had as a crew, undermining the essential hierarchy and willing obedience essential on a ship. As we approached port, the crew's resistance to taking orders came close to mutiny under the impetus of a ringleader called Murin. At our mooring they refused to furl the sails neatly, heaving them brailed. They said it was unnecessary work. I must admit the mate had been treating them harshly when we had difficulties taking the towline aboard. Now they refused to work under his threats and demanded to be discharged then and there. I could not accede to their demands and had the signal "Mutiny Aboard Ship" hoisted to alert the authorities.

Understanding the signal, Murin urged them to take the poop deck and, arming themselves with whatever came to hand, they advanced towards the stern in a compact group. I stepped forward and drew my revolver on them, ordering them to raise their hands to show submission. All stopped except Murin, who continued coming at me, shaking his fist and shouting to the others to follow him. A movement to my right caught my attention and I glanced down to see a rifle barrel held in a female hand. Ginny had taken up arms to defend me. I was caught between humiliation at being defended by a woman and pride that she dared take the route of masculine violence rather than rely on feminine charm to change the course of events. For the time being, I forgot the dichotomy: survival was the present problem. Whether it was surprise at this turn of events or genuine fear of a furious female, I do not know, but Murin and the others who had started to follow him were nonplussed and raised their hands.

"Murin is the ringleader. Clap him in irons."

"Get moving," added Ginny in a harsh voice I had never heard before.

I told Ginny to watch the rest of the crew while I ushered Murin aft. With rifle unwavering in her hand, they looked at her without moving an inch. I think they were more afraid of her eyes than the gun.

As the mate appeared with the irons, Murin broke out into a furious tirade of curses and then suddenly pulled out a knife, pushed the mate against the bulwarks, and opened his stomach with four fast passes of the blade. I could not pull the trigger, and it was not the revolver that jammed.

In the tumult which followed, I heard Virginia call my name in shocked incomprehension. I stood paralyzed, not seeing the hands pulling Murin away or hearing the mate's cries.

Murin was subsequently condemned to death, but I heard he escaped from the prison.

I could not understand what had happened to me, but its effect on my relationship with Ginny was painful. My stomach cramps came back too. We had always been equal partners in bed, but now I could do nothing unless she feigned submissiveness. I felt I had failed as a man, so I was trying to compensate by winning her over, but Ginny did not like playing the loser. The result brought neither of us satisfaction. I remember someone in New York telling us that in the earliest societies the organization had been matriarchal, a system which could not last because men have to dominate women in the act of copulation, so it was unnatural. Still, in my weakened mental state, I feared that Ginny might come to dominate me and my protective action was based on that fear. We grew apart and my desire was smitten with solitude. She gave more and more attention to the children.

I engaged another mate but retained the same crew, a contestable decision taken primarily because Virginia argued against it. I thought if I could re-establish my authority I might make her my lover again.

We crossed the equator, observing the normal initiation ceremonies for first-timers. Then it was the standard route across the trades and running down the roaring forties past the Cape of Good Hope for Tasmania. The only difference was that rumors about the coming comet put the fear of God into the heathens in the crew. I berated them for their superstitions but later found my wife trying to explain the phenomenon to the same men. It humiliated me, but I pretended not to have heard.

After rounding Tasmania, our course took us north through the perils of the Pacific islands. Stories of cannibalism sent shivers through the crew as we passed the infamous Solomons. If we should hit a coral reef, they would be the only place to land. Just south of the Gilberts we rescued a boatload of elderly natives who had been drifting helpless for more than forty days after strong winds had blown their canoe far out to sea. They had suffered horribly and the danger they had been in made me realize the relative insignificance of my own problems. In Yokohama I managed to find a ship to take them back to their own island and raised funds for their passage. That incident was precious to me, a harmonious chord in the dissonances echoing around the ship.

After the unfortunate events at our departure, I had all of the seamen's knives gathered and had the smith break off their points before returning them to the men. No legal use of a seaman's knife requires it to have a point, so an easy conscience can see no injustice in this measure. I let it be known that the possession of a pointed knife would be considered a challenge to my authority. Ginny maintained that I was punishing innocent people by sharing my suspicion against the whole crew, but I considered Zelanski guilty of rebellion when I caught him with a knife he had ground back to a point. He was put in irons, but the Yokohama police refused to take him off my hands except while we were in port. I knew his presence aboard was going to polarize the crew once more. The local press heard about Zelanski and must have interviewed some of the crew because they printed the whole story of our problems since leaving New York. I did what I could to protect the ship's reputation in a long, open letter to the newspapers, affirming my total confidence in the crew.

We took on ballast for the passage to Manila, where we would load sugar and hemp bound for the United States. I would try to have Zelanski arrested there; in Japan they could not be persuaded to change their decision.

Rumblings of discontent moved through the crew, slowing the work of setting sails. I had to resort to the steam winch, as they would not exert themselves to do it by hand. I hated to replace blood and muscles with boiling steam and iron. The children normally assisted in the manoeuvres of arrival and departure, but this time I sent them below. Ginny stared sullenly as the tension mounted. No songs to ease the effort were heard as the cable was hauled short, just the sinister clicking of the pawls and groans from the heavy hemp rope. When the cable was up and down, two Japanese agents came out in a boat to put Zelanski aboard. I had specified that he should come chained, but he was not, and the moment he was aboard he grabbed a belaying pin and threw himself at me. Virginia cried out a warning and I managed to evade him until he was seized by the officers. With the madman chained to the shrouds, I fetched my repeating rifle and took a position on the poop deck where I could survey the whole ship. I wanted no more surprises. The calm manner in which I conducted the rest of the operation had its effect on the crew and we sailed in a state of armed peace.

That evening Ginny submitted to my refound vigor, urged on by Zelanski's shouted oaths from the shrouds. Afterwards I went to stand personal guard over the prisoner, instructing Ginny to remain below with the children. Going below at the midnight change of watch, I found her sleeping in the children's cabin. I ended the night alone in bed but at peace with myself.

Was it the comet's passage? We did seem to be travelling under a bad star. Whatever it was, it was to dog the ship all the way back to New York. We even came close to being incinerated in the most awful natural catastrophe in the history of mankind, the eruption of Krakatoa. Our route from Manila to the Cape of Good Hope took us right through the Sunda Straits.

For two centuries this volcano island had been covered in undisturbed tropical vegetation, and it had been thought to be extinct. But if a serene and equal humor is desirable, Krakatoa was only pretending to have one. When it did loose its temper it displayed a telluric power such as the world had never seen before. It had been grumbling angrily for two months, but nobody took it to be anything more than an old man's muttering.

"He's just remembering the old days."

As we passed through the straits, the sea itself seemed to tremble at the old man's anger. Why did the sea tremble if it was nothing important? On the air was the distinct smell of sulphur, the smell of the pit. I took a sounding and found the bottom much closer than it should have been according to my chart. What was stranger though was that the tallow with which the lead was armed had melted. That explained the bubbles we saw coming to the surface, the sea itself was beginning to boil. The crew moved fast enough now when I called for extra sail.

We saw the flashing orange and red flares of the explosion from far over the horizon, lighting up the great black clouds of spectral dust pouring into the sky. Soon that dust was coating our sails, and glowing cinders were falling on the deck. There was no need for me to order the crew to throw those cinders overboard and keep the decks well wetted with the fire pump, the danger and its remedy were obvious. Ginny and the children huddled in a hatchway, too fascinated to go below.

For days the sea supported a carpet of dust, and each wave coming aboard left a coating on the ship that at first threatened to block the scuppers. More days were to pass before I had a glimpse of the sun and was able to establish our position with a sight. I was fortunate that the prevailing wind cleared the sky for me, because that cloud of dust travelled round the world for years, discoloring the sky. Also, we were well out at sea, where the tidal wave caused by the explosion passed completely unnoticed. When compressed by shallow water, the wave reached unheard-of proportions, wiping out whole towns and throwing their debris far inland, as far away as Chile. In Sumatra, the Dutch gun foundry was discovered one and a half miles inland, and many ships were dropped onto hillsides, never to see the sea again. In the neighboring islands alone more than thirty-six thousand souls were drowned.

I learned later that a fissure had opened at the base of the island, below sea level, allowing water to pour down into the primal fire below, like a female intrusion into a masculine force. The resulting explosion blew off the whole top of the island, because the crater above had sealed itself long ago, bottling up the pressure. The roaring inferno raged for thirty-six hours and could be heard over a hundred miles away.

Many deaths were caused by that release of anger, but secretly I envied it. I could not talk about it with anyone, but the accumulated anger of my childhood was an essential source of energy for me, too.

All those deaths, which are so many failures, do not speak to me of a benevolent Creator. My dream is of a world in which the same people, the same animals, and the same objects remain forever: moving, evolving, but eternal. If there really was a creation, it should have been once and forever. If I die, it will be a defeat for me, a failure. To last would be the proof of winning. That is the success I seek: to last, with the others or not.

As though in reply to my blasphemous thoughts, God sent the sea to punish me. With the *Northern Light* using the Agulhas Current to push us around the Cape, a violent storm blew up from the opposite direction, building up enormous disordered waves. Seas born in the southern ocean run all the way around the world, so they have ample time to grow to their fullest stature. We fought to keep her up into the wind, but the strain became too much for our repaired steering gear and it broke again, leaving the ship lying across the seas. Waves broke on board and rolled her over on her beam-ends. Both the steam pump and the hand pumps had to be employed to keep the holds clear.

The end of the storm at sunrise revealed a new threat to our survival: as we had pumped, we had pumped out dissolved sugar, leaving us with a thirty degree list to starboard. The only answer was to jettison the hemp stowed in the 'tween-decks to counterbalance the lost of weight in the holds. There were so many bales floating on the sea that we could have walked on them to Port Elizabeth, which might have been the best thing to do considering the state of the ship when she was finally towed in to that South African harbor.

It took two months to complete the repairs.

One of my officers fell ill soon before our departure, forcing me to find a replacement. The choice I made proved to be in keeping with the rest of this voyage: disastrous. He was called Henry A. Slater. It was not until later that I learned that, even before we left port, he had plotted to add to his already long list of crimes, of which I knew nothing at the time—their plan was to murder me and take the ship, Slater to have Virginia as his share of the booty.

After only a few days at sea, Slater began to show his characteristic insubordination. Calling the whole crew to witness my action, I logged him and gave him a good dressing down. The reaction on his part was one of open defiance, so I had no choice but to imprison him, keeping him under guard for the remaining fifty-three days of the passage back to the United States. Ginny begged me to show clemency, but after one and a half years of problems I was in no mood for forgiveness.

As soon as I discharged him in New York, refusing a reference in his seaman's discharge book, Slater started a process in the federal courts, accusing me of false and cruel imprisonment. I took the action lightly and paid him the five hundred dollars compensation. Had I realized the bad reputation it would bring to my name, I would have followed Virginia's advice and defended myself more vigorously. Afterwards she tried every means to establish my innocence, and I had to borrow to finance her activities, but the smell of guilt clings to a man no matter if his innocence is established. My stripes never recovered their original shine even after the publication of this article, which should have removed all trace of tarnish:

New York, 12 January 1884. Henry Slater has paid a visit this day to M.B.S. Osborn, editor in chief of the *Nautical Gazette*. He told him that he has undergone all he can support and that he has had enough. He added that if Mr. Osborn would listen, he was ready to unburden his conscience. In consequence, Mr. Osborn had Slater's statement taken down by a stenographer and affirmed before the editor who is also a Notary Public.

This is the substance of his affidavit:

"I was mate aboard the square rigged ship *Northern Light* of which Joshua Slocum was Captain. During our trip from Port Elizabeth to New York, I was, under the orders of the said Captain Slocum, imprisoned and put in prison. I heard the first mate, Mitchell, say to Captain Slocum that he had heard me say that I would kill Captain Slocum and his wife once I was out of irons. I believe that was the reason I was kept prisoner. Since my liberation I have learned that Captain Slocum gave orders that I should be allowed on deck each day and be given sufficient quantities of food and water. Mitchell said to Captain Slocum that if I was allowed on deck I would start a revolt and have all of the officers murdered. I do not blame Captain Slocum for the treatment I suffered...I am not responsible for starting the process against Captain Slocum and I do not want this action to continue. I realize now that Captain Slocum and myself were dupes of those who should have protected us and that all of their affair was got up to extort money from Captain Slocum by men who want to share it amongst themselves afterwards...'

Slater affirmed that he came to me of his own free will, said Mr. Osborn. He realizes that he has placed Slocum in a bad situation, and himself at the same time. He admits that he did not know what he was doing. He signed many papers but did not know what they were.

I have never been a braided bully; I command wooden ships with a fist of iron, which is necessary. I have never approved of the weak-willed bowing and scraping which leads to the command of iron ships, I am proud to say.

I had to sell my shares in the *Northern Light* as she was sunk in disgrace, towed off ignominiously to have boilers fitted. Virginia reassured me this was the only honorable course.

Invitations to society gatherings had almost dried up, making us aware that we would have to make a fresh start. When an invitation arrived for the inauguration of the Metropolitan Opera, I refused to go, feeling I would be a usurper among high society: I was beginning to accept other people's opinion of myself. I insisted that Ginny go, however, for she had done nothing wrong.

I spent the evening wandering the East Side of Manhattan quays without purpose, joy, or sadness, as if tranquilly awaiting the arrival of more bad news. I paid no attention to the Negroes selling their roasted corn or the harebrained doctor giving out cups of coffee, thinking a seaman would drink that instead of alcohol. I walked behind the municipal cart, with its water tank washing down the road, careless of its puddles. The enterprise was typical of this world: to a real problem of dirt, they applied a cosmetic solution, thinking that if something shone for a few minutes it was a good as clean. I had no regret at not accepting the invitation, being in no mood for enjoyment.

My reflections took me deep into melancholy. I missed my former social success, now diluted like the detritus around my feet. I looked around me to see where I was and found I was nowhere, back in the ranks of the anonymous. On long days at sea I had stayed on deck all through storms, knowing that if I went below for a cup of tea, it would take even more courage to return to the battle.

With such thoughts in my head, I stopped by a Jewish restaurant I knew where pickled gherkins came straight from a barrel and the sandwiches were stuffed with spicy smoked meats. Waiting for my rye bread and gherkin, I wondered why the Jews had to dress up their differences so ostentatiously that it became an embarrassment to everybody else. Did their conviction really need to be so adorned? Glancing up, I saw myself in my captain's uniform, reflected in the mirror behind the counter: another unwelcome line of thought.

The only free seat was at a table already occupied by a middle-aged man, but he invited me to sit with him, making an exaggerated salute to my scrambled egg. On his knees he balanced a pile of apparently identical books which kept threatening to overturn as he launched in to an animated soliloquy:

"Captain, you are of a race apart. Permit me to salute you with my pen. You are of a race on the verge of extinction, a race of men tempered with courage, a race of men who cannot continue because they are so rugged. The strongest knot is a lashing made without fid,

128

rope, or tar. That magnificent knot is called courage. God makes it out of seamen."

I was not sure I was following all of this.

"You are of a savage but brotherly race whose credo I know well, Captain. Goodbye to the shore, goodbye good times, for us there is a greater love. Tie a knot on the past, our life is all fresh starts. Carry your heart into the future, and spit into the wind. The coast is gone, we need it no more, the open sea calls us."

I chewed on my gherkin, noting the look of envy he cast on my gold braid.

"You are eddies in contrary currents. Your enthusiasms and despairs are without a country, always between leaving and arriving. You, like me, Captain, have seen those calloused hands building miniature ships in bottles? Like a prisoner in love with his prison, he makes a model of it in case he should ever have to leave. But torn between two poles, he revenges himself by putting his prison in prison itself, in a bottle."

"Would you like another cup of tea?"

"Landlubbers know nothing about your voyages, you men of the sea. Your incessant oscillations between monotony and excitement, joy and sadness, calm and agitation, inertia and activity, security and fear; privation and excess. That is why you seem so calm when faced with what a landsperson finds exciting. Your lives head on to naivety and cynicism, childishness and heroism, Captain."

He held out to me one of the books he carefully removed from the pile on his knee, kept there, I realized now, to preserve them from the grease on the table.

"This is yours for a miserable twenty-five cents Captain. Do not thank me, the author should efface himself before his work."

He pocketed the money and quickly left table and restaurant.

Moby Dick was a source of encouragement for me for the rest of my life. At different times I was Ishmael, Queequeg, Starbuck, or Ahab. One particular phrase haunted me, from when they were adrift in a damaged, sinking boat:

> There, then, he sat, holding up the imbecile candle in the heart of that almighty forlornness. There, then, he sat, the sign and symbol of a man without faith, hopelessly holding up hope in the midst of despair.

Unfortunately, I never saw Herman Melville again, though I thought of him every time I read the book or ate a gherkin.

Without thinking, I followed a crowd moving towards an enormous tent. I would go and see what it was. There was the hoarding: "The Wild West Show," starring Buffalo Bill himself. It appeared to be more popular than the opera. I returned to the hotel to find out what this book I had just bought was about.

Ginny's and my desires kept each other in sight but were well apart. We needed to conserve our energy to maintain our hope. We had hoped to win but now were concentrating on not losing. A poor victory perhaps, but considering our defeats defending honor, it was a victory nonetheless. My hardened hide did not prevent me from seeing the light of beyond infiltrating through my thinning foliage. My forties were giving me an unexpected reception and I entered them without enthusiasm but calmly, grasping for every glimpse of color. Ginny had her grey times too.

We evaluated what was left of our opulent past: just enough for a ship a quarter the size of the one we had left. Every option in steel was rejected. We had known our best times with wood and would remain faithful to it despite the recent setback. We are made of fibres like wood; nothing about a man links him to metal. At sea one has to become as one with the ship, so it makes sense to choose a compatible material. Ginny and I had enrolled our love and rocked our children on a wood deck in the shade of sails to the tune of wind in the rigging. Our shared determination to start again simply needed to be equipped with the right tool.

The ship we finally found, the *Aquidneck*, approached closer to perfect beauty than any other product of the hand of man. After she was registered in our name, we went over her, incorporating her every corner into ourselves. Our hands caressed the polished patina of her woodwork, only leaving one piece to respond to the call of another. The dozen years of our conjugal fellowship lead to complete agreement on our findings. Ginny moved ever more slowly, as if she wanted our tour to never end.

Captain Cheeseborough had had the *Aquidneck* built in 1865 at Mystic, Conneticut according to the caprices of an old man. The clipper had as much of the luxury of a private yacht as was possible in a commercial ship. He had taken no account of cost in his determination to build an outstanding ship, finally paying fifty thousand dollars, an immense sum for a ship of her size. In a good breeze she could show a clean pair of heels to any steamer afloat. She was built low with just one deck, one hundred and thirty-eight feet long and thirty on the beam. Ginny did not object to my comparing their respective features.

"Nicely curved stern and firm bow."

"That bowsprit's impressive too."

We admired the silver eagle with outstretched wings that decorated her transom.

"I think you've inspected that stern long enough now, Josh."

We went down to our new quarters laughing together for the first time in months. In the middle of the day, like young lovers, we took possession of the bunk in the master's cabin. Our games were punctuated with further bursts of laughter as other comparisons to our new ship were made. We laughed until we cried, tears of hope and tears of regret.

Back in the main cabin, with its polished parquet floor, Ginny mused about redecoration, demanding that we should paint deckhead, doors, and bulkheads white, with the mouldings sky blue and gold. I brought her attention to the mizzenmast penetrating the centre of the table and we were soon checking the mattress again.

I sat on one of the revolving chairs bolted to the saloon deck and listened while Ginny poured out her remaining sensuality through the keys of the piano. Even after making love, I desired her as much as ever. A canary in a cage hung under the stained-glass skylight joined in the concert. There seemed no doubt this fresh start would bring us happiness again.

We decided that during the weeks required for a refit, Ginny would go to her relations near Boston to rest and recover her health after the rigors of the last voyage. Her leaving involved no separation: we would simply both be in two places at once.

The ship had been laid up for a long time, and a thorough examination showed much of the standing rigging to be rotten, caulking that needed tightening, and some of the copper sheathing requiring replacement near the waterline. When the family rejoined me, I had almost completed loading a cargo of flour for South America. The revitalized Virginia was looking as attractive as the refurbished *Aquidneck*. In New England she had bought fashionable new clothes and learned the art of applying make-up.

131

All through the trip to Brazil, Ginny was more attentive to me than ever. She still needed to rest, so the children had to learn to amuse themselves without her help. But they were entertained by the many evening concerts during which she improvised pieces dedicated to each of us. I noticed the children's tunes always sounded sadder than mine. She laughed as she tried to explain that their's were in a minor key and mine in a major; I did not understand.

"They are minors, you see, Josh, and it's very sad to be a minor."

When I put the children to bed I asked them what she had meant, but they knew no more than I.

The whole family enjoyed our stop in Pernambuco, moored behind the sheltering reef from where we could make excursions to a coconut-covered island to gather shells, singing our respective tunes at the tops of our voices. Our master musician had taken the time to teach them to us, and each had made up their own words to suit the rhythm. Now they were our own personal anthems.

Somewhere off Santa Catarina Island, five hundred miles south of Rio de Janeiro, Ginny suffered an attack of quinsy and took to her bed. The children missed the cookies she normally made fresh for them each day and the sudden absence of music brought a grey air of depression. By the time we had arrived in Buenos Aires roads, Ginny had recovered enough to talk about salting some fresh butter for the return trip. I went ashore to clear customs, with a much lighter heart.

Before I had reached shore, I saw the code flag "J" hoisted on the *Aquidneck*. This was our private emergency signal. Half an hour later I was at Ginny's bedside: she had suffered another attack. For two long hours, her tears flowed down to her blue lips as she struggled to make words. I think the tears were from her inability to speak as much as from the pain.

With the children gathered around the bed after their supper the storm in her heart seemed to calm.

Then there was not a breath of wind.

No more Ginny.

She had not even been allowed to get past thirty-five: I had been allowed just thirteen years with the woman of my life.

I stitched her beloved body in sailcloth, and we laid her to rest in the soft earth of the English cemetery in Buenos Aires, under the Southern Cross.

While my head and heart wandered stunned through memories

and my eyes saw only Ginny—on the *Pato*, on the *Washington*, on the *Amethyst*—laughing, talking, and smiling at me, my old cramps took advantage of my distraction to mount a new offensive. The pains grew worse until I was scarcely able to move. Was death's appetite insatiable? I had no will to fight it if it should want me too.

Ginny had taken all my love with her into death. Losing my loved one, I lost all feelings of love for my children. There was nothing I could do about it: it was just gone. In this desperate condition I should never have tried to navigate, because I ran the *Aquidneck* onto a sandbank. Was it me or was it Ginny trying to hold us there with her?

What little liquidity I had left was needed to refloat the ship. No money could refloat my Ginny though.

Against the counsel of experience, I accepted a cargo of pianos from Baltimore. I would have accepted anything. The difficulties of securing such a cargo presented a risk it would have been better to avoid, but we took to sea with fifty new pianos, and one old one which now stood silent. After several days of fine breezes the wind heard the rumor of my Ginny's death, and the waves set to battering the ship with the froth of outrage on their lips. As the bow pierced a particularly angry breaker, the wind urged it on and the bowsprit broke.

"Captain, the stays are going to give."

"But..."

"Lively does it."

The fore-topmast collapsed and swung in the rigging like a Damoclean sword.

"Where is my wife? Go and fetch her here right away."

We had to turn and run off before the wind before all the rigging gave way. A form in oilskins ran to the helm.

"Ginny, put the helm up and bear away."

She carried on into the wind, so it could not have been Ginny. I ran to the helm, pushing the imposter aside.

"Go and find my wife or you'll soon be joining the masts at the bottom of the damn sea."

The creature crept towards the companionway. As the hatch opened, I heard a chord of music: that must be Ginny practising. I fought with the helm to turn her away from the agents of death trying to board us over the bow. Suddenly the wheel spun freely under my hand—the chains had broken under the strain.

"Where is she? Ginny! Ginny!"

The wind screamed back its reply and the ship rolled like a stubborn child. As soon as the foremast fell, the main and mizzen followed, having lost their forward support. The conductor had brought down his baton and the orchestra in the hold burst into tune, a tune the Devil himself would have been proud to have composed. And was that Ginny I could hear playing along with them?

"Ginny, Stop! Stop! We'll lose all our music if you wreck the ship."

There was Victor's tune, and Jessie's, and then mine: she was calling us to join her.

"Ginny, no! Don't take the children."

The deck vibrated with the noise. The whole orchestra of devils joined Ginny in a huge crescendo and then I heard no more.

When I came too there had been calm weather for several days. Our cargo had been completed destroyed when it broke free. Under jury rig we were heading for the Antilles. I asked the children if Virginia had been hurt, but they only cried. So, she really was dead. The memory of Buenos Aires swept back into my unwilling mind with fresh force. My solitude stood thick around me like prison walls.

I took that imprisonment badly: What was my crime?

I would have my revenge on death.

Alone.

CHAPTER SEVEN

Courage

*M*y widowerhood isolated me in a cloud of indifference.

I went through the ship's repairs like a somnambulist, passing her into the shipyard's hands like the seamen who had given my father their boots without asking how he would mend them or watching the work, just dropping them off and collecting them when they are fixed. I managed to stay clear of the rum at least. Life went on around me, but there was no life in me: I was sailing on automatic pilot.

Early ice, which could easily have been avoided if I had been thinking, kept me frozen in Boston for weeks. An obliging relative took in the children and I visited them frequently, but there was a distance between us. The absence of their mother seemed to have change their identity so that I scarcely knew them. I was no longer their father but just playing their father in a play which lacked its central character. The audience was not impressed by my act. I walked them around Boston in a fevered search for any form of distraction, anything to keep them from examining me too closely. Close inspection would have revealed my internal injuries, and children do not like their fathers to be ill. An ill mother is disturbing, but a father must be resplendently healthy to reassure his tribe. If he is too old or weak to hide his condition, then he is pitied, not for his present state but for not being what he was.

"Do you remember how strong he was?"

A father who accepts he is ill or old angers his family. His patent decrepitude forces them to stop depending on him. He is relatively fortunate if he can lay the blame on age or illness; a father who fails in the office of provider without any excuse is treated as a cad and rejected by family and society. Failure in this office is totally unacceptable.

I was already guilty of not providing the children with a mother. There was a lot of talk at that time about the Mormons, the women condemning them with scorn, while the men seemed to quietly envy their polygamy. If I had embraced their faith the children might still have a mother now.

The men in the family tried to keep me away from their daughters, but the women promoted their offspring more or less discretely. Is it possible that these paragons of virtue, these strongholds of decency, could imagine I might harbor carnal desires behind my uniform of correctitude?

My nights were polluted by dreams of those female forms bursting free of their corseted constraints in a wild dance where my own body could choose which one to violate, which mystery to invade, which source to drink from. My heart mourned for Virginia, but my body missed her in a quite different way, and the body can be very insistent.

I became fascinated by the accounts of those sorcerer women who made such a scandal at Salem two centuries ago. Women whom evil had stripped of all virtue to the point that only fire could drive out their contagious debauchery. Those writings fed my basest masculine imaginings, after which a few hours of calm would return to my fiery solitude.

At that time, Boston was full of Negroes looking to find freedom and fortune in the North with the Yankees. The Bostonians had been fierce abolitionists during the war, but having to suffer this black tide was quite a different matter. They had been against slavery, in the South; they favored the political emancipation of Negroes, in the South; they were for Negroes, in the South. But what did they think they were doing coming north to New England? I must admit that my own Quaker origins were brought back to the surface by this tide. God had always been the light, and the Devil the Prince of Darkness. A pure soul is white, sin blackens it, and baptism washes you clean. An innocent man is whiter than white. White is for virginity, black is the color of death. The white Bostonian population became more circumspect about the equality guaranteed by the Constitution. Exceptions were sought, differences invented. Arguments were put forward to demonstrate the connection between the color of the skin and the color of the soul. The solemnity of the hymns was compared to the heavy sensuality of Negro religious music. It was whispered that their men's violaceous penises had acquired their legendary dimensions from the insatiability of the females' appetites.

The effect of all of this on me was to allow female Negroes free

136

entry to my dreams. They knew no segregation: Negroes and Salem witches alike shared the favors of my fevered attentions. A clarinet played the music for the chorus of black and white, which formed the prison bars of my solitude.

I tried consulting a spiritualist, hoping that a contact with Ginny would free me from my nightmares, but the attempt was unsuccessful. The dreams continued, becoming more and more involved, until one night I thought I saw Ginny's body amongst the female crush, though I could not get to her; like the horizon, she was always the same distance away, no matter how far I went towards her. So I started taking cold baths to put out the fire of evil which was only making me feel guilty. Deprivation of this nighttime satisfaction encouraged me to seek something more palpable during the days. The hunger brought on by my dreams needed to be fed on real flesh. The many inhabitants of my imagination needed to be driven out.

A large family reunion was organized to take place in Lowell, Massachusetts. I collected the four children and we travelled together to the Merrimack House Hotel on Lowell's main street. The town, sited at the junction of the rivers Merrimack and Concord, pleased me immediately with its bustling activity. The cotton mills where busy and buildings were going up everywhere. The one hundred thousand industrious inhabitants seemed well organized into an hierarchical system almost as efficient as a ship's.

The family received us heartily, especially once they found we were staying in a hotel. Salaries in the town were good, but accommodation was limited. My cousins lived in the best quarter, around St. Peter's Church, happily for them. Further north, the inhabitants of Chinatown were crowded like the crew of the forecastle. There were no Chinese in Chinatown; it took its name from the fact that the immigrant French Canadians who lived there were willing to work for low wages, like the Chinese. A cousin who often visited the area on business told me how they were split into two squabbling factions: those from the Montreal region, who mixed happily with the Irish and managed a certain amount of English; and the pious faithful from Quebec City, who wanted a church of their own with a priest from home. Apparently they did not trust the purity of a sacrament delivered in an accent different from their own. The Montrealers used the church of St. Peter, and the Quebec City faction the church of the Immaculate Conception.

I found myself becoming more interested in my first cousin than her explanations. She did not lack charms, generous and well proportioned charms. To be charmed by them more often, I asked her to act as governess to my children while we were in Lowell. She accepted my offer immediately, saying her sewing business would come to no harm if left for a time. I paid her, but she would almost certainly have done it for nothing—no money, that is. At that time there were four women to every man in Lowell, which ensured a healthy widowed captain all the female attention he could wish. In that puritan climate my widowerhood weighed heavily on me; there was no outlet for physical desires but marriage.

Cousin Henrietta Miller Elliot had originated from the same corner of Nova Scotia as myself: the Annapolis Valley. Her family had moved to Ontario early in her life, in hopes of making money at mining. She claimed she was pleased with their move to Lowell because it brought them closer to the sea again. I learned from another branch of the family, with a daughter of their own to promote, that it was the proximity of her much loved younger brother working on the East Coast rather than the sea that had attracted her to Lowell.

As Lowell had a large garments industry, I decided to equip the children with winter clothes there. Out shopping all together, I could not resist the temptation of browsing in Sargent's bookshop. I found several books for the children, and a copy of Mr. Stevenson's latest novel, *The Strange Case of Dr. Jekyll and Mr. Hyde*, I bought as a gift for "Hettie," as I was now encouraged to call her. In return for my gift, she hired a coach to take us on a tour of the town. All the children wanted to sit up front with the driver, leaving us alone in the back. She talked about the cotton industry, how the raw cotton was imported from the South to be woven and printed here, how good prices straight from the factories meant great opportunities in the garment trade, how the "mule spinner" strike of 1875 had started when the owners decided to cut wages rather than endanger their profits when prices had fallen. I did not follow her story; I followed the curve of her thighs under her skirt and the swelling of her breast, almost too full for her twenty-four years. She talked about the racial disagreements fostered when the companies imported cheap Canadian labor to break the strike and the American workers switched to the machine tool factories and the leather industry. This last comment caught my attention and I told her how my father had worked in leather in Nova Scotia; she stopped the coach in front of two big oaks and lead us into a shoe manufactory, doubtless thinking it would please me.

The odor of tannin and acid soon drove the children out, but I stayed to see the assembly line, doubtless to please her. Rows of well oiled machines worked without rest, each attended by a devoted servant. Hettie appeared to know every detail of their working, explaining how similar machines could bring immense profits to the garments trade too. That is the type of thinking behind the American industrial revolution, an elitist revolution which brings freedom to the few and ties the many in slavery to machines. I was not against it since I had always seen myself as one of the few. After the workshop we went to examine the final product in the attached showroom. The work was certainly neat enough, but were these boots as solid as handmade? I did not even ask the question, fearing a lengthy and detailed answer. A pair of soft ladies' boots in fine leather attracted my attention. They were the same style as Virginia had bought before our last trip. I bought them for Hettie. The gift shocked her into silence on the way back to the hotel. As the children tried steering the horse, I steered Hettie's charming disturbance towards the subject on my mind. The warmth of the hand which stole from her muff to rest on mine melted the winter in my heart. Now it was warm, like on another 31st of January, in 1871 in Sydney.

The wedding was set for February 22, 1886, two days after my birthday.

Hettie's family were pleased with the engagement so long as they thought I would sell my maritime interests to settle in New England and help start the much desired clothes factory. I had to apply all the authority of my superior age to convince my fiancée of the absolute necessity of a woman's moulding herself to fit her husband: the only way to maintain conjugal felicity. Taking her for a walk to the confluence of the town's two rivers, I recited many historical examples of failures met by couples who refused to respect this law. As she remained refractory, I told her she was indispensable to the pursuit of my career, a far nobler calling than the confection of cotton clothes. She responded to that argument, flattered to be made so important. I should have realized that with women one does not win anything but time. I was almost disappointed with her when she gave in to me. Ginny never had.

The 22nd of February found the couple exhausted by preparations. We had hardly had time to talk together. Hettie had to organize
every last detail of the ceremony, from the invitation list to making
herself dresses for her family and the bridesmaids. In tight groups,
Hettie and her friends whispered to each other the secrets of married
life. With me it was only the accommodation on ship and the
frequency of our returns to Boston.

Her father pressed me to allow her to invest a portion of her dowry
in the Lowell and District Telephone Company. Their talking
machines were the latest fashion amongst the rich. I would have
preferred her to cut her lines to Lowell but finally relented; the
Aquidneck could have used that investment herself.

My future father-in-law also presented to me a bright spark named
William Burroughs. He claimed to have invented a "comptometer"
which would revolutionize every office by making accounts auto-
matically. All he needed was a little more money to complete its
development. I told him clearly that I had neither the time nor the
money to waste on that sort of lucubration. The father-in-law became
gloomy and accused me of a lapse into papism in not taking enough
interest in worldly success. As a good Protestant, he equated material
riches in this world with a guarantee of salvation in the next. The only
other world in which I would like to secure a place is the one where
Ginny is, but I could hardly tell him that.

All I wanted from the day was the social sanctioning of the satisfaction of my desires, the end of the physical aspect of my solitude.
Hettie was more than twenty years younger than me, with a fit and
healthy body: I should be able to count on her for stimulation for the
rest of my life.

I paid little attention to the ceremony itself, my thoughts centring
on what would happen once the ceremonies were over. The lace
modestly covering the decolletage of her white satin dress attracted
my eyes rather than concealing anything from them. Even at the most
solemn moments, I was wondering how it would feel to have my hand
between the cool of that satin and the warmth of her flesh, that hand
she was now holding to slip on a ring. Marriage came just in time to
save me from the sin of mental rape.

A maternal branch of my wife's family, the Gringas, from the
Beauceronne region of Quebec, brought a special delight to the
service with their particular wedding gift. They had hired a singer

from their own town who filled the church with vibrant emotion. Emma Lajeunnese progressed later to an enviable singing career as Emma Albani, backed by Queen Victoria's patronage. Her celestial voice floated immaterially to every corner of the church.

With so many French Canadians there, the reception was a jolly affair. I discovered the Gringas were related to Venant Kerouac; so the captain had not finished with me yet. I told them about the letter we found on the West Coast, but they had not heard of a Angelina Desmarais. That would have been too much of a coincidence. Thoughts of the old captain made me wish I could talk with him again now and seek his advice. I was afraid I might have made a miscalculation in my navigation and might be headed on the wrong course, because although I was there with Hettie, I still felt alone. Instead of a remedy, perhaps I had only found a placebo, and that would be a hard pill to swallow if it were true.

I used the excuse of the children to leave the revellers to their celebrations. I was anxious to proceed with my cure. The new Mrs. Slocum would have stayed with her friends all night. At Merrimack House, young Garfield cried so pitifully we had to take him into our bed. Hettie seemed pleased to have him there between us. She chatted on about the famous brother who had not been able to come to the wedding but whom she hoped to see in Boston. I could barely hear her above the sound of blood pumping through my veins. In the morning Garfield rushed off with the other children to satisfy his young appetite in the dining room, leaving me with my old appetite and a full meal to feed it on.

I took my meal, but it proved to be strangely unappetizing. There was none of the sauce I had been accustomed to. The offering I brought to the table, my fine set of cutlery, was not welcomed with thanks either. I learned she had been long accustomed to eating with her fingers and felt no need for other utensils. We shared the meal it is true, but it was a frugal wedding breakfast. The social legitimization of my appetite did not guarantee its satisfaction. I carried on sadly but without regret, returning to the table as often as possible. The only way to overcome a hunger is to feed it. You have to create your souvenirs before you can become attached to them. I turned my back to her so she could not see the melancholic look in my eyes; and there on the bedside table was the book I had given her as a present, *The Strange Case of Dr. Jekyll and Mr. Hyde*.

The biggest deception came from having to limit my horizons to suit hers. Ginny and I had always been able to climb to the masthead and see new lands far beyond the normal horizon. I sometimes wondered if her ghost was not at work, keeping me down on the deck to remind me I could not climb without her help.

Victor and Garfield joined us on the ship, very glad to be back at sea. The two younger ones stayed with their relatives. Hettie was more relaxed with them than with me, devoting much of her attention to winning their approval. She was closer in age to them than she would ever be to me. The arrangements of the accommodation did not suit her, she said. I explained to her that I was a man, a father, a captain, and a faithful husband, but that I was continuing my life, not starting a new one. Destiny may impose changes on me, but only destiny has the prerogative. My intention was to pursue the same destiny with another wife, not to seek a new destiny. She insisted on at least disposing of Ginny's clothes; they did not fit her anyway. It was true: the two women did not have the same stature.

We were not as happy as we might have hoped, but it seemed to me we had all that was needed to be happy one day. In the meantime, we had to do the best we could together.

A cargo of oil awaited us in New York, so we left our moorings under ballast without wasting time looking for Hettie's brother. I did not want to miss the inauguration of the Statue of Liberty either. Hettie was thrilled with New York. She took the two boys to visit every attraction. I thought it was she who sought their company, but later they revealed to me that it was rather the reverse.

We proudly took our place in the parade of ships which made up part of the celebration of the opening of the famous edifice. To please Hettie, I rented a hotel room for a few days while the cargo was being loaded, hoping this would encourage the honeymoon to shine on our nights more brightly. A waste of money: Hettie did not refuse herself to me, but pleasure refused itself to her unless she took it firmly in her own hands. She preferred to control my pleasure in the same way too. Without being actually disagreeable, the situation disturbed my masculine pride. She was virile enough, but I could only have a secondary role in her passion play. The matrimonial pleasures I had missed so much since Virginia's death were becoming matrimonial duties.

The dangers of sea brought a welcome change to the situation. In direct contact with the old sea dog in his own environment, she partly surrendered to his command. In the heart of a gale, her pleasure came completely under my control. She wrapped her arms and legs around me and clung like a peggy to the mizzen. I remembered how I had clung to my father's leg on the my first trip to sea. With the situation out of her hands, she could abandon herself to the captain's orders.

The trip to Montevideo was marvellous: gales all the way. And what she learned on that voyage she never forgot. I had thought she might become a new partner to me, but she restricted herself to being irreproachable in all she said and did. She did not impose her equality on me but, by resignation and submission, chose not to displease, which is not the same as pleasing.

We flew along in strong free winds, but the ship shared my growing-grey faults. Until then I had always looked to the future, but now the future was chasing me, throwing itself at me. Like my life the *Aquidneck* was not totally watertight. The recent change in my life and the long stop in New England had blown several of my specifications, and seams had not been properly caulked but just stopped up with tar. With gales constantly throwing water over the stern, the susceptibility of the deck was revealed. At least with this light cargo we should stay afloat, but after pumping for thirty-six hours we still found four feet of water in the hold. We must be pumping the whole of the Atlantic over the side. The water level started to rise again as soon as we stopped pumping. We searched for the point of ingress in vain, scouring the deck for a fault. As she settled in the water, more and more waves broke over her: we were becoming dangerously heavy. The water surging noisily inside her endangered our stability. Would cutting the masts help her to stay upright?

Hettie and I were clearing away one of the boats when she moved a coil of rope and almost broke a leg in the hole that was hiding beneath it. The hole! It was blocked temporarily and soon the pumps were sucking air. With the return of good weather, a thorough repair was made and I went over every inch of the deck, showing my sons how to detect cracks and recaulk them properly. Hettie oscillated between fear of the sea and reaping the rewards of that fear, between the attractions of land and the gifts of the sea. I was forever comforting and caulking.

After discharging in Montevideo, I took on a full cargo of baled hay for Rio de Janeiro. Unknown to us, a cholera epidemic broke out in Argentina while we were on passage and the Brazilians responded with arbitrary quarantine restrictions that were disastrous for my business. We were stopped and diverted to Ilha Grande, to the south of Rio, for the ship to be disinfected and the cargo discharged into quarantine. Under the guns of the armor-plated warship *Aquidaban* we anchored at Ilha Grande January 7, 1887. The anchorage was already crowded with diverted ships. The next morning, armed officers came alongside and ordered us to leave immediately, the port had been closed that morning. I explained we had arrived the day before.

"Gentlemen, please believe me. Ask aboard the *Aquidaban*."

"That is not relevant. I cannot change my orders, Captain."

He gave me a wink and rubbed his thumb across his fingers in the age-old sign, but I was sure of my case and already angry at the delay. Why should I provide his daughter with a dowry? Why allow this mosquito to suck my blood and infect me with his filthy disease? These officials with authority but no accountability are like a plague killing everything they touch.

"I arrived before this order was made, gentlemen. I must insist in the name of my family that you permit me to stay."

"If you insist then, Captain, you can leave immediately. Otherwise I will signal the *Acquidaban* to fire on you."

The anonymous Napoleon even insisted the whole crew should be lined up so he could check them against the list, strutting along as he inspected his "guard of honor." Without my wife and children aboard, would I have tried outfacing his threats? Without Hettie's eyes on me would I have swallowed my pride and paid? Who can say, but I did neither; we weighed anchor and headed back for Rosario.

The epidemic proved to have been only a mild one, only one case in Rosario. The closing of the ports had all the appearance of an act of revenge on the Argentines, who had closed their ports to Brazil some time before on a similar pretext. The sensitive Brazilians had not liked this obstacle to their sugar trade and so decided to teach a lesson to the whole of South America without going to the expense of a war. I always prefer a more straightforward approach. Closing their ports just at the beginning of the season, when Brazil received most imports from the south, was so much admired by the Argentines that the Buenos Aires government declared a two-day public holiday in their honor. A good sense of humor is needed to keep a captain cool in this sort of situation.

Our forced return sent the motorized coast guards into paroxysms of laughter when they learned we still had our full cargo. In Rosario a local merchant pretended sympathy for our plight but also said: "*Caramba!* I have suffered losses too and there is so much hay about now."

I preferred to lay the ship up rather than accept the prices I was offered. The price would go up again when the Brazilian ports reopened, and I would lose less if I waited long enough.

I had to wait three months. The cholera had disappeared long before that, but there was a snake in the grass: the Brazilians wanted to have their own corned-beef factories working before they opened up for competition. The sailing world was profoundly discomfited by this loss of trade, especially since there were now fifty-seven refrigerated ships running fresh beef from Argentina to England.

Queen Victoria's Golden Jubilee found us floundering. Steam already dominated industry and was rapidly expanding its territory over the sea. If the Queen of England was intent on ruling the world with steam, what chance did we have?

Steam did nothing to facilitate the finding of crews for sailing ships either. They preferred twenty days of loafing to three times as many risking their lives in the rigging before returning to their beloved whores. With the type of crews we were left with, a long spell at anchor was not a good thing. Our Finns soaked up so much alcohol that they went on the rampage in a fit of ethylic madness. We had to call on the assistance of officers on three other ships before they were brought under control. They were in such a dangerous temper that I dismissed them all and engaged local men. I would have done as well to keep the drunks. All the prisons had been opened during the cholera epidemic and gallowsbirds haunted every port, trying to leave the country before they were rounded up again. The mate was as vigilant as possible in his selection, but two of these creatures were actors enough to pass his inspection.

Dangerous Jack's sabre-scared face was almost level with his bull shoulders, while Bloody Tommy's slim form coiled like a snake about to strike. Their shared penchant for sheep was revealed when Hettie found them committing their acts of bestiality on the ewes brought aboard for the pot. She was sick for a week and any approach by me brought on the same attacks of nausea for some time after. The meat she would not touch. Her rejection of me I bore well, because the waters of the River Plate had sent Ginny's ghost to haunt me. Memories of our times together made me indifferent to Hettie's attractions. Ginny would have been wrinkled by now, but I knew age would never have dampened the fire it seemed impossible to kindle in Hettie.

At the end of April, the *Aquidneck* closed on Ilha Grande for the second time with the same cargo of hay in her holds. Unwelcoming mists veiled the hills. Within a few days a whole fleet of hay-laden ships had joined us. The acrid smell of fumigants hung over us until the fresh breezes of the passage to Rio blew them away in mid-May. Hettie took advantage of this further delay to reintroduce her plans for a clothing business somewhere in New England. When she mentioned the "family circle" though, it spoilt all her arguments, for that phrase brought to mind an image of myself and the children huddled around Virginia's deathbed. She could make no appeal against such memories. Boils started breaking out on my back. Her words and ideas were filled with the same grey banality as the Ilha Grande climate, where rain and mists still hung every day over the hills. Ginny had always brought color to our lives. She had played melodies where Hettie was a monochord. The two boys seemed to think just the opposite: they were fascinated with Hettie.

The fort at the entrance to Rio de Janeiro bay forced us to stop again. We had certainly not sailed faster than the telegram sent from Ilha Grande to notify them of our clearance. The details of this further annoyance were made important by the precarious pecuniary position of the ship. To stop a ship they fire a cannon, and for this undesired service they charge eight milreis. If a second or third shot is needed to bring about the correct response, then the charge goes up to sixteen or thirty-two milreis. However, American ships are exempt: my American ship stopped at the first shot, but they had the gall to fire twice more anyway and charge me thirty-two milreis.

After paying, we were generously permitted to weigh anchor and proceed to the berth reserved for us in port. Our cargo was delivered ashore without defects, complete with all the rats and fleas loaded with it in Rosario three months ago, all perfectly healthy in spite of their long trip and the fumigants.

While the ship was discharging, I was invited to attend a condomblé and went along out of curiosity, having heard of these quasi-religious gatherings before. I had intended only to watch, but when I was told the dancers often communicated with the beyond, I felt I must try. I was given a bitter drink and then joined the whirling dancers in their accelerating spirals, spinning to the music's insistent beat. Sweating black bodies surrounded me. A hand passed me a tortoise shell filled with small bones to shake, soon replaced by a bone-filled skull. As my body filled with the strange rhythm, the boils on my back danced and shook too. I put my ear to the skull and there was Ginny's voice coming from inside, singing a song of love. The boils ran frantic around my back and each shake I gave the skull brought Ginny's voice clearer and louder, singing our love to me.

My boils were cured, but reality thought one good thing was all I deserved. We had moved to Antonina in Paranagua Bay for a cargo of mate tea destined for Montevideo. The villains in the crew had got it into their heads that a large quantity of silver was hidden in the captain's cabin. In the quiet of the night they tried to carry out their plot to murder us and find the treasure. Hettie woke me, saying she could hear noises. I had just finished telling her how silly she was and not to wake me again, when I too heard a step over our heads. Nobody had any business on the poop deck at night. Arming my pistol, I surprised them before they could reach us. Bloody Tommy was carried off to hospital, his stomach ripped open by one shot but still screaming and swearing. Dangerous Jack lay dead on deck, with his cutlass still in his hand, his blood mingling with that of a butchered sheep. The infamy of his perversion followed him into death. The bodies told their own story, and I did not expect to be involved in an inquiry. But I was wrong. I had to place the ship under a pilot while I waited on the authorities' pleasure, and the *Aquidneck* made its return trip without me. I must have been questioned by every official in town before the "investigation" was over. Hettie was pleased at the chance to be ashore again, sightseeing with the boys.

During this enforced stay in Paranagua, I discovered there were many fine woods available, which put me in mind of the profitability of my old trade. The problem was there were no boats large enough to carry good lengths out to the ship, so I determined to use this wasted time to build one. I found these notes in my diary:

Engaged local sawyers to reduce 40 ft. lengths of Spanish Cedar into planks.
The plans are complete; like a dory.
Found some thick iron-wood planks for the bottom.
Today found the curved pieces I need for frames.
Started planking.
Can see her shape now, looks good.
Check the measurements again and she will fit exactly into the 35 ft space available on deck.
Saw some excellent timber today in the village of Guarakasava.

Once we started running timber out in the dory, I placed Victor in charge of overseeing the loading while I checked each piece before it left the shore. When I returned aboard one evening, he came to me with something to report.

"Until now I was naively convinced that all Brazilians are honest, Papa. I thought such good boatmen must be honest. But I was wrong, Papa. This is not Eden. Do you know what I saw?"

"Calmly now, Victor. Tell me what happened."

"It was the tallyman, Papa, the one who counts the logs for the dockers' payments. When one end entered the ship, he counted 'uno' and when the other end of the log passed he counted 'dos'."

He was the same age I was when Captain Kerouac started my training. I told him:

"Victor, tomorrow morning you find another teller yourself and remove this bandito. Can you do that?"

He did it and the replacement proved satisfactory. It is a hard task to face a man and tell him he is dismissed. I was proud of my son and promised him that soon I would make him my mate.

After celebrating a tropical Christmas, we completed the loading and weighed anchor. Crossing the bay, I could see the current was driving the ship towards a sandbank. I called the orders to tack, but as we did so, the wind failed completely. We were no longer moving through the water, but the water itself was moving us straight for the bank. Up forward, Victor saw the situation and had the anchor dropped immediately, but the current had churned up the soft sand so much the anchor would not bite. The *Aquidneck* bore down on the bank, until a sickening, cracking shudder announced our grounding. No wind and the anchor would not hold. I had left just after high water to take advantage of this very current that was now holding us on the bank. I stood mouth agape, unbelieving, lost, because there were no orders I could give, no action I could take. Victor took control of evacuating all hands to shore in our boats. For days, I stayed on that river bank watching as, a few cables away, my pride, my livelihood, my home, and my status slowly broke its back. I could hear her groaning in agony as each vertebra snapped during her long, slow death. I winced at each jolt and my own back bent in sympathy.

It was many days before I could straighten my own back again. The family left me alone to suffer the paralysis of my defeat. I came close to giving up then, to submitting to fate. How much courage it took to pull myself out of that depression, to find the energy to act again. I saw that if I did not do something soon, anything, I would sink broken with my ship. Doing something would eventually bring back my courage. On the outside I became the energetic Captain Slocum again, the brave and competent father of the family, knowing no fear and immune to setbacks. Inside, Joshua lay weary, unwilling to fight again, but he would have to follow when he was ready. The body would solve the soul's problems.

I have already published a record of what followed under the title *The Voyage of the Liberdade,* my first book, the first *Slocum* on my bookshelf. I took the account from the log and my diary, but I left out most of the personal details. As with my later books, my purpose was not to reveal myself, but the passage of time has left me less shy, less proud, less concerned with making myseif a hero. It all seems less important now.

So, there we were, in involuntary exile in Guarakasava. Audacity and courage were the only cards we had to play. Sometimes you have to look for your fortune inside yourself. I explained my project to the family and they listened in silence, fearing that if they did not share my conviction and enthusiasm I might take it as an affront. Long months of Robinson Crusoeing lay ahead, but the plan to build our own boat and sail it to North America would be an exploit which might restore our social standing, whereas to return in disgrace as passengers on a steamship would finish us completely. From failure, we would fight back to win success. I emphasized the importance of polishing our image as great sailors in order to avoid falling into the darkness of other people's indifference. I stressed the "our" and never mentioned the "my."

By the time I had finished talking, the boys were already seeing themselves as heroes. Hettie concentrated on our chances of survival. I replied with an account of the worldly rewards that would greet us five thousand miles away. The prospect of fame dried her tears, and she asked what she could do to help. I invited her to put her seamstress's talent to work building the sails.

Those first weeks were joyful ones, all of us happy to be busy again. Each day we worked at rebuilding our hopes within sight of the wreck of our past. The immense attention given by the press to Fridtjof Nansen's expedition across Greenland's snowfields spurred us on. Surely our exploit would bring us even greater renown.

By mid-April the boat was ready. We launched her on the very day Brazil announced the freeing of her slaves. In honor of their new-found liberty and our own, we named her the *Liberdade*: the boat was our own announcement of freedom.

I already had dreams of writing an account of the voyage for publication and my diary served partly as a draft for that book. Much of it never saw print and all was changed.

I have rigged this record with the web of my life aboard a boat built with my own hands to carry my family home. All seamen commit an error of navigation sometimes, so please give indulgence to my literary mistakes...

If we succeed in this adventure the benevolence of the Gulf Stream will have to be thanked for sending fair winds to carry us to a safe port. Providence will decide...

Within the family, there are cross currents, adverse winds, and frightening waves...

The essence of this story is the author's devotion to the spiritual beauty of the oceans, which have always seduced his heart... An ocean whose waves are inevitable, regular, ephemeral.

If only father were here to admire my new creation... Captain

Kerouac would smile his approval, I am sure... The lines of a Cape Ann dory are easily recognizable but what would they all think of her junk rig?... The sails Hettie has worked so hard at will serve us well. She jokes that her sails will last longer than my hull... Hettie worries about Garfield's safety when we are at sea. I promise her I keep an eye on him...

I am not well. Have had to place Victor in charge of the boat. Surprised to find Hettie quite content with the arrangement... Three days of fever but it is finished now. A few drops of arsenic soon take care of malaria...

Another stupid delay by the authorities. We finally have to pretend to be going on a fishing trip in order to get a sailing permit. We can use the nets anyway...

Mrs. Slocum has provisioned the boat: 120 lbs. pork; 30 lbs. beef, both salted; 20 lbs. salt cod; two jars of honey; 200 oranges; six stalks of bananas; and 120 gallons fresh water. A small pannier of yams and some cane sugar stalks arrived later. To add flavor, Brazil nuts, pepper and cinnamon. A little table salt...

Garfield has declared he will save space by drinking sea water. I shall have to be careful he does not try it.

To properly describe our life on board, I shall have to explain our arrangements. The light provisions were stored at bow and stern, the heavier ones centrally and as low as possible to help the boat's stability. A sole was built over the top of the heavy stores with a canvas-covered cabin top standing one foot above the deck. This provided us with a living space four feet high and twelve feet long in the middle of the boat. The coachroof and much else was built of bamboo. Hettie gave this lashed-up structure an old-fashioned look; I do not think she was entirely convinced of the explanation I gave:

"You have to consider the advantages of bamboo. It is supple and bends under strains rather than breaking. But that is not its most important virtue. I learned the secret of building coachroof spars and rails with it in Hong Kong. You see, between each knot there's a chamber of air which can support several pounds in the water. We have at least a thousand of those chambers. If the boat should capsize..."

"Josh. You told me..."

"Listen Hettie, Listen until the end of the explanation. Victor understands, I think."

"Excuse me."

"So, if the boat capsizes, the flotation in the bamboo turns her back up the right way."

"Are you certain, Josh?"

"Hettie, please. I know what I am talking about."

Then it was Garfield's turn to be afraid. We had caught a small shark equipped with multiple rows of shining, pearly teeth: pearly in color but razor-sharp to touch. This one was delicious, although many are spoilt by an ammonia taste. I showed Garfield how to use the dried skin to polish the model boat he had made. This little boat danced along behind us in the *Liberdade*'s wake until another shark bit it clean in half while Garfield was watching.

"I think we're too close to the sharks in this little boat," he said.

After that I banned the sport of trailing an arm or leg in the water, and the washing bucket was dipped in the sea on the end of a rope. After seeing the fate of Garfield's model, nobody was tempted to disobey that rule.

The west wind which has been blowing all day is the tail end of a pampeiro. It has kicked up a big sea, rolling us and pushing hard on the rudder as the crests sweep past. Majestic violence…our boat leaps from one wave to the next, supple as a fish.

Of all the waves which battered our boat that day, often standing her on her nose, not one swept the deck. Hettie clenched her teeth and took the sheet, paying out while I bore off. The *Liberdade* felt like a flying fish, trying to leap out of the water and fly. My pleasure in her performance was answered by a thin smile from my wife. I put my arm around her and she wiped her nose on my sleeve. Garfield imitated her action on Victor's sleeve starting the two of them on playful pushing and shoving. My thoughts went to the other two children ashore—and their mother.

It takes courage to face a gale at sea in a small boat, but it takes even more courage to run off before it. We had been on course for home.

I have found the joy of sailing a small boat again. Now I can enjoy the pleasure even more by sharing it with my family… Victor makes me proud and I am astonished by Hettie's willingness to continue… The South Atlantic rollers roll right up to the shore. We have to continue along the coast. It is impossible to run for shelter, the waves break on the ten fathom line... This morning a violent squall fell from the mountains ripping Hettie's sails to shreds...

Fortunately we met an old acquaintance, Captain Baker, on the steam packet *Finance* headed for Rio. He offered to take us in tow. Hettie was shaking with fear and fatigue by now, so she and Garfield were taken aboard the ship, leaving Victor and myself to handle the boat. She would have to be steered on a precise course and my experience was needed for that. Victor stood watch over the tow cable, axe in hand, ready to cut us free if anything should go wrong.

"Look out," called Captain Baker, "when my ship starts moving we might pull that dinghy right out from under you."

"Just get on with your post round, Steam Baker, and watch your course with my wife and child aboard. I'll look after this end of the tow."

He opened up the valves and as the *Finance* picked up to her full fifteen knots, the *Liberdade* did not falter. To be towed in a small boat by a steamer is always dangerous: many do not survive the experience.

The tow was one and a half inches in diameter and ninety fathoms long. When the steamer lifted her stern on a wave, leaving the *Liberdade* on the other side, it pulled as tight as a harp string. As we ran down the face of a wave ourselves it fell in slack coils at our bow, but not for long because the steamer's next plunge pulled it taunt again dragging us ahead with a violent jerk which made the whole boat shudder. This process was repeated at every wave. In those circumstances it was imperative to steer a straight course: the slightest veer would have capsized us. As I was the only one who could take such a responsibility, I was the one at the helm for the entire forty-eight hours of the tow. I knew what I was doing and was managing perfectly well, so Baker's streaming of oil to take the tops off the waves only exasperated me. I would rather have the waves than his oil all over my boat's freshly painted topsides. But we had no sails, so I had to persevere.

I had arranged the tow rope so it came from the bow and looped across the hatchway before being made fast. That way Victor could stay in the shelter of the cabin with his axe but still cut us free instantly should the need arise. I feared that my young mate might be overtaken by sleep, put his head under his wing, and retire, but my

153

calls of "Ready, Victor?" always met with an instant response. With the rough, jerky action of the boat, I suppose sleep would have been impossible even if he had not been so vigilant. I had the benefit of frequent saltwater soakings to keep me awake, consoling myself with the thought that such heavy dowsings might wash off some of the oil coming from our "savior." It was a humiliating test to put a boat to, but it proved the efficiency of her lines.

The morning after our arrival in Rio, we read about ourselves in the *Opiz*:

We have the greatest confidence in this American sailor, audacious and cool. We hope to hear all the newspapers of the old and new worlds soon proclaiming their happy arrival at their destination in this marvellous little boat. We will take part in the celebration of their glory.

After these flattering words and others in the same vein, the only problem was to convince Hettie to put to sea again. She had happily repaired the sails, but the thought of leaving set her to trembling like a jib in stays. Playing the card of parental responsibility, she reproached me with putting the lives of my two sons at risk, especially considering one was scarcely old enough to be left alone. The children were ready to climb aboard so I ended the argument prematurely by ordering her aboard.

So far as I was concerned, we no longer had any choice. Our project had been proclaimed to the press and we could not abandon it at this early stage without being ruined forever. We had to succeed for the press.

During solitary nighttime watches, I was already seeing myself selling copies of the book I would write. A certain amount of glory would lighten the solitude in my heart. I had failed to keep what I had by serious endeavors, so I would try a little folly instead. I seemed to remember that old Melville had said something like that in the restaurant; or was it in his book? I would have to reread *Moby Dick* as soon as I had some free time.

27th July 1888. Contrary winds and current force us to anchor and await a change. Last night a large whale blew into our waters and surfaced right under the boat with a heavy blow. Everybody was shocked. I evaluated the monster at between fifty and sixty feet. When he took a turn around the boat we felt very small. Twice he

154

was so close I could have touched him with an oar. After that first hit we were sure he was about to attack us but I suspect he was just curious to see what had got in his way.

Thought about *Moby Dick* again. I was glad this whale was not white.

Lost one anchor in the collision and I suspect some damage to the keel. Not taking any water.

Garfield has been crying for some days but today Hettie's good humor returned and his soon followed. Hettie sometimes favors me with tender caresses but it is impossible to respond to her in front of the children out of respect for decency and the memory of their mother. There will be privacy in the future though.

A fresh breeze from the south permits us to weigh anchor and head towards the more favorable Trades of the tropics.

28th July. Midnight the breeze turns east, pushing us towards the shore. Have had to put on more sail to weather Cape St. Thome... Pushed by current into turbulent shallow waters twenty hours from Cape Frio... The Southern Cross is lower each day. The S.E. Trades are setting in now. On route and making good speed with "waves gently carrying us home" as Garfield says... Arrived in Bahia do Todos Santos.

A charming port, sheltered by beautiful country and a heady mixture of bloods. The atmosphere sooths the senses, even Hettie feels it, but in a different way. The women here are perhaps the most beautiful I have ever seen, strolling on the quay, dancing up town, returning to drink, love, and then refresh themselves in the bay's lazy turquoise water. The immodestly amorous throng reflected every color, from morning café au lait to nighttime café noir, with a pearly bead of sweat shining here and there as witness to excesses. A port which invites you to stay forever, to sit and eat San Salvador pepper fritters while watching pass the samba-swaying bodies of the least shy girls I had ever met.

Hettie displayed a passion to be off sailing I had never noticed before. With Victor constantly distracted by laughing females, we hauled the boat ashore to repair the damage done to the keel by our whale friend. I did most of the work myself, as Victor kept disappearing, to return with shining eyes but too tired to work. Hettie worked with a new zest, arranging stores and materials from the easy-going

Brazilians. They applied the freedom they had won from the Portuguese to every aspect of life. Even the authorities were polite to us, presenting Hettie with a rare white flower when we left.

Heading for the open sea through the triangular sails of the local fishing boats, lanteen rig imported from Portugal, I could not help thinking of Defoe's hero Robinson Crusoe, who had stopped at Bahia in search of slaves for his plantation. I hoped that would be the sole similarity in your voyages.

Victor and I keep four-hour watches. In good weather we have to fight the intense sleepiness brought on by staring at the compass. We even fall asleep during the day. We have established a method of signalling so the helmsman and lookout can call the one off watch without disturbing the others. We are tied by a cord. Two pulls means it is time to change watches. Three means come quickly, there is a problem. We attached the cord to any arm or leg before turning in so we can be woken easily and silently...

The system only failed once. I pulled and pulled at the rope to find there was only an empty boot on the other end—Victor's ruse to gain a few more minutes in dreams of Bahia girls. I knew that was what he was dreaming about because that was where I went too. All we had was dreams, for although Hettie showed her normal shipboard willingness there was no privacy on board our little boat. We also had signals for good news, particularly the arrival on board of flying fish which need capturing quickly before they flap themselves back into the water. Fresh fish made a welcome change to our diet...

Half way between Cape St. Rogue and the Amazon. Strong E.S.E. wind for two days. Turning into a gale. Waves are building...

The boat has started taking water...

Hettie is courageous. Garfield helps bail too. Victor and I are exhausted from steering, changing sails and bailing...and we will have to make for land.

That was an error we all remembered for a long time. Closing the shore, the boat suddenly lifted and then slid down the face of an exceptionally long wave. This was a danger we had not expected. The waves were surging past us and breaking just a few fathoms ahead. We must have been over a bank although I had not thought to find one there. The next big wave was already building behind us when I saw that it would break before it reached us and carry us rushing and tumbling in its white water.

I put the helm hard down in an attempt to turn our bows into the wave. The rest of the family could do nothing but hold on and pray. We were completely buried, losing sight even of each other, then after what felt like minutes but could only have been seconds, we emerged gasping for air. The waves were arriving one after another. The water was brown with churned-up sand and white with foam. In this perilous situation, sometimes buried under breakers, the next moment balanced high on a wave, we fought helm and sheets with all our strength, easing her forward gradually in search of deeper water. How long the struggle lasted I have no idea, but finally we came out of the maelstrom into relatively smooth water. The *Liberdade* shook herself clear of water and was sailing again with the sea below and the sky above, where they should be. We looked behind us.

The whole horizon was lit by phosphorescent foam. As the heavy rainclouds passed to allow a little light, we had the first view of the assembly of dangers through which we had passed, and one spot in particular where a half-tide rock sent foam shooting a hundred feet into the heavens. The black of that rock stood out from the flowing foam like the entrance to hell. We had never been in so much danger, but we had survived. The light weight and suppleness of our little craft had saved us from destruction. The flotation in the bamboo super-structure had proved its worth a hundred times, bringing her upright again when she would have rolled over. I was astonished how well my theory had worked in practice, although I would have been quite content for it to remain theory.

19 days out of Pernambuco and we have had Barbados in sight since dawn. Delicate blue hills, green fields dotted with white houses. Huge windmills looking as old as the hills keep watch. Definitely the most charming spot in the Antilles. By communal assent we make a tour of the green fringes of our coral waters, keeping well clear of the many reefs. Entered Carlysle Bay at midday. One hundred miles made good each day since Pernambuco.

I had many acquaintances in Barbados who soon were paying us visits. They had all known Ginny and were unsure whether to offer consolations for my loss or congratulations on my remarriage. Hettie was obviously upset at all the praise for Virginia but managed to maintain her dignity. She also found some nocturnal spice on the island.

The *Condor* was in port, commanded by an old friend who, along with his young wife, had almost succumbed to the island's famous wrecker. The two women became inseparable. During the days they disappeared on long excursions, and whatever they did on them had the two giggling together all evening. At night Hettie became a firebrand. I never asked what they did during the days, but I know when we two captains met for our breakfast of fruit juice and cinnamon toast we both had particularly happy faces. We decided to stay until the worst of the hurricane season was over.

7th. October. Unhappily we leave Barbados today.

12th. October. Mayaguez, Puerto Rico.

This was to be our last stop under the tropical palms of the West Indies and all of us made the most of it. Never have I seen such an hospitable port for seamen. The polite and helpful officials showed every courtesy, which made a welcome contrast to our struggles in South America. They were of admiration and curiosity for our *barc pequeno*. The American, Dutch, and French consuls rivalled each other in attentions to improve our stay. Only one incident clouded my happiness.

Some photographers had requested permission to take a picture of the boat with her captain on deck, but through a misunderstanding we were absent when they arrived. Anxious to have their photograph, they recruited a Negro to pose in my place. The picture was printed in the Paris and Madrid press, accompanied by a flattering description of myself and special comments on the healthiness of my tan. The rest of the family found this extremely droll, but I failed to see the funny side. I was working hard to become famous and somebody else was taking the credit. Fame is like cinnamon: one is never satisfied. A little more cinnamon to finish the toast, then a little more toast to finish the cinnamon; a taste of glory to regain renown, then a little more, just a little bit more. There is never "enough, that will do."

Seem to be clear of the thunderstorms around Cuba now. We do not want to stop again until we reach a port on our own coast. Impatient to see the Pole star climb higher. We have a tendency to sheet in too hard hoping to accelerate ourselves home. We had been going to stop at Nassau but now we'll go straight on.

Soon we were in American waters again.

Two days sailing at good speed through the Bahama Banks took us to Bimini. After that only a small push would take us in sight of the American coast. The wind veered from its normal N.E. to S.E. as we passed Bimini, giving us a smooth crossing of the Gulf Stream's tireless current. The first day with the wind free and the current under us we made 200 miles. Quite a performance for such a small boat. During the second night we were bowling along at the same rate when she hit some flotsam. The *Liberdade* leaped up over it but the keel received a heavy knock. I had to go into the water to clear away the damaged section and afterwards she seemed to go even better. The only problem is that if we hit anything else carried by this oceanic river the hull itself is more susceptible to damage. We are rolling and pitching more but the speed is still good...

On the western boundary of the Stream, steep waves run from all directions creating a wild disorder beyond my ability to describe. The *Liberdade*'s motion is neither poetic nor pleasant. The wind has backed to the N.E. again so its right against the current. I am uneasy with our damaged boat in these steep seas. Green water coming on board at times...

A bad sea has broken aboard, damaging the coachroof. Have had to run off to make repairs. The stew on the stove might be over salted now...

We see the hills of America ahead...

We have travelled over 5,000 miles now. Closing the coast we first distinguish forest, then fields, finally the comforting spectacle of a village. We are off Bully Bay in South Carolina...

At nightfall Cape Roman was clearly visible to the north. The wind has failed as we approach the coast, forcing us to anchor in four fathoms. 20.00 on the 28th. October 1888.

We had taken fifty-three days of sailing to effect our exploit, already famous in the foreign press for a total expenditure of less than one hundred dollars.

The intracoastal waterway took us north to Chesapeake Bay. I have delicious memories of drifting along slowly with the lightest of breezes, so tranquil that ducks came to perch on the stem. They only left if the rifle appeared. We had bought a huge turkey, so on

Christmas Day we feasted on roast turkey and plum pudding. Each mouthful had the special taste of our own country, which was seasoning enough. We were home: safe, sound, and noticed!

We sailed on up the Potomac to complete our trip, alongside in Washington, D.C., on the 27th of December.

Hettie's body had become lithe and tanned, and I was proud of her for staying out the trip when the temptations to quit were often great. Victor had become an accomplished seaman and Garfiled was learning, well into his apprenticeship.

I had chosen Washington, knowing it would be filled with journalists covering the first Pan-American Conference. As our journey had embraced the three Americas, I was given a reception to satisfy all my desires. My future notoriety seemed assured. While Hettie, Victor, and Garfield folded sails, coiled ropes, and generally tidied the boat, I occupied myself with my future, receiving the gentlemen of the press. Many political bigwigs wanted to be seen with this symbol of unity, and I welcomed them: they could give me the support necessary to revive my sailing career. Thanks to the timing of our arrival, the whole world's press came to write about the exploit of Captain Slocum and his family. In London the story came alongside accounts of Jack the Ripper's morbid doings. Fame knows no morality.

We received telegrams of congratulations in seven different languages.

After this brief journalistic flurry, I would have to profit from the interest by writing a book. News does not stay news for long; paper more durable than newsprint was needed to perpetuate the voyage.

Through the winter alongside in Washington, Hettie sulked over my newborn glory. Even the celebrated Civil War photographer Mathew B. Brady came to take my likeness. Invitations fell like rain, begging the honor of my presence at smart society receptions, so I was often away. Hettie wanted to accompany me to these gatherings, but I explained to her that glory, if it was to become a marketable investment, must not be diluted.

"But while you're boasting about 'our' exploit, in the warm, to those bare-shouldered women, I'm getting stiff from the cold in this floating glacier."

"It's very stuffy in those places and you know you hate tobacco smoke."

"And the smell of roast beef too? You might not have noticed, but we are still eating salt beef."

"I'm soon going to start writing the story of our adventure. Everyone says it will be a great success."

"If we don't have to eat your paper and drink your ink first to stay alive."

"I will be content with a pencil…"

"And we can boil a chart for dinner."

Our relationship was cooling despite the approach of summer. But the interest shown in me by Washington society filled the voids created by Hettie's bad humor.

Leaving the Potomac for New York, Hettie and I found ourselves alone on the *Liberdade* for the first time. The family from Boston had taken the children to join their brother and sister. There was a hygienic silence on board. Hettie's own internal waterways were leading her back towards her family, while I was heading for the consecration of my fame in the influential and rich society circles of New York. When the desire for matrimonial pleasures came upon me, I found she no longer tempted me. Her back bent in the galley seemed far removed from me upright at the helm. The final straw came just a few days after our arrival in New York. I was still planning my own visits to the press when I read the following in the *New York World*:

> Certainly people talk much about Captain Slocum and his marvellous little boat the *Liberdade* but the "World" wanted to know what the Captain's captain, Mrs. Slocum, has to say on the subject. So a reporter was charged with visiting this little boat where she rolls and pitches in the tide washing the grey rock quays of the Barge Office, near to which the *Liberdade* is moored.

Not only had my wife received a journalist aboard, but she had not said one word to me about it.

> "Would you like to come in?"
> It was with these words that Mrs. Slocum received our reporter. The mistress of the house was in the minuscule cabin, sitting on a plank stretching from front to back about three feet below the deck. Apart from lying, this is the only possible position.

This reporter's lubricity leaped out from between the lines. It was making me sick just to read it. He was intruding on my private domain, my wife, and my adventure, feeling himself quite free to strip them all.

Mrs. Slocum is young, robust, with a pleasing figure. Her face with its ash eyebrows, sparkling eyes...

I was being cuckolded in public.

...a remarkable well shaped nose, an open smile...

What openness?

...and a chin which reveals both gentleness and firmness. This is the truth of her oval face, bronzed by months of sea breezes and the tropical sun. Yesterday she wore a yachting suit in marine blue serge, the short skirt and blouse decorated with narrow white stripes. In her long brown hand she held a sailor's hat...

The lines in the newspaper danced before my angry eyes, brimming with tears of rage. I wanted to both efface it completely and take in every detail. By studying every word with a magnifying glass I sought to find what exactly had passed between this scribbler and my wife.

Mrs. Slocum has a deep, grave voice even though she is from Boston where women normally speak on a high pitch...

There was no doubt left. Only love or lust makes a woman's voice deep.

She has sweet manners and is shy to talk about her trip...

As if an adulteress would want to talk about her husband.

"This is an adventure I would not like to repeat, yet now it is completed I feel a certain satisfaction in having done it. Here, next to the hatchway were two big barrels of fresh water..."

I rushed through the remainder of the evil article, feeling I wanted to throw overboard each item as it was mentioned.

"...the books were behind us and here the stove I cook on." And Mrs. Slocum showed our reporter a simple iron pot on three legs, inside which a handful of charcoal can be burnt. Our hostess continued, "When we reached the colder regions in November, we used it as a brazier, standing it near the door...."

The credibility of my version of events was being put in jeopardy now.

"Did you not sometimes feel tired and alone during the trip?"

"The feeling of isolation was strong at the beginning, but it went as quickly as it came. As to tiredness, that was mainly due to the impossibility of taking any exercise. The deck is too narrow to walk on and you cannot even stand inside...."

When a wife criticizes her husband's work to another, she is betraying him.

"Did this feeling of isolation affect you from the beginning?"

"Yes. When we left Rio de Janeiro they gave us a big farewell party. The Marine Office gave us a permit excusing us from harbor dues and allowing us to fly the Brazilian flag...."

I always stressed our American colors.

"The Brazilians thought it a great honor to allow such a small boat to carry their national colors...."

I suppose they were wrong!

"Then when the land disappeared below the horizon?..."

Go on, tell them how you broke down.

"The sea was an image of desolation. Yet after a few days I learned to love life aboard...."

I did not have to read this.

"I got used to the limited space and felt not only content but happy. We had plenty of books when we left, we obtained more in the ports we stopped at and the ships we met at sea gave us magazines...."

She begged for them, much to my disgrace, and then only read half. That is the truth of it, Mister reporter.

"Wherever we stopped, they showed the greatest interest in us. And when we went ashore we were received in the most charming manner...."

I seemed to be a captain who specialized in stopping in port.

"Will you be leaving for another voyage, Mrs. Slocum?"

"Oh. I hope not. I have been away from home for three years since I was married...."

A wife's home is wherever her husband might be.

Mrs. Slocum told our reporter that she is going to Massachusetts...

So she was giving him her address too.

"I will go by train. I have had enough of sailing for now."

She did not know how well she spoke. Steam would take this notorious infidel away: she had topped infidelity with disloyalty. I gave her the price of her ticket and instructed the cab driver to wait with her until the train left.

I cried bitter tears: less for the loss of Hettie than for having failed to find another Ginny.

Before throwing away the guilty article, I checked the byline again for the hundredth time: Arthur Elliot. Through the tears of her departure, Hettie had begged me to believe that he was the long-lost brother she had hoped to see after our wedding. I had no reason to want to believe her.

CHAPTER EIGHT

Disarray

I had wanted to be enviable, outstanding, brilliant. All I managed was to make a faint glimmer in the shadows, to arouse only passing curiosity. But it was not through lack of effort on my part that I failed. No, I was still convinced I could catch success if I ran hard enough. Herman Melville himself had taught me the importance of appearance. I did my best to astonish the other guests at the receptions to which I was invited.

In 1889 the salons and clubs were buzzing with the complaints of disquieted financiers upset by the collapse of the Suez Canal Company and jealous that France now had a tower to top Chicago's thirty-story skyscrapers. I was always presented as a famous, even heroic, captain. Each host wanted his function to be the best, so the importance of each guest was inflated. As they presented it, the *Liberdade* had braved the Leviathan and journeyed through hell on a trip which put the Argonauts to shame. I was not one to gainsay them. I had yet to learn that living only for the admiration of others inflates the ego until the little child who lives in the heart of all of us is crushed. I tried to keep the conversation on the subject of sailing, forcing the other men to hide behind their cigar smoke while the women competed to compare their lily-white skin to my tan.

I never refused an invitation. They made me feel important and, apart from the boat, were all I had to live for. The show I could put on was the only canvas I had to spread to the wind. The imperatives of my financial situation also made the sumptuous tables particularly important. Glory and hunger were not the only winds blowing me from one reception to the next, though: the New York oligarchy employed the best musicians. Those concerts were like safe harbors for me in the vanities of my social wanderings.

The Vanderbilts had the greatest success of that season with a

165

whole evening devoted to the New World's premiere of a work by a European composer named Richard Strauss. The music brought me no pleasure that evening though. I wanted to be soothed, reassured, but this just challenged me, and frightened me, even. I could recognize all the famous people of the world called to life in the music, but search though I might, I could not find me.

The final applause made me realize the ephemerality of the fame I had achieved. Anonymity had not yet arrived to poverty unsustainable, but I could see that the currents of time were pushing me towards a backwater. Not only was I receiving fewer invitations, but other guests were no longer crowding round to ask me questions and hear my tales. Like any object of curiosity, once the curiosity was satisfied, I would be dropped.

After the concert, Mrs. Vanderbilt invited all the musicians to join her guests, a privilege which was normally reserved for composers, conductors, and soloists, but it was becoming chic to overlook social differences and ignore prejudices (many musicians were Jews) during a buffet. This fashion was never taken up by the aristocracy, who felt threatened by any hint of socialism, but it served the enlightened pragmatism of the new-rich like the Vanderbilts. These great owners understood that an annual picnic for the employees impresses them and costs less than an increase in wages. I wish I had known that trick when I was hiring large crews.

I think musicians felt more at ease with me because I was obviously out of place too, but whatever the reason, I soon found myself surrounded by them. They were fascinated by the stories of my marine exploits; many of them were recent emigrants from Europe and had their own vivid memories of the horrors of the Atlantic crossing on an immigrant ship. Many expressed an interest in seeing the *Liberdade* but by the end of the evening only one violinist was prepared to make the walk, Mabel Wagnalls.

Mabel, I was told, played piano and violin and also composed. She was less than thirty but already considered to be a flower amongst American musicians. I was even more impressed when I heard she had written a book, a "musical story." So much talent under that long black hair. The violin case she held could have been modeled on her own body.

As we left, Mrs. Vanderbilt was there to shake the hands of her departing guests. Holding mine she quietly hinted of seeing me again soon for a grandiose project she had in mind. I thanked her for her hospitality, praying, in vain as it turned out, that her grand project might involve something profitable for me. Parties and concerts were all very nice, but no offers of employment came from them, no proposals to finance my next ship. If only I could be like the people whose company I kept, but my identity was being crushed under the weight of the show I was putting on. I needed some of the Vanderbilt gold to lighten the burden.

My young companion walked slowly at my side, laced around her violin case. I did not understand all she said about music, but it was clear she had a great passion. That a young woman of less than half my years could know so much and express her opinions with so much authority filled me with astonished respect. I had often been impressed by Virginia's ability at the piano, inventing new melodies, but she did not have this woman's knowledge. I could admire her freely because her talents were outside my domain, and so she could attract without challenging. A single child, she spoke about her parents with rare devotion. She told me something of her early travels in Europe with her mother to study music. Her father's business interested me more at the moment, he was co-founder of the publishing house Funk & Wagnalls, publishers of the famous *Literary Digest*. To be published by them was the final consecration for a writer.

We walked the length of Bierstadt to Fulton Market, preceded a few inches by the violin case, carefully tacking around the detritus littering the tramways. Hundreds of horses stood immobile before their carts, not even troubling to lift their heads to the passers-by. On our right, awnings reached out from the tenements to cover stalls and shop fronts. The horses on that side had their heads towards the tramway and their sterns to the shops, where food was being unloaded to stuff the Manhattan rich and make the Brooklyn poor jealous. Across the tramways another row of horses stood facing the first. They were waiting for their carts to be loaded from the ships, lifting an occasional wary eye to the bowsprits waving menacingly over their heads.

Peripatetic merchants pushed their barrows of oysters and sausages, each shouting the unique advantages of their wares. The smell of spiced sausage fat floated over the steaming heaps of dung and empty oyster shells. Potato peelings and cabbage leaves soaked up the stream of urine running between the cobbles. We stepped aside to let a tram pass, the advertisement on its side claiming that children clamor for "Castoria" caster oil. Mabel pursued her involved musical discourse without once putting down a wrong foot, flicking her hair like a horse's main to emphasize the important points, ignoring the comments from the porters and stallholders in praise of the more outstanding features of her anatomy.

She did not stop until we reached the *Liberdade*, squeezed between a steam tanker and a gravel barge, that had been once a proud sailing ship. I offered her my arm to help her aboard, but she preferred to keep both hands on her violin case. I showed her around the boat, pleased with the opportunity to show my own erudition and enthusiasm. The night being mild, we sat out in the cockpit. Suddenly there was nothing more to say: a long silence, and then she made her own tour of the *Liberdade*, leaving me to care for the precious violin. She asked if she could return the next day with a writer friend. I would be spending the day aboard anyway. I walked her back to her tram.

The friend, Sydney Porter, proposed making a photograph of me on the boat with his box Kodak. I had seen one before in Washington and had been tempted by its relative simplicity. Now the small photographic films were readily available in drug stores. Amateur painters were laying aside their brushes in favor of these magic boxes, which were more faithful to reality and easier to master than watercolors. Mabel bustled, helping her friend to set up his equipment, constantly counselling him on angles and adjusting my pose between shots. She expounded on how she saw her role as musician and composer as being like a photographic instrument. She called it musical imagery. She sought to transpose the surrounding reality into music and words, arranged according to her own personal light.

Sydney now suggested he could have the best of his pictures printed as postcards bearing the legend, "A Souvenir of the Exceptional Voyage of the *Liberdade*." He was convinced I could sell them easily, having seen the large number of people who had come to view her since the New York *Herald* had printed a long article on the voyage. I had never hinted at my financial problems, yet Sydney offered to have the cards printed on credit. I accepted.

Three days later, Mabel arrived with a package of cards bearing a flattering likeness of the great conqueror. I offered her one immediately, but she said she had already put some aside for herself. An autographed copy was accepted, though. She installed a small folding table she had also brought and spent the afternoon negotiating the sales of cards and visits aboard the famous boat conducted by the famous captain himself.

At supper time we packed away, and I offered her a meal in the restaurant from which the smell of smoked meat had been drifting across to us all day. She thanked me kindly but explained she had to return home to practise; tomorrow she would be leaving on the Fall River Line with the other musicians for a concert tour taking them to Lowell, Bangor, Boston, Nantucket, and New Bedford. Did I have a message for anyone? No, I did not.

Over the following days I grew increasingly indolent, almost broke with no invitations. The effect of the *Herald* article was wearing off and my post card trade languished, the guide languishing too from being unable to tell his story. Outside all was flat calm, but in my head a storm raged. Would anyone ever give me a command?

My courage and ability had been vaunted in the press and around the high society salons, but I was still left to wallow in my little boat in the port's fetid backwaters. I was in hell and could see no way out.

I will sleep all the time until I reach irreducible insomnia. I will not wash. I will become such a tramp that the newspapers will take an interest in me again when they see that the most miserable of hobos is in fact the most famous ship captain. Glory will open its doors for me again. I will be offered the command of the most splendid clipper. I will make my excuses but they will insist; I will hesitate but they will offer me shares. I dreamed I would have to fall as low as possible before I could be recognized again.

My discouragement walked me the length of Chatham Street to the Bowery. Poverty looked at me from every side. The dirtiest jostled with the most wretched. The half-drunk robbed the dead-drunk. No stench could stifle the noses of this army of deserters who no longer knew what they were fleeing from. Flight had become a reflex, an action with no reason.

A missionary overtook me in my ambling walk and stopped to offer me the hospitality of one of the numerous refuges standing side by side all the way to Mulberry Street. Between the Jewish and the Italian quarters, the remnants of society grubbed in the rubbish for a morsel of nourishment before fighting for a place in one of these hotels of misery. A shelter had to be found before two o'clock in the morning, before the police swept the roads and alleys clean with their long maple truncheons. I refused the missionary's charity, preferring to be alone with my disenchantment.

By the time I reached the Bend, it was difficult to distinguish between bundles of rags and clothes still enwrapping some tatter of humanity. I realized I could never be more miserable than these creatures. Nobody sees these people: you try to forget what you saw and pretend you never saw it.

Rage began to gnaw at my disarray.

I kicked an old broken boot out of the gutter. A shrill cry came from it, followed by the bloody rat I had disturbed. I have always hated those vermin. I turned away from the rat's limping flight and prepared to kick the boot again, but suddenly my anger turned to tears. I had just recognized the very kind of boots my father had made in my childhood. I did not have the courage to look for a maker's label. I rushed back to the *Liberdade*.

A letter awaited me there, stamped with the Vanderbilt monogram. It was an invitation to join a select group of excursionists. So that was all the special project was. And as good news never comes singly, the Smithsonian Institute offered to pay me for the transport of the *Liberdade* to Washington and the use of her as an exhibit.

I left the boat in Sydney's care before joining the happy elect the following Sunday. Sydney took care of the transportation and gave me an advance on the calculated revenues. I signed over the payments from the Smithsonian to him with the understanding that he would pay himself back for my advance, the transport, and the postcards. He thought there would still be more to come; for a time I could forget about failure.

The Vanderbilts had had a private railroad built from New York to their Shelburne estate near Burlington on the banks of beautiful Lake Champlain. The luxuriously appointed coaches with their wainscotting, bevelled mirrors, and rich velvet furnishings comforted me. This was where I was meant to be, and destiny had simply made a temporary mistake with my career. The entourage and the admiration and interest of these great people convinced me that fate would correct its mistake in the near future and perhaps even spoil me a little to make up.

When a lady rustled her way across to me to ask about my next command, I replied, "My sailing career has to await the imperatives of my writing career, madam."

"Listen everybody. Do you hear what the brave captain has declared? But the sea will miss you, dear sea dog."

"I only hope my literary activities will not keep me from my oceans for too long."

The Vanderbilt's white train pulled across the calm Vermont farmland, leaving a trail of black smoke from the coal shovelled into its fire by Polish railmen. The valleys of my childhood in Annapolis passed the windows of my mind. I imagined that far valley welcoming back one of its sons a writer. This picnic brought back my confidence and the satisfied feeling that I would soon be gathering the fruits of a fertile labor.

Like the sword, the pen is often taken up with the intention of changing fate. I did not like the route my fate had been following lately, so I had to challenge it to a duel.

I found myself back in Boston with hardly a cent.

Aunt Noémie gave me a room in her house in East Boston. As she was a great gossip, she kept me up to date with the children's activities. I decided not to visit them in this impoverished state, but Victor came to see me from time to time. I was glad to be close to them while the world's influenza epidemic was ravaging New England. I wanted to be there just in case.

At Shelburne, I had elevated myself to the status of writer. Now I had to make it true, but I did not seem able to steer a pen across those featureless white sheets of paper. I diverted myself with a new Oscar Wilde, *The Picture of Dorian Gray*.

All my days were passed dried up before accusing blank sheets dampened only by occasional tears of jealousy at the thought of Mr. Wilde's character. Why could I not be offered the opportunity of a similar compact; why could I not be young, begin again, and make myself a talented writer? I was being sucked down into a vicious whirlpool. I had to start writing to get the image of Dorian Gray out of my mind. I told myself I certainly had a book in me, something worth telling, and that if I could not get it out I would have to remain silent forever. I had hoisted my colors: now I had to produce my painting. Without a ship to command I needed a new identity, but changing from the course I had followed for forty-five years made me panic.

I set to with all the application of an old seaman working at decorating a whale tooth; designing the cover. I sketched the outline of a small sailing boat lost in the fog. I carefully illuminated each letter of the title. I changed the style of calligraphy for my name. I found it too short compared to the title, so added the word "Author" after my name, and then "by" in front. I tried endless variations, never being completely satisfied with the placing of my name and title. I had the feeling of performing a rite that only published writers, that is to say, initiates, knew: that of choosing the jewel box, or coffin, of one's own eternity. On what lay within that cover would depend my perenniality or my condemnation to anonymity. According to the humor of my disarray, I gave more importance to my name or to the title depending on which I thought would carry the other further. The dilemma was reduced when I realized the book would be about me anyway.

When I was finally satisfied with a cover design, I placed it in full view on my desk. The desire to see that cover in bookshops made the ink boil at the nib of my pen. She was like a woman who made me listen long to her clarinet before I took my pleasure.

For two months I wrote every day.

In the afternoons I would go to the library to consult other authors, comparing my own writing to that of the greatest. I did not look to take inspiration from them, only advice. My writing twisted between an account of the *Liberdade*'s voyage and reflections suggested by the events. The more I write, the more I have the feeling that all books are just words in the great book of culture. My memory includes that of all who went before me and committed themselves to paper.

I never received any formal tuition in writing, but I have read, and reading gives me the right to reproduce; that is, I allow myself to use other writer's thoughts but not their style—which is what the whole world does. Once an idea is put out into the world, it becomes communal property. Wanting to be completely original is what had kept my paper blank for so long: I had been paralyzed by the fear of saying something that had already been said before, rejecting all I had ever learned. Even your own book no longer belongs to you once it is published; but it is good to see your own name on the cover.

After all my work, the unforecastable winds and tides of the world's economy came to threaten the publication of my manuscript. The London and New York stock markets were falling in 1890, and selling books at a loss had forced many editors into less noble trades. With the whole of my life wrapped up in my manuscript, the refusal of it was equivalent to a nullification of my existence. Rejection followed rejection, but then destiny in the shape of influenza gave me the opportunity to publish at my own expense. Aunt Noémie died of the fateful disease, leaving in her will a sum sufficient to save my dignity, much to the disgust of the family, who considered my investment a waste of the money.

Standing tall, the dollars in my pocket and the manuscript under my arm, I walked slowly and solemnly to the editors Robinson and Stephenson of Oliver Street. Publishing at your own expense does not mean you have no talent: many great writers had started that way.

My book arrived in time for me to celebrate Independence Day with it. One hundred and seventy-five well-printed pages bound in a strong green cover; and there on the spine, my name.

The economic crises may have halted the sale of books, but it did not stop the critics from commenting on the virtues of what was published. One in particular wrote with an enthusiasm that was useful for me years later. In its July edition, *The Critic* printed Joseph B. Gilder's article, in which he said my true qualities as a captain are undeniable, affectionately referring to me as "this indomitable old seaman":

The Voyage of the Liberdade, a description of a sea journey by Captain Joshua Slocum, is a gripping sea tale, a moving evocation of a seaman's life, written simply in a direct style which does not spoil its humor, poetry and deep insights...the same type of account of a real life adventure as Melville.

In spite of the quality of my book and its author's needs, it did not sell. When the economic situation denies a meritorious captain a suitable command and an author his readers, misery leads on to bitterness. I was tired of having no status. Success should be rewarded by status to satisfy justice.

The book still did not sell.

I used it as a visiting card to show people I was not the nobody appearances might lead them to think I was. Seeing my reflection unexpectedly in a shop front window, I thought I had become Melville or that Melville had come to take me over. At the lowest ebb of my wanderings I spoke of my book as my latest work, a follow-up to *Moby Dick*. I thought of myself as one of his creations, so my book

173

was one of his books really. With the few cents I earned from sales, I moved from one cheap boarding house to another, muttering to myself the words he had given me in New York:

"Captain, you are of a race apart... You are of a race on the verge of extinction, a race of men tempered...the strongest knot is a lashing made without fid, rope, or tar. That magnificent knot is called courage... You are a savage but brotherly race."

Eating a dill pickle, a poem came into my head:

Goodbye to the land, goodbye good times,
For us there is a greater love.
Tie a knot on the past,
Our life is fresh starts.

Whose braid was that reflected in the mirror? Was it him or me who said, "You are eddies in contrary currents...incessant oscillations between monotony and excitement, joy and sadness, calm and agitation, inertia and activity, security and fear, privation and excess."

Ahab, Joshua, Ishmael, Herman, Queequeg, Slocum, Starbuck— I had to remember my lines.

One line haunted me again, but I do not think it was one of my lines; perhaps it was my friend Queequeg?

There, then, he sat, holding that imbecile candle in the heart of that almighty forlornness. There, then, he sat, the sign and symbol of a man without faith, hopelessly holding up hope in the midst of despair.

I bought a smoked herring from a barrow boy, wrapped in a page of yesterday's *Boston Globe*. Sitting on a mooring bollard to chew my herring, I read the greasy sheet. I could not believe it, but there it was: Herman Melville dead. Abandoned, what would happen to me now? Looking up through feeble tears, there was the *Morrissey* putting to sea, perhaps heading for the Bay of Fundy. But what a *Morrissey*, she was only a ghost now, too: not a sail set, not a square foot of canvas in her rigging; she had no rigging to carry it, no masts. Only a haze of smoke hung over her deck: the traitor had turned to steam. On her deck I made out a crew of identical puppets, all dressed the same, all moving in unison. They had their backs to me, but I still recognized their shoulders: they were my grandfather's. Then the hundred grandfathers turned together and they were no longer him, but Melville, Herman Melville!

"Herman! Melville!"

No response. They ignored me. My voice could not carry to where they were. The Melvilles turned their back again and the grandfathers walked away from me.

Everybody had walked away from me, everyone had abandoned me.

I had worked so hard to get out of the ranks of the masses and now I was buried again, imprisoned behind them. Lost: all my buoys, lighthouses, and landmarks had been removed. I was incapable of steering my life without them; I was aground on the reefs. My claims to any identity as a deep-sea sailing captain fought a duel with the reality of my present condition, and reality gave no quarter. Like two rats in a barrel, one would have to kill the other.

Far from receiving a command, I found myself taking orders again—in the depths of a ship, in the depths of a steamer. At the service of steam, muscles knotted, skin black, lungs filled with dust, throat dry, and eyes running, I broke the back of my shame shovelling coal! They called it "Cape Horn berries." Cape Horn!

The hardships I had suffered off Cape Horn seemed like a lost paradise now. If only the roaring forties would whistle through here and clear it of those lumps of petrified death, this filth which greeted the way for progress. If the wind would only come and pirate this ship, I could join her crew and snap my fingers at coal.

A few weeks of this humiliation was all I could take. I went ashore and washed myself clean of coal's grime once and forever. I wanted to see the children, but the new mother had returned to Lowell with them. Only ten years before, I had arrived in New York from the Antipodes in command of a great ship: Captain Slocum arriving triumphant from Hong Kong. Invitations to dinner! Now I could not afford the fare to travel sixty miles to see my children.

Unemployment haunted the streets and alleys of every city in America, and the situation was not much better in Australia where thousands were going to escape starvation here. Bankrupt bankers dishonored accounts, taking even the successful down with them.

I shared the remains of a salt cod and a handful of beans with a type who liked to be known as "Mr. W" for some reason, although his family name was Judson. He spent all his time drawing and redrawing a crazy design, like two snakes covered in teeth, twining and biting at each other. He was convinced it contained the secret of an invention that would make us both rich. Like I was convinced I was a great captain, I thought. In our condition it was imperative to cling to something. He had the advantage over me of hope for the future, whereas I was thinking only of my past. He had spent all his money in Europe trying to patent his great invention, but everybody had laughed at him. It had not shaken his hope though and he was now trying America.

All novelties fascinated him, and he talked to me for hours of the wonders of Europe: the iconoclastic music played by Mr. Satie in a bistro near the Bastille; a sacrilegious painting he had seen of a woman as seductive as any sacred image; a savage from the Pacific islands with a flower behind her ear, painted in colors which challenged nature herself. He rejoiced in the scandal that canvas produced, especially since its painter had been a banker and courtier who had abandoned wife and children for the girl.

He begged me to give him my help to patent his design in the United States of America, but though I found the man sympathetic, his "invention" meant nothing to me. He said his "Eclair" fastener would replace all the buttons in the country, but as far as I could see, buttons worked perfectly well, so why try to change what had already proved its worth?

From my youth I had had sound premonitions, but now my vision seemed to have faded. I had caught the pox of defeat from that filthy coal dust. An insidious illness was settling in my eyes to hide the future from them: they could only look backwards now. Inertia. I whirled around on the spot, trapped in the eddies of my own backwater, unable to see a way out.

Somebody from the White Star Line recognized me, although I do not know how in the condition I had fallen to. I was offered the command of a steamer. I hid behind my sails and refused the commission. Inertia and fear of the new dominated me, not pride. I feared to try in case I should fail. It takes more courage than I had then to risk failure. I could jump for it and save myself from drowning, but I did not dare make the attempt in case I should get my feet wet.

Word passed around that the McKay shipyard was looking for carpenters. At a time when the metalworkers union was threatening a strike, I felt I could find myself again by staying true to my principle of each man for himself and work with that most noble of materials: wood. Manual work distracted me from the abyss of despair, and I was praised for the depth of my mortises. The appetite for life began slowly to return. I straightened my back and threw off the load of inertia, working steadily with the smell of sawdust cleansing my nostrils.

On the tenth day of my convalescence, they started talking to me about the union. Then I was questioned on the church I belonged to. Then it was suggested it would be better if I paid my fifty dollars membership fees and joined the union. I explained to them that the fruit of my work was mine alone and, as they would doubtless remember, being such religious men, the Bible supported me in that view. I was naive enough to tell them that the good quality of my work was the best guarantee for me of continued employment. The discussion became heated. They played their theme of workers' solidarity, even citing the latest Papal encyclical to support their case, but out of context. I did not want solidarity with a bunch of idlers who spent more time talking than working.

I stopped listening to them and continued with my work; continued, that is, until the foreman came to tell me I would do better to stay at home tomorrow and forget about working at McKay's, for the good of everybody.

I remain of the opinion that a workers union ought to aim at accomplishing the best quality work rather than serving the caprices of second-rate wasters. It is by his work that a worker protects his employment and his dignity. This "brotherly" action only proposes mediocrity disguised as solidarity. For refusing to join the ranks of the union movement, I found myself back in the ranks of the unemployed.

I stared at the water in the harbor.

The following weeks are lost to my memory, hidden in a thick fog. My eyes were dimmed by the shame of uselessness: I was useless even to myself. My pride had already been damaged by the discovery that I was not indispensable. To be useless was ceasing to exist; I was a ghost with no feelings of pain or pleasure. I do not know what it was like really: only memory confirms our existence, and as I remember nothing of that time, we might as well say I did not exist.

The first clear sensation of returning to life was the cry of a baby. I saw a mature man with a young wife in a landau. Then came the powerful cry which reawoke a soul wandering in oblivion. Captain Eben Pierce recognized me: it was he who had persuaded me to try the Russian coast fishery when we met in Hong Kong. He was dressed in his best, as if coming from Sunday church. He presented me to his wife and newborn son Jan. The mother calmed her baby while the captain and I walked the length of the quay.

He had no illusions about my condition, understanding the debilitating disgrace uselessness involves. He tried to bring a little dignity to me by talking to me as a fellow captain, discussing our various meetings in North Pacific ports and mentioning various whaling masters out of Bedford. He reminded me of my different commands, and we both lamented the coming of steam. He had become rich in his chosen whale oil trade but never asked how I had come to fall so low.

Arriving back with the now quieted Jan and his mother, Captain Pierce asked me directly if I could do him a favor.

"Me? Do you a favor?"

"Listen young man (he was several years my senior), if you have a little free time, perhaps you could disembarrass me of an old boat which has been dragged ashore on a piece of land of mine at Fairhaven."

"Disembarrass you?"

"Yes, yes. If you can do anything with it, so much the better for you. There are doubtless some good pieces of timber you could sell."

"Yes, probably."

He gave me his card. "Come to the house tomorrow, we will make some arrangement."

The chance of some sort of useful activity cleared my vision and brought my heart back to life. I had no idea what awaited me at Fairhaven, but at least I was going somewhere to do something.

I moved into a small summerhouse near Captain Pierce's house and lived there like a hermit for thirteen months, not lonely at all.

Thirteen months of solitary confinement.

Thirteen months of sarcastic comments from the neighbors.

Thirteen months of patience.

Thirteen months of giving adult dimensions to the model my father had destroyed.

Thirteen months without doubts or lassitude.

Thirteen months of concentration on my last chance.

Thirteen months when poverty was replaced by voluntary hardships.

Thirteen months of giving to my boat everything I could earn in the nearby shipyards.

Some time later, people came to remark on the similarities between my *Spray* and the converted Norwegian herring boat *Gjøa* in which Amundsen finally made the NorthWest Passage: the same chubby bow, the same square stern, the same exceptional destiny. At that time there was nothing exceptional about the *Spray* or her captain, but I felt my destiny to be tied to this boat. My survival depended on hers, so I must save her; I was rebuilding myself, too.

Thirteen months of cutting out all the rot.

Thirteen months of building and shaping fresh with good American oak, recreating something sound. Hammering in the caulking to make us watertight, survivors. I did not save her: we saved each other.

The ever growing astonishment of the increasing number of visitors convinced me I was doing the job right. Retired whaling men from New Bedford brought me their advice—and their envy at my still accomplishing something when they only had their pasts. I understood them well. Their lives were a lament for harpoons which would never taste whale again, sunk in nostalgia for the golden days of whaling and the fortunes they had earned and then wasted on illusory luxury. All the talk was of that still recent past when New Bedford sent out four hundred whalers, when the quays were filled with thousands of barrels of oil, when the owners and captains were disappointed if the profit on a voyage was less than one thousand percent.

Thirteen months during which my heart beat inspiration into my hands: from stumbling block to solution, from fear to audacity, far from the anxiety of emptiness, uselessness, and futility.

Thirteen months of happy labor filling my life.

Thirteen months of celebrating each advance and looking forward to the next day's challenges.

Finally yoked oxen pulled her down towards the water, in the midst of a procession of admirers. The *Spray* laughed in her pride at having beaten fate. Her reprieve was cheered by a crowd of mill workers in French and Portuguese.

She floated like a swan and the crowd drifted off.

The survivor swung her thirty-six feet and nine inches of length, fourteen feet and two inches of beam, and four feet and two inches depth of hold in the passing offal. Would reality soil our dream?

The beautiful pine mast was our Statue of Liberty. I had lived at one with this boat ashore, and now she floated alone, suddenly independent of me and my dreams. A sadness like the "little death" that follows lovemaking filled my heart. She bounced happily at her mooring pile with no sign of gratitude to me. We had reached this point together and now she was satisfied. I would have to start another project with her to bring us together again. It surprised me to find that I seemed to be submitting to her demands. We would see about that. Why had she left me alone now, after I had done so much for her? During the months of work my disarray had dissipated in the healthy fatigue of work. Now the boat was afloat, my dream was accomplished, and I had to find a new one. But I did not have one. I had no ideas at all, and the absence of a dream was rapidly turning into a nightmare.

The children came to visit me from time to time. During the rebuilding these visits had always brought me pleasure. The admiration they showed for my work made it easy for me to respond to them. Now, when I took them out along the coast or in the bay, I felt they were no longer impressed; they remembered far more important ships I had commanded and the perilous adventure of the *Liberdade*.

I decided I would improve the fishing techniques on that coast. That would be something more outstanding. I announced my theories to the world, assuring everyone of the sure success of "Slocum's New Methods." I set myself an objective, something to aim for. I spoke with confidence, but left it to my imagination to work out the details of any real innovation. I tried modifying the shape of the hooks. I experimented with different baits. I fished when the others were in harbor. I was attempting to be different, but I only became a spectacle. I was not talked about, just gossiped over.

The general direction I was taking was right: there was room for improvement in their methods. But I stumbled over the details. I remained a captain, someone above the melee of details who sees the whole picture, more at ease in command than in minute execution. It is true, the rebuilding of the *Spray* had required the working out and completion of details, but that was a sort of rediscovered childhood, a pause in my life. The more old fogeys there were around, the younger I felt, capable of completing a task they mocked. I had wanted to impress them just as I had wanted to impress my father. The construction or reconstruction of a boat is a prolonged activity which becomes incarnate in an object whose beauty and performance can be

180

evaluated—beauty and performance which reflect on the builder. Building a boat is turning a dream into reality. It is, in the end, a dream object, a dream work, a dream accomplished. Ultimately, the reality is like a dream.

My theories and experiments in new fishing techniques suffered a discouraging lack of concretization. I managed to capture the attention of ex-whalers recycled into coastal fishermen with my ideas, but I could not capture the fish with them. Day after day my barrels remained empty. Why did trivial details have to spoil the pleasure of my plan? Nature sardonically stripped me of my rigging.

A boon came then, just in time: a second edition of my book. In spite of the failure of my experiments, I could not feel more at ease. In that milieu, the singularity of being a published author raised curiosity if not admiration. Then I realized that it was foolish of me to try to distinguish myself with fishing amongst fishermen. The key to any success I might have lay in the amalgamation of my two disparate talents. I was a good sailor and my writing was well spoken of, even if it did not sell very well (another detail). My book had been an account of a voyage made under exceptional circumstances. If I should die now, all that would be left of me would be that account; the perenniality of an exploit was only assured by a book.

Having rebuilt the *Spray* with determination and against all the opinions of the experts was not enough. Certainly it had taken courage, but it lacked temerity. Courage commands respect, but temerity quenches the ordinary man's thirst for novelty and adventure.

A letter arrived for me from Boston, from the musician and writer Mabel Wagnalls whom I had met two years before at a New York reception. A letter from a former life, it brought back another aspect of my former life I had almost forgotten: women. She wrote of how upset she was by the death of Mr. Stevenson in Samoa. I had introduced her to his writings when I gave her *Treasure Island* and *The Strange Case of Dr. Jekyll and Mr. Hyde* from the *Liberdade*'s library.

My humor became effervescent, as though I had been given a transfusion of new blood. I closed myself in the *Spray*'s cabin with my letter, completely intoxicated, stunned by the turbulence of feelings which seemed to be dragging me inexorably toward an unknown which was equally seductive and frightening, the dreadful reef of love. I was encircled by an infernal whirlpool of thoughts: I was Stevenson leaving England for daring to love a woman who was not free. The roundelay set Mabel's violin humming: Stevenson going to ruin his health at Hyeres, my own misery on the quays of Boston; scraps of Mabel's deep voice, and Virginia's enigmatic smile, the smells of South Pacific ports, the treatise of the dead writer on books and men. The *Spray* began to creak to the same rhythm as though she were agreeing with me. But agreeing to what, exactly?

What business had I falling in love with this young woman? Nature and the laws of man would have to be set aside. The whole stream of my life was suddenly concentrated in one definite course. I would sail around the world to conquer her. With the wind filling the sails and ruffling Mabel's hair, we would encircle the entire globe in one uniting embrace; slowly, wave by wave, in the intimacy of our small boat. We would audaciously live out a forbidden love and shake to the anger of Nature until we finally overcame it. The whole world would exalt with us. Mabel would transpose the immortality of our happiness into a sublime symphony and I would write the book of our love. The *Spray* creaked her complicity. The calm already invading me was but a precursor of the beatitude promised by this dream.

Instead of my usual long walk, I sat out on the coachroof. I saw the people ashore active around their houses. I saw the shadows of their dreams decaying in the reality of toil. I did not want my dream contaminated by them. I went below and closed the hatch.

In the cabin I abandoned myself to my new dream, embellishing it through that long, sleepless night. In the morning I wrote to Mabel, inviting her to visit me so she could inspect my new boat. Several weeks went by before she could come. I let them go by without me. Like a squirrel I buried stores in every corner of the boat, dreaming of spring even though it was a preparation for winter.

The violin case was the first thing aboard, the same one she had carried in New York. Her legs pressed through her skirt as her stepped across from the row boat which had brought her out. As in New York, the case seemed to be there as a shield to protect her heart. Hair hung down her back in long silky waves, waves to roll me through a night passage. She was more frail than Virginia, her lips less full, but there were the same nut-brown eyes above the same strong cheeks.

"Good day, Miss Mabel. Welcome aboard."

The light in her eyes drew me straight towards the reef.

"Good day, Mr. Slocum. But what am I saying? You're Captain Slocum more than ever now."

"Thank you. Come below and sit down for a moment."

I did not dare show her around the boat just at the moment: I knew I would not be able to even mention my bunk without faltering.

"But you have plenty of room here. The other boat was not this comfortable."

"You had a good journey?"

"There was a lot of us, of course. You know we are playing in New Bedford on Tuesday."

My letter of invitation had been very correct, but I had not expected a reply in the plural. I had seen no announcement of a concert.

"How is your friend Sydney?"

"Well. And your family?"

"You know...the family..."

Mentioning my children and Hettie made me feel as though I was being accused of a crime I had not yet committed.

"Would you like tea?"

"Oh yes, very much. Let me help you."

The *Spray*'s constricted comfort at least mean we would have to come into close contact.

"But why are you clamping the kettle like that?"

"What? Oh, I see, well, a boat can always roll about, so you have to take care."

"Oh, I see."

"You have to keep an eye on things on a boat."

I carried the tea things to the table and back again several times, and each time I passed her, she gave off a scent of fennel and lilac, scents which stirred my memory. I tried to keep the conversation off useless recollections and on boats.

Between practices and concerts she passed most of her free time aboard. Teaching her the working of the boat, she showed the same aptitude with sheets and halyards as Virginia had. I knew that Ginny could never be jealous of Hettie, but with Mabel I was not so sure. But Ginny was on the other side of my life, on the other side of the mountain. Now I had passed the summit and was no longer climbing, just trying to ease the way down.

On the third evening, sailing some miles from the coast, we dropped all the sails and let the sea roll us together. Then that difference in our ages came to separate us again; I could see it coming,

183

reflected in her eyes, but I refused to recognize it. She closed her eyes so as not to see it herself and gave me a smile of absolution.

She went down to the cabin for her violin, returning with it clutched tight in her arms in a way which made me jealous of the thing. She set it vibrating to a melancholy melody as new to me as the feeling of humility that now came over me. The vigor of her vibrato shook her left hand with spasms of passion while the bow in the right searched out notes, ever seeking. She clung to her instrument and music in the same way I had caulked the holes in my own life with this little boat, and with the same passion.

And the same solitude.

We returned under reduced sail and so spun out the day, to fend off the sadness of tomorrow. She confided in me her ambition to become the first female composer of a major work in the West. She was accumulating notes. She promised to include what she had improvised this evening in her first concerto.

She took the helm while I removed a few scratches from the violin case with sandpaper. Putting a polish back on the case, the idea for *Spray*'s future formed itself fully in my mind. The rebuilding of *Spray* had not been a work in itself, but merely the preparation for a work. She was my instrument: now that I had something to play on, I had to produce the work, a sonata in thousands of movements for solo man and small boat.

I told Mabel my thoughts.

"You're right Joshua. And perhaps our two works will be played together one day."

"Mabel, I propose a pact. Look, your case is like new now, take it back and give me the helm."

"Thank you. I prefer it that way."

"You have to write your concerto so the whole world will recognize you as a great woman, and your music will make you immortal."

"And you? You will finish your sonata by making a circumnavigation alone?"

Would the absence of witnesses to my future accomplishments render them useless, non-existent?

"Yes, Mabel. You know, going round the world in the opposite direction to its rotation, I might be able to slow down time."

"That's not necessary, Josh. You won't be too old for me when you get back. The problem now is that I am too young for you. You know that the dreams you keep become prayers, and the prayers you stay faithful to become reality. Your enterprise is a prayer as tenacious as a thousand-year rose."

(Years later Mabel had a book published entitled *The Rosebush of a Thousand Years*, in which she wrote, "Dreams long dwelt on amount to prayers and prayers wrought in faith come true.")

"You have to turn your back on me now, Mabel, and I understand that. But I will go around the world and come face to face with you again."

"Then I will be able to face you properly."

"Is that a pact, Maestro?"

"It's a pact, Captain."

She left us with a present of her book *Miserere*, a musical story she had recently published. Inside the cover she wrote "Wishing you a safe and successful journey," and then, touching my arm, she said: "The *Spray* will come back."

CHAPTER NINE

The Exploit

Seeing another copy of the account of my world voyage on a bookshelf, I am assured that the trip was not made in vain. My name is perpetuated through it. As with my previous book, it tells little of what I felt, though. There is more of that in my diary and the mail I sent and received: recurring themes of the people I have known.

11th. May 1895. All the journalists coming to interview me before my departure interrogate me on the difficulty of survival alone on a small boat. They forget I have been initiated into solitude ashore. Now I prefer my solitude to be on a boat. I am less alone aboard with the memory of Mabel's voice than I was in Hettie's company. Poor Hettie.

The only female effluvium that come to inhabit the *Spray* are those of my dear sister, Virginia, and Mabel. All three are in harmony, applying their gentleness to my wounds. During the day I sail between harsh reminiscences of my father's stern indifference and the hope that my children never see me in that way...

20th. May 1895. I am erasing sad childhood memories one by one. Seeing my childhood haunts again brings them back to be dealt with. I devoted the whole of yesterday afternoon to hunting for the last momento of my childhood: the treasure I hid on the day we left the farm. The barn has been demolished and I had difficulty locating where the old store would have been. Memories are often as deceptive as the people they nourish. Close to doubting myself, I finally found it, much closer to the surface than I expected and surprisingly close to the house too. Perhaps it is because a child's world suffices him that it seems so large, or perhaps it is because his steps are so small.

The lard bucket was rusted and the handle broke as I pulled it from the red soil. I remember I buried it "forever." Only fifty years later I was putting an end to forever. But the lard had faithfully preserved my treasure: the lobster claws, the rusty old knife, a new cent whose provenance I can no longer recall, a pot of mulberry jelly, pieces of the milking stool, and the cup, my cup, the cup Elizabeth filled with warm milk while I looked, the warm milk and Elizabeth's warm body.

My nausea came back. Disintering the treasure of my past, I suddenly felt I had violated Elizabeth's grave. I quickly reburied the lot and fled Wilmot Township, condemned to the present. But the present brings me closer to the future when my exploit will accomplish my new desire for me.

New York. 15th. June 1895

My Dear Captain,

Your Maestro hopes this letter reaches you in Yarmouth before you leave.

My health is good in spite of the periodic cramps you know about. Otherwise no problems. But I cannot choose the time or the place I have these little illnesses. We spoke a lot about that at sea, remember?

I have just read Mr. Mahler's second symphony. I found some of the ideas I wanted to use already there. I am still mad about it.

I have been told that new ideas often come to the surface in different places at the same time. So be careful. Do not lose time, in case your exploit should be pre-empted by another. That would be awful, Captain.

I have thought a lot about what you said when we came back to the coast and you might be right: I might have a tendency to interest myself too much in the totality of your personality to the detriment of certain details which are inevitable in people like us. But it does not surprise that, for your part Captain, you are attracted to one part of my personality. In music, it is the mysterious assembly of connected notes and the secrets of the rhythm that attract and charm. Do you not agree?

5th. July 1895. Between anxiety and the Gulf Stream. I keep crossing the tracks of steam packets and the fog increases the risk of a collision which would be fatal for me. The fog finally lifted today, I even saw the sunset. As it disappeared, I turned towards the east and there on the end of the bowsprit the full moon was rising with its frank face I seemed to recognize from somewhere. "Good evening sir, very pleased to see you again."

From then on I regularly held long conversations with the man in the moon. He always kept my confidences to himself.

8th. July 1895. The fog has cut off conversation between the man in the moon and the man on the sea again. Waves are growing big and I feel more alone. I am plumbing the depths of solitude. There is the boat it is true, but I feel like a small insect clinging to a leaf blown far away from his home.

I am becoming afraid. I know that from the power and precision with which my memory works. The fog cuts off the future and the anger of the sea threatens my present, so my memory takes the helm.

All sorts of events from my past, insignificant or important, large or small, extraordinary or commonplace, come back to me with astounding clarity. Certain episodes I had not thought of for so long return with confusing force. Voices I heard long ago beat at my ears like waves breaking over my head, voices from the four corners of the world...

10th July 1895. Have found how to silence the voices filling the boat. I order my own actions in a loud voice. The defeat of silence diminishes the disquieting affects of isolation. But the ridiculousness of the situation makes me realize again how alone I am.

I will try a new method, singing. I sing every song I know to the wind. My voice always put people to flight before, but the dolphins and turtles do not seem to mind.

The following letter reached me four years after it was posted:

Fayal, the Azores via
St. Pierre-et-Michelon
26th. November 1895

Dear Courageous Captain,
I hope you remember me, Antonio de Pico. I am the one who asked you last year, while you were in our port, to take myself and

my sister to Lisboa. I wanted to tell you we understand why you refused us.

At the time we were upset that you refused us, but after your departure, when the weather was very bad, we no longer regretted not being with you on your boat.

On the second day of the storm my sister found some pieces of a boat on the shore and started to cry as she thought of all your kindness, and you dead at sea. She was very upset and me too but less than her. That is normal for seamen.

I am working now on the Grand Banks and the mate spoke to us about you alone on your boat, which he had met in Gibraltar. I was so happy and wrote to my sister to tell her you were still alive. Thank you for not dying,

Antonio de Pico, your friend.

I was very touched by that letter, but it also recalls a strange episode in my adventure. Goat cheese and plums can sometimes carry you to the borders of reality, or irreality. Who knows if our internal eyes see true? At the time I sent an account to the *Boston Globe* and I mentioned it in my book. Here is the original version from my log:

27th. July 1895. I am still shaken by yesterday's strange event. During the night I started to be attacked by stomach cramps. The wind was already fresh and starting to increase. I needed to reef but the cramps were growing stronger.

I shall just have to put down what I remember. Being clear of land I should have dropped all sail and stayed down in the cabin until I felt better. I am a prudent Captain. But in spite of the gale blowing up I left all sail on. A mistake I can only blame on the cramps. I just balanced the sails and went below where the cramps forced me to collapse on the sole.

I cannot say how long I lay there half-conscious. When I came back to myself I felt the boat pitching into a heavy sea. Glancing out through the hatch I was stupefied to see a man at the helm.

He held her on course with a firm hand. I was completely bewildered by what was happening. He was dressed like a foreign seaman with a big red cap pulled down over one ear. Most of his body was hidden behind a thick, bushy black beard but he seemed familiar; his face reminded me of Captain Kerouac, my first captain, but his hands, they were my father's with the left ring finger missing, cut off when he was working on a piece of sole leather which was too dry.

"Senõr," he said, doffing his cap, "I have not come to do you any harm."

It was true the look in his eyes was a friendly one.

"I have not come to do you any harm. I have sailed much, like you, but I have never been anything worse than a contrabandista. I am one of Christopher Columbus's crew, the pilot of the *Pinta*, and have come to help you. Rest easy, senõr Captain, I will steer your boat tonight."

I thought clearly he must have the Devil in him to carry so much sail in such bad weather. He seemed to read my mind, for he exclaimed:

"The *Pinta* is there in front of us and we have to catch her. We need all sail. *Vale! Vale! Muy Vale!*"

He cut himself a serious-sized quid of tobacco, and once he had worked up some juice, added:

"You were wrong to mix plums and cheese, Captain. You need to be sure of the origin of any cheese you eat. *Quien sabe?* Perhaps it was made with goat milk which would make it capricious."

I could not manage to say a word of reply. Cramped with fear and cramped with pains in my stomach, I lay down where I could in the cabin, on the sole near the hatch, my eyes fixed on my strange visitor. He chuckled and then began to shout a song to the moon:

> *"High are the waves, wild and sparkling.*
> *High is the roaring of the storm.*
> *High the cry of the seagulls.*
> *High are the Azores."*

I prayed he might stop. I was suffering enough already.

Heavy sea broke over the deck but I kept drifting into a delirium where the noise was of grain being poured aboard from a high quay.

When I awoke this morning the *Calentura* was gone. The *Spray*'s deck has been washed so thoroughly by the waves it is as white as shark's teeth. There is no trace of the pilot of the *Pinta* but the boat has kept her course all night. Somebody must have steered...

26th. September 1895. Forty days out of Gibraltar. In a few days or a week at most I will have completed my second crossing alone in *Spray*, but in the Trades this time. The calms of the doldrums have been trying, but I escaped without a hurricane.

I was counting on this crossing to provide me with a moving story to send to the newspaper at home. They said the previous one was a little dull. It is absolutely necessary I find something piquant to arouse their interest or they might want to drop me, making my adventure sterile and pointless. If I recount my private thoughts about life, people, solitude and love—I know it is in fashion amongst writers, but they are people who can be excused for having disorganized lives. I am a Captain and feel I would loose my dignity by baring my soul. So I keep that for my personal log. Only real accomplishments should be proclaimed. The day everybody reveals his passions in public, an epidemic of the soul will start. Our emotions, our sentiments, our ambitions, our desires, our delusions, our feats, and our selfishness will bring out a medieval, contagious purulence. The virtue of our civilization is based on discretion....

2nd. October 1896. Re-reading what I wrote on the danger of promiscuity in human feelings, I am no longer so sure. During this long solitary crossing, which is almost over now, I have met with several steamers. Most make a polite salute but not one has stopped for a conversation. When I was on the big sailing ships it was normal, in the doldrums, to take the time to stop for a gam (my old black cook called it a jam). Then one spent a fair time visiting each other's boats in a climate of brotherhood, sharing libations freely....

5th. October 1895. We are there! The anchor is down in the port of Pernambuco. Half way between Boston and Cape Horn on my route via Gibraltar. My exploit is no longer just a project, a promise nor a boast as some people maintained. The reception I received here proves that. Here at least I am a hero, which helps me to forget my financial situation.

There is nothing waiting for me here from the *Boston Globe* though. I fear my articles might not be good enough. I may be wrong though; for some reason the Brazilians have forwarded my mail to Rio....

6th. November 1895. Arrived in Rio's beautiful bay yesterday. The money I have received from sales of my book in Gibraltar and Pernambuco will be enough for the essential purchases I need to make here. I can laugh at my present poverty because I know the exceptional voyage I am making now constitutes an investment whose dividends will assure me financial security for the rest of my days. Though I have to live parsimoniously now, I am buoyed up by the hope of improving my situation so I am not depressed as I was when wandering uselessly in Boston and New York. The prospect of wealth is sufficient for me to be able to bear my present poverty. There is mail too.

Philadelphia
July 14th. 1895

My Dear Captain,
Your Maestro sends to you two copies of the same letter; one to Gibraltar and the other to Brazil since at the time of writing this missive I no longer know if you have been able to respect the itinerary you left with me.

I am in Philadelphia for a special concert at the French Consulate. The 14th of July is the national festival for these experts in the art of seduction. But do not fear, the mustached diplomats have only profited from my musical talents. Excuse my flippancy, it must be the influence of those frock-coated messieurs' champagne. But it is you I see in the bubbles in my crystal glass.

I am a little jealous of you. It seems to me your exploit is advancing much more quickly than my work on the road to glory. I cut out your articles and preserve them with care. They have even been writing their own articles about your project and past, but you probably know that.

I have thought a lot about our interest in each other. It might be wise if we give the fruit time to ripen. It would be silly to pick an apple while it is still green and lose the pleasure of eating it red and ripe. But I know that famished stomachs demand to be fed. Is that not so Captain?

I have had a completely crazy idea I hardly dare tell you about. Tell me what you think of it. Our destinies will rejoin each other to perpetuate themselves. Let me explain. What if my musical talents join your courageous sailing in an opera? I will compose an opera based on your adventure.

I do not know if it is the musical project itself or what it symbolizes which makes me so excited, but I am full of it.

Does this shock you? Please answer me openly, Captain. I certainly know such an initiative would put your family relationship in peril, that is why you must not hesitate to answer me immediately as to if you approve or not. I will understand if it is no. With regret but I will understand.

You know Captain, more and more people are struggling to live openly what they think and feel secretly, and not only the artists who live without fear of law. But there we are, I think the champagne bubbles are making me a little bold. But surely we are intimate enough to be bold.

All my tender friendship,
Mabel Wagnalls
(in complete harmony)
P.S. I have already been inspired to write one air for the opera: one on the violin, representing my role.

Now I had all the more reason not to think about my present poverty. In the same accumulated correspondence was a letter from my wife.

Lowell, Mass.
30th. June 1895

Hello Joshua,

The papers tell me you are still safe and sound. I am glad about that.

While you are away travelling, life is not so easy for us here. I have to do a lot of dressmaking to repay my family for the kindness they give to myself and your children.

Do you think you will make enough money to send us some soon? In the fall all the family will be going to school and we need to have some money for that. I calculated that you will have to send at least thirty dollars before the summer ends.

I do not talk much about your strange idea of sailing alone for no purpose. Some people say it is better than your doing nothing. But you could have found work here and provided for our needs.

The children say hello. Especially Victor who has finally found a ship. I write this for him because one stamp and one envelope is all we can afford.
Think about us a little,
Your wife Hettie.

I had to take a rest in Montevideo to wash away the cold sweats caused by my stranding on the Uruguay coast. I told the story of that mishap in my book and would rather not even think about it now.

3rd. December 1895. Mabel's clear display of affection (an opera is quite a thing) and the triumphal reception I received in Montevideo have filled my veins with courage again. I know that I am not doing all this for nothing. I will not turn back now.

The Royal Mail Steamship Company has been re-fitting *Spray* for me for nothing. What is more I have been given twenty pounds sterling and an ingenious little stove which will be marvellous in the cold weather awaiting me around Tierra del Fuego.

It has been a great joy to meet my old friend Captain Howard and open my heart to him. Far from New England, conventions and social prejudices do not stand between us here.

Together we sailed up the River Plate towards Buenos Aires. I had not been back there since Virginia's death. I did not know how I would be able to face the anchorage where my sons hoisted the "help" flag recalling me aboard the *Aquidneck* to share Ginny's suffering. I left the navigation to him. I felt sick. My breath was short and I could not co-ordinate my movements. Howard insisted I show him the exact spot we had been anchored and brought the *Spray* up there. I fell into a desperate torpor, unable to feel any emotions, sitting like a statue of myself. Captain Howard made a brave gesture, he put his arm around my shoulder and held me tightly against himself, like a Latin father might take his son. No man had ever dared be that intimate with me. I thought tears would come and wash away my last trace of masculinity, he dominated me so much. But no tears came; instead a gentle smile came to my lips and the wrinkles of my fifty years fell away like breakers after a storm.

I had the feeling the four million Argentinos in the towns around us were basking in my calm. Howard removed his arm. I walked slowly around the boat holding onto any prop which came to my hand.

When I returned, my friend was busy lighting the new stove. I put a hand on each of his shoulders and he stopped moving. Through his shoulders I felt the familiar curves of Virginia in one hand, the promise of Mabel's in the other. I knew, through the fingers clasped firmly on my captain accomplice's shoulders, that Ginny was still with me and she was ready to accept Mabel too. Hettie could stay in Lowell.

Suddenly I had a huge appetite, as if I needed to feed all these people in my head too. While my friend tended the first I set to making a memorable fish chowder, a wedding feast for all my companions. Consolidating my intense happiness I arranged morsels of pork in alternate layers with slices of onion in the bottom of the pot. It all curled up into smiles on the slow fire. Then came a bed of potatoes to receive the fish. A libation of salt and pepper to make peace with this region of suffering. I sang a song to each layer as it went into the pot. We both laughed as I poured thick cream over the lot. Howard prepared the croutons—broken ship's biscuits. Then we left the happy pot to stew slowly and prepared the table in the cockpit....

20th. February 1896. Fifty-two today.

The *pamperos*, winds cruel as fate, force me to heave to off Cape Froward, the most southerly point of South American mainland. Cape Horn lays ahead. I feel this bad weather is going to continue, another initiatory ritual. Gale after gale, I brace myself with the knowledge that each one I overcome makes me more fit for the next. At the end of all this initiation I should find a treasure of serenity, then I should be able to vanquish fear of myself, of other people's opinions and of Nature's bad humors, like this solitary seagull who has decided to differentiate himself from the flock by daring to go higher and further, by braving the winds the others fear. He is on my deck now, sheltering from the storm with me. He has certainly earned the pieces of ship's biscuit I feed him. A gesture of solidarity. The other gulls who prefer the gregarious security of the cliff will never know the taste of that biscuit. My marginal gull has initiated himself into superior pleasure, but he knows he has to pay the price.

On this day of my fifty-second birthday, I take a close look at my past. Each time I have had to face a fear and overcome it, I have succeeded through my differences.

As a child I was ready to renege on my masculine role to the extent of taking pleasure in typically feminine household tasks to obtain Elizabeth's particular affection. The warm milk of our complicity left me with no feelings of guilt. Perhaps our attitude to each other did not conform to social norms, but I managed to remove all fear of losing her love.

It was daring to sneak behind my mother's half-open door that enabled me to overcome fear of the female body.

In Westport I disobeyed my parents' orders, to lead my gang on daring adventures which taught me about courage and failure.

If I had obeyed my father I would not have had the advantage of overcoming the normal fears of leaving familiar surroundings.

All my life I feared not being equal to the ability I claimed for myself, but I never let it show. Without that difference of behavior to the other young seamen, I would never have been able to climb the ladder of marine hierarchy so fast.

I still remember the sound of a clarinet in San Francisco, my way of overcoming the fear Mr. Hearst caused over being attracted to his wife. Hatching my nascent sexuality between impious legs. There I learned the difference between desire and love. No woman is unique when it is just a matter of desire. With love they become indispensable, for a while.

When I put flight to the fear of having a woman on a ship, I acquired a difference which most other captains envied: a life of daily love in the midst of maritime accomplishments. They had to feed their desires with memories of home or expensive contacts of the type which can be made in every port.

All my commercial successes are attributable to that difference in me which allows me to suppress the fears caused by earlier failure.

My failures have mainly been due to the opposite of difference. When I have too much fear to dare to be different, then banality fails me. When I had fear of solitude after Virginia's death, I precipitated myself into the commonplace by marrying the first pretty creature I found. That was a test I failed. The solitude continued as a punishment for my lack of originality.

This boat, carrying me around the world towards the consecration of all my differences, even though we are full of fear of what lies ahead, would still be rotting in Fairhaven if I had not overcome the fear of ridicule when everyone mocked me during the early months.

And the voyage of the *Liberdade*—it had been necessary to overcome my own and my family's fears to turn that into a success.

I still fear Cape Horn, the Pacific, the Indian Ocean, iron and steam. I fear Mabel's youth and talent. Have my differences carried me as far as they can? And if I fail in this last chance to prove I am exceptional?

The wind is dropping at last. Excuse me seagull, I need to hoist the foresail.

Two months later after difficulties enough to make anyone give up, I cleared the Strait of Magellan. Many people remember that part of my tale.

Greenwich, England

Three passages of the Magellan Straits will never fall from memory.

The first is its discoverer's.

The second is Francis Drake's. He travelled the whole length of the Straits without any charts in six days.

The third is Captain Slocum's which, from a strictly maritime point of view, is considered the most remarkable.

W.S. Barclay, geographer
New York 1939

Passing Big Borgia, or Despair Island, we contemplated the virgin world of sharp mountains, glaciered peaks and terrifying rocks which struck Magellan's eye.

I disembarked at a small bay which is the famous spot where for years passing ships have kept the custom of leaving their visiting card in the form of boards painted with their names and the date of their anchoring.

Many are rotting, but amongst them is the name of Captain Slocum's brave little *Spray*. A man of different temper to all others.

Felix Riesenberg.

4th. May 1896. I have written nothing since I doubled Cape Pillar to clear South America on the tenth of April.

I want to make the maximum of notes before going back to the sea for the long period of solitude which will take us to Tahiti.

This evening is my last at anchor on Robinson Crusoe's island, Juan Fernandez.

For fifteen days and nights the Pacific did all it could to hide its treasure from me behind contrary winds and currents, roaring its disapproval of my chosen destination. My morale suffered almost as much as the sails, both needing constant repairing.

Long will I remember the relief with which I humbly greeted the blue mountains of Juan Fernandez appearing over the horizon. They hid their peaks from me in the clouds, but I still bowed to their feet. You can laugh at Oriental salaaming, but sometimes protestation is the only adequate expression of respect.

The wind finally moderated just before nightfall, leaving *Spray* just a few miles short of the anchorage. There was a faint flow from the settlement at the bottom of the bay and I sent a shot echoing around the cliffs in the hope of raising a tow but no response came. All night I sat in the calm listening to waves breaking on the rocks with no means of getting myself clear.

Just before dawn a boat pulled out from the village. There were six oarsmen in the boat and I could see they pulled real oars on thole pins. They moved together like well trained seamen. I deduced from this that I had met with civilized people again, nothing to do with the Fuegians who had tried to attack me a few weeks ago.

Their leader—his companions called him "El Rey"—spoke English. All the rest seemed quite content with Spanish. I felt more than the simple joy of reaching land—they had all heard of the *Spray*'s voyage from the Valparaiso newspaper and were eager to hear my news. For weeks I had been a nothing at the mercy of the whimsical humor of that tyrant the Pacific. Now suddenly I was the center of the world, albeit the rather small world of Juan Fernandez. The island was long famous for being where the English sailor Selkirk had been thrown ashore. His adventure on the then deserted island had been the inspiration for Daniel Defoe.

My visitors climbed aboard to give the *Spray* and me a respectful inspection. I made them coffee and doughnuts, something they welcomed as a great treat. Finally they took us in tow and worked us in to the anchorage.

I soon learned that the "king" was given this courtesy title by his subjects on the basis of having lived there longer than anyone else—thirty years. Once the anchor was down I was inveigled into producing another batch of doughnuts while my visitors told me something of the island and its history. The governor, it seemed, was a descendant of the Swedish nobility and his daughter entertained herself by riding the island's wild goats, a feat I thought impossible until I saw it for myself.

The "king" told me he was native of the Azores but had learned his English during many years of travel. He had even commanded a whaler out of New Bedford, so we had many common themes to talk about. He had married his Carioca and brought her to settle here; now she lay in the gothic splendor of the mountain peaks he could leave no more for he could not take her with him.

The tremendous success of my doughnuts was made understandable when I learned the only meat on the island was wild goat, so they were forced to eat very lean normally. The suet in my mix was a luxury to them. As I had a more than ample provisions, I saw the opportunity of making a little business. I hung a scale under the boom and started a brisk trade. Before nightfall every household on the island was equipped with the makings and receipe for Slocum's doughnuts.

That trade actually turned out to be more profitable than I expected. I did not ask much for my suet, but they paid me in old coins from a galleon sunk in the bay. I carried away all sorts of coins from my "Treasure Island" that sold for unexpectedly large sums over the years. The islanders had filled my purse but I was able to give them a pleasure they would certainly miss once their supplies of my suet were consumed. I have always found it difficult to establish a fair balance between the legitimate enjoyment of a profit and the suffering inflicted by a one-sided deal. One man's profit becomes another man's pain, like cause and effect—an effect, it would be good to see removed from human life. It seems impossible to gain without stealing from someone; arguing for the necessity of trade does not remove the discomfort.

I can scarcely describe the beauty of this island with its fertile valleys fed by crystal streams. Many of the calamities which pollute the mainland are unknown here: beer, rum, police and lawyers, for example. The only fashion in clothing is that they be comfortable. There is no doctor, but health laughs out from every face.

Why did Selkirk leave this island, I ask myself. For the same reason I will: the pursuit of a goal.

All forty-five residents have given me the honor of an invitation to their houses, built from flotsam and the remains of a ship driven on the coast. King Manuel Carroza's resembles a pinnace, its one door furnished with a brightly polished copper knocker. A huge flagpole stands guard before the entrance, alongside his pretty whale boat painted red and blue.

The day before yesterday I made the pilgrimage to Selkirk's lookout at the summit of one of the mountains. There he spent many a long day watching for the ship he was sure would be sent to rescue him. There is a commemorative plaque:

"In memory of Alexander Selkirk, seaman. Born at Largo in the county of Fife, who lived on this island in complete solitude for four years and three months. He was cast ashore here in 1704 by the wreck of the *Cinque Ports*, of 96 tons, 18 cannons, to whose crew he belonged, and was rescued by Drake the 12th February, 1709. He died lieutenant aboard Her Majesty's Ship *Weymouth* in 1723 at the age of 47 years. This plaque has been erected close to Selkirk's lookout by Commodore Powell and the officers of Her Majesty's Ship *Topaze* in the year of 1868."

Where in the world will they erect a plaque carrying my name and for what reason? And why do those who erect historic plaques give themselves as much importance on them as the hero's to whom they are dedicated?

I also visited the cave Selkirk lived in. It is still dry and habitable. It is situated in a splendid sheltered position little frequented, in the shadow of the majestic mountain protecting it from the sea's storms. The island is fourteen miles long by eight wide. It belongs to Chile despite the three hundred and forty miles which separate them. Chile had once used it as a prison island and the caves, used as cells, can still be seen.

I leave tomorrow.

I must leave tomorrow.

But how sad to have to tear myself away from these present joys. The children, all the children, came down to the boat at dawn to take me to gather wild fruit for my stores. We found quince, peaches and figs, the children filling a pannier of each for me. I would give anything to be able to participate in those children's pure enjoyment of life. All their lives they have heard only Spanish, so any word of English releases cascades of laughter which climb and run around the mountains like wild goats. What they do not know gives them no fear, it makes them laugh. If I could only laugh at the unknowns which await me.

A beauty from the island has made me a new foresail. I would like to be rolled up in it with her. The spice of her skin and the sweet smell of the fruits have revived appetites in me which will only be an embarrassment at sea. I will definitely leave tomorrow, Mabel.

5th. May 1896. The "king" has just left after watching my last night with me. He told me the beauty who sewed my sail was the first child ever born on this island, a fitting reply by man to the island's own beauty. I say goodbye to her paradise and hoist my sails in pursuit of my own....

24th. June 1896. For more than a week I have thought of nothing but my arrival at the Marquesas. My forty days at sea since Juan Fernandez have whetted my appetite for life and emphasized my solitude.

The hero sat and looked with equanimity at the waves breaking all around Nukuhiva, waves which would not be wetting me for a while, now that I was at anchor inside this great horseshoe almost ten miles in circumference with two islets guarding the entrance. A door to paradise, but an earthly paradise which has to be carefully cultivated before it will bear fruit. I learned here that constant weeding is necessary to protect one's happiness from indolence, chronic ill-nesses, dependence, religion, and insular envy. Waves of depression threaten to overwhelm a solitary on his motley quest. Creeping idleness is the hardest weed to uproot.

The small port swarmed with vagabonds toadying to the authorities, all fat and drunk on palm wine. The women hid in the shade, giggling amongst themselves.

The civil servants seemed to be fighting to overcome their boredom by producing reams of useless paperwork, or perhaps they wanted to be revenged on the world for being posted so far from their beloved metropolis. My arrival made the locals greedy for what I might bring them and the officials bitter because I was able to leave. They took great pleasure in informing me I should have gone to Tahiti first to obtain a permit, as everybody surely knew. They laughed at the strangeness of my foreign ways (that is, non-French ways): my clothes, my language, my American nationality, my inexplicable solitude, my ignorance of local regulations; in brief, I must weigh anchor right away.

A sorry-looking fellow with sharp features and European manners discretely hinted to me that if I could give him a lift he would show me a bay on the other side of the island where there were no officials to cause problems. We loaded up his carefully tied parcels and slipped quietly out of the bay.

Throughout the passage he spoke little, but when he did it was in astonishingly genteel English. His ways both disturbed and fascinated me. He was filled with either chronic pain or well contained violence, I could not tell which. From his mouth muttered maledictions, and his eyes sent out a call of distress each time they swung my way. Constantly fiddling with an old pocket knife, he had whittled the butt of one dinghy oar into a tiki by the time we arrived at Taiohae Bay.

He had been correct, there was no sign of an official there.

During my short stay in Taiohae valley, I completely forgot the outside world, caught as I was in the spell of an all-sufficient present. The whole valley was wrapped in the calm of a dream. The people rested in the cool of the river bank, waiting for the coconuts to fall from the trees and roll down the steep hills to them. Life was carnal in this land of flesh. Her Majesty Flesh was served in every way not requiring too much effort. She was rested, fed, oiled, cooled, caressed, loved, tattooed, soothed. She was propitiated with incense of sandalwood ground in palm oil, offered bananas, and lobster in coco-milk. It was an endless orgiastic banquet, an enjoyment of every moment, but always quietly, without excess, perfecting the enjoyment of the body by sharing it with everyone.

My passenger explained to me that officials never came across the mountains to inspect the village of Taipi. Maoris occasionally came on their little white ponies to trade or look for a wife, but the locals enjoyed a reputation of cannibalism and the officials were too fearful to follow the same route.

The softening idleness of the valley must have worked its way into my brain, because it was not until I had left that I made the connection with my hero Melville's novel. That was why it had all seemed to be so familiar.

Some months later a letter reached me from my vagabond passenger:

Do you remember the devil you carried to paradise, Mr. Hero Slocum? I salute the exploit which united with my misery for a few days. As you are now famous, I know you must certainly be rich. I find myself in the nadir of glory and at the end of my savings.

As I write to you there are coconuts and banana trees before me. Everything is green. Do you remember those bright points of red, the hibiscus, mixed in with that green? But you should see the big patches of blue: not the sea, but the mountains in the background, so high they threaten to crush us. Little Vaitani whom you know so well is bathing in the river at the moment. That little bisexual is always so cheerful. She has the fullest breasts imaginable, inviting you to come and lay in their shade. She is dressed only in the bronze of her tan and the velvet of her hair.

Things have changed here in the valley; the police have planted their filthy boots here. If one of them should see Vaitani now, he would slap an indictment on her for offending their stinking public morality in the person of himself.

Police in the colonies are like excrement on a banquet table.

Contrary to you, glorious Captain, the little, dearly bought fame I had has been usurped by jackal profiteers with no taste. My health is exhausted by my poverty, so I allow myself to offer you the opportunity to relieve my misery somewhat. I have several canvases which would doubtless interest some of your American compatriots since their appurtenance to the New World saves them from the European prejudices now precipitating me towards a most painful death.

But before I hasten my departure, I have painted a canvas which has taken me a whole month, day and night. I tell you honestly I will never paint such a canvas again; all my remaining strength has gone into this one. I offer it to you for a sum I allow your American generosity to decide upon. You can also let me know if any of your friends are interested in my work.

The one I offer to you particularly is a large canvas. The two top corners are chrome yellow, with the title on the left and my signature on the right like frescoes on a gold wall. To the right and low down a baby sleeps, then three kneeling women. Two figures in purple regard their reflections. An enormous figure, in spite of perspective, squats with hands raised in the air and watches astonished as these two dare to think about their destiny. The figure in the centre picks a fruit; two cats near the child; a white goat. The idol with arms mysteriously raised seems to indicate the beyond. The squatting figure listens to the idol. An old woman on the verge of death accepts it, resigns herself. At her feet a strange white bird holds a lizard in its claws, the uselessness of vain words. All of this passes near a stream you know well—you remember, the one at the end of the clearing? In the background are the sea and the mountains of the next island, all in tones of blue and green. The figures stand out in orange.

I have called it, 'Where do we come from, where are we, where will we go?'

I will never paint such a tableau again.

With my best regards, I remain an admirer of your exploit and ask you in turn to recognize mine. More so since I suffer natural, artistic and social torments. But we are of the same breed, the same durable wood.

Paul Gaugin

P.S. Send me the money with the least possible delay, I will forward the canvas as soon as I receive your rescuing payment.

It was unfortunate for both of us that fame had failed to bring me any pecuniary reward by that time.

17th. July 1896. Apia, Samoa. Arrived at Stevenson's island yesterday. I have venerated him for so long but he died before I could meet him.

I must say I am not doing very much, and my idleness has nothing to do with recovering from the thirty days of good sailing which brought me here. Good sailing but several brushes with whales I did not like. Mabel knew I expected to collect mail here but there is nothing from her.

For a month dodging coral reefs I have imagined that letter

waiting here for me. I can face storms, sharks and monotony if she is waiting, but with nobody waiting I go nowhere.

This morning a funeral went down the river. All the mourners cried honestly, in silent sadness. The dead man was surrounded by love. Did he know that when he was alive? Some times when life is difficult, it would be good to profit from all that love which only appears too late. Is it better to live in an emotional desert or to be buried in love?

With the new steamers, mail should not be late arriving. Perhaps Mabel forgets to support my work in the excitement of her own, yet I never miss one occasion to send her news and reiterate ever more openly the fascination she is for me. I certainly left her to make this trip, but that was only so I could find her again back at the starting point.

Not one word.

18th. July 1896. Still nothing.

I feel more alone than at sea. I dreamed of funerals all night. The *Spray* was made of porphyry with her rigging in copper and gold. I stood embalmed at the helm, dressed in the Captain's uniform I had made in Hong Kong after buying the *Northern Light*. The apparition attracted crowds as it floated down the Potomac. A fast steam launch circled the boat. The people in it were agitated, some laughing nervously. Some made great signs with upraised arms to the crowd as though conducting the lamentations. I could not recognize them, the boat moved too fast and I could not turn to look. My children were brought out (they trailed a model boat behind the launch), but they struggled to escape the sarcophagus. The next launch brought my sister Elizabeth and Hettie. Hettie tried to call to me but the seamen stopped her. Suddenly Elizabeth was white with consumption; she laughed and plunged into the black water. A rainbow of orange and gold reached from shore to boat with Ginny walking and smiling as if all were normal. She kissed me and then went down into the cabin. Soon the smell of cod pie reached my nose. She came back to my side whistling an air I knew well, but formerly I had heard it played on a clarinet. From behind me she picked up a violin case and placed it on the coachroof. Then she plunged into the darkness of the water too.

The wind started to blow stronger, phosphorescent waves growing higher. My floating coffin stayed steady, unmoved by the seas. The violin case opened and the wind whipped away the tiara of flowers with which it was filled to reveal Mabel sitting in the bottom. Salt rain fell from the storm clouds, filling the violin case. And Mabel could not swim! I wanted to carve the tiller with my knife but I could not move. Then Mabel was sailing ashore in her violin case.

The storm grew worse, with great rolls of thunder. Suddenly I could move and the thunder was reduced to somebody knocking on the hull. I was still trembling when I stepped out on deck.

The visitor supplied the counterweight of fame to help re-establish my inner equilibrium. No news is worse than bad news sometimes. Some certainty to remove my anxiety; lack of news was unbalancing me. My visitor, Fanny Stevenson, was the living souvenir of the author I had read with such pleasure. She had been his companion, now she was as devoted to the memory of her dead husband as she had been to his person when he was alive.

She invited me to her home in Vailima to relax in the past owner's furniture. Her admiration for my exploit made me forget temporarily the sadness of my epistolary silence. Often in her conversation about the great man, she repeated the phrase: "Our tastes were the same...our tastes were the same."

In Samoa my name was never recorded at the post office as a receiver of foreign mail. On my departure, Mrs. Stevenson gave me four beautifully bound volumes of sailing directions for the Mediterranean with the following inscription inside the cover of the first:

To Captain Slocum,
    These volumes were read and re-read by my husband and I am certain he would be happy to know they are in the hands of one of the travellers of the sea he esteemed above all others.

I left Samoa, taking my nightmare with me. I had put off departure until the very end of the favorable season, in case a letter should arrive late. The medicine of fame conferred on me by famous people had not cured the vertigo caused by uncertainty but it had eased the symptoms. Anyway, in Australia, surely, I thought.

In Australia they had two telegrams.

27th. November 1896. Two months in Sydney already. Two

months of illness and cures. My health worries me. I lack tone and am frequently subject to heavy headaches. Two months of discord caused by the ambiguity of the letter I finally received from Mabel and memories of my engagement to Virginia. Everything in this city, and especially Manly Bay, reminds me of the confident audacity of our desires. I have met with several members of the Walker family and they have been very kind to me.

I am also troubled by the attempts of a seaman called Slater, whom I had disciplined on the *Northern Light*, to discredit me once more. Most of the population admired me, but this ignoble individual seeks to tarnish me again. He has brought up the old story again and twisted the reality of events to his own advantage. I continue to ignore the presses' questions on those sordid events.

I have to write Mabel to tell her my work is bringing dividends even before it is complete. The Australian journalists know about me now and most are printing favorable reports of my exploits in spite of Slater's troublemaking. What I am hoping is that the public will remember me.

Sydney
2nd. December 1896

To the phantom who haunts the boat and the dreams of Captain Joshua, the too-discrete musician Mabel,

I hope you received my last letter with list of expected stages for the rest of my voyage and likely times of my stops. Just in case, I will enclose a copy with this letter.

You doubtless remember what I told you of the happiness I knew with my first wife, Virginia. I must tell you sincerely that you too have become an important part of my happiness. Here in Sydney, Virginia and I spent so much time together before our two lives were married into one. Now I see again the places where we told each other of our hopes and I feel an overwhelming need to relive those promises for the future with you. I expect you will find it somewhat indecent for me to avow a feeling you might not necessarily return, but I do not want anything to happen to me without you knowing my heart. I believe we could make a duo to sing our lives with complete harmony in a naturally pure key.

Re. the newspaper clippings you enclosed with your short letter regarding this Scandinavian chemist who has left his fortune for prizes for all important human activities, can you find out if music and seamanship are included in those activities?

I have tried to find somebody here who knows this new work you are playing with the New York Philharmonic but nobody in the Australian musical world seems to have heard of a composer called Zarathustra.

I want you to know I feel a certain pride, which I hope to hear reflected in your music soon, at being followed by journalists and cheered by crowds. People pushing to look at me helps me to forget my internal turmoil.

I enclose some clippings. They are to assure you of the importance of your friend Joshua, so you may keep them. One day we can collect them together in a big album, one page for articles on your music and the next for those on my exploits and, I hope, my writing. These come from the *Sydney Daily Telegraph* and the *Sydney Morning Herald*:

Reception for Captain Slocum
The *Spray* towed in to port.
Welcoming address.

Sydney. For this occasion a welcoming committee rented the steamer *Minerva*. She left Circular Quay with one hundred and thirty aboard to cross Sydney Harbor and head to North Harbor where the celebrated *Spray* is anchored. The Captain was on board and responded to the acclamations by saluting with his flag, a tradition many of our yachtsmen would do well to recall.

We were permitted to attend the official reception ceremony. The Captain came aboard the *Minerva* where he was acclaimed with unreserved enthusiasm (contrary to certain rumors). Our co-citizen F.B. Evans, elegant as ever, made an eloquent speech.

In substance he declared: "In the name of everybody assembled on the boat, all the others who dearly wished to be here and the whole of Australia, I wish the most cordial welcome to the intrepid Captain Slocum. And it is not solely in his capacity as an exceptional seaman that I say this in everyone's name, but also in his capacity as an American par excellence." The crowd joined Mr. Evans in clamorous applause.

A shield and telescope were presented to the Captain who responded in substance: "I express thanks for the reception you have given me. I hope to satisfy anyone who only knows of me by the lies I am told a certain individual is spreading in the newspapers. But your very presence reassures me of your confidence. I have not come all the way to Australia to be welcomed by the injustice of his silly talk." Once more the crowd were unsparing in their applause. The Captain concluded by praising from the bottom of his heart the generosity they had shown.

Another launch passed close to the *Minerva* during the ceremony crowded with passengers who saluted me by waving their arms and shouting several loud hurrahs. But bad faith and calumny is to be found in journalists too, unfortunately. Read this other clipping's false account of an event which was entirely favorable to me.

The Johnstone Bay Sailing Club specially chartered the *Lady Manning* to follow yesterday's regatta, carried away once again this year by the yachtsman V.T. Appelbaum jnr., who declared at the end of the race that he still could not understand why Baron Coubertin had not included sailing amongst the disciplines being revived in Greece.

At the end of the regatta, the steamer went to Bradley to allow the passengers a sight of the *Spray*. As it passed a little distance from the *Minerva*, where a pseudo-official reception committee was gathered, the *Minerva* induced the *Lady Manning* passengers to call hurrah in honor of this Captain Slocum, concerning whom one of our valiant police, once a seaman serving under this individual, has denounced for sordid behavior in this newspaper recently.

One remembers the accusations of unjustified cruelty in his testimony. The self-styled "hero" Slocum has still not deigned to reply to those accusations and continues to ignore our reporter's questions on the subject. The *Lady Manning*'s passengers remained silent. On the *Minerva*'s bridge a member of the committee called out, "And now, Belmain people, three cheers for Captain Slocum."

This untimely appeal released several hostile demonstrations aboard the *Lady Manning*. A second appeal only accentuated the boos, and in spite of the acclamations shouted by the people aboard the *Minerva*, they could not overcome the cries of reprobation.

The truth is that any few signs of reserve were expressed by polite silence.

Let me finish by recounting an episode which reveals in a tangible way the admiration I receive without dwelling on this jealous gossip by certain malcontents in the gutter press. I had explained publicly how my sails were ripped off Cape Horn and the difficulties I had in repairing them and re-rigging the *Spray*. A few days later, a new suit of sails was delivered on board, a present from Mr. Mark Foy, the respected proprietor of Australian stores and Commodore of a yacht club.

Though these testimonies might help me to support the absence of a response to the questions I ask as regards your disposition towards me, they cannot replace you. I suspect *Spray*'s compass of following the one you have installed in my heart.

Your Joshua Slocum

P.S. They have raised the maximum speed for motorized vehicles to fifteen miles per hour in Australia now—real calamity.

I spent a large part of the southern summer in Australia and Tasmania. It was from there that I wrote to my son Victor, asking him to circulate the letter among the other children.

Dear Victor,

There are things a father must tell his children to help them with their lives and to ensure that they understand his. It would be in vain to attempt to follow the course your father has taken if you do not know where he is headed and why. You have all sailed enough to understand that.

All around me in this paradise called Tasmania I see many happy families. I cannot hide from you that I envy the fathers surrounded by devoted children—like you perhaps envy the children you know who are fortunate enough to have a rich and attentive father. But how many do you know who have a famous father, because I am becoming one.

If you could see the crowds who come to hear my lectures you would be proud of your absent father. I ornament my expositions with magic lantern images of the stages of my solitary tour of the world, and this new process brings great success. If I manage to go right to the end of this exploit, we will throw ourselves into a Great

American Tour with this type of lecture/spectacle. Be assured, it works very well. We could even take a musician with us to entertain the audience during pauses. Your father knows that times have been hard for you over the last few years. Papa knows. But I am less responsible for that than people probably lead you to think. Remember, if you do not behave like everyone else, you are made into a black sheep. Do not refrain from replying to your father's detractors that he is surpassing all the other fathers in the world and the glory he is being drenched in in the world's most dangerous seas will bring all of you a fortune which will make all of you powerful, respected and envied citizens. You need not be ashamed of your father as you may have been tempted to be.

You must understand that your father has acted with dignity all his life in a trade which is being inexorably soiled by steam. My present boat does not have the stature of our old ships, my sails cast less shade, but I have stayed faithful to the wind, the wind which has carried us to the four corners of the world.

Leaving you for so long does not make me unfaithful to you; on the contrary, I have kept the family's dignity intact for all of you by investing my efforts, my pains, my perils, my solitude in the pursuit of the assured ease of a fame which is no longer a distant prospect. While I write now I am already beginning to gather the fruits. Understand your father's feelings.

For several years you have suffered from my absence. They have been hard years for me too. But you will gain by it in the long term. When I have left this world, my memory will stay with you for as long as you live and you will grow old passing it on to your grand-children. For a long time hence it will be an advantage to be born with the name Slocum. Remember that when you doubt your father's actions. And tell yourself that all trace of your friends' fathers will have disappeared as soon as their wake is over.

Another thing I want to tell you: a father is not always destined to be there every day to educate the young who become educators in their turn—sometimes the vicious circle of apprenticeship has to be broken while something new is accomplished.

Not all fathers have the same destiny. But your father's is almost accomplished. If the reward for my effort comes in time for the 1900 Paris Exposition, you will be able to meet the children of a painter I met in the Marquesas who share in fame as you will.

Do not forget there is a time to learn, to know and to teach, but it is also necessary to act. That is the way for all humanity. And remember the order of those steps is not always the same.
I would prefer to be able to tell you all of this face to face.

Do not listen to the evil gossipers; they are either jealous or mediocre, two calamities you must strive to avoid.

Have sufficient confidence in me to regard the years of my absence as a necessary sacrifice so we can escape foundering in banality.

More your father than you think,

J. Slocum.

It was long after I died before my children came to understand the real meaning of those words.

Victor had grown old in turn by the time he received this letter from an old Australian who was only a nipper when I gave my first lecture.

Launceston, Tasmania

Mr. Victor Slocum,

I must tell you I have all your illustrious father's books and that they occupy pride of place in my house.

I must tell you I knew your father well. My friends encourage me to write to you all the details of his visit here which remain in my old memory. They may be of use to you. My friends think so and I agree with them.

I remember the arrival of your father's little boat at the mouth of the River Tamar caused quite a stir in our town of Launceston. I can tell you it was the pilot station at Low Head that told us the news that the Captain wanted to ascend the forty-four miles of river to our town.

I believe that every one of the twenty thousand souls in our beautiful town were looking out for the arrival of the Yankee skipper. He ascended the whole river without a pilot. That takes plenty of nerve. I have seen many ships go aground in our beautiful river, because the ebb tide can reach eight knots.

During the week he stayed here, your father allowed people to visit his boat if they paid a fee. You may not believe it, but long queues formed to have a close look. Not only did the skipper open the boat to the curious, but he also gave public lectures to tell us all of his remarkable exploits. I managed to sneak in to all of them. Please forgive me, but I did not have the money.

There is no need to tell you that for us young children this was a wonder, to be so close to danger. It seems funny to be telling you all this so many years later. I was sulky with my father for weeks later because I wanted to be Slocum's son. I hope you can excuse me for that now.

Sitting writing to you, some other details come back to my mind. I remember your father was always very kind to us children. He showed us his route in our school atlas and told all the details of his adventure in the Straits of Magellan. I still remember the softness of his voice when he told us that he never felt alone and that when he was at sea he went to bed without fear, counting entirely on the boat. He spoke to us about the peace of the great oceans. One night he ended his tale on a serious note: he told us to become so admirable that our parents would praise us. I finally understood what he was saying long afterwards when my own children had grown up in their turn.

I must tell you that this Yankee with his acid humor was the only hero we had ever come close to. Before he left, we decided to make him a gift in keeping with our veneration. We made a tour of all our mothers, aunts and cousins, begging them to supply the *Spray* with as much jam and jelly as we could poach. Your father certainly had a feast for a long time.

If I manage to remember any more details, I will write to you, and if you have any questions to ask me you only have to write and I will reply immediately.

Good wishes,
Burford Sampson

I do not remember which one of the children this Mr. Sampson was, but I do know that if I had been able to stop my voyage and settle somewhere it would have been Tasmania. The country is splendid and the people honest and cheerful. A Scottish lady lent me rooms for my first lecture. There was a gentleman who had been a travelling speaker for years and his advice was most useful when I first had to expose myself to an audience. I never stopped feeling ill at ease before starting a lecture but I did learn to conceal my nervousness. He taught me the trick of speaking to one person in the audience at a time, pretending the others are not listening.

13th. April 1897. The summer draws to an end. My headaches are returning.

I found a note left on the boat for me yesterday:

"A lady sends Mr. Slocum the attached five pound note as testimony of the admiration inspired by his courage which has made him cross the sea in such a small boat alone without any sympathetic presence to come to his aid when danger threatens."

I think I know who left it. I do not know if it is my voyage itself, the publicity it attracts, or the darkness of my solitude, but women are showing a lot of interest in me. Several could have written this note but I think it was the governor's daughter, Margaret...

15th. April 1897. It was the governor's daughter. She came aboard without appointment late yesterday evening. She wanted more to receive my attentions than to give me hers. She left very happy, but she is so young, so fresh, it makes me feel clumsy in my old age. I am sure that women who admire a man strive to have that admiration returned and very often have only one way to achieve that.

Now, if Mabel were here...

25th. April 1897: Back in Sydney. Finally another letter from Mabel, amongst several from creditors:

Dear Captain,

Your last letter was very touching.

Do you know the papers here have been spreading doubts about your survival? I must say I was gravely upset by such rumors.

You are a very dear friend to me, without doubt the most precious of my friends. But it is so long since we saw each other.

Perhaps the solitude of your boat suspends time for you. If that is so, you were right to leave. Here in New York time flies as if it did not want to linger in such a busy city. I have the feeling of being pushed forward with each stroke of my bow, each chord on the piano. Perhaps we are no longer on the same date, writing to each other from one year to another. I might use that idea in a future work.

My friends tell me I am changing rapidly as I mature. One thing is certain, I am much less timid, which has something to do with you. You know what I am talking about.

Hawkes has finally agreed to publish my string trio, with two public recitals arranged for next fall's season. You see I am faithful to our pact. One questions always troubles me: do we not put too much emphasis on life after death when investing so much in a work or an exploit? In constructing for oneself the basis of later fame, a lot later and perhaps even too late, could it be that our present slips through our fingers? I confess to having difficulty in sacrificing the pleasure of a party with my friends to lock myself up scribbling some "work." Perhaps with your age and experience it is easier.

Your attachment to me is most flattering. Your friendly interest in my person gives me the feeling of being important. It is true that at the time we knew each other fame was not near for either of us. Now that they write about you in the newspapers, you might find me less interesting. Much more so, since your marvellous voyage must have brought you into contact with many fascinating and beautiful women. You are a man who is sensitive to feminine charm, which is said without meaning any offence. Your kind letters to me make no mention of your encounters. Why is that? But I stray.

I hope we will meet when you return. If I knew the exact date and place of your arrival I would make it a duty to meet you since it seems that would please you. But we know neither the place nor the time. There we are.

One thing is certain, you will find me much changed. I am rounder and have cut my hair. My mother hates it, but my friends like it.

Continue to write. It is important to me.

Take plenty of time to visit the world. I have bought an atlas and have drawn on it your track since our separation. I have copied the lines of your track onto a manuscript to look for the possibilities of a melody in it.

To the pleasure of hearing from you again soon, Joshua.
Your friend holds your affection as a constant theme.

M.M.M. (Maturing Musician Mabel)

I could not see what I had been looking for in this long-awaited letter. She wrote to me, politely. Nothing was broken in our pact. I decided I still had every reason to hope, and hope is what counts.

Redoubling my efforts to make the American continent aware of my exploit, I wrote a long letter to Joseph Gilder for publication:

Moored to a coconut tree
Keeling, Cocos Islands
20th. August 1897

I doubt you ever expected to receive a letter from this little island kingdom.

I have just completed in three weeks a trip equivalent to an Atlantic crossing. Three weeks of good weather heading north.

I had free time to read both day and night, only leaving that agreeable occupation to trim sails, eat or rest. The *Spray* ate up the gales almost as fast as I ate the jam I received in Tasmania at the end of my lecture tour.

Adventure is without daily event much of the time. Only in hindsight is it interesting or romantic. Then time is condensed, squeezing out the insignificant moments. The daily reality is normally prosaic and non-picturesque. Life itself is a similar adventure. It is exciting if one overlooks the majority of days, it is boring if one dwells on them.

I am happy to tell you I passed through the islands of the Great Barrier Reef without incident, contrary to some rumors I have heard.

I stopped in Queensland to give lectures augmented by my normal magic lantern show. In Cooktown I moored the *Spray* in front of the monument erected to Captain Cook from where I could contemplate the same rocks he had looked on.

I gave one lecture in a Presbyterian Church, the proceeds going to charity.

I arrived at Thursday Island in Torres Strait on the 22nd. June. My American compatriots should know that I was the only American ship in harbor that day to join in the Jubilee celebrations for the good Queen Victoria when we enjoyed a display of Australian Aboriginal dancing.

Ten days later I sighted the great island of Timor and on the 11th. July I had Christmas Island abeam. Heading west, *Spray* and I entered the Indian Ocean. I had to navigate the next five hundred and fifty miles very precisely in order not to miss the low lying Cocos Keelings.

The first sign of land being near was in the form of a tern which flew once around the boat one morning and then headed west with a business-like air. I climbed the rigging and with the increased height could see coconut trees apparently planted in the water some miles ahead.

It was exactly what I had expected to see, yet still the sight of them right on my course made me shout for joy. I must admit I was proud of my navigation, and why not? It is only human to be proud of yourself when you do something well. I abandoned myself to a celebration of my own ability.

My mooring lines were made fast to a coconut tree on the 17th of July.

These islands form a strange little world belonging to the descendants of the first settlers, a Scottish family. Here things are not done as elsewhere. The women, often completely naked (which does not excite desire as one might think but rather cools it), wear the trousers in the hierarchical sense. The men perform the menial tasks.

The miserable Fuegians would be astonished to see the "master" of the household gathering coconuts under his wife's supervision.

I have heard it said that a missionary is bubbling with zeal to come here and convert the happy indigens. If he does ever set booted foot on these isles, I hope he is not of the brutalizing species which have poured out like crabs over so many other beaches to destroy happiness. They are swarming over most of the Pacific now.

The conversation I once had with you on the subject of the sea often comes back to me. My soul may not be a pure one, but it is certainly clearer at sea than on land. It is worth mentioning that I feel more pride aboard the *Spray* than I ever did on the great sailing ships I commanded. I believe it is due to the constant responsibility entailed by solitude. I suspect it is the same in other walks of life.

I understand that New York ladies now go yachting. They could also study navigation. My first wife, Virginia Walker, was born in New York State, even though I met her in Australia, and was able to take on the navigation of our ships. A woman who understands her husband's work understands him much better. Perhaps the reverse is true too.

When I return I would like to talk to you about my idea of using my talents by sailing a school ship around the world. I would love to teach celestial navigation to our young chaps. I will choose a good sailing ship, a clipper, which will be able to rival steamers without any of the inconvenience of the latter.

The comments raised by my voyage/exploit often make me smile. One would imagine from them that I am engaged in a serious study of the limits a man can go to in facing perils. Those are the benevolent comments. It is an interesting idea, but I never started on this voyage with any such purpose in mind. It is simply a matter of accomplishing the unaccomplished. Afterwards it might be interesting to study my reactions, draw lessons and share them. But you have to swallow food before you can discover how well it nourishes.

I take things as they come. Now I am beginning to understand many things I had not suspected. I would have to give a whole different set of lectures to explain that to people. After the account of the voyage I intend to publish, do you think there would be a demand for a more reflective work?

Captain Joshua Slocum
(on his way back)

5th. October 1897. Almost two months rest at Mauritius.
I have not forgotten that the United States is still far away but I have to await the season for favorable winds, so I spent the time on agreeable activities. I walk everywhere, in the most charming company. These vanilla-velvet skins would excite the most sated. And those almond eyes, laughing innocently at the boldest thoughts. Is it my sea-dog imagination, my past sexual privation or the spice of the islands which inspires this appetite in me which demands to be fed. But appetite seems to increase with eating. I really need to work at a fresh abstinence to prepare myself for the icy mists of the Cape of Good Hope. For the moment the table is set though, and I am not yet full...

18th. October 1897. Today I visited Rose Hill, Curipepe and

some other picturesque sights. We came back through the botanical gardens near Moka. The proprietor had discovered a new plant that very morning and seeing me asked if he could name it "Slocum" in my honor. He was pleased not to have to torment his mind trying to think of a suitable name to latinize. How everything changes with fame and the mysterious charm of coming from far away. I know back in Boston where I had suffered so much from anonymity a gentleman had paid thirty thousand dollars for a flower to be given his wife's name. It was not such a big flower either, while "Slocum" is bigger than a beetroot....

29th. October 1897. The heights of Moka have sunk below the horizon behind me. I had to write to Mabel to tell her about my lecture at the Opera at Mauritius. A floating opera. She will no doubt enjoy my description of the cocktail of beauties who made up the Lord Mayor and His Excellency the Governor General's entourage. They themselves treated me as an equal. She should have seen me in my new suit....

1st. November 1897. I have passed by Reunion. The pilot came out to meet me, so I was able to give him a Mauritius newspaper. I did not stop. I hold my route for Cape St. Mary, toward a Madagascar now officially French....

9th. November 1897. A violent south-west storm in Mozambique Channel for the last three days. I am battling to reach the shelter of the African coast. The *Spray* and I fight to get south.

I finally reached Port Natal in Africa on November 17, 1897. Fifty years later to the day, my son made a speech in London to the famous Royal Geographical Society:

On this 17th. of November in 1897 my father arrived in Port Natal where he was met by the members of the Port Natal Yacht Club. Here is an original photograph of him in which the *Spray* can be clearly seen at the quay.

I would like to reveal to you some of his tales of that visit.

It was in the building you see in the background of the photograph that my father was presented to the Right Honorable Harry Escombe, prime minister of the Colony. He later told my father, "You are the sort of man I would like to hunt lion with."

They say the prime minister had a great reputation for hunting, although not in the field, and as a card player for his ability at bridge. This prime minister even offered to round the Cape with him, playing cards to pass the time. Happily the Captain forewarned that Mr. Escombe would win his very sloop from him before they have even reached the Cape....

That remained to be proved.
I understand the *Spray* had a good time in Port Natal...
I would like to have seen you there in my place, eh!

...but the best of things must come to an end, and on the 14th December, 1897, our hero stowed his dinghy on deck and then, getting underway with the morning's land breeze, soon found himself at sea with his solitude again, as the Australians say...who are obviously not numerous in this circle....

Little today.

The Cape of Good Hope was now the last important point to pass. After Table Mountain he counted on the Trades to return him rapidly to the fold. From Durban to the Cape he had to travel eight hundred miles of often inhospitable sea. You all know that violent winds frequently sweep the Cape. My father suffered a serious storm every thirty-six hours on average. We will never know, but it may have been as a result of meeting my father in South Africa that Rudyard Kipling wrote "Captain Courageous." He published it a few months later...

My son, by linking me too much with other famous people, you shade my own glory. Too many famous people together make each other look dull. And I am not famous just because I met these people.

Christmas Day, the third since he had left, the sea was rough and confused. Not the time for plum pudding. But after the Cape was doubled, my father was happy, considering that stage practically completed. You also know that it is precisely at the Cape that an imaginary line separates two climates: to the north, bright weather and settled winds; to the southwest, weather with gales blowing from the Horn.

The *Spray* was becalmed under Table Mountain. A tug prowling the area in search of sailing ships in trouble brought the sloop into port in default of a larger client...

Is it really necessary to give this sort of detail? You would have done better to dwell on what I told about a contemplative rest facing the Cape, savoring my rounding of sailing's greatest headlands.

The *Spray* entered the Alfred Dry Docks the next morning, where she stayed for three months, entrusted to the port authority while my father took the opportunity of a free railroad pass to cross the country in all directions from Simonstown to Pretoria.

I would like to recall one episode of his stay. In Pretoria my father was presented to Mr. Krüger, President of the Transvaal. His Excellency was cordial at the beginning of the interview but when he learned that his visitor was making a tour "round" the world, his mouth closed like a clam and his eyes shot fire, my father says. My father was amused by the situation because he was curious to know the true views of the head of the Boers with regard to the sphericity of the Earth. It was publicly rumored that Mr. Krüger believed the Earth to be flat, but the Captain had first thought it was a joke to make the Dutchman look ridiculous...

You should have told them about the tense climate at that period. It was no time for jokes. You have to remember the Boer's claims to independence, the whites legislation being preached in Rhodesia by the Bulawayo Literary and Debating Society, and the massacre of British troops on the Benin border.

During his stay, three Boers wedded to the President's views were preparing a paper to support it. The three disciples came to ask my father for arguments in favor of their thesis. He replied that the experiences of his own voyage would not permit them to prove the world was flat. They had a bad time of it. My father, who always had a dry sense of humor, invited them to appeal to the resources of the age of obscurantism for the pursuit of their researches and left the three sages absorbed in the study of the *Spray*'s route traced on a map of the world— mercator projection showing it flat.

The next morning one of the sages said to my father, "If you respect the Word of God, then you have to admit the world is flat."

The Boers' view did not prevent me from frequenting the company of people like Governor Sir Alfred Milner and astronomer Dr. David Gill with whom I passed long hours "in the stars," discussing methods of navigation. Dr. Gill joined us when his studies into the mechanisms of malaria allowed him the time.

Before leaving the subject of South Africa I must mention an event which I enjoyed at the time.

The British sense of humor had not lost its vigor despite the difficult situation in the area. When I was still a young lad in Nova Scotia, I had been fascinated by the adventures of Mr. Henry Morton Stanley and particularly his comment on discovering Dr. David Livingstone. When I was staying in the Hotel Royal with Colonel Saunderson, his son, and Lieutenant Tipping, I had the good fortune to be introduced to the great Mr. Stanley, a living legend. The heroes of legend do not so often descend from their pedestals to mix with ordinary mortals.

"Captain Slocum."

"Mr. Stanley, I presume."

He did not flinch. I suppose everybody he met must have greeted him that way, but I could not resist. After a long silence he said.

"You came alone, I believe."

"Solitary, in fact, Mr. Stanley."

"For myself, Captain Slocum, I can afford a crew."

"You have a large ship then?"

"You are still a little green concerning Africa, Captain. Believe me, fifty canoes would make a lot of *Spray*s."

"Especially if they pass over one of your waterfalls, I imagine."

Unperturbed, he puffed away on some disgusting tobacco which served to keep all flies at a distance.

"And you have sailed many seas, Mr. Stanley?"

"The perils of Lake Tanganyika are other than you imagine, Captain."

We sipped cloudy tea, the steam and smoke enveloping us. Neither of us was willing to show our admiration for the other's accomplishments. After inspecting me from head to toe, he broke the silence again.

"What an example of perseverance."

"You have done more in the jungle."

He had broken the impasse and now we could speak freely. He asked me if my boat had watertight compartments. I explained that as the whole hull was watertight from end to end, it was one large watertight compartment.

"And if you hit a rock or shallows?"

"I avoid them. The land is always the danger for seamen."

After a long pause he said slowly, "And if a swordfish were to pierce you with his spike?"

"Sir, the swordfish must first face me in a dual. Ever since the times of the pirates, all seamen carry a strong sabre and the swordfish know it, believe me. More tea?"

He accepted my defence. The conversation slipped into a repertoire of jokes told against President Krüger. My idol had received me into his company.

I wrote to Mabel frequently during my time in South Africa to assure her presence on my arrival back in America. I elaborated a code of telegraphic messages to ensure that the trial of three years of separation would not prove a waste. My returning to the United States had only one point: rejoining Mabel. I had left in accord with our pact of accomplishments. This rendezvous I intended to keep.

10th. April 1898. St. Helena, a sort of nowhere. Have spent a night in a room haunted by Napoleon. Haunted by failure. Haunted by the ship grandfather Southern had sailed on, the *Bellerophon*, bringing him to his exile. Not happy thoughts to sleep the night with. Returning to the *Spray*, I finished the bottle of port I had opened to toast my companion, the Pilot of the *Pinta*, when we sighted land.

Now there are the normal excursions, lectures, dinner with the governor and departing gifts. All I can think about is leaving, finishing.

I spent quite some time in the company of the Pilot of the *Pinta* around this period. I lived for nothing but the arrival in Fairhaven, but my apprehension grew as the distance lessened. Yarning the Pilot prevented me from dwelling on an outcome I was far from sure of. Would my efforts reward my departing prayer, as Mabel had said? I concentrated so little on what happened around me that old *Spray* will have to finish the story:

At last the Pole Star shines on my heavy hull again. It must be a full two years and a half since I last saw her. She will be the one to lead me free of these Antillian reefs. The master shouts to me, "Come on old girl, one more wave and we will be clear." I follow the North Star clear of the reef. To my way of thinking, he relies ever more on me these days. When we dropped anchor in Grenada after forty-two days at sea, he turned his back on the journalists come to beg an interview. That is not his way at all.

He still gives his lectures, but his mind is in the future; I do not know if he remembers the past right. Now here we are eight days in port through calms, and him pacing the deck furious. He reads, then throws down the book and it is out on deck again looking for a breeze. Yesterday he kicked me!

The middle of June and I am doing my darndest to get us home when something breaks. I wallow in pain and despair. What will he do to me if I fail him? Calm down and think. Yes, I can feel now, my forestay has parted. That is why I cannot pull. Now, though, he is climbing my mast with a new stay. He must have forgiven me.

Now we are reconciled but both tired from that battle to save my mast.

The wind plays in my rigging and the waves slap my bow. We need that noise, but we surely tire of it.

Passing Fire Island, I had to make a quick rummage to check that he was still with me. He was so silent, I thought he had gone.

My bowsprit swings, searching for a sniff of Fairhaven. My anchor hungers for a taste of mud again.

If he is kindly to me, he will take me back to the place I was reborn. But he is not happy, so perchance he will not be kindly either.

He speaks again at last. "We still have a few miles to add to our forty-six thousand before we reach Fairhaven. Do you think the old lock-keeper is still there?" So, he will take me back.

The beginning of July, I dance along the coast to the Acushnet River. The old lock-keeper is gone. But the cedar pile I was tied to, she is waiting for me still. She has taken something of a list to port, perhaps a respected bow, but her seaweed tresses have grown long.

Between the river's mist and the smoke from New Bedford, I cannot take a clear view of how my old home lies.

He has not spoken all night, but I can celebrate on my own, dancing a jig with my old Poverty Point pile.

Under Mabel's inscription in her *Miserere* I added:

After her world tour the *Spray* returns safe and sound as you said she would. Dear book, I return you to your author, but only so she can place you in *Spray*'s library herself for a second time. You have travelled the Strait of Magellan, past Cape Horn, you have seen Juan Fernandez, St. Helena and many other deep-sea islands. You have cleared the Cape of Good Hope unharmed to rest passive in your box while the Captain waited for the wind or faced long nights of gale. For long weeks, dear little book, no human breath ruffled your pages with a comforting chord, the only music coming from the waves. You have seen solitary atolls in the middle of hostile oceans, protected from the clamorous wave by a ring of coral. Not all rings have the virtue of growing stronger with time.

CHAPTER TEN

Frustration

I had not put a foot on shore.

For three days I stayed aboard, vexation building in my bones. I looked to the bank, but there were only the normal idle loungers.

When a boat came out for a look, I went below. When I finally tread the soil of this ungrateful county which has better things to do than remember me, it will be because I have run out of provisions. Occasionally I answer them briefly. Then one of them lets slip that a lady had arrived at the LaCoste Hotel and was asking after me!

At the hotel, "Certainly we have a Mabel Wagnalls registered. I'll have a message sent up." All that anxiety, all that doubt, and she had kept the rendezvous.

"You have finally decided to land then, Captain."

She came up behind me as I waited at the reception desk. I had gone round the world to find her face and there she was, at my back.

"I knew the *Spray* had returned."

I was struck speechless.

"Shall we go out to the terrace, Captain?"

"Yes, yes, if you like. You had a good trip?"

"Yes. And you?"

"As you see."

"I had some difficulty freeing myself from engagements, so I am late. But there we are, I am here now."

"I see, not too tired?"

"No. And you?"

Sitting in the wicker chairs our eyes met directly, searching for answers; both pairs were full of tears. Four hands remained locked on four chair arms.

Night fell; Mabel came back with me to the *Spray*, which quietly creaked a welcome to her, "I have came back, see."

"Me too, I have come back to see you."

The conversation remained at the daytime level.

The night brought us a long chaste embrace, silent and soothing: an intense sharing because both of us continued to guard our disguises, our outward identity. The linen and satin of her musician's dress pressed against my salt-encrusted jacket, but our faces revealed everything stowed away. Our breaths exchanged the winds and storms that had raged in my heart over the three years of our separation, but our contact passed no lower than the heart. It was better not to banalize the mutual admiration that had joined our destinies together.

I wanted durability with Mabel, such as I had known with Virginia. I found that better adapted to my age, needs, and thoughts.

I had made my tour of the world alone.

She had written her opera.

It remained for the two of us to make our accomplishments known. An unknown work is a pleonasm, a sketch, a failure.

Mabel would return to New York to complete her opera by having it played. I had to complete my tour by having it trumpeted.

Unlike the English, Australians, and French, the Americans distrusted my claims. They had a long tradition of practical jokes and journalistic scams. Pretended balloon voyages and trips to the moon had taken them in and they were wary. My story sounded equally tall to them. In short, they took me for a fake. In each port I visited I had to suffer being taken as a simple crackpot or fight the insinuations of elder brothers, the old deep-sea captains, who suspected me of inventing the story to cover diamond trafficking with South Africa. It took me many years to overcome widespread cynicism.

I had been expecting a triumphant arrival, horns welcoming me into a paradise of glory, but I did not even rate the front page of the local Newport newspaper, and the *Boston Globe* gave me a mention on the back page. The New York newspaper relegated me to a few summary lines on my claim. The *Times* ignored me. Even William Randolph Hearst, whom I had guarded as an infant, only had room for the Spanish–American War, which had just been blown open by the explosion of the *Maine* in Cuba. The Americans were leaping at this excuse to extend their empire, and righteous indignation filled every page. There was no room for my little nutshell in such times.

Glory has the habit of running in the train of war, and my boat did not have the knots to buck the current of history and pursue it. I could not claim the laurels I had won in my personal battle but had to stand aside to watch the heroes of the war march by. I should not have been forced to stand idly watching the parade. I should have been leading it. On July 3, 1898, I wrote to the *New Bedford Standard*:

> From an honorable Captain of our Merchant Marine, having recently proved my capacities by a solitary voyage around the world, I address this message to all my friends and creditors, to our Government Representatives and to my co-citizens of the same belief. Like so many of you, I long to make myself useful.... I have passed most of my life in the Philippines, China and Japan. I am not a fanatic looking for a scuffle, but trying to make myself useful to my country. Does Mr. McKinley not need a pilot for Guam and the Philippines?

The Pilot of the *Pinta* thought it a good letter but it bought no response.

Victor and Garfield, now aged twenty-six and seventeen, brought their stepmother to visit. Local journalists rushed to see her arrival aboard, scenting a story. Hettie arrived in tears. The next morning one of the papers made that their headline: "She Thought She Had Lost Her Husband Three Times."

For me she had long been dead.

> Their reunion was moving. Captain Slocum declared to his eldest son, "Vic, you could do it too, but now you cannot be the first."... the Captain showed his family his album of foreign press clippings....

> Thus they dismissed the most remarkable voyage ever accomplished.

> Then he told us about his plans. He told us he intended to pay all his debts plus the legal rate of interest. We also learned of his intention to depart imminently for New York where important work awaits him.

Hettie begged to accompany me to New York and I decided her presence might well be advantageous. It had earned me one mention in the press already, so the image of the captain flanked by his welcoming wife could serve my plans well. It gave a reassuring aspect to the solitary sailor story. The temporary presence of Victor and Garfield would have a similar effect.

My lectures did not achieve full audiences but sufficed to provide the minimum needs for a man of my status. I bought myself a new hat, shoes, et cetera, but clung to my old salt-stained suit with the pride of a battle-bloodied uniform: a signature suit.

The family and I settled on the West Side. Mabel had her studio there, to which I discretely retreated whenever possible to fill myself with her music.

I still liked the idea of a school ship as proposed in my letter to Mr. Gilder from Cocos-Keeling. It was a project that would be useful to society, bring me national prestige, and provide a reasonable means of subsistence. I would have a respectable command again, a spring-board for attracting crowds. Mabel encouraged me to concentrate on writing an account of the voyage and reflective notes on the subject. She felt my journalistic resumés did not do justice to my achievement. I was afraid all interest in my exploit would wane if I took the time off the write.

By the end of October not a single leaf remained on the trees and not a cent was left in my pocket.

I presented my proposal for the school ship before a large number of sympathizers gathered in a Carnegie Hall room. I longed for a proper command again; I proposed the building of the ship on the lines of a clipper but with some important modifications of my own. The ship would be designed to carry three hundred crew/students around the world on a two-year course. My son would rejoin me as mate. I previewed a program divided between study, manual work and recreation. The aim for the formation of young seaman capable of sailing and navigating the sail ships which would inevitably come back into style soon, even for ships of war. Diverse options additional to those specifically nautical were also foreseen. Thus the student could choose courses in literature or other branches of culture, perhaps music? Places would not be exclusively reserved for males. I spoke of the ability of women on a ship in spite of prejudices, citing Virginia's many skills. I even said I could not conceive of such a project without girls. I spoke with force and conviction.

The response left me feeling old and weak. It would not work, it would not pay, it was not needed. Sail was finished.

Hettie returned to her sewing needles in East Boston. For the sake of appearances I went with her for a few weeks, condemned to listen to my in-laws' gossip. Mabel was away on a long concert tour. On her return I sailed the *Spray* from her pile to Eire Docks, Red Hook, South Brooklyn.

My friend John Gilder's brother worked with the *Century Illustrated Magazine*. Through his influence I was asked to draft a series of articles describing my odyssey. I replied to the invitation the next morning. My memories could now be transmitted to others to live on in them. I even allowed myself the indulgence of astonishment that the invitation had been so long coming. My naive excitement burst out in my acceptance.

I have made a trip beyond anything even the Emperor of Germany could accomplish, starting by building the boat myself.

My story will live on. I do not think my record can be beaten whether for courage, endurance or tenacity.

I must tell you the most interesting and instructive parts of the voyage have never been mentioned by journalists. The way they quote me is so inaccurate I am discouraged by them. They only look for the worst moments, which drives me to despair.

Your offer gives me new hope.

If you come aboard *Spray*, gentlemen, I can show you the interest my voyage has raised in foreign countries, especially the British ones.

Without wishing to boast, I know it would be difficult to better the voyage I have just completed, the account of which you will have for your magazine.

I know that certain journalists have been ironical about my boat. Gentlemen, my boat and I belong to each other entirely. The proof is that she is as well kept today as the best ship afloat. Her bilge is so dry I keep matches there. Her hull has not the least trace of worm, she is perfectly healthy. The boat is as good if not better than the day I put her back in the water after having rebuilt her with my own hands.

As for me, I feel ten years younger than the day I cut down the first tree to reconstruct her with.

The series of articles was published from September 1899 to March 1900. Mabel sent me the seven copies of the magazine for my birthday (I had to forgive her for being late). She had the habit of circling in pencil any other article she wanted to draw my attention to. Here are some of the subjects she picked out, one from each issue: the invention of the new miracle medicine aspirin (she often suffered from migraine), France still torn apart by the Dreyfus affair (anything concerning Jews interested her), a criticism of Oscar Wilde's latest play, *The Importance of Being Earnest* (she tried to keep up with all new books), a report on Johann Strauss's funeral (a death which touched her heart), an advertisement for the sale by post of a book called *The Realization of the Possible* (in spite of knowing my reluctance to read while I am writing), a note on the latest efforts to record sound (she often deplored the fact that certain inspired interpretations could not be recorded for posterity), and a sketch of the first feminist congress in London.

I envied Mabel's freedom to display her feelings in her music while I felt the need to hide my own in my writing. I was discovering the difficulties of providing an honest account of events—they are not always simple. The only thing I could do was present my own point of view. I tried to be true to each moment, hoping that one day a coherent synthesis would appear of its own. Only when it was all down on paper would I be able to step back to take an overview.

Writing for the magazine brought me more satisfaction that I had expected. This was the first time I had attempted it. I reflected long on each episode and then just let the words flow on their own. With a subject I knew so well, the phrases fell into place. The ship bearing my ideas sailed freely over waves of words, borne on the tide.

Writing resembles sailing: it requires tenacity and discipline. Mabel's well informed criticism was of great help. Whenever she was free of musical engagements, she would join me aboard with some pickled gherkins to read the latest pages of my offering; I was working on a book now, too. It was her support that pushed my pen to retravel the journey described in the *Century* articles and to expand the story to full book length. She compared my writing to Defoe's.

At the beginning of summer I submitted the manuscript to the editors and then hoisted sail. Mabel joined me at Martha's Vineyard. Our relationship had developed into something which satisfied us both without either of us losing our heads. She pronounced herself delighted to join me further by writing the preface to my book; I was to feature in her next work.

However, two letters of bad news awaited me at the post office; the editors had turned down Mabel's preface and Hettie announced her intention to join me.

At the end of summer I returned the *Spray* and Hettie to Boston and then went to New York to resume my parenthesis with Mabel. But all that awaited me there was a return of my neuralgia, with a knot in the back of my neck and both eyes trying to escape from their sockets. Not only was Mabel delayed in the Mid-west by an extended tour and a visit to her parents, but the pleasure of having my account published in the *Century* was overshadowed by having to cross swords with a journalist who was trying to pick faults in the details I wrote. Here is one example of this jackass's pusillanimous writing in the *New York Times*:

The articles in which Captain Slocum recounts his voyage are certainly interesting; but they lack something, the absence of which is a hard test for the credulity of all those amongst us who possess, or claim to possess, a certain knowledge of things concerning the sea. Captain Slocum claims, on several occasions, that the *Spray* is so well balanced as to be able to steer herself or, to make the claim explicit, that he trimmed the sails, lashed the helm, and that the boat thus remained on course all night while her "Captain" slept tranquilly in the cabin. It is really difficult to credit this account. We do not go so far as to say the Captain has mistreated the truth or even that he is deceived in good faith concerning the *Spray*'s intelligence. We content ourselves with expressing regret that he has not revealed how this miracle was achieved. The strangest things can happen at sea.'

Two days later the same paper published my reply:

An old sea dog honors me with his criticism.

It is very possible that what happened during *Spray*'s voyage seems inexplicable to some sailors, even very experienced ones; and I only regret not having met them before they wrote their articles. I would then have been able to take them out on *Spray* to demonstrate to them what my boat is capable of. In the present state of things, it is not in my power to be more precise.

This sailing boat, rebuilt by a single pair of hands, has gone around the world and is now perfectly sound, watertight and solid.

She does not make a single drop of water. Some might say this is impossible too; however, it is a hard indisputable fact.

The story of my voyage is constructed on the same seaworthy lines: that is to say, it is completely water-tight, as your navigation officer can discover if he really wants to test the patience necessary to realize a voyage around the world.

This is typical of the restraint I felt I had to show in this overcivilized world. Truth is almost made a lie by edulcoration and politeness. Compare it to the first draft, written with my true feelings showing:

There are real seamen and there are toads who only have watched from the shore.

Why do you give an envious fresh water amateur the opportunity to dispute the experience and courage of a real deep sea Captain, who at least has the decency to sail before writing on the subject, before your readers?

Writing is a noble art which cannot just be picked up by anybody, an art which has to be defended from the attacks of envy and cupidity. Doubtless your journalists have to write something. In that case they should restrict themselves to reporting the facts rather than set themselves up as judges of far better men.

If what happened on the *Spray* seemed inexplicable to your bath-tub sailor then he should take the trouble to find out rather than airing his ignorance. If this so-called journalist dares to doubt what I say, then he should come to see me. I would have taken him for a trip at sea to demonstrate how it is done. But then he would have been sea sick.

This unpretentious sloop, re-built by the same hands that hold this pen, has sailed around the world in precisely the manner I have recounted.

I have always been susceptible to criticism, which makes people think me irascible. But what do they want? The implacable sea seeks out any sign of weakness and seamen properly fear it so much that they flee any uncertainty or wavering.

I never forget anybody who has crossed me.

The scepticism and arrogant criticism which greeted the publication of my articles and book brought back my neuralgia, pumping to the beat of my perverse destiny. It would be a couple of years before I discovered what lay behind this unwelcome reception. It was explained to me, with supporting proof, how a certain man had been so eaten up by envy that he set in motion the contestation of my accounts. Eben Pierce's generosity had been nothing more than condescension. He thought his charity extended to introducing two shorebound wrecks. Jealousy started when those two wrecks became seaworthy again. Now he was doing all he could to prevent me from reaping any reward for my endeavors. And I had always been thankful to him. Unfortunately it had only been one of those acts of charity intended to make the donor feel more powerful. An old man frequently needs to show he still has some power. He had used his power once to get me started; now he was using it to stop me from going further than he had intended.

I was preparing to leave for the village of my birth when I received the first author's copies of *Sailing Alone Around the World*. There were to be five editions in my lifetime. My best chance at immortality lay with that anchor and seahorse-decorated blue canvas cover. This was a far greater exploit than the *Liberdade*. I immediately read it right through to see how it stood up to the test of print. I felt it had passed, which brought a feeling of relief, such as when a great storm has ended. Temporarily I could consider my destiny assured: every time someone reads the book, the existence of Joshua Slocum enjoys a reprieve. So long as it is read, I can continue to roam the seas. Only when the last copy is destroyed will I finally fade into the ranks of the anonymous dead.

Mabel hugged to her breast the copy I dedicated to her—my name pressed against her beloved flesh. She read out some of her favorite passages, which she remembered well, having spent so long helping and encouraging me with them.

The prospect of lecturing at Westport daunted me, but I was given a warm welcome by the people who knew me when I was young. In the end I had to give three lectures because the whole population wanted to hear, with many coming back twice. It was a pity I had no copies of my book to sell: I believe everybody would have bought one. All the older ones had some anecdote to tell of my childhood, claiming they had known then it foreshadowed an exceptional future for me. A past had to be fabricated in keeping with my present: this "blue nose" who was emblazoning their blazon had to be a hero from birth.

Then came an old aunt to reveal to me, in hypocritical confidence, the way my mother had mistreated my father. Now I was left to carry the burden of guilt. I could not correct any wrong I had done to my father because the protagonists in the drama now revealed to me had long been dead and could not forgive me now.

Not even the adulation of the whole world can compensate for the absence of a parent's praise for a child's accomplishments: even a fifty-year-old child. I should have been able to present my books for my parents' admiration. My immediate family did not stint their praises, but it seemed to me that sycophantic interest influenced their attitudes. I left Westport pleased with their praise but dubious as to their motives. Ahead of me lay the reception of my book by the press. I wrote to my editors:

> I fear to be stung to bleeding if the literary priests of the *Boston Daily Evening Transcript* attack me, but am a little reassured by the advertisement in the window of a Boston bookshop proclaiming our book "the best story of the sea ever written."
> So much for Boston.
>
> A friend introduced me to the chief editor of the *Herald*; he had many excellent things to say concerning the publication but, so far as I know, has not pronounced them outside his office. Many people think I will have a full house for my nautical lecture at Tremont Hall in Boston next month. The seats are fixed at between twenty-five cents and one dollar, and it seems they are really curious to see my stereoscopic views. If the people of Boston do not give me a full house I will still clean up. Anyway, whatever happens, I will do my best.
>
> I have to say I have not received any of the criticisms I expected concerning my "master work" and I hope never to do so.
>
> Without pretending to be an accomplished writer I am certain not to bring attacks on the reputation of American deep-sea Captains.
>
> I have been around the world in my little boat but it is now that I feel most threatened by reefs.
> Captain Joshua Slocum

But I need not have worried:

> A book of the greatest interest for all who love adventure.
> —*New York Times*

His voyage was thrilling, his book is even more so.
—*Nautical Gazette*

Read it again three times since your departure for Canada, and each reading brings me still closer to my favorite Captain. A little more patience with me, Joshua.

Your Maestro Mabel

A second reading is even more enjoyable than the first since one discovers details which first passed unnoticed...and allows one to admire the form of the account at the same time as the story itself.
—*New York Mail and Express*

And it seems you did not have time to come and see us when you gave your lecture. Why? I was ill, as you must have known. The family took your book away, but Victor was kind enough to lend me his copy. I do not know when I will have the time, but I will try to read it if possible. Will your success bring us any material benefits?

Your Wife (Hettie)

No literary tricks, no great pieces of heroism, but an irresistible impression of boundless courage and imperturbable selfconfidence.
—*The Nation*

In spite of all the publicity surrounding him, his humor has not been altered. Here is an author who ought to enter the Hall of Fame.
—*New York Evening Post*

I was in the house all day, but having started your book at breakfast I sailed with you until night for forty thousand miles and want forty thousand more. We were Jules Verne's British editors. Your exploit surpasses his fiction.

R.B. Marston, M.P.
Sampson Low, Marston & Co.

Sailing Alone Around the World was soon published in England, where it received the same unanimous praise.

Nobody who has read Mr. Slocum's account would tolerate any manifestation of the doubt with which the ignorant so often greet great actions.... The story is true from first to last line; it is written

in such a direct style, as straight as a marlin-spike, and yet full of details showing a discrete poetic sense and a passionate love of Nature live in the soul of this "blue-nose" Captain.
Sir Edwin Arnold
    —*The Daily Telegraph*

I can now offer my contribution to your glory, at least I hope so. The hero of the opera I have nearly finished is a solitary navigator who writes...knows great love, as I hope I am correct in thinking...keeps this news secret for now, as we keep everything secret...I am going back home to Lithopolis to work there for a while.
    Your Musical Mabel

Happiness returned to my life.
The Paris Universal Exposition was approaching rapidly and I badly wanted to participate in what I felt was a major world event. I wanted *Spray* to be illustrated in the pages the new century would turn. But the French still considered American exploits to be amusing colonial curiosities, interesting only for amusement while relaxing from engagement in the great European enterprise of civilization. For them the past had to be distant before it was credible and it had to be European to be taken seriously. They preferred a replica of a Viking longboat to *Spray* even though it would not have accomplished one-tenth of her travels. The horses of the Spanish Riding School in Vienna where the French Republican Guard were trained still looked down on the American quarter horse, and the Eiffel tower still stood higher than New York's skyscrapers.
Paris and I were never to meet. I leafed through the prospectus and read reports in the press. Mabel should have had the chance of presenting her music there too and we might have been able to meet a sculptor I was sure I would get along with, Auguste Rodin. I had seen only illustrations and copies of his work, but I felt his hands could certainly hold a tiller or steer a woman the way I did.
Mabel shared my feelings:

Lithopolis

My Dear Captain,
    I received your letter with great pleasure, although sharing in your disappointment at the news you relate.

I understand how you must feel. I would have loved to have shown you the work of the impressionist painters I discovered in 1893 during my visit to Europe with Mama.

Sydney Porter writes to me regularly and always asks for news of you. Do you know he is now famous in the world of letters, writing under the name of O'Henry? He should be coming to visit me in Ohio soon with a companion who sounds as fascinating as yourself, one Richard J. Jones. I will tell you all about him.

You expressed some curiosity about this little town of Lithopolis, so let me describe it to you. Imagine 300 inhabitants in less than 200 houses, often mended, for no new ones are built. It costs less to leave town or die than to build here.

Nobody moves into Lithopolis—one has to be born here. It is more exclusive than the St. Nicholas Club in Manhattan.

The surrounding hills cut with the ravines of streams would delight the impressionists, particularly Corot.

At the end of the main street, at the top of a small hill, the cemetery shaded by its pines and elms gives Lithopolis an air of dignity and destiny.

The general store sells ploughs and coffins side by side. The silence of the four churches is broken only by bird songs and the thump of the tomb engraver's mallet.

I expect to spend all summer here, which means I will not see you until the autumn.

I pursue my literary and musical endeavors.

My mother, who is right in most things, says one can substitute perseverance for genius. If she is right, I should be able to profit from this summer's work.

Success in Buffalo.

Mabel

Another disappointment soon followed: Hettie joined me in New York with Garfield. She and the youngest boy installed themselves in the intimacy of my sloop. Knowing I was going to the 1901 Buffalo Pan-American Exposition, she hoped to attract a little attention to herself by accompanying me.

I fitted the dinghy with a one-and-a-half horsepower motor with which Garfield towed the *Spray* up the Hudson and through the Erie Canal. Hettie boasted she was not once seasick.

From May to November the *Spray* and her master became fairground attractions.

The promoters of the Exposition concentrated on "Progress in the Western World." There was little place for the apotheosis of the nineteenth century when the wonders of the twentieth awaited. It was an ode to metal, machines, coal and steam, to giganticism—to a puerile, rusting dream. Intoxicated with speed and noise, they relegated me to a sideshow. The metallic and electric imbroglio needed to be set off against touches of folkloric anachronism. Visitors were invited to "shake hands with the valiant Captain, man of indomitable heart and nerves of steel [they had to have metal everywhere], veteran of the oceans, a man of strong soul and exceptional character."

We were moored between the triumphal arch and the blinding electric tower with its thousands of lamps shining like so many fallen stars. Nearby forty-two Indian tribes were exhibited like me but made a great deal more noise about it, perhaps to exorcise the spirit of the lights. Under the cupola of the temple of music, an orchestra endlessly repeated the Latin American rhythm of Victor Herbert's "Pan Americana." They even had a ballet—which danced to the glory of electricity, steam, and modern technology—that they hoped to take on to Paris.

During this time, Mabel's music remained unknown and she could not come to taste of my fame since Hettie was gorging herself on it.

In the central alley the curious could stare at Eskimos in furs with imitation ice igloos, next to Polynesians in raffia, South American hidalgos, Hawaiian dancers, macrocephalous dwarves, artificial incubators for premature babies—all dominated by Chiquita, the human robot.

A visit to the *Spray* was listed with the attractions alongside the "Voyage to the Moon," and the "Authentic Mexican Bullring." An immense history and noble geography had been reduced to a few acres of indigestible agitation seasoned with the whole world's spices: a southern plantation with Negroes playing banjoes, an Hawaiian village, the East in all its splendor, Old Nuremburg, the inevitable Buffalo Bill, the spoils of the Spanish-American War, Cleopatra eating sausages with Geronimo, and Captain Slocum with his wife on the celebrated *Spray*.

Like the others, my exploit was reduced to the level of a curiosity. Adventure reduced to clowning: thus the mob cage and tame anything that shows up their mediocrity. By paying to see the freaks, they had the feeling of controlling them. In this way, heroes are imprisoned by the homage paid to them.

I still thought popularity was the same as achievement then.

All day long I answered visitors' questions and autographed copies of my book while Hettie pocketed two dollars for *Sailing Alone Around the World*, one for *The Voyage of the Liberdade*, and twenty-five cents for a brochure called "Sloop *Spray* Souvenir."

That brochure was a good example of my mistake: a panegyric of my exploits and myself which I had Hettie sign. Inside each copy I glued a piece of canvas labelled "from the mainsail ripped entering the Pacific." Under the title was written: "Prepared, classified and annotated by Henrietta E. Slocum." I had her say: "Here is a collection of articles and commentaries relating to the celebrated voyage of the *Spray* around the world, as recorded in the most important newspapers. Attached is a souvenir of the *Spray* in the form of a piece of her original mainsail ripped beyond possible repair in the storm of the 4th–8th of March, 1896, off Cape Horn, a veritable hurricane. Fans of the *Spray* coming aboard with their knives and having a lively taste for a moment are behind the preparation of this souvenir."

Under Hettie's signature I did not refrain from letting fly some darts at the detractors and critics who tried to rob me of the fruits of my courage by not understanding how it was all achieved. The when, what, how, and why, of an exploit are indissociable, but the newspapers always simplified to the point of making my claims incredible.

In September a young anarchist assassinated President McKinley in the centre of the Exposition. The President had signed the *Spray*'s visitor's book on the previous evening, so we were flooded by a morbidly curious crowd eager to see his last mark on the world. Theodore Roosevelt took his oath only steps from the boat.

At the end of the Exposition, Hettie and Garfield returned home. I replaced them with a horse.

My new "tug" followed the footpath faithfully, acting as though she had been waiting to perform the task for me. I recognized myself in that horse as she hauled along boat, captain, and his reflections. She too would soon be replaced by machines, betrayed, as Cape Horn was being betrayed by the Panama Canal and condemned to memory. What worth is it to be most fearful cape in the world if no one comes to be frightened?

The three volumes of visitors' signatures had somehow banalized my exploit. Was it worth sailing for this? I would trade my tiller for a plough.

I had crossed the seas, now I would trace my furrows on the land, planting my hopes there...tearing up the weeds of frustration.

CHAPTER ELEVEN

Adrift

Now I had money again, so I was able to buy one of the oldest houses in Martha's Vineyard, right in the centre of the island at West Tisbury. That old house had been drifting just like me; putting it back in condition would help rescue both of us. Inside, great oak beams and joists gave it something of the feel of a ship, with spars over my head. So I did not retire to Hawaii as I had always said I would. I had always liked the climate in Hawaii, but for a certain musician established in New York, Martha's Vineyard was easier to visit.

I was approaching my sixties without joy. I even had regrets.

The old whaling men on the island betrayed their past by amassing stock in U.S. Steel. After making their fortunes in wood, they should have stayed faithful to it.

These pillars of the small island's society regarded me as no more than a curiosity, as though it was more estimable to be rich than renowned. Only members of the common mob become pillars of it.

During the first year, I left the *Spray* dandling in her nearby retreat at Wood's Hole on the mainland as a shelter for Mabel's discreet visits. I went to those meetings with so much anticipation that, as often as not, I received very little pleasure from them. Mabel took no umbrage at my bodily silences, being content to listen to my dialect of intentions.

I struggled to anaesthetize my nostalgia, regrets, and despair and create a catharsis for my inexorable aging by forming thousands of plans for the future. When it was not the school ship, it was exploring the Amazon, growing hops in New England, or market gardening. Mabel always listened to me attentively, showing her gentleness by going along with each of my follies, never bringing up the subject of the last meeting's plan. When she saw my imagination was running down, she took out her violin to play the tune of her own troubled soul.

242

The retired seamen of the island made themselves drunk on tales of the sea, all talking at once and nobody listening. Sober, they panicked at the threat of a coal miners' strike like they had in their first gale; their shares might suffer if steelmaking was affected.

Only landlubbers showed any interest in my tales of the sea. I started to frequent the farming community. They at least listened when someone spoke. Otherwise I busied myself around my small farm. I refurbished the house and added new rooms, and I applied myself to the roof, giving it a more Oriental tilt. But the inside of the barn was more like a maritime museum than a store for land implements. There were more shells, dried starfish, and other bric-a-brac from the beach than fodder.

My wife sometimes came to join me in the country and then we were more in demand socially. She grew loquacious concerning "our" life at sea, and "our" maritime exploits; this made me even more interested in agriculture.

Birds lived in huge numbers in the branches of the oaks and pines around the house, certain of not being disturbed by the sound of our conversation. I made more noise when I was alone.

I started planting trees with great enthusiasm. Like my world trip and the book, they were a way of perpetuating myself. The treasure I had hidden during my childhood could only preserve events. Now I sought to have my exploits grow. Sea salt might keep me well, but it would be safe to root my renown in the land too, where it could multiply. But then came an event which returned me to my former love.

I was pruning my apples trees when the famous journalist and writer Clifton Johnson arrived to photograph and interview me. It had been a long time since such an important person had shown any interest in me. I replied to his questions with complete sincerity, taking the trouble to give detailed answers so he could understand everything. Some of my answers surprised me. The quality of the interlocutor must have been transferred to me in the questions.

I enjoyed the interview so much, I offered to take him out on the *Spray* to add some action to the words (why did I not ask him to help prune the apples?).

Some weeks later his eulogistic article appeared in *Outing*. The respect he showed for me was flattering, but I was troubled by the ending:

When I first saw the *Spray*, she was rolling gently in a creek on the coast of Massachusetts near Wood's Hole. Other boats were moored nearby. The *Spray* could not rival them for grace or style, but she has the engaging look of a real family boat; one felt she had been built as a marine home capable of facing all weathers, all seas, and not just for summer outings along the coast.

It was a real pleasure to climb aboard and discover all the details of her equipment.

It was also a pleasure to take an improvised dinner with Captain Slocum which he quickly prepared in the small galley, and another pleasure again, when night fell, to settle under the awning and sleep aboard.

But what was best was to take a trip on the old *Spray*, as her owner affectionately named her, and make the crossing from the mainland to Martha's Vineyard…His house is one of the oldest on the island; built in the form of an ark framed in oak, with curled up boards, tiny windows and open hearths. It has a dilapidated air now, empty and abandoned, but the Captain knows how to handle saw and hammer so it will not take long to make it comfortable.

In a single session he has become an enthusiastic agriculturalist, proud of his well kept garden and intent on making the surrounding fields fruitful under his hand.

Martha's Vineyard is an Eden for him and it is probable that the sea will never see him again.

In the same issue of *Outing* was a long article on the new U.S. distraint on the Panama Canal, reminding me again of how the Horn was condemned to the same bitter isolation as myself.

His way of talking about the *Spray* made me realize I had abandoned her. Not even in my most secret sexual escapades had I ever felt so unfaithful. I was treating her like a causal call girl.

The trees could grow without me. Anyway, planting trees was something anybody could do. Living aboard the *Spray* and sailing her again might astonish anew. My only repose lay in loyalty to my comrade in arms; to abandon her might imperil the perenniality of our survival. Our twin destinies were close coiled and both of us were beginning to creak.

By 1903 my life was exhausted by an erosion of pleasures, caused by the disappointments of repeated setbacks. The sound of potatoes growing or hay drying was an oppressive void, an emptiness with only memories to fill it. At harvest time, instead of drying my beans, I went to catch a shark at the Sippican Casino at Marion, to the great relief of bathers, as the *Vineyard Gazette* recorded. This curiosity raised a momentary interest in me which I profited from by announcing a lecture for the following Thursday at the Agricultural Society Hall in West Tisbury. The newspaper advertised it for me:

> Do not forget to go to Captain Slocum's lecture at the Agricultural Hall. This lecture, "A Voyage Around the World," will be a real feast for our citizens. They will see one hundred lantern slides projected, as the circulars announce, showing the places visited and people met, savage and otherwise, during the voyage.

I rarely gave lectures now. Several times I had been invited by the Lyceum Bureau in New York, and thus by the greatest impresario of the times, Major James B. Bond—for a quarter of a century he had handled the greatest, the likes of Mark Twain, Cable, Whitman, Stanley, Peary, Henry Ward Beecher, and William Dean Howells. He asked me to make a lecture tour but it never succeeded. Shortly after this failure, Major Bond published a book entitled *The Singularity of Genius,* in which I spoke of his disappointment in these terms:

> Captain Slocum, who conceived the idea of sailing alone around the world, is the most recent and most remarkable of those who make up the short list of temerarious adventurers who have achieved something which no man has done before and thereby acquired worldwide celebrity.
>
> What is more remarkable is that Captain Slocum is capable of writing and describing the incidents of his voyage and his marvellous adventures in such a picturesque and clear fashion that he charms and inspires his readers as nobody else has done or will do.
>
> It is really marvellous to hear his detailed descriptions of the dangers from which he has escaped and also to hear him reply smartly to all sorts of questions asked him by listeners who have experience of the sea. I have listened to this sort of tournament for hours and never has the Captain hesitated for an instant before furnishing a reply which goes right to the target like an arrow.
>
> If all of this had happened twenty years ago, it would have made a fortune for Captain Slocum and the Lyceum, but it is impossible

at the present time. Why? Because in the present state of things the lecture circuit is in the hands of agents representing organisations who assemble committees of enterprising citizens desirous of doing something for their towns, persuading them to create a fund for a series of lecture and other attractions.

This has gone so far that, once the newspapers publish articles on an exploit as heroic as Captain Slocum's and circulars announce his intention to appear before the public to give lectures expounding his adventure, these local committees inform the Captain that there is already a series of lectures in the town. Which means that an independent lecturer or presenter of any type of spectacle, whatever its merits might be, is boycotted by the committee in every town in the United States containing between two thousand five hundred and forty thousand inhabitants.

Long months without news of Mabel did not favor my conversion to a routine farmer either; but two drops can make the cup overflow.

The island had no time for anything but Captain George Fred Tilton. He was everywhere, the endless topic of conversation. They criticized him, envied him, admired him: there was only him. He had been a simple whaler who had had the good fortune to command the last great sailing whaler out fishing, the *Charles W. Morgan*. The eponymous owner made his money at the cost of the lives of whales and seamen, and then invested his gains in a chain of large stores that condemned all the smaller shopkeepers who stuck to their traditional ways to closure. The ship was transformed into a floating museum where the brave Tilton recounted his travels to paying visitors. Unfortunately the *Spray* could not hold many people, and I did not benefit from the backing of a magnate like Morgan.

Tilton came to West Tisury almost every weekend for the horse races. He had transformed an area behind the village into a race course where the local farmers gave themselves the airs of rich landowners, riding their own horses while the wily Tilton won on frisky mounts brought over from the mainland. I campaigned with the mayor against this practise. My adversary treated me like an old fogey who was trying to stop Martha's Vineyard from acceding to inevitable and desirable progress. They mocked me in the street and voted for him, forcing me to retire to my old *Spray*, to the detriment of my plough, which rusted without me.

The other drop was the sudden publicity surrounding a poor Gloucester peasant. I know now he had attended my lecture at Gloucester; inspired, he started making various solitary trips in a boat a little smaller than mine, even crossing the Atlantic from Gloucester, U.S.A., to Gloucester, England. Nothing to eclipse my sailing around the world you say? This stubborn man had lost all his fingers some time before in a particularly painful incident off the coast of Newfoundland. Forced by danger to continue rowing, his fingers had frozen to the looms of his oars. Thereafter, a solitary trip was enough to make a hero the press praised to the skies: hearts bled for the pathetic Howard Blackburn.

I refused to see the proper admiration due to me overshadowed by pity for a poor man's stumps.

Towards the end of July 1903, Mabel paid me a visit. I had spent all summer playing tourist along the coast, selling my books and samples of the shells I carried as ballast. I returned to Kennebunkport to meet her.

Her fine lips, arched nose, dark eyes, and hollow cheeks had grown more serious. From the start she talked a lot: too much. She raised a mountain of words between us I could not tunnel through. I wanted to take her in my arms, but she was occupied, enthusing over some opera she had been to, *Pelléas et Mélisande* by Debussy. I had wanted to run my wrinkled fingers through her hair, but she had cut it even shorter in the latest fashion. I wanted to tell of the distress of a wandering nobody, but she insisted on marvelling at the first radio transmissions between North America and Europe.

When I mentioned my loneliness, she replied by telling me of her exciting meeting with the Italian singer Caruso, who had accepted to sing my part in her opera; it was to be presented by the Kansas Opera Guild.

I had to be content with her presence, to limit my desires to what was possible. I invested my passion in a chowder of cod, potatoes, onion, cream, port, and cayenne pepper, working slowly to keep her with me longer. She filled any silences that might have brought us closer with impersonal babble about her game of naming all the domestic animals at her home after opera characters.

Had I become an opera character too?

For several months Hettie settled at the farm, taking in boarders;

the *Spray* and I lived at Menemsha Creek.

Nobody talked about me any more, except to mock my making chowder for tourists—and to gossip about my extramarital travels. The old crabs envied our autonomy.

Doubling sixty, I thought of Cape Horn. I knew I would never see it again.

No news from the Pilot of the *Pinta*; but I thought I saw Bully Hayes on the quay yesterday. It was too dark to be sure.

Going back to the farm with a cod for Hettie and her guests, I found the house empty. The door stood ajar, a cat curled in Hettie's favorite chair. I decided to forget Hettie and adopted the cat. We shared the cod.

The cat settled in my old jacket, so I took him aboard. He let me warm the joints of my old fingers in his fur and purred.

The Trades waved us on as we slipped through them to the Antilles for the winter.

When we returned in the spring there was only one letter waiting for me. The Smithsonian Institution were asking about the disposal of the *Liberdade:* it was no longer of interest to them. I replied:

> The *Liberdade* no longer exists as a boat. If someone can demolish the hull and gather the pieces in a corner, well stowed in boxes, I will gladly pay for the operation and remove the packages when possible. If not, let the executioner do his work.

Would all the witnesses of my past thus disappear, one by one? Even the memory of their existence? Even the idea of thinking about them?

I was beginning to forget them myself.

It could not have been Bully Hayes I saw on the quay. I met him on Grand Cayman and he had not been in the area—just somebody who looked like him I suppose.

One day in the wet summer of 1905 (I think it was 1905), I received a card cordially inviting me to the world premiere of Mabel's opera in Kansas City. If you think I was pleased at another monument to my glory, let me tell you: it came like a condemnation to oblivion.

Mabel and I had often discussed possible titles for the work. The one I had always preferred was the most simple: "Joshua!"; I was prepared to tolerate "Joshua...Alone." But the invitation from the director of the company informed me the opera I had inspired was called "Solitude West."

I kept that card so as not to forget all those traitors who had stolen my exploit, my suffering, my chance of survival, to make something of their own of it. I will revenge myself on those unscrupulous thieves pirating my memory, these Enrico Carusos, Emma Lejeunesses (yes, her again, she always turns up at the worst moments of my life), and Mabel—yes, Mabel who refused herself to me and then stole my identity. Bully says I should go and pirate it back again, stage a raid on their opening night.

I am making money for the trip selling sea-shells, but disguised with one of Bully Hayes' headbands. He and I and the Pilot of the *Pinta* make a jolly trio on board the *Spray*.

They tried to break into prison to release me last night, but there were too many guards for them. I cheered them on, but they had to run for their lives in the end. Yes, me, in prison. Charged with raping a young girl from New Jersey. Perhaps she was raped on my boat, but it must have been Bully or the Pilot, not me. I think it was a plot by the singers to stop me from attending the premiere. I have been held here so long I will never see the musical result of Mabel's pillaging. I know I did it for her, but it was not so she could run off with it. Our agreement said plainly that each should make their own fame, not that one of us could steal the other's.

Bully and the Pilot say it is a plot, too.

They cannot break me out, so I have to make this painful crossing alone, forty-two days going nowhere. And no library on this ship, just one book of poetry by Rudyard Kipling. I have four of the poems off by heart now, reciting them out aloud to an audience of four walls: "The Rhyme of the Three Sailors," "The Bell Buoy," "The Long Trail," and "The Virginity." The walls will know them by heart soon if I do not get out of here right quick.

Good news. President Roosevelt has taken a hand in the affair, even invited me to his house; something about me taking his son sailing, I am not sure exactly. Bully and the Pilot do not understand it either.

November 1909: we anchor in Vineyard Haven. Twilight hides us from the houses perched like crows on the bank, watching us. I told my two companions to stay inside; I think I can see some people hiding behind the lobster pots on the quay.

I creep back inside myself and pretend I have not seen them.

As the three intruders climb silently aboard, I recognize them. At a word from me, my companions slip on deck to let go the moorings.

The wind blows fresh from the southeast.

I had better go on deck and give orders to this crew. There are five to organize now: Bully, the Pilot, Elizabeth, Ginny, and Mabel. I have never had so many on board.

As we leave the mouth of the river for the open sea, we see Hettie standing on a rock, dressed all in green. She waves, but there is no room for her aboard.

The wind is increasing, a gale coming.

This is no time to bear away. "Sheet in, sheet in!" The weight in the rigging pulls groans from the *Spray*.

The only way to find some calm is to go through this gale. The mast creaks its consent; the halyards and sheets squeal. The befouled hull cries out to return: she has known oblivion before. Is it too much to ask her to face it twice in one lifetime?

I stand fast at the tiller and grip onto my dignity. I pull my hat hard down, and head for the darkest centre of the storm, holding firm to my dignity: sailing. *Spray* heels more; upright at the helm. One day one has to face…face…the waves beat my face. With dignity: take the waves, don't turn your face! Am I alone? Where are you, Elizabeth? Ginny! Mabel!

Bibliography

ADAM-SMITH, Patsy, *The Shearers,* Nelson, 1982.

ANTIER, Jean-Jacques, *Au Temps des grands voiliers,* Éditions France-Empire, 1971.

_____, *Les Prisonniers de l'horizon,* Éditions France-Empire 1971.

BERG, Donald, *Country Patterns 1841-1883,* Antiquity Reprints, 1980.

_____, *Houses and Cottages 1893,* Antiquity Reprints, 1983.

_____, and Steven J. RAKEMAN, *The 1870 Agriculturist,* Antiquity Reprints, 1980.

BOSS, Judith A. and Joseph D. THOMAS, *New Bedford, A Pictorial History,* Donning, 1983.

COLLIN, Gaston, *Défi Pacifique,* Boréal Express, 1978.

COURRIÈRE, Yves, *Le Démon de l'aventure,* Plon, 1987.

CYRULNIK, Boris, *Mémoire de singe et paroles d'homme,* Hachette, 1983.

DALLET, Jean-Marie, *Je, Gaugin,* Robert Laffont, 1981.

GARLAND, Joseph E., *Lone Voyager,* N.B. Robinson, 1984.

_____, *Down to the Sea,* David R. Godine, 1973.

GAUGIN, Paul, *Oviri,* Gallimard, 1974.

GORSKY, Bernard, *Trois Tombes au soleil,* Albin Michel, 1976.

GRAFTON, John, *New York in the Nineteenth Century,* Dover, 1980.

GRAVELEAU, Max, *L'Embellie sur la mer,* Arthaud, 1978.

GREENHILL, Basil and Denis STONEHAM, *Seafaring Under Sail,* Patrick Stephens, 1981.

GUIMARD, Paul, *L'Empire des mers,* Hachette, 1978.

HARRIS, John, *A Century of New England,* The Globe Pequot Press, 1987.

HOLTZ Kay, Jane, *Lost Boston,* Houghton Mifflin Company, 1980.

HORTON, Marion, *Do Dreams Come True,* 1925.

JOHNSON, H. and F. LIGHTFOOT, *Maritime New York,* Dover, 1980.

KOXAK, Jaromir, *Bateaux,* Gründ, 1973.

LABORIT, Henri, *Éloge de la fuite,* Robert Laffont, 1976.

LAWRENCE, D.H., *Île, mon île,* Stock, 1985.

MELVILLE, Herman, *Taïpi,* Folio, 1952.

MERLE, Robert, *L'Île,* Folio, 1972.

MERRIEN, Jean, *Les Drames de la mer,* Club les Amis du Livre, 1961.

MICHENER, James, *Cheasapeake,* Le Seuil/Points, 1979.

MOITESSIER, Bernard, *La Longue Route,* Arthaud, 1971.

PROTEAU, Yves, *Les Grands Voiliers,* Conciliuem, 1984.

RIIS, Jacob A., *How the Other Half Lives,* Dover, 1971.

SABATIER, Robert, *Les Années secrètes de la vie d'un homme,* Albin Michel, 1984.

SIZAIRE, Pierre, *Le Parler matelot,* Éditions Maritimes & d'Outre-mer, 1958.

SLACK, Kenneth E., *In the Wake of the Spray,* SheridanHouse, 1981.

SLOCUM, Captain Joshua, *Sailing Alone Around the World,* Norton, 1984.

_____ , *Seul autour du monde sur un voilier de onze mètres,* Chiron-sports, 1980.

_____ , *Le Voyage du Liberdade,* Gallimard, 1980.

SLOCUM, Victor, *Le Capitaine Slocum, roi de la mer,* Amiot, Dumont, 1953.

SPINNER, *collectif,* Spinner, 1984.

STEBELTON, Sue, *The Wagnals Memorial,* 1988.

STEVENSON, Robert-Louis, *Dans les mers du Sud,* Folio, 1920.

STONE, Irving, *Depths of Glory,* Doubleday, 1985.

SWANBERG W.A., *Citizen Hearst,* Bantam, 1961.

TELLER, W., *The Voyages of Joshua Slocum,* Sheridan House, 1985.

_____ , *Slocum, homme de mer,* Chiron, 1964.

TILTON, Capitaine George Fred, *Cap'n George Fred,* Dukes County Historical Society, 1969.

TOYNBEE, Arnold, *L'Histoire, Elsevier Séquoia, 1975.*

VILLARET, Bernard, *Sept Histoires des mers du Sud,* Editions du Pacifique, 1972.

VOSS, Captain J.C., *Aventures de mer,* Ouest-France, 1983.

WALLACE, F.W., *Wooden Ships and Iron Men,* Mika Publishing Company, 1976.

WHITAKER, Richard, *Sydney Side,* Gregory's, 1986.

WOODS, Shirley E. Jr., *La Saga des Molson,* Éditions de l'Homme, 1983.